LITTLE CENTURY

LITTLE CENTURY

ANNA KEESEY

FARRAR, STRAUS AND GIROUX   NEW YORK

Farrar, Straus and Giroux
18 West 18th Street, New York 10011

Distributed in Canada by D&M Publishers, Inc.
Printed in the United States of America
First edition, 2012

Library of Congress Cataloging-in-Publication Data
Keesey, Anna, 1962–
    Little century : a novel / Anna Keesey.
      p.   cm.
    ISBN 978-0-374-19204-4 (hardback)
    1. Orphans—Fiction.   2. Rangelands—Oregon—Fiction.   I. Title.

  PS3611.E3455 L58 2012
  813'.6—dc23

                        2011046308

Designed by Abby Kagan

www.fsgbooks.com

1 3 5 7 9 10 8 6 4 2

For my only Joaquin

Soto! Explore thyself!
Therein thyself shalt find
The "Undiscovered Continent"—
No Settler had the Mind.
—EMILY DICKINSON, C. 1864

PART ONE

ARTEMESIA

1

THOUGH SHE WOULD NOT HAVE ADMITTED to any fixed expectation, Esther is still confounded by what meets her at the end of her journey. The hands at the Two Forks ranch, it appears, can be called *boys* or *fellows* by Pick, or *buckaroos* by Vincent, but not *cowboys*, except in fun. They are not boys, anyway. They are laboring men in flannel shirts and leather vests and boots worn down at the heels. They have brown necks and cheeks that look chapped, as if they have employed shingles to scrape away their beards. They may be strong—they must be, if they direct cattle about—but they don't seem very likely. They are lackadaisical, on Esther's first morning in the high desert, at the task of fitting boards over the windows of the Two Forks house, which have been shattered by vandals.

"Buckaroos don't like to do anything excepting to ride and to wrangle," says Vincent, who helps run the ranch. "They want to act like they never seen a hammer. And of course they'd rather take out after those sheepmen and separate them from their slingshots. It's a dull job to clean up when you want to hit back. But Pick works them, and they do what he says."

Last evening, at the end of her four-day journey to Oregon, in the windy winter dusk, she was greeted by destruction. As Vincent drove the wagon into the yard after a cold and dusty trip from the train station, she saw no welcome party arrayed on the steps, but lamps swinging, the yellow beams crossing into and out of the stripes of light coming from the house, and a number of bare-chested men kicking glass with their boots. She held her valise on her lap and hugged it. Disorder? All right. But damage, ill will? Bad neighbors? She had not imagined this when she decided to come west.

And now, despite hours of grateful sleep after the discomfort of the train, the morning seems no more promising. Esther pulls her coat around her and sits down on the bitter iron of a wagon tongue. Before her are miles of gray plain roughened with brush, rising into a blurred olive band of vegetation and other bands of smoke and slate blue too far away to be consequential. And beyond these the three rocky peaks Vincent calls the Sisters array themselves in robes of ice. Esther has never imagined a land so fruitless. Under snow is thin, silky dirt, and under that, rock so rough it catches the leather sole of one's shoe. It is eerie rock; it has flowed from inside the earth through some unnatural crevice, blackening the landscape like Hades's chariot. The shrubs are plentiful yet parsimonious, flexible but dry. Here and there, like scarecrows with giant heads, windmills brood over the plain.

Vincent hands her a cup of coffee, and the heat feels good through her gloves. She thanks him and tastes it. Bitter, manly, and scalding, not like tea. "What did you mean just then, about sheepmen?"

"Herders and owners of sheep. Not so many around here as cattle, but there's some."

"But why would sheepherders break your windows?"

"Don't care for a cattleman."

"Oh." She's embarrassed to say she doesn't understand, but he sees this and comes to her aid.

"Pick leads the way around here in keeping sheep off what's cattle ground."

"Do they try to come onto his ranch? Isn't that trespassing?"

"Well, that land ain't legally part of Two Forks. Most of this desert around here belongs to the U.S. government. But McKinley don't give much of a damn, and since cattlemen's taxes been nursing this town along for years, it's just fair we get first crack at the open grazing. Last week Pick had the buckaroos mark out some territory by burning what they call deadlines on the trees up there in those hills. Bunch a sheep came up there—local stockman named Brookie Duncan runs 'em—and the buckaroos chased 'em all down, shooting and hollering and scaring the bejesus out of the herder boys. He takes a large pull of coffee, and shakes his head. Maybe it wasn't that nice. But you give them boys a penny and you'll be out a dollar."

And the shepherds responded by breaking the windows. "But why slingshots?" she asks.

"Can't waste the ammunition to shoot out a window, they're too poor. And they don't really want to hurt anybody. I don't think they do. Well, they're not likely to get much of a rise out of your cousin. Ferris Pickett's nothing if he ain't cool."

She's perplexed, a little thrilled, by these doings, but she hopes the sheepherders have vented their annoyance and won't come back. Pick, her cousin, does seem cool. He will make sure everyone behaves, certainly. His house alone is a testament to his competence and certitude; it is by far the largest place she has ever lived in. Inside, the wallpapers and carpets are scarlet and blue, almost royal, and the furniture is rich and polished. Outside the house is broad and formal, with massive front doors, a dark mansard roof, and bright white paint. Above the veranda runs an abbreviated balcony with an iron railing, like baroque black lace. But for the large metal windmill twirling beside it, this house would look suitable commanding a large lawn with redbuds and lilacs in one of the better areas of Chicago. Even with three of its large windows cracked or shattered, it is impressive, even haughty, as if it has mustered itself out of the dust and then been surprised by the humble neighborhood.

Vincent follows her gaze. "Pick built it a while back, when he was young. Well, younger. He's thirty now. He wouldn't go for so much gewgaw anymore, now that he's grown. Say now—" He gestures east with his bearded chin. "That claim of yours is a pretty property. It sits on a lake, most of the time."

She pictures a piece of land rising and flying away from its lake like a magic carpet. "Most of the time?"

"It's a playa lake. It's not there all year. Comes and goes, so they call it Half-a-Mind. You can water stock all spring at Half-a-Mind, but come August, you're sure to go begging. There's a place to stay, though. Miller built a cabin on the claim before he absquatulated."

"I'll live there all the time, then? That is—all the time?"

"Now, that depends on what you mean by *live*. You're supposed to spend six months of nights there and grow a crop. But the law don't say you have to eat or keep your clothes there."

"I don't think I know how to grow anything. Except marigolds."

"Oh, I'll show you. Anyway, you can eat with Pick and me and the boys. You're only a mile away."

A mile! And not a cable car anywhere. She ventures, "I saw there weren't any ladies at breakfast."

"Hah! Nope."

"You aren't married?"

"Me? Nope."

"Isn't Pick married?"

"We're not much good at marrying at Two Forks. Maybe it's a problem with the well." He laughs. "No, sir, you're the first female we've convinced to stay with us for long."

For long? Someone has been and gone, then. But she never imagined that there would be no women on her cousin's ranch; it had not occurred to her. For most of her life she has known mostly women and girls. Her mother, her school friends and teachers, and her mother's friends. But there *is* a town here, somewhere. There will be—well, people.

Pick, tall and soft of footfall, appears behind them, resettling his hat on his fair hair. "You're ready," he says to Esther. "Good. We'll go over to the claim."

"Better take a sidearm against you got a jumper in the shack," says Vincent. "Nobody's been in there since Miller lit out."

———————

Yesterday, after collecting her at the station up in Peterson, Pick took her to a parlor at a nearby boardinghouse. She was given hard-boiled eggs, toast, and tea, an odd lunch, like something served to lady convicts. While she began, with great self-consciousness, to peel an egg, Pick said, "You're older than I thought. What are you, nineteen? Twenty?" This observation was neither friendly nor otherwise.

"I'm eighteen." Had he not read her letters?

"Well, you're taller than most girls. Maybe that's it."

"I was almost always the tallest at school. People asked me to reach for things."

He nodded.

"And I suppose wearing mourning makes everyone look older."

"I guess that's so."

She tried again. "At the station just now, I wasn't sure who you were, if you were my cousin or not."

One of his cheeks rounded and tightened, and he gave a side-ways laugh. He had many wrinkles around his eyes, though he was young. "Who did you think I was?"

Having just taken a bite of egg, she put her fingers over her mouth. "You didn't say."

"Did you think some other man might be looking for you at Peterson depot on the fifth of January? I'm Ferris Pickett, all right. But I'm called Pick."

Pick. It sounded like the name of a man who took care of stables or shined shoes. She would learn to use it, though. *When in Rome,* her mother would have said, raising an eyebrow, *unless the Romans are scoundrels.* He wore a blue shirt and dark, pointed boots, but his riveted trousers were work beaten. His brow was broad, and pale where his hat shaded it—she had already seen this in men on the train, nut-tanned faces with porcelain brows—and his eyes were light and set far apart under brows that slanted down and outward, suggesting the faintest anxiety. If he had a beard with his golden mustache, he would look a good deal like Ulysses S. Grant.

When her mother died a few months ago, leaving her alone in the world, Esther wrote to this distant cousin on her father's side who raised livestock near Peterson in the middle of Oregon. As far as she knew, he was the only living person related to her. His letter back to her was brief.

I can't offer you any work to speak of unless you can wrangle a cow but it's an up and coming town and maybe you'd like the change. We've got plenty of room in the house and plenty outside it.

Since Esther's home was the rented second floor of an apartment house off Damen Avenue in central Chicago, the only cows she'd ever known were those bawling and stinking behind the barricades at the stockyards, and one particular enemy who had stepped on her foot at a county fair when she was a little girl. But like other eighteen-year-old persons, she was not averse to the sweeping decision or the dramatic gesture, and she had always admired Nelly Bly, the newspaperwoman who had gone around the world in every manner of conveyance. Now that her mother was gone, to go away had for Esther the allure it often does for the terribly hurt. Cow wrangling, certainly, certainly—though if her cousin required her to count pins or skin monkeys, she would have been ready to accept that as well.

Assurances had been offered, of course: *whosoever believeth shall never die*, and so on. Yet when Esther sat in church with her mother's friends and associates, she looked not at the jeweled figures in windows lit by the winter sunshine, but at the cracks between the stones of the floor. As she looked, they seemed to grow larger, into nooks and caves that might easily hide her dead: the baby brother who had arrived blue and winded and stayed only four months, the thin papa with the white mustache whose heart slowed, crawled, and could not begin again, and now her mother. The cracks were cold and deep. Couldn't she slide in there with their poor bodies and be dead? But that afternoon she boarded the streetcar back to the apartment she'd shared with her mother, where some sheets were hastily thrown over the furniture, and took out her mother's book of addresses and found him.

As she drank her tea, Pick rubbed at his jaw, as though he felt something there under the skin. "And since you seem to have survived the crossing, you must still be Esther. You had a long ride, didn't you? Did you feel a little dull, cooped up all that time?"

She nodded.

"I guess there wasn't much for you at home, was there? Not much to stick around for?"

It was true. Her mother was gone. She died one morning in August while Esther read a book and ironed a dress. Flu had weakened her, but she died of a stroke. A stroke, as one would make with a pen. "Your mother must have been very tired," said the doctor. "Some people are susceptible to events of the brain." Never again would Esther see her wise brown eyes or the wary smile that lit them, often for nothing, often only because Esther was talking. This glint of sympathy from Pick pushed tears into her eyes, and she had to clamp down on all feeling, as though stuffing an animal into a box. "Oh—well. I did want a change. As you said."

"You've had a hard time. But this is a good country for someone alone. We're all equal out here, and everyone makes his own luck." Her mind tried to grasp this. Could luck be made? "No one cares if you're poor or crippled or an Indian or an orphan. As long as you can do some work and be a decent neighbor, you'll get ahead. In fact—listen, Esther. I've got an idea."

She put down the egg.

"It has to do with fooling someone who deserves like the devil to be fooled. Maybe you played at pretending not so long ago. You ever try to fool someone?"

"Now and then, I suppose." Once, at the Lake Michigan shore, she had floated on her stomach and pretended to be drowned.

While she floated there, it suddenly came to her what a terrible thing she was doing to her mother. She was relieved when she surfaced, spluttering and paddling, to see that her mother had been not in the least taken in. From the shore she looked at Esther, stretched, and made an elaborate dumb show of yawning.

"Well, down the street is the land office, where people claim homesteads, and in it there sits a little clerk who wants shaking up. He's drunk on his duties, to speak poetically—I don't mean actually drunk. But he's got all the maps and the stamps and the ink he can play with, and he enjoys himself. If we pull the wool over his eyes, we'll have a good joke to take back with us to Century."

"Century?"

"That's our town."

"Oh—this isn't our town?"

"We've still got a bit to go to reach Century, and then a little more to Two Forks. A couple of hours, it'll take in the buggy. Shorter if you're riding. What do you say, Esther?" he asked, smiling. This smile was cheeky, mischievous, though the impression arose from the high placement of his neat, pointed eyeteeth and he may have been unaware of it himself. "Feel like helping out your old cousin?"

He wanted her help to conspire against a bully. Nelly Bly would leap at such a chance. She smiled back. "If I can."

The land office was empty of people but full of business. It was a high, narrow shop fitted with shelves on each wall, full of official reports and stacks of papers, the highest reached by rolling ladder. Filling the lower shelves were great leather-bound books, much larger than usual, stamped with gold lettering and frilly with the edges of pages. On a table sat a broad map box that, with its stack of drawers and gleaming veneer, would look grand and official if there weren't sleeping on top of it a fat little dog with protuberant eyelids. The dog's lips twitched as it dreamed.

"Wilbur, where are you?" called Pick toward the back room.

Behind the curtain there was silence, then a neat, tripping step, like a goat. A shadow clawed at the muslin and then became a clerk who presented himself at the counter. He was towheaded and sulky and had crumbs on his cheek. "Pickett," he said.

"My cousin would like to file on a homestead. Esther Chambers, Wilbur Grist."

Mr. Grist stood still for a moment, looking at Pick. Then he reached out and shook hands with Esther.

"I think you know the quarter section she wants," said Pick.

"I'm not sure I do."

"Miller's spot near Half-a-Mind."

"Is that the one you want?" Mr. Grist asked Esther.

"Yes."

"Well, it's the only piece left with water on it east of the mountains. As no doubt you know. Miller just gave it up for good a week ago. Of course, he's been gone some time to Prineville. After he lost those oats, he had to look for work. His wife's working in the hotel. Not the nicest place for a woman."

Pick said, "Perhaps Esther will do better. She's a smart young lady."

"That I don't doubt," said Mr. Grist. He brushed the crumbs from his cheek. "You do know you've got to spend six months a year on the place for five years?"

"Five years."

"Yes. You do know that?"

She didn't know it. But she tried to look authoritative, undeterred, and she blundered ahead. "Oh, yes."

"It's a long time. Longer if you're young, if you understand me."

Pick patted Esther's arm and shrugged. "Well, it's not as bad as all that. If she gets tired of it, she can turn it back to you, Grist. Or buy it, of course."

Relief rushed over her, but Mr. Grist was still skeptical, as though determined to disapprove of Pick. "At a dollar and twenty-five cents an acre? What have you got here, Pickett, an heiress?"

"Nothing like. Are you, Esther?"

"No!" She had a bankbook, of course. Perhaps a half year's worth of money, if she didn't have to buy her lodging. Her mother's furniture, hers now, stored in a Chicago warehouse.

"Either way, when you get a deed to some land, then you've got something." Pick's tone was uninflected.

Mr. Grist went to a rolltop desk and took a ledger from it. The desk was shiny with varnish, and he paused to rub a smudge off the wood with his shirtsleeve. He carried the ledger back to the counter and opened it. "What was your date and place of birth?"

She had rehearsed this part, on the street. "On the twelfth of November, eighteen seventy-eight, in Chicago, Illinois."

". . . Chicago, Illinois," said Mr. Grist as he wrote.

"She's an orphan, Wilbur. She doesn't have proof."

Mr. Grist laid down his pen. "Pickett."

"Wilbur."

"She'll have to swear."

"She's prepared to swear."

With a sigh Mr. Grist took a Bible off a stack of books and dropped it in front of Esther on the counter. It was black, the leather faintly pebbled, the edges of the translucent pages a powdery red. She put her hand on it. She had never sworn to anything before. There was a little wheezing noise. The dog had woken and was panting, his popped eyes giving him a look of pathetic surprise.

"Twenty-one years of age?" asked Mr. Grist. The dog hacked and slobbered. Mr. Grist put down his pen and went to it. "Tut, Nick. What's in your throat?"

"I don't think I can," Esther said to Pick softly.

"Well, you don't have to. It's asking a lot on short acquaintance, I know. But I'll get you out of it right quick." He was undemanding, relaxed, even playful. He closed one eye slowly, a parody of a wink, and she smiled.

Mr. Grist was running a finger around the inside of the dog's mouth, which seemed to calm it. Now he turned back. "He gets a bit choked up on his own hair sometimes. Ready, miss?"

"Yes," said Esther. She wiped her hand on her coat and placed it on the Bible.

"Speak up?"

She cleared her throat. This was a new place, and a new life. Who knew what risks might be required?

"Twenty-one," she said.

"Sign here."

Esther. Chambers.

At the livery stable Pick retrieved Vincent, an old man with a long beard that was crimped as though he'd been sleeping on it. Esther had never seen such a beard, yellow-white, like ancient linens in a forgotten closet. Vincent was pleased to meet Esther, he said, he surely was. Horses were brought out and hitched to a buggy, and Pick helped Esther onto the front seat next to Vincent. He himself rode a saddle horse called Lobo, a large russet animal with a deliberate gait and a bright white star between its eyes. He led the way back to the station, where they claimed Esther's trunk and valise. When he had remounted his horse, he came alongside Esther, his face thoughtful in the shadow of the hat.

"Now, remember what I said. You can just hold that claim down until I get the jack together to buy it. A couple of months, maybe. That way no one else can sneak it out from under us." Vincent watched Pick and combed his beard with his hand. "Vince, she took Miller's claim."

"I did gather that," Vincent said, nodding. "Glad she got it."

In a rush she said, "I want to help."

"You are helping," Pick said. "I appreciate it. And I understand it might disturb you a little, not to follow the letter of the law. Nobody really likes it. But out here there's laws and then there's laws. This is a strange sort of country. Some think it's devilish. They say it won't provide. It won't provide roses and strawberries, that's for sure. It's for independent folk. And if you want to be independent in the high desert, there're things you've got to do."

"I understand. I do. And thank you for inviting me," she said. "You didn't have to."

"Well, what goes around comes around. And you're grown, aren't you?" He cocked his head, eyes amused. "It's not like adopting a baby in diapers."

2

NOW—ONLY A DAY LATER—she sits sideways behind Pick on the wide, muscled tailbone of Lobo. Her dress is rucked, her exposed petticoat a mess of coarse eyelet, and her shoes uncovered to the tops. She clutches the back of the saddle. It curves like the edge of a bowl, so it's hard to hold on to. Her feet are going to sleep, and she can't see much of what's ahead unless she leans back precariously. The house recedes. The buckaroos become tiny, even those standing on each other's shoulders nailing boards over upstairs windows. She cranes her neck for a glimpse of the town, but sees nothing. A little smoke in the sky, over there. As far as she might walk to, or even see, to one side or the other, all is gray and sleeping under a shiver-thin coverlet of old snow.

After a quarter hour's quick bumping, the bay horse descends a short hill and turns. In front of them are banks of broken reeds, then a snowy flatness. "There's your lake, Esther. Half-a-Mind."

A lake? A pond. In Chicago the lake is a sea, plied by glinting steamers, the far shore invisible behind a compelling line of horizon. Here some handfuls of snow scud on a patch of dirty green glass. Lobo's progress flushes small birds that loop out over the lake and come back to the shore behind them. Beyond Half-a-Mind a great bank of earth rises like a cut loaf of peasant bread. "Peterson Bluffs," says Pick. "Look there."

Fawn-and-white animals are scattering up the bluff's far side, and while Esther is still focusing her gaze, they disappear. "Deer?"

"Antelope."

Antelope! As if it were Africa!

The abandoned cabin is not locked. There is one glass window and one made of thin oilcloth, which admits a blurred amber light. The walls are made of stacked desert rock mortared with mud, with rails of twisted wood on top of that, and a plank floor. There are chinks and gaps in the roof, and the corners of the room are failures, so a pole of light stands, like a broom, in each one. Against one wall is a platform with an old mattress upon it; against the other is a cookstove. Opposite the door, a table has been rigged by jamming one edge of the lid of a packing crate between the logs of the wall and propping up the surface with wooden legs. A white crockery cup on the table, saucerless, is lined with dusty, stony soup. There is room for bed, stove, table, Pick, and Esther, and that is all. It is the size of her mother's pantry in Chicago. She blows into her gloves.

Pick lifts the mattress and drops it, and the dust billows. "We'll get this swept out for you. Look, Vincent's got the stove set up, and here's your coal. We've got a chair for you over at the ranch. It'll be like a playhouse." He seems to be talking to himself. He has probably never said the word *playhouse* in his life. "We'll fix it up for you." He pushes the door closed and opens it, examining the track it drags on the floor. "It's less than a mile back to the ranch, and you'll just be here to sleep. We'll patch these gaps so you stay warm. You can use the water from the lake for now—we'll knock a water hole for you. Miller never dug a well. I plan to get one dug soon's the ground softens up."

This ground, soft? But by then she won't have to be here anymore. Pick will have bought the land for himself. A few steps off from the cabin stands an equally destitute little shed and a bit of fenced clearing. The path beside it leads in one direction to a narrow privy and in the other down to the lake. Pick points to the water. "We'll plant you a little patch of something, over there, to satisfy Grist at the land office. What do you want, snap peas? Sunflowers? Rye, maybe? We'll hope for a wet spring, and wild hay this summer." He is becoming enthusiastic again. "By next year we should be set up to irrigate some of our own hay with lake water. That's the thing, Esther. You've got to know where your winter hay is coming from if you want to succeed in cattle."

She nods, as if she does want to succeed in cattle.

He rubs his jaw and looks down toward the lake. "Listen. I've been thinking. You're pretty forward in your schoolwork, aren't you?"

"Yes," she says. "I've been ahead in everything but Latin, but that's because—my mother." In the months after that terrible August, when she stayed with the family of Mr. Fleming, her mother's employer, there were mornings when she could not wake, when no one could rouse her, and Latin, her first subject of the morning, suffered. She wants to go on and tell him about her subjects, about how praised she has been, but he's gotten what he needs.

"That's fine. What I'm thinking is this. We've got a school here, a fine school. Miss Fremont is held to be good, she's out of Boston. But it's a little odd if a girl who's supposed to be twenty-one is going to school."

She sees that this is so. What is someone like when she is twenty-one? Not in school anymore. Engaged, usually, or at least being "finished." Involved in clubs and societies, traveling, giving parties, going to parties, practicing the piano, sometimes learning a skill like nursing or operating the telephone exchange. Twenty-one is a free and confident age. She can't possibly mimic it. She is too young, she doesn't know how to do anything, and she is unnerved by this whole new place. "I don't think anyone will believe I'm twenty-one."

"Sure they will, when I tell them you are," he says.

"But I haven't finished school," she says. "I haven't been graduated."

"Well, nearly, right?"

"Yes. Nearly." What is the significance of nearly? Nothing. She thinks of the other girls from her class, in white, in June, without her. She waits a little while, then clears her throat. "Then what will I do if I don't go to school. Will I just—" She looks around. "Just sit here?"

He laughs. "All right. Sorry. I know it's not funny. Well, Vincent can sure use you, if you don't mind working. And if you think you need lessons, we can have Miss Fremont meet with you. She won't mind accommodating. It could be—oh—you want to brush up. You're thinking of becoming a teacher yourself, something like that. Would that suit?"

"Oh—I have thought of it before. Becoming a teacher."

"No one says you have to, of course. And there's plenty for you to keep busy with. You can help Vincent if you're inclined, and the ladies are always getting up something—a dance or making a quilt for somebody. But the first thing is to get four legs under you so you're not always up behind me." He leads the way down the path to the lake, and she follows.

"A horse for me?"

"Sure."

"I've never ridden. By myself, I mean."

He actually stops. "Never ridden a horse? How'd you get around?"

She stops, too, so as not to collide with him. "Walked? Or rode the cable car. I once rode a bicycle. And I've ridden a pony before."

"Have you?"

"At a birthday party."

He sets off again. "Huh. Well, fall off a few times, then you'll know how to ride a horse. It's called the Academy of Ouch That Hurts. Watch out for this barbwire."

"Pick. If you needed the water, why didn't you take this claim yourself?"

"They think I have my share."

"But in the first place."

"That was back before the government let that section go for claiming. We're at the mercy of Washington, D.C., most of the time. They open this and close that, and we don't exactly know from year to year what there will be to graze on. Besides, though, I came of age in a dry spell. Half-a-Mind was like that soup cup on your table, full of dried-up nothing. I took the quarter section with the spring on it."

Reeds brush her skirt, catching at the cotton, and she struggles to keep up with him. He knows where to step so that he doesn't mire down in the crumbling, cold mud, and he seems deft and light. His legs in his pants, his haunches, are hard. He is not only handsome but he has a bearing. There seems to be nothing ill formed or extraneous in him, nothing excessive or demanding of note. He is as precise in thought and action as a fine oiled clock. This is what men who work outside are like, she thinks. Her throat feels flushed. A bubble of feeling, desperate to break, rises inside her.

At the lake's edge he shades his eyes. "I'll be damned." A gray-and-white edging is just visible along the edge of the plateau. "Those Cruffs don't know when to quit."

"What is it?"

"Bunch of sheep and bunch of boys who run them."

"Oh—the ones who broke the windows?"

"No. Those were Duncans, I believe. The Cruffs don't go out on that kind of limb. But these fellows are making camp up there in the bunchgrass I'm saving for spring. They ought to know better. You wait a little while." He turns and strides back up the path toward the cabin.

"How long will it be?" she calls.

"Just until I come back."

"I'll go with you."

"It'll only take a minute."

He departs. She moves along the shore, slipping now and then, her shoes crunching the milky ice. Mud swirls up from the lines of shattering and releases a dank scent that mingles with the tangy breath off the desert. A few geese pass high above, scorning the lake to go farther south. Well, if she were a bird, she wouldn't land here, either. She picks up a light cratered stone and throws it as hard as she can. It lands on the thin green ice near the center, breaks through, and disappears. On the bluffs the sheep still make a subtle gray motion. Up there, she supposes, are people and a dog. If she stands still, she can hear—oh, almost—the little shouts, the tiny barking.

Oregon, she sees finally, has been misreported. On the train from Chicago she spoke at some length with a conductor who told her what she could only now call a tale. "They say it's a garden," he said. "I ain't been out there myself, but I heard of a tree, and from it they made boards for a whole street of houses. One tree. 'Course that's just what they say. I'm a city man, I wouldn't know the difference."

But everyone else had said so, too. Oregon would not be Chicago. There would not be smoke and iron, brick and business, and people brushing by gaily on the way to parties. There would not be dismal railed yards where someone had thrown out the slops, nor raw, muggy cemeteries where people rubbed the backs of their necks with large, limp handkerchiefs. On the train she got out her map and imagined it. There lay her Oregon, embroidered with its tiny unknown towns. It was furred with evergreens and speckled with lakes, with patches of blue flowers and waterfalls sending up silk tendrils of mist. The roads and the houses were there, too, like satin stitches and French knots, and smaller yet the people, their limbs finer than hairs. And there was Esther herself, black triangle of skirt, a fair braid looped up, a single stitch each of blue eye. She was merry, the little thread Esther, swinging a pail of milk, which she had obtained from a friendly cow. She sat in the sunshine on a rustic bench in a green dell. She was making a cheese, like a peasant girl in a story. How *did* one make a cheese?

Even yesterday, when she had ridden half the day through brush and sand and snow, passing blistered little station houses with signs reading FREMONT, BROWNING, GASPER, and JACK-HIGH, she had still hoped. But her Oregon was a mistake, a fiction, and presumably all those who had been fooled were too ashamed to send the news east.

And even if, in Chicago, she had been warned that Oregon was a desert, she would not have understood, for this is not the voluptuous desert of the *Thousand and One Nights*, with piles of glittering sand, nomad tents of purple and gold, and green oases where one bathes and eats grapes. This Oregon is terse and indifferent. It is parchment. It is a moon.

She turns and, despite his discouraging, runs to follow Pick. He is already out of sight up the trail. But it's not so far to the top of the bluff. She has run farther. Besides, it feels good to run. She is panting and damp when she rounds the last bend in the trail. Her ears ache with hot blood in the cold.

All around her are drowsy, munching sheep. They smell like the worst corner of a livery stable, but their faces are benign. Their foreheads are broad and their horns curved as though tucked behind their ears, their eyes are wet and nearsighted, and many have curls of wool on their cheeks. Their skin is loose and stacked in folds around their necks like the skin of a hippopotamus. One sheep is achingly broad in the belly. Her spine seems bowed. Esther puts her hand on the ewe's side, and the animal looks around at her hand and moves forward a heavy step. Surely the lamb will come too soon, before winter ends. Or are lambs supposed to be born all year? She doesn't know.

A little farther along she meets a sniffing black-and-white dog, which surveys her with clever, judgmental eyes. But before she can extend her hand, she hears a whistle, and the dog wheels and flings itself away. She follows it toward the edge of the bluff, where the sheep thin out.

Here there are two wagons, built up on the sides and roofed like the carts of peddlers or gypsies. From each juts a thin black stovepipe. Near them two men in overalls and blue sweaters stand talking up to Pick, who still sits on his horse. The dog lies down on the grass between them. Esther draws near.

"Too bad things are so poor up in Morrow that you boys have to stray down here to pasture the woollies."

The two men—a man and a boy—don't even shift their feet. The older one, thin and losing his hair, rubs his widow's peak. "We don't lack for feed in Morrow," he says, stolid but calm. "Our bands happen to be growing at a great rate. That's luck that doesn't come often, and we've got to spread out onto whatever is still free range. And of course up here on the bluff we aren't having the coyotes to worry us. The dogs can run them off."

"In Peterson County we don't consider these lands to be free."

"Well," the boy puts in, "when Peterson County is elected to Congress, it can fence off what it wants to, but until then these are free-range lands, and the marshal will back us up." His shoulders in their blue wool are awkward, as though their breadth is new and he is not used to carrying them.

"The marshal, is it?" Pick gives a dry puff of laughter. His horse takes a step forward and he draws back on the reins. "There's no call to talk of marshals. And after those capers at my place the other night, you all are fortunate I think so."

"Not our business," says the older man. "We stay out of all that."

"And I'm just up here to have a civil conversation."

"We know it," says the man. "Don't we, Ben?"

"He's civil all right. But he ought to know the law." The boy chews his cheek, looks past Pick at Esther, and says, "Somebody lose a tame crow?" His eyes are dark—brown, probably—but the whites are very bright, and Esther has the impression of lamps flaring under the frowning olive brow as if from under an eave.

Pick turns his head. "That's no crow. That's a blackbird from back east. Michael and Benjamin Cruff, my cousin Esther Chambers. She's unfortunately lost her mother and has come to stay."

Esther moves up to stand next to him, and the boy drops his brown stare.

"I'm sorry to hear it. How do you do," says Michael Cruff.

Esther nods. Crow, indeed. They are the scavengers, not she.

The boy says carefully, "Pleased to meet you."

"Anyhow, don't mind Ben," says Michael with a gleam of irony. "He's always bucking for a fight."

"Doesn't bother me," says Pick. "But if he flaps that tongue around some people, he's liable to find himself bucked out in smoke." He takes his foot out of the stirrup and leans down to give her Esther his hand. "Well, Blackbird, how about a perch?"

Michael steps forward and holds her foot in the stirrup as she steps up, turning to sit sideways. When she is settled and has hold of the saddle, Pick says, "Be seeing you boys," and they ride off, the sheep shuffling apart before them.

When the Cruffs are out of earshot, Esther asks, "What does that mean, to be bucked out in smoke?"

"Oh, that was a joke. A fellow bucks out in smoke when he loses a gunfight. It's an old-time expression. You don't hear of many gunfights nowadays. Nobody's a good enough shot anymore."

3

LATER, AFTER PICK HAS RETURNED the girl to Two Forks and Vincent's care, and eaten a plate of potatoes, he rides out to the lake again. January is the dead dark of winter, and even he, notorious for not feeling the cold, would rather be at home, messing around with his accounts or reading or having a smoke with his foreman, Teddy, and the other boys. But he's too impatient for cards, too prudent also, since he knows the value of a dime and knows that his buckaroos have up their sleeves some tricks peculiar to the saloons of Klamath Falls and Winnemucca that he himself would have to learn the hard way. No, better let them whittle one another's paychecks. The boss ought to keep to himself.

In among the brittle, tinkling aspens at the south end of Half-a-Mind, where the ice on the lake is broken and the water shows through, he finds what he's looking for. A thaw a couple of days ago softened the iron mud here, and the mud took down the splayed clefts of sheep. He surveys the prints, looking for marked hooves. He isn't above the cloak-and-dagger himself, and his buckaroos have done him the favor, now and then, of sneaking in and putting cuts into the hooves of the bellwether sheep in the bands of the Duncans, the Cruffs, and the other sheepmen who winter near Two Forks. And here is one—it looks like it, at least. And another. Yes. Well, well, my lads, he thinks. One of you went and had a drink of my water, did you? But you won't have Pickett in a sack for long. No dumb drunk shepherds will disturb his peace and foil his progress. This is cattle country, and when the Far West Navigation and Railway puts a freight line down here, the train won't be taking sheep as cargo. Pick will guarantee that.

The Chambers girl is a great bit of luck, an unlooked-for advantage, and though he doesn't believe a word of what the reverend spouts in church on Sundays, he feels encouraged—by heaven, by the world itself—in his efforts. She's got this whole side of the lake now, and that's a fine development because she is a family connection and can be made his ally. It's proper, because if anyone has a real claim, a moral and heart claim to what water there is on this desert, Pickett feels himself to be the foremost candidate. He is not like these sheep bosses from California or the little shepherds who just got here from Europe on the last boat. Even the cattlemen up from Wyoming have to line up behind Pick. He was born here, and he learned to walk and talk and ride here. His father was a foreman on a ranch over in Deschutes County, and Pick played and rode and then roped with buckaroos from his first tooth onward.

Until he was twelve, that is, when his father's heart gave out. After that Pick's mother—who insisted on calling him Ferris, his given name—took her surly son west to the Willamette Valley and installed him in the home of her sister and brother-in-law. This was a turreted manor on Center Street in Salem, where the sound of passing carriages was the percussive line under all daily activity. Pick's aunt and uncle had no children and tried to take charge of him, but he refused to be cherished. While his mother, hair ropy and untended, sat in her room writing out the receipts for every dish she'd ever learned to cook, he spent as much time as he could out of the house, and he slept on a bedroll in the sunporch even in the worst weather. In that wet valley, where the green-black fir whooshed and shuddered all winter and the leaden clay stuck between the heels and soles of his boots and weighed him down, he had no horse, but walked to school like a girl, carrying books and a lunch pail. For a while he wore his father's stained leather hat and sat bunching it in his hands while he studied, but the children in the town school were debonair and questioning, and they shamed him for it, such a big hat, when a man ought to wear a bowler, and a boy his age a cap.

At fifteen, at his mother's insistence, he went to the university not far away. Its prim buildings were arranged along a gravel footpath; their tall windows were gabled and glinting and occasionally appeared to manifest the bewhiskered ghost of a founding missionary, which electrified the undergraduates and caused some of the faster ones to pursue the forbidden late-night séance. To him it was all silliness. In classes with these town boys, it seemed to him that all the business was the business of crowds. Politics was for crowds, law for crowds, newspapers the organ of crowds. Theology was for crowds of women, and of men who were like women. Medicine was all right, if you wanted to live at the beckon of every drunk and hysteric for miles around.

Outside the university, more people. Constant construction took place in deep mud, where everything would rot and have to be rebuilt. And nobody seemed to notice this corruption. Gabbling and planning, they flung themselves into change, cultivating busyness like a cash crop, and when they'd made their lives as complicated and fussed-up as they could, they ran over and put their noses in at someone else's door to recommend more complications. The newspapers were the worst. Many people wrote things down, all opinionated—women, opinionated—and the editors ranted on in what was known as the Oregon style, calling each other corrupt and dastardly, calling each other bandit, boondoggler, miscreant, scoundrel, puppet, preacher, and brothel keeper. It was only because they lived so close to one another that they had to indulge in all that verbalese. If they had more space, they could just do, and never say. Above Pick's head in the street the trolley and telegraph and telephone lines made a vibrating mesh, as though somebody had dropped a wire cake safe over the whole town.

Above the wires, all winter, the sky lay like a mat of begrimed wool, prodded by the black tips of the Douglas fir. Rain pecked at the roofs. Windows streamed with water, wood bloated, rain barrels slopped over in the yards, wool coats smelled as if lain on by dogs. People now and then shot themselves, and Pick didn't blame them. In the spring the air was full of white mist, and plants grew with obscene haste, hollyhock and cornflower, wild pea, valerian, fluffy, draping roses. When the wheat came in, it poured. His uncle made jokes as Pick hoed the kitchen garden. *Don't catch your foot in that melon vine, you're liable to get drug to death.*

Too much of everything, and everyone too blithe. Even when valley people were unhappy, it was from discomfort, not danger. They were damp or they itched, so they whined and wheedled, but they were easily distracted by any novelty. He remembered, always, the desert of his childhood. The vast quiet, the singular negotiations between a cold, calm man and a colder, calmer plain. One coyote on a ridge trotting that low-slung thousand-mile trot. The unexpected thin blue of a host of camas flower making the most of a dry creek bed. The simple white skull of anything.

When he was seventeen, his mother finished dying and he went back over the mountains and hired on at his father's old ranch. People remembered that his father had bossed cruel and useless loners and shaped them up into buckaroos, and they saw Pick coming up to be that same kind of man. Later his aunt and uncle, persistently fond, settled money on him. He took a claim even farther out in the desert, where there was not much feed, but what there was he wouldn't have to share, and he bought land surrounding the claim and got more when he could. He hired Vincent, an old hand who could remember when Pick was a little boy and so hungry he ate with two forks. So the ranch was named before there was a building on it.

The only subjects he had thought much of in college were agriculture, biology, of course, and architecture and engineering.

These last two, by and large, were for housing and moving women—people who didn't sleep on the ground or ride a horse from place to place. After college he kept a few notes and plans on those subjects because he knew that one day he would build a house to protect a woman, and then he himself would no longer sleep on the ground.

4

THE BUCKAROOS have found various ways to delay work on covering the windows, and the next morning, as Esther reads the *Century Intelligence* and *The Oregonian* at the kitchen table, they are still hammering away and discussing the project in loud voices. She covers her ears and studies the tiny print, trying to make sense of the news from the Philippines. The war was a topic that had interested her mother, but one upon which she had to keep silent while working at Mr. Fleming's office, as they did not see eye to eye. Esther didn't pay much attention then—all wars seemed just more evidence of the moral turpitude of adults—but now, for her mother's sake, she reads. There is a boy-faced island revolutionary, Aguinaldo, who insists he was promised independence for his nation, and U.S. admirals who insist with equal vehemence that he was not. He has no proof. He claims he was told that the United States' promises were good ones and did not need to be written down.

Well, someone was lying. Or was it just the newspapers themselves that were mistaken? It was impossible to tell. Still, those people in their island home catch her fancy. She imagines they have wonderful flowers there.

The hammering, finally, has stopped, and she folds the papers, turns out the lamp, and goes out. The raw pinewood covering the broken glass looks tidy but sad, and the house is a blinded matron bravely wearing its patches. Esther feels tender toward it. She scuffles in the yard and turns up from the dust a triangular shard of glass. She buffs it on her coat and looks through it. Now the house wavers a bit, and the mountains look like mountains underwater. A buckaroo—Teddy?—walking across to the bunkhouse looks far away, like someone from another time.

Vincent wobbles into view, and she puts the glass in her coat pocket.

"Do you know yet who did it?" she asks him, gesturing toward the house.

"Maybe we do. We'll see."

"But can't the police catch them and make them pay something? They shouldn't be allowed to get away with it."

"Pick likes to handle things in his own way. It's a small town, and he don't want to ruffle the wrong hen. Especially when we've all been asked to commingle and socialize with the lot of 'em." He holds up a paper card, a printed invitation. Esther reads it. There will be a dance in town Friday evening at the school building, potluck and raffle. "You can make your debut. D'ja ever reel?"

"Reel?"

"Virginia reel."

She hasn't. She's never heard of it. She knows several variations on the waltz, can polka and cross-step polka, and has laughed herself silly castle-walking around the dining room with one of her friends. But who knew what they did for dancing here? To Pick, later, she says, "Must I dance?"

Pick laughs and nudges her. "A girl of twenty-one doesn't know how to dance? They must not be much civilized back east. We'll just let it around you're shy. You are, aren't you?"

"I don't know."

"There'll be a lot of cowboys in, but just tell them you won't dance with a man unless he's washed since Christmas."

He doesn't seem concerned. But even if the dances were familiar, she'd still be nervous. There had been years now and then when dancing school was too dear for the family purse, and she has been always conscious of how she lags. She is awkward for eighteen, let alone a well-grown woman. She is not eager to leap out of a wagon, go into a roomful of strangers, and begin disporting herself to unknown music.

When she goes up to the spare room, she kneels in front of her trunk. She fondles its contents: books and ink and pens, pastel crayons, stockings and underclothes, her old bear with the felt paws and the crude patch over the stuffing that protrudes behind one ear. The framed photograph of her mother, looking young and rather serious, and her amused, white-mustached old papa. She holds it close to her face, as though to inhale it, so close she can see nothing but the dark grain of the paper behind the glass.

Deeper still she finds, wrapped in white tissue, her red wool dress. It was delivered from the tailor the day her mother died, so she has never worn it. Esther and her mother chose the cloth together—it is the best red, hearts-of-cherries red, and the wool so fine and light in the hand. This poor dress. It had meant to go to school and be admired, not packed away. She bends close and smells it, thinking it might remember Chicago and the quiet, sunny flat it had occupied so briefly. But there is just the insignificance of stored wool. She stands and shakes it out and holds it up against her. In the small mirror she can see only the bodice blazing against her skin. The gathers at the armhole and waist are delicate and regular. Well, someday she may wear it, if she is ever no longer mourning.

Shivering at the mirror in her underclothes, she pins up her hair. It looks fussy, not elegant and sumptuous, as she would like, but it is better than having the whole lot come loose and hang like so much ashy embroidery thread. She is indeed tall, and broad shouldered, with snowy eyelashes that disappear when seen straight on, so that her slate-blue gaze is as bald as a statue's, an effect softened slightly by the girlish ripeness of her cheeks. She pats them, a little brutally, to bring up the color. "Hello. Good evening. Yes, just arrived," she says.

She finishes buttoning her chemise and then her corset over her meager, wide-apart breasts, nipples cold as pennies. The corset brings her bosom into a high and pretty place; her throat and chest are milky. As a matter of pure fact, she is not truly homely, but she cannot feel that, especially now. Last summer her mother pinned a little postcard picture of Saint-Gaudens's *Diana of the Tower* above her own desk and told her, "This could be you. Look at that leg she's balanced on." Leaning over her shoulder, Esther studied the leg, the high chin, the authoritative hand drawing back the bowstring. But the praise came from her mother, who loved her and who has now died. Long in the neck, long of hand and foot, bird boned in the wrists, Esther's body has been slow to make its crucial changes, and the work is still manifestly in progress.

In resignation she steps into the circle of her better black skirt, buttons it at the back, and then puts on the charcoal waist that goes with it. She can hook most of the back before twisting it around her waist and putting her arms into the sleeves, but she cannot reach the bit just below the collar. She goes down to the kitchen, where Vincent is solemnly combing his beard, and shyly presents him with her neck. He coughs, draws back a bit so he can focus— "My eyesight ain't so good"—and attaches the hooks.

Pick has changed out of his work clothes but for the hat. He wears a fine brown sack suit and a paper collar, and with his straight nose and the gold brush under it, the white forehead and fair blue eyes, he has a look of distinctive masculine decency. It is reassuring to her. Out here in the West, many men seem costumed. Vincent, for instance, with his strange long Confederacy beard, and Teddy the foreman, who sports a bowler above his dungarees and chaps. Some of the buckaroos, those with uncertain pasts, wear vests of spotted fur.

"Well, those aren't the happiest rags I ever saw, Esther," Pick says.

He means no harm, she knows. But she feels a more handsome girl would make something interesting of black clothes. "My mother said black never became anybody, least of all our family."

"How long is it you've got to wear the weeds?"

"A year altogether. It'll be a year in August. But I can change to something not all black when spring comes."

"They wear the gray," says Vincent. "Gray, and lavender and white. I seen the Godey book, so I know some of what's in fashion."

"Where the heck did you see the Godey book, Vince?" Pick asks.

"Elijah Jacob had it in Odell Underwood's back a month. Buying a hat for Phelia, and she's particular. I'll say she is. Particular like I need a shave."

Pick says, "If I were a mother"—in the corner Teddy, polishing his boots, gives a snort, and Pick eyes him—"if I were a mother, I wouldn't wish that drabbery on a daughter. Can you wear jewelry? Hold on a minute." He goes into his study, where his big rolltop desk can be seen through the doorway. He opens a drawer and takes out a box, extracts something from it, and puts it away. He returns holding a ring in his fingers.

"This comes from my mother's side, so I suppose it's yours as much as mine. I'm not likely to wear it. It's some Chinese doodad."

It is one large pearl, pink in the light from the kitchen stove, and on either side of the pearl a little carving: a willow, a pond. She tries it on her ring finger, then on her middle one. But it hangs loose on her knuckle.

"Oh, well. Too big," says Pick.

She's afraid he will decide it's not right for her and take it back. "Wait, wait." She closes the ring in her hand, darts out of the room, and thumps up the stairs to her trunk. There she pulls out the little embroidered pouch that holds her mother's few bits of jewelry. In it is a silver chain that used to hold Esther's father's pocket watch, which her mother had worn around her neck. She threads the pearl ring on the chain and goes back down. The ring hangs on her breast, glowing.

"Good, then. I'll go roust the boys. Hold my hat."

When Pick has gone out, Esther puts the hat on. It covers her eyes. She pushes up the front with her finger and looks at Vincent. "It's like being in a mushroom. Why do they wear something so big?"

"The buckaroos are coming," says Vincent. "They hear you, you're liable to hurt their feelings and make them quit."

Esther takes off the hat. "They wouldn't!"

"You watch out. A buckaroo's pride is a delicate creature."

This is a new thought, that buckaroos would bother to have such a thing as a pride. She gives the hat a spin on her finger, but it wobbles and falls. Guilty, she brushes it off and holds it in both hands.

Pick puts his head in at the door. "Temperature's dropped. You're going to need another scarf. Then come on out to the wagon."

Esther follows Vincent to the door of his room. He brings out a length of wool knitted in black-and-cream stripes. As he arranges it over her head, he says, "Oh, yes. A pride as tender as the inside of a foot."

Century is smaller, even, than Peterson. It was foolish to hope otherwise, for a town with no train depot would of course thrive less. Two streets crossed with two streets, like tic-tac-toe on a tablet of yellow dirt, and on those streets as many sandy sagebrush lots as buildings. There is no brick or stone—everything is made of wood and seems vulnerable to being blown down by any wind or wolf happening by. Church. Hotel. Saloon. Some sort of milliner. No library. No restaurant. No telephone exchange. A tiny building with a bell shocks her by turning out to be the school, where the dance is to be held.

At least she is too cold to dread strangers. She wipes her nose with her handkerchief and goes into the schoolroom. The desks are pushed back into the corner, but the walls are still hung with portraits of the presidents, who do not deign to look downward, like guests pretending they are not hungry. Pick's party is a bit late, it looks like, for upon their appearance there is a relieved burst of talk and a movement toward the tables set up in the center of the room. A number of people look at Esther with some surprise and interest, and she smiles, hoping to make a good impression. She touches the ring around her neck and then, knowing how such ornaments tend to dangle in the soup, tucks it into her collar. Very few other women are wearing jewelry at all, and most of the dresses have the fussy, amateur look of homemade and made over. The colors are pretty, though: bright pink, fairy-tale blue, a child's garden of flowers. Vincent escorts Esther in, takes her coat, and sees that she is seated at a long table next to a young lady whose wine-colored dress trimmed with gray lace, bright auburn hair, and refined manner mark her as some species foreign to this place. On each table are dishes of beef and dumplings, cooked corn, stewed apples with what looks like onion, and bread that smells wonderful. Several dishes of wan butter are scattered about on the calico tablecloth. Esther, momentarily enthralled by the prospect of hot bread and butter, remembers herself and turns sideways to shake her neighbor's hand.

"I'm Jane Fremont. I teach the school," the young lady says, with a look that suggests the school is an animal prone to hydrophobia.

A portly man sitting across the table is Mr. Cecil, the editor and printer of the *Century Intelligence*. He holds a pale yellow derby hat, which he can't find a place for on the table, and he looks around with an aggrieved air before putting it in his lap. Then he takes up his knife and delves into the butter, chasing the skittering dish around the table. "When I was last in San Francisco," he tells Esther, "I couldn't sleep for all the butter I had. There's more butter on the steppes of Siberia than in Century, despite all these cows."

Jane Fremont takes the dish from him and places it near Esther's water glass. With her cool glance and long neck she is like one of the swans that swim in the park ponds in Chicago. She laughs often, and her laugh is like a soft honk. Her russet eyebrows are as high arched as naves, and they remain at that amused peak when Mr. Cecil, gesturing with his knife, begins to introduce Esther to the assembled citizenry. This seems natural. He is the only newspaperman in town, and he seems to know everyone.

"There you have your cattle people," he says, indicating a cluster of well-dressed men and ladies and plump children, busy and animated in the center of the room. "You'll meet them because Pick's in cattle, though I can't say he's friendly with every last one of them. Those fellows by the door are homesteaders, though I'll lay you ten to one they'll be something else next year, it being a dicey matter to grow anything on the high desert. You need a fallback—somebody in the family with a paying job, or a good breeding animal to keep you afloat. You can tell a homesteader by his clodhoppers." Esther is mystified until she realizes he is referring to the men's inelegant footwear.

Jane Fremont looks tart. "When one is pushing a plow, clods must be hopped."

"Oh, I imagine so, Jane. I'm sure you're a regular tap dancer. Jane farms, too, you know, as well as teaching school."

"Do you?" Esther tries to imagine this.

"Yes, I do. A few things do grow here, though it's a desert. And I'm proud of my shoes."

High up in the room, near the stove, are the sheep people. Esther looks carefully to see if any appear to be criminal vandals. But no—they're very like those in cattle, though perhaps there are more single men and fewer babies. "Those are the Duncans," says Mr. Cecil. "Brookie's the heavyset one, the curly blond. He's a decent fellow, but he's got a temper on him." Brookie—whose sheep were driven off by Two Forks buckaroos. "And over there you have your Cruffs." He taps the table with his knife.

"I thought I had met the Cruffs up on the cliff near my claim," Esther says. "Perhaps I was mistaken."

"Oh, I daresay you met some. The Cruffs are Irish, you know, Irish and Slav, and they're abundant. I think there are perhaps five, but we don't see them all together often. They have very brown skin for Irish—that's the Slav in them. They're really from Morrow County, and they just stop in Century a few times a year on their grazing rotation."

In the next hour, between bites of roast beef and onions, she is introduced to a number of other citizens, including the Reverend Endicott and his wife. Delight Endicott is large eyed and dainty, with blond fur on her cheeks, like a French shepherdess with muttonchops. She murmurs her pleasure in meeting Esther and shakes hands by placing a soft little collection of fingers, gathered in an ivory mitt, into Esther's palm. She condoles with Esther over the damage to Pick's house and hopes that as the winter advances, tempers will settle a bit. Her husband, the Reverend Endicott, is one of those tall redheaded men who lose most of their hair early. He says he will speak to them of honor and self-discipline in church. He hopes to see Esther there. Esther would not miss any regular chance to be among other people, but she doesn't put her enthusiastic answer in precisely those terms.

During this encounter a little woman holding a packet of papers joins them with an air of controlled excitement. "Jane, Delight, Reverend. I must speak with you. I've just received new materials from my comrades in the East. You will find in here," she says, caressing the papers, "several detailed programs that may be used to promote purity of mind and body among the children in church and school. We will raise Century's children properly. We won't have any more such business as night riders and window breakers." Her front teeth push forward actively, so that deep creases run from the corners of her mouth to her chin; when she speaks, she resembles a wooden puppet working its peg-hinged jawbone. This unfortunate feature ages her, for she can't be more than forty. She sighs, as though she's encountered some rare luxury. "Just think. The moral sweeping that will take place when women receive the vote may be begun now at school, with the tender generation of the new century!"

"Invigorating notion," says Reverend Endicott somewhat vaguely.

"You do keep up, Violet," says Delight. "We would be so back-ward without you."

When Esther is introduced, the woman, a Mrs. Violet Fowler, turns to her eagerly. "I heard you were coming. I am longing to discuss with you the progress of temperance in Chicago. In a place as out of the way as Century, we need nothing so much as fresh blood!"

When she has moved down the table to another diner and the Endicotts have gone as well, Jane Fremont says in a tone of deli-cate civility, "I put it down to Violet that suffrage has a poor repu-tation in Century." She explains that a now-expired mayor saw fit to make Mrs. Fowler the postmistress, and since she has never shown any inclination to relinquish the position, there is no escape from her.

Esther ventures, "I suppose it's providential he didn't make her the minister."

Jane Fremont lengthens her face. "I shan't sleep tonight."

5

AFTER DINNER the tables are cleared and then taken wholly apart, as they are only long boards laid across the pupils' desks and covered with cloths. At the front of the schoolroom, near a lithograph of the Arc de Triomphe, a few men have their ears to violins or are blowing long, reedy notes on harmonicas. Vincent is taking his accordion out of its box. When Esther and Jane come back inside, shivering, from shaking off and folding the tablecloths, Pick is standing in a cluster near the cloakroom with a number of other cattlemen. He is packing a pipe with tobacco and listening to a young rancher with flaring nostrils and spiky dark hair, whom Jane identifies as Carey Stoop, of the cattle Stoops. He has a high flush in his cheeks, and speaks in a tone earnest, innocent, and angry.

"I told Michael Cruff one day," Carey Stoop is saying, "that they can overrun Ireland if they want to, but here we don't have the forage. And he says he doesn't know why sheep should have to make all the adjustments and cattle none. And I says, look, it's a question of prior claim."

"We been here," says another man.

"That's what I indicated to him," says Mr. Stoop. He enumerates on his fingers. "We get set up, we get the Bannock out, we get the Paiute out, we put up barns and windmills, we organize the towns, we pay the taxes. And then it's, well, you can't run your animals on this hill, well, you've got to allow for those coming in from California. And he says why shouldn't we make a bit of way? He says isn't it a big desert?" His nose flares again, and his handsome cheek is flushed. "And I say to him, if there's one crea-ture on earth I don't have to step aside for, it's a woolly from California!"

"Hear, hear, Carey. That's right," a couple of men say.

"Yes, but where do you suggest the sheep go?" asks Pick genially.

A few shrug, but several of the men laugh, as though they've thought of something but decided not to say it.

Mr. Stoop shows no such restraint. "Blazes, that's where."

"I'll tell you, Pick," says one. This is that tiny Mr. Jacob, of the cattle Jacobs, no taller than a boy, but taut, as if leaning forward in his boots. "Back in Kentucky we used to get big messes of spiders in the house every August, and the quickest riddance was to sweep them into one big bag and burn it."

A long note, thin and tangy, is drawn from the fiddle at the front of the room. The fiddler sings,

"Sometimes it's dreadful stormy and sometimes it's pretty clear
You may work a month and you might work a year
But you can make a winning if you'll come alive and try
For the whole world over, boys, it's root hog or die."

The tune is lively, but the folk are languorous with supper, still chatting. So Vincent goes forward, gives his accordion a blaring squeeze, and says, "Look, you—this one's a reel," and shortly they begin to fall into two lines and do their duty.

Violet Fowler presents herself in front of the gathered cattle-men. Several of them look at the floor, having the need to scrape their boots, but Pick takes Mrs. Fowler's arm and joins the line with her. She telegraphs pleasure with her head nods and her spritely air. Carey Stoop has left off his tirade and is watching the young ladies who are dancing—Jane Fremont and a half dozen other girls from all around the room. He has no sweet-heart, thinks Esther. Probably he is too loud and drives them away.

For the next dance, having divested himself of Mrs. Fowler, Pick returns. "This one's easy," he says to Esther. "It's pairs, and you take turns coming forward, bowing, coming back, swing your partner, and circle hand to hand. Come on." He takes her hand and joins one of the squares. She looks at him wildly, and he says, again, "It's not hard. Vincent's calling it."

And it isn't too hard. She listens to Vincent—"Swing that lady by the hand"—and watches the other dancers, and watches Pick. She knows how to curtsy and to be swung. *Do-si-do* is a droll circumnavigation of one's partner. By the time she is circling, taking one person by the hand and then the other, she is beginning to feel better. No one notices her, really. They aren't thinking about whether she's twenty-one, only of whether they can clasp the next hand offered and keep the circle intact.

The voluble Mr. Stoop, now happy and eager, has Jane Fremont by the elbow and is carefully watching his own feet. Jane, who apparently need not think of the dance in order to perform it, regards his bent head with what looks like irritation. Esther herself is taken around the waist by someone else, and someone else again.

There is a woman across the circle, dark hair rolled up Gibson style, a splendid dancer who moves without thought. Her body seems a bit too much for her clothes, her short red jacket binding at the bosom and across the back, and her black-and-white-checked skirt just a little too short. She is both taut and radiant as she swings and turns. Anticipating the beats of the tune, she is always where she should be, but casually, her mouth open in a smile, eyes half closed. Her skirt is still spinning one way while she turns and curtsies to the other side. Esther tries to mimic her and gets lost. "That was my foot, Delores!" someone teases the woman as she passes, and she throws back a saucy, black-eyed smile.

Finally Esther must gesture to Pick that she is winded. Jane Fremont, too, means to sit out, and she and Esther leave the floor together. Nearby, a little girl, dark haired and long in the waist, holds a spoon loaded with stewed corn in the position of a primed catapult. She puts her tongue in her cheek and aims. A couple of boys who appear to be in her sights jump up and down and cheer. Esther's hand flies to her mouth, but she can't help watching. Delight Endicott, quitting a conversation, holds up her lace mitts like helpless paws and calls out, "Marguerite!" and Reverend Endicott, nearby, reaches for the little girl's shoulder. But Marguerite lets fly. The corn sprays and pelts the boys, who heave with laughter and shake their fists. High on the wall, bits of corn festoon the waistcoat of Rutherford B. Hayes, and Violet Fowler, departing the dancing, appears to have gotten a kernel in the eye.

Delight Endicott attends to Violet's eye with an embroidered handkerchief. Then she takes Marguerite by the hand, gives her a rag, and points at the stewed corn on the floor. Her fair hair bends over the dark one, and she chastens the child in a voice lilting but determined.

Jane Fremont shakes her head. "If you think stewed corn is bad, you should see what the little hoyden gets up to when she's supposed to recite her ABC's."

"She doesn't resemble them, does she?"

"The Endicotts? Oh, but she isn't theirs. They board her so that she may go to school here. She's really Delores and Fred Green's child—did you see Delores there dancing, in the red coat?"

"Oh, yes! She's wonderful!"

"Well, they live all the way over in Jack-High and have a little baby. Jack-High has no school to speak of, so they send Marguerite to ours. You'll see Delores. I think you will. She has a little business of chickens, and she comes around to the bachelor ranches to deliver eggs."

Esther nods, and nods again when Jane rises to dance again with Carey Stoop. Boarded away. What would that have been like? Esther's own mother had loved her in a distracted way— always busy, rubbing her face with a sleeve while she sewed, letting Esther know with a look that impudent little girls should not interrupt important discussions between a working mother and her competent charwoman—but Esther knew that in her mother's pell-mell days at home and at Mr. Fleming's office, days she considered successes if no debt was drastically overdue and neither house nor office was uninhabitably dirty, nothing gathered her thoughts like braiding Esther's hair, no place was as peaceful as the chair beside her bath. And Esther herself, measuring and pouring her bathwater from a wooden cup, was anchored by the peripheral view of her mother's brown mohair skirt, her narrow-shod foot bouncing slowly as she read the *Inter-Ocean* or *The Advocate*. If Esther had been separated from her mother at that age, she would have hurled corn, too. Now, of course, there is nothing to throw.

A waltz begins, that floating, sweet rhythm. The fiddle is plaintive. A few minutes ago she was at least pleasantly contented. Now certain of the notes dip into her like ladles and come up full of loneliness. The people in the room recede. They are strangers, every one.

She stands and slips into the cloakroom and closes the door behind her, then opens the door to the street. It is silent outside. Cold flows in. She finds her overcoat on a hook with many others.

Out across the schoolyard she walks to the top of Main Street and down it into the racing wind. The moon looks near and bright, shadowed only now and then by blowing clouds, and underfoot the snow and sand make a feathery squeak. Esther walks past storefronts that look like playing cards stuck into the dirt. Apparently everyone is at the dance. No one stands in a doorway, no one washes a dish in the backroom lamplight. Even the hotel burns no lamp, having presumably no guests.

In Chicago, over the years, her mother took her to several parties given by old friends for the weddings of their children. Esther, child of a late marriage and therefore younger than the others, mostly sat near her mother and watched, though some of the awkward younger brothers, conspicuous in groomsmen's dress, had taken her around the floor now and again. She had not been comfortable there, but at least it had been familiar. People had known her father when he was organizing workers, and they were fond of her mother. There was some agreement on what one valued and how one behaved. One believed in the progress of the working-man, in orchestras, in cleaning up the milk supply so that poor children would not get sick. One went to see exhibitions of science and to flower shows but could not afford opera and thought much of popular music maudlin. The friends of one's family had sometimes been born abroad and knew how to make varieties of exotic cookies and cakes, if the ingredients could be found. And everyone read more than one newspaper, and no one spit in the street, and if a child was born with a harelip, one sought and paid a surgeon.

Here—who knows what they believe, other than sweeping up spiders into bags. Perhaps it's just that she knows no one. But she feels abraded, skinless, cold, and lost. Her head aches. Why did she think there would be something for her here? She is a fool, a bumbling child. But the thought of that long journey back exhausts her. And she promised Pick—as much as promised—that she would help him for two months. Better make it three. Three months for Pick to get the money together to buy the claim outright. She cannot go back on her word. Anything is endurable for three months, isn't it?

Her eyes are streaming with cold, and it is hard to move her mouth. But as she looks down Second Street, preparing to turn back, there is a light, many lights. She goes a little closer. It is a store building, with the usual false front standing up in front of a little attic. The front is lettered in what might be red: PEASLEE'S CENTURY EMPORIUM. But this sign seems to be studded with tiny apertures, for yellow lights, like little stars, shine out here and there among the letters. Nail holes, where something was hung? Pecked by birds? Chewed by mice?

At least she is not alone in this emptiness. Someone else has need of silence tonight. Someone else's heart keeps a vigil between the desert and the dancing.

6

THE MARE Esther is to ride has a bad eye, nearly filled with a blossom of white cataract that matches the salt of white spots on her brown rump. Vincent explains: she was culled from a band of wild horses that live on the range to the east of Century, a weakling filly and easy prey for coyotes. But the hands over on the Jacob ranch who raised and broke her found that she lost her frailty with regular feeding, and her shyness became bitter will. She puffs out her massive belly when she doesn't want to be saddled and sucks it in again later so the loose saddle will slide sideways and dump her rider into the dirt. She affects a tubercular wheeze when faced with an ascending slope and makes a federal case of her tender feet when asked to cross rocky ground. She gives a martyred whicker when other animals are being fed, treats interlopers in her stall to sighing exhalations from both ends, and defends other mares by rushing at inquisitive stallions with her pink muzzle contracted and her large teeth bared. For this last habit, as well as her general girth and crankiness, the Jacob hands named her Duniway, after a well-known suffragette who'd gone around the country disgracing herself but now stayed at home in Portland. For their trouble with the mare, Elijah Jacob turned over the money Ferris Pickett paid him to the bunkhouse and the buckaroos bought bottles of Monongahela and toasted the departure of Duniway over a few hands of Low Chicago.

"Mules don't have young, so she can't be a daughter of mules," says Vincent. "But she's got mule in her. Must have ate one."

Esther clasps her hands in front of her face and blows on her gloves. There are many horses at Two Forks, but she has come to understand that the buckaroos aren't in a hurry to lend to a beginner their trained cow horses, who may be spooked and ruined by Esther's incompetence.

Vincent glances at her. "Don't worry, though. She's resigned herself to a rider, and for all her guff she's got a nice gait. She'll ride like a Pullman car."

He has run the mare in circles on a long rope to tire her out, and now he helps Esther aboard. He hitches her knee up on the battered sidesaddle and says, "Pardon my grab." He explains how he got the saddle for her at a bankruptcy sale. "Ferris meant to put you astride like a buckaroo. I said Ferris, you dumbhead, you can't do that. She's a girl, and from the city. She don't want to go astride!" He tucks his beard into his vest with an air of satisfaction.

Esther is queasy. With her knees hitched up both on one side she feels she might topple over, and the mobility and muscle of Duniway are threatening. How strange it is to sit atop another creature and give commands. And yet one doesn't know what the creature is thinking, nor what it pleases to do, and the commands could come to nothing if what pleases it is to prize one off on the nearest fence post. Yet none of the girls she knows at home ride horses, and there is something extremely romantic about the sidesaddle.

When she feels Esther's weight, Duniway sags her back into a deep curve and casts an invalid's eye on Vincent. He is unmoved. "Switch her hind end," he says, and Esther switches with the twig he has given her. Duniway extends a broad, flaky hoof and begins to walk around the corral along the fence. Esther rolls from side to steep side of the sharp withers, far above the ground. From the sagebrush interrupting the fence line beside her to the distant white points of the mountains, it is a view that makes one glad for leather gloves. She says so to Vincent. "Everything's sharp."

"It's volcano country, that's why. You look enough, you'll find pieces of obsidian just sitting around."

"What's obsidian?"

"It's a rock made of black glass. It'll cut you if you don't watch out."

How unpleasant. Bobbing along, momentarily bemused, she sees that it would be possible to be even more betrayed by Oregon than she herself has been. She says, "Imagine if someone filed on a claim and it turned out to be full of obsidian."

"Well, he wouldn't grow much, except maybe arrowheads. Uh-oh. Watch her!" For Duniway has veered out of her circular pattern and is making for Vincent, pressing him toward the fence. He scrambles up and pushes the mare away with his foot. Esther pulls back on the reins, then loses her balance, drops them, and clutches the front of the saddle. Her stomach is high under her ribs.

As she recovers, she hears, "That's a good place for those reins." Pick is pausing on his way somewhere. "On the ground where the mare can get tangled up in them and fall and break both your necks."

Esther leans forward over her hitched-up knee. "I can't get to them."

"That's right. And that won't be so nice when you've got a spooky mare in the snow a couple of miles from home." He gives the sideways smile.

"I'm sorry."

But he has gone on toward the barn.

The first time she falls, Vincent is near and is able to catch her. The second time, Duniway, atrot, plants her forelegs and jerks to one side. Esther is flung forward. She grabs the mare's neck, twists, and falls flat on her back. Her breath leaves her body. In shock she looks up at Duniway, who gives her a casual look out of her good eye and then closes it.

Esther's breath returns, and she sucks in air and, with it, pain. Don't cry, she thinks. She gets to her knees, then stands, bent, her chest aching. She clamps a piece of her skirt in her fist.

"This mare's a tartar today," Vincent says. He is holding out his hand. It takes her a moment to realize he's offering her not comfort, but another boost onto the mare.

But soon Esther is making short expeditions into the desert. Wind and occasional motes of shouting at the ranch behind her are the only sounds. The knee she has high on her saddle aches, but she is relaxed, one hand grasping the knotted reins, the other reaching to comb through the coarse yellow-gray strings of mane. There is a beautiful stiffness to the hair as it grows from the curve of the neck. Though Duniway is not a pretty animal, her neck is generously arched, her muzzle spotty, prickled silk. On her Esther is above the snowy dust and the lacerations of the sagebrush. Like a chessboard queen, she can travel in any direction and go on as long as it suits her.

In those first days, Pick often turns and nearly treads on her, she shadows him so. He is surprised and amused, and then merely surprised. She keeps close to him as though to a hearth. When he plans to ride the range, desperation goads her, and she asks if she can accompany him. "Sure, come on," he says. "But put on your whole kit. I plan to be out quite a while."

They pass south of Half-a-Mind and south of the crumbling, upthrust Peterson Bluffs, where the Cruffs earlier made camp. They are gone now, or at least the sheep are gone. Beyond the bluffs, it is as if they have passed a reef into the open ocean, for the wind pours southward in a glacial flow, unimpeded by the forms of the land. They ride through hummocks of brush woolly with old snow, like huddled animals, like the hedgehogs in English children's books. She opens her mouth to make this comparison, but the impulse withers. He might not understand what she means, or if he understands, he will wonder why it is of significance, that things resemble other things.

He stops the bay at the edge of a gully and looks down into it at a flurry of tracks along the bottom. His wrists rest on the saddle horn, one on top of the other, and they do not move as he points one gloved finger down at the tracks. Then he pulls his scarf down from his mouth to say, "Let's get these cows out. It's warming up.

If it rains while the ground's still frozen, they'll get washed to Nevada."

She holds on to the edge of the saddle surreptitiously as Duniway puffs and clatters through the rocks. This motion is becoming familiar, the feeling of elongating and contracting as the mare reaches forward to clamber up a slope, her hindquarters tucking up after. The smeary white cloud in Duniway's eye does not impede her, apparently, at least as to navigation and identification of palatable foliage. Now she halts and reaches out her head. Esther fights with her for a few unnerving seconds, pulling back on the reins until all her weight is in her single stirrup, while Duniway, her lips distorted diabolically by the pressure of the bit, continues to work her head toward a clump of grass.

Pick calls back, "Choke up on her."

Esther chokes up the reins and wrenches the mare's head uphill. Munching the few threads of grass she's had time to procure, Duniway proceeds as though nothing has been fought and nothing decided.

"Will she always do this? Do as she pleases and never mind me?"

"Depends on how you train her. You can braid a switch on the end of the rein. Noggin'll split the leather for you, or Vincent."

She fingers the long curve of the reins. If only the mare would just obey and not need whipping. "What sort of cattle do you have?" she asks him. He tilts his hat back a little to answer her in an easy flow of detail. She is proud to have found the right question.

His cattle are Herefords, good specimens, most of them. About seven years ago he'd pulled together the money to buy a couple of excellent bulls, and since then he's seen quite a bit of improvement in the conformation and health of his calves.

Esther has been introduced to these bulls, Waterloo and Knock-Knock. They are both bulky and calm, with huge white heads and tiny, innocent eyes, unaware that their drooping anatomies are a bit vulgar. Waterloo, with a pad of fat behind his head and a wobbling white dewlap, is as stately as a judge. His horns are bent toward the ground, as if he has grown his own yoke. Knock-Knock is thinner and younger, glossy amber-brown, and very muscular. His head jerks when he trots. "Look at him go," said Vincent. "That's how they named him." Knock-Knock and Waterloo enjoy a luxurious existence, each grazing and being fed alongside a small group of superior cows in his own lot near the house. Pick often goes out to enjoy a consultation with his "associates." This morning Esther saw him brushing Knock-Knock, using long strokes while scratching the dense white forehead curls with his spare hand. He seemed to be speaking to the bull, which dozed under his ministrations.

The other cattle are vagrant in the winter, Pick says, though in January, February, and March his buckaroos put out hay around the range for early mothers. In the spring all the cows in that country, ten or twelve thousand, are rounded up and separated by the brands burned into their hides. The Two Forks brand is simple—a double Y flipped upside down, burned on the right hip. The new calves are gelded and branded, and all are turned out to eat spring grass and get fat. In the fall, when they are hearty, a selection is cut out and trailed to market. How far? Hundreds of miles. Most of the Two Forks cows go to Winnemucca, Nevada.

"Wastage, though. That's the problem. Even if you trail them slow, they waste along the way and get to market a lot skinnier than when they started off."

"But why don't you take them to Peterson and send them from there?"

"Oh—that little train you came down on can't carry the weight. The tracks are narrow and they didn't build it that well." They have ascended a small ridge now, and Pick points west with his leather glove. "But if we can convince the railroad we've got a thriving situation here, they'll run the freight line they're planning right through Century and on down the valley. It'll pass between Half-a-Mind and Two Forks. Those beefs will ride in style."

"How will you convince them?" Until recently she would have thought that a railroad exists, as streets exist and telegraph lines and buildings. But since she has seen Peterson, and Century, where there are hardly any paths that can be called streets, and telegraph lines hang low between raw poles, and buildings are constructed over the heads of the occupants, she can imagine the railroad being someone's dream, a tentative plan, flexible and impressionable.

"We're talking to them. Those of us who've got a lot of land of our own—Elijah Jacob, Carey Stoop. The railroad wants to know Century's a thriving town, orderly, with a future. That means we've got to have range as well as private land, and it can't be bitten down by sheep. I've just had a letter from the representative of the railroad, and he'll be in town in a couple of days. I'll take him out to a meeting with the cattlemen, and we'll see what we can do. Maybe you can help me."

"Oh—how?"

"I don't know. Maybe you can use your new whip to scare sheep with." His statement is interrupted by a bawling ahead. They move up a little higher, and there a little group of cattle are standing close together, looking shaggy and miserable.

There are three with pugnacious little horns—steers—and a heifer. One of the steers hangs its head. The flesh of its flanks is cut and welted. "I think this one's hurt," Esther says.

"Stay back, then. He's like to go on the prod." Pick moves Lobo closer and examines the steer from above. "Well, I thought the sheep were departed, but I guess not."

"What's wrong with it?"

"Slingshot. Somebody took a slingshot to it."

"Oh—those who broke the windows?"

"Probably. Those were Brookie Duncan's boys. But there's a few outfits roaming around right now—we run into them now and then and send them packing. And who knows—this could be a bit of payback from the Cruffs. That Michael is a reasonable fellow, but the younger one's a hotheaded little so-and-so. Well, we'll see who gets the jump next time."

"Why do they keep on? What have you done to them?"

He shrugs. "I've let them know where I don't want them to graze, and they don't like it. But if they cross those boundaries, they know what'll happen."

"The boundary of Two Forks?"

"No. I'm talking about the federal rangeland. Those pieces aren't mine, in the eyes of the government. But they're not doing anything with it, and I've been looking after it and running my cows there for ten years. I'm keeping the sheep out as a matter of my own . . . discretion."

"Oh. Well, what *will* happen if they cross the line?"

He rubs his chin with his glove. "Something they won't like, that's all. Here, lead us down. I'll bring up the back."

"What is it—why is it that we don't want the sheep?" she asks awkwardly. "In the first place, I mean."

"Besides that they're ugly and dumb? They ruin the range. In one hour they can crop down a pasturage that won't regrow for a year. And cattle won't sleep where sheep have slept, and they won't drink water sheep have fouled. That's what people say, anyway, and I've seen it myself."

"Really? How can the cattle tell?"

"I don't know. Smell, maybe. The way you can smell a person, sometimes, and know you don't like him. In any case, the cattle belong to this country, and the sheep don't. So my little laddies and their stump-jumpers had better stay out or watch out." His voice is musical, scathing, and deep.

"They should leave the animals alone," she says.

He laughs. "The animals are the whole point."

Still. Cattle and sheep are not interesting, like cats. They are not beautiful like horses or deer, nor companionable and clever, like dogs. Their eyes are set too wide on their poor broad heads, and they are clumsy, and their skins are loose and given to drooping and bunching. They constantly cut themselves on barbed wire, and the wounds are carbuncular and hard and take a long time to heal. Because of their smell, they are plagued by flies. Surely it is beinghood that looks out through those wandering, rheumy eyes, but they are beings without faculties, with no way of escaping their servitude, the milking, the shearing, the butchering, the eating. They have no wild place where they belong, like the antelope that run on the bluffs. They are lowlanders, chattels. Some people may be fond of them, especially if they are crucial to business, like Knock-Knock and Waterloo. But they can only live the way other creatures decide they should.

She has paused so long, staring into space, that Pick is looking at her with amusement, and his sharp smile, so seldom seen, startles her. My, he is handsome. She feels suddenly conscious of her posture, of her waist and hips as they rock above the saddle. In a flush of unease she leads the way down to the desert floor.

They usher the cattle toward Half-a-Mind for watering. The cows move toward the lake in an arc. The business of cows seems to be one of circles within circles, the animals rotating in the herd as they come up to drink, and the herds rotating through the rangeland, and all of them circling through the year. The circle ticks around and tolls each autumn when the animals are sold and the money counted. Sometimes it is enough, Pick says, and sometimes it isn't enough. Meanwhile, the new calves are beginning inside the mothers.

Thin white trees, bearing a few pale pods like paper coins, are scattered along the lake's brief south shore. "Aspen," says Pick. The cows quicken their pace when they smell the water. But Pick stops his horse and swings down. He bends and looks at a winter-dry plant, then pulls it up and puts in his pocket. "Larkspur. This one's dead, but they still scatter seeds. Larkspur's deadly to cattle."

"In Chicago they grow it in the gardens."

"One's fellow's bouquet being another's poison," he says.

One fellow's—her body prickles with memory, hearing her father's voice, a few ghostly notes from her babyhood. One fellow's—that is all she can remember. They are riding through the aspens now. Among the trees she is emboldened. "I can swim," she says. "So you won't have to pull me out of Half-a-Mind the way you saved my father. Though that was a river, not a lake."

"What's that?" Pick says. "Your father?"

"The way you pulled him from the river when you were a boy. What river was that?"

"River. Huh. I don't remember."

"The river my father almost drowned in. You put out a branch and brought him in. He spoke of it. My mother told me."

She is surprised at his reaction, for she has heard this story many times. Her father went west once, for a visit with cousins he had never met. He was in his thirties then, and it was a year or so before he would marry Esther's mother, and he spent a good deal of time in travel. During his stay in Oregon he encountered a shallow and sparkling river that became dark and forceful in places, and while exploring the rocks along its banks, he slipped and fell into the water. He had never felt anything so cold, her mother said. The water came right out of a hole in the mountain, hardly water, really, but something between water and snow. Then he felt a poke in the side of his head, and there was his cousin Ferris, who was a little boy, nine or ten. He had a long stick, and he'd come out onto the wet rocks in his bare feet and wedged himself in between them to offer his help. Her father let go of the rock, and his cousin pulled him in hand over hand. Her father told the family he was a brave, strong boy, but they would not praise him. Her mother was interested in this detail, and never forgot to mention it.

"I can't say I remember that," says Pick. "That family got split up. Your dad—wait, now. He was my mother's cousin? My grandmother's cousin, I think. She didn't have that many. Most of the family came west and spread out, but I think somebody in your dad's family wasn't well enough for the journey and they stayed home. That's all I know. I never met him."

"But you did. He remembered you. Didn't you ever save anyone when you were ten years old?"

"That would have been back in Long Crossing."

"To him you were a hero."

"Maybe I do remember. Yes. Barely. I think he had a new coat, a sheepskin coat that got ruined."

"Did he? I didn't know that." Her heart surges up in wonder and delight.

"I wish I could tell you more," he says. "After my dad died, we hardly ever talked about the past."

"That's so strange! We talked about it all the time."

"I wonder why."

Because someone was always getting buried there. Interred by time. Leaving fewer and fewer traces in the present. She is perplexed that he doesn't want to save anyone, or know what came before. But perhaps with such uneasy events around him, he can only pay attention to the present, and himself.

As they ride back toward the ranch, more reveals itself in Pick's memory. That sheepskin coat, and a city man's shoes. A greenhorn who had probably followed a butterfly out into that mountain river. And a chair? Something about a chair? A rocking chair, the strut broken. The man sat in his suspenders and white shirt and carved a new one out of a stick of pine. He thinks of saying, *Could your dad carve wood?* But he doesn't. These recollections are barely conscious, they flicker around his other thoughts like water sliding over rocks, and it is one of his peculiarities that he is loath to ask questions. And there is another reason he does not speak. She resembles something, someone. The dense sparkle of the lank hair, the impatience modulated by uncertainty, and, worst, a place between her eye and temple where the bones form a locus of familiarity. He cannot describe the feeling he has when he sees that place—who could? For it is where he played as a baby, turned against his mother's breast, sleepy, his hand wandering over her face. To see that old terrain repeated in the plain countenance of this girl sets his spirit worrying. A sidelong view of her is a misstep. It keeps him cool toward her, which doesn't help matters. For, being who she is, his coolness makes her turn her dangerous eye upon him again and again, searching for a key.

7

LEARNING TO RIDE A HORSE has situated Esther. She is not as lost as she felt the night of the dance. And she is determined to be useful, to offset any regret on Pick's part that she is here. For several mornings running she asks, "What is there to do today?" and she is put off, but one morning when Vincent addresses himself to the laundry, she falls in with him and begins working, and he doesn't send her away.

Almost immediately she regrets the choice. Her mother always sent the laundry away to be washed, and Esther never paid much attention to it. Now she sees how dirty clothes can be, stiffened with dust, winter sweat, and tobacco juice, and she learns that one must first brush the horsehair off the calves of dungarees with a piece of burlap because mere washing won't loosen it. Several great kettles are set to boil in the yard. The thin handles of the water buckets, even when wrapped in rags, bite into one's fingers, and one must bend one's knees so the water doesn't slosh over and freeze on one's stockings. Carry water, carry water, carry water; soap, bluing, starch; stir, wring, rinse, wring. The clothesline is strung between the corner of the bunkhouse and a fence post, and when she and Vincent have hoisted twenty-five or thirty pairs of wet pants and overalls over it, they have to cover them with clean old sheets so the wind won't dirty them when it leaps up full of snowy dust, as it always does. Then the sheets themselves have to be washed, a detail that secretly brings Esther to the brink of insanity. She thinks of Cinderella. The writer Mr. Perrault failed to say that when Cinderella was made to slave for her haughty sisters, the worst part of it must have been the tedium.

Her mother would have liked that idea. But there is no one here to tell it to. When she has ventured to say what her mother would have thought of this or that at Two Forks, the men—even Vincent—treat her as though she is complaining, and tell her, "You'll get used to it. Everybody does." At Two Forks she has no one to turn to with the contents of her heart, and it is beginning to stiffen and freeze over. Her feelings are a humiliation, a mere waste of heat.

"It's time to meet Delores for the eggs," says Vincent. "Keep stirring. I'll be back." He goes out onto the road, pulling a small cart behind him, and Esther stirs and watches, wanting a glimpse of the woman who was so adept on her feet at the dance. There is a wagon crossing at a distance, far off up the rutted drive, and the woman turns her head. Esther has the sensation that Delores sees her standing in front of the clothesline, but perhaps not, for she is very far away. Strangely, though, she does not stop the wagon, though she must be able to see Vincent coming with his cart. The dark head turns away, and the wagon goes on toward town.

In a few minutes Vincent is back, scowling. He says to Pick, who has come in from the pens where his best bulls are kept, "That dang woman went and skipped us. And I'm all but fresh out of eggs."

"Did she see you?"

"Must have. And I'm already sweet enough to go out and meet her, so she don't have to come all the way to the house."

Pick looks in the direction the wagon went and then back at Esther, and he chews the side of his mouth. Then he shrugs. "Guess she didn't like your looks today, Vince. Maybe she means to stop on the way back."

"Maybe so, but we've got new boys working, and I need ten dozen."

"Send Esther after her, then. Make sure she stops on her way back. And I could use a few things from Peaslee's. How's that mare treating you these days, Esther?"

"Oh, I can do it. I know I can do it," she says hurriedly. "Just let me get my hat."

But she has been in town only for the dance, and they made that trip in the dark. When she has saddled Duniway and is about to mount, she asks Pick, "Is the town that way, the way she went?"

Noggin Koerner, who is loitering nearby, turns over his coffee cup to empty the grounds, and he laughs. The skin of his face is tight, as though someone has grabbed a fistful of his scalp at the back. But why should she know where anything is? She'd like to put Noggin Koerner on Michigan Avenue and let him find his way out of Chicago.

"Go northeast on the wagon track until you see it. It'll be hard to miss. And when you get back, you can get your things together. Vincent's almost done out there at Half-a-Mind. You can go out tonight and start counting your six months."

Already? She's been assuming it would take much longer. But no doubt Vincent hurried. Cattle, as long as they are living, need water, and she has seen that Pick likes to keep things moving.

It isn't far to town after all. She never leaves the wagon ruts, and Duniway is dutiful, if reluctant, casting her eye to one side and then the other but apparently seeing nothing in the way of foliage worth lunging for. As Vincent has taught her, Esther keeps the reins low in one hand and tries not to show daylight underneath her, though it is difficult in the sidesaddle to sit that lanky trot. But she perseveres, and soon the white windows and little green bell tower of the church are discernible through the cuttings made by wagons in the brush. She is curious to see Century, what there is of it, in daylight.

As she passes a livery stable, the first building on the street, something—a hen—blusters into the air from the sidewalk. Duniway leaps violently sideways. "Oh! Wait. *Whoah.*" Esther has apparently earned a small measure of grim competence by now, and by standing up in her bottom stirrup and flailing for a grip on the far side of the saddle, she manages not to fall. But during these acrobatics she loses her hat, and her careful roll of hair descends onto her neck. Duniway comes to rest against a hitching rail beside the livery stable. Esther immediately dismounts, as if fleeing the vicinity of a live volcano.

Apparently Duniway's encounter with the villainous hen has stimulated her digestion, for now the mare lifts her tail. A cascade of green manure balls hits the snow with a wet, thudding sound. Esther loops the reins around the ice-gray rail. "Fiend," she breathes, in smoke, but Duniway's white eye shows neither guile nor guilt. She just stands there, now all contentment, her neck steaming. Esther pushes her hair up and stabs it with the loosened pins.

The hen is still in the road, belaboring the hard mud with an officious little beak, until Delores Green steps into the road and picks it up. The little girl from the dance, Marguerite, lets go of Delores's skirt, runs forward and picks up Esther's black felt boater, and gives it to her. Shaky, Esther places it on her head. Marguerite reaches up, and Esther crouches a little. The little hands are busy, poking bits of hair under the felt.

Esther nods. "Thank you. That'll stay, it feels like."

Delores says, "I hope you aren't hurt." It is clear that she means to be kind or make amends, but she is constricted by something. On her smooth olive skin her features are placed in some kind of exquisite ratio, as though drawn by an artist bent on giving her a charm unalterable by age. But no warmth reaches her eyes, which are shining, black as licorice drops. She makes an effort to smile. "Hens can be very tiresome."

"I'm learning that," says Esther. She introduces herself. "I remember you from the dance, Mrs. Green."

"Oh—do you?" It would be natural to say she remembers Esther, too, but her expression is still flat, even closed. She is one of those people, it seems, in whom distress appears as a shroud across the face. But what kind of distress is it?

Esther says humbly, "Vincent—Vincent Delaney at Two Forks—asked me to remind you to stop on your way home, and that he hoped to get an extra two dozen."

"Two dozen. That's fine. It won't be 'til dusk, so he'll have to watch for me." Clearly, she does not like to come all the way down the drive to the house. To save time, Esther supposes—the ranches and claims are often far off the main road.

At this moment a large lady awash in glinting copper skirts—ah, Phelia Jacob, the eminent cattle wife—takes up a conversation that the uproar has interrupted. "It's what I was saying, Delores. That hen's off her head. My helper girl says she started off well but now has laid all of two eggs in a month's time, and she's not getting along with my birds, so I'm bringing her back to you. I want a different hen, one that will be quiet and lay."

Delores regards Phelia with incredulous amusement, and suddenly she resembles that adept, gleaming dancer Esther saw the other night. Her laughter tumbles down a scale. "I think you must have done something to upset her, Phelia. You've had her for two months. And in *my* coop she laid eggs."

Phelia's voice grows pinched with self-righteousness. She expects Delores to take her seriously, to buckle under. "Whatever she did before—and by the way, I've no way of knowing if that's true—the fact is, she doesn't lay now. A hen is cheap, of course, and I could afford not to mind about it, but it's really the principle of the thing, Delores, if you mean to run a fair business, and a Christian one."

Esther is intimidated by Phelia's breadth and confidence. But Delores will not placate her. She ignores the implication that she is lying, and she says merrily, but with some gravity in her voice, "No, Phelia. The principle is that you yourself chose that hen from several others, she was healthy and a good layer, and if you don't like her now, you can sell her to someone else or eat her. The principle of the thing. My goodness, Phelia. What rubbish."

"Oh, why do I waste my time." Phelia clamps the hen under her arm, turns her own broad, coppery bottom, and departs.

Delores's husband, Fred, pushes backward through the door of the livery, balancing a heavy sack in one arm and a dark, wiry baby boy in the other. He drops the sack beside Delores and gives her a sunny, expectant look. "Here's your feed, my dear." A clutch of brown hair sticks out above his ear, and she reaches up and puts it behind. The baby, seeing Marguerite, pumps his little body up and down in his father's arms.

Marguerite reaches for him, but Delores takes out a pocket watch. "Mrs. Endicott will be waiting at the piano for you."

Pulling a fistful of her mother's checkered skirt, Marguerite says, "I want to stay with you."

"That's as may be. Piano lesson." But she leans down, and Marguerite bunches out her little lips, and Delores kisses her. "Rabbit away, rabbit."

Marguerite hops down the board sidewalk, banging it like a drum with her boots, and then trots toward the church. Fred, Delores, and the baby watch her go, the baby with his hand in Fred's beard. Esther feels herself superfluous and drifts over to her mare, who is savaging the hitching rail with her enormous teeth. But Delores comes over to Esther as she prepares to mount and steadies the stirrup for her. "I do apologize about the hen," she says, still opaque in her tone.

She doesn't like me, thinks Esther. She is dubious about me, and I've done not the least thing except to dance badly. But she hurries on, as Pick may be waiting for his—she takes the list from her pocket—baking soda, chloroform, and bullets. She leads Duniway down the street. Here is the false front of Peaslee's Century Emporium, yellow, it turns out, and the lettering in dark rose red. In daylight, the stars she saw are just small dark spots in the sign.

The door of this store has no bell, and it swings open silently. No one is to be seen in the front room. Between the front and back rooms, holding a red calico curtain aside with one hand, Jane Fremont stands talking to someone who is out of sight. She is laughing in a pained way and speaking all at once. "I won't ask you to betray anyone's confidence. But you must tell Mr. Silver Hairbrush that I can't accept such presents. Joe, it goes on and on. Think how you'd feel if you were courted by a will-o'-the-wisp." Some reply Esther can't hear makes her laugh again. She lets the curtain fall and turns. "Miss Chambers! What a pleasure to see you so soon. Have you been doing your shopping in metropolitan Century?"

"I just needed to see Mr. Peaslee, but I was waylaid." She describes the encounter. "So in the end Mrs. Jacob kept the chicken."

Jane presses her lips together and shakes her head. "Well. Phelia seems to feel that the richer she gets, the more likely it is the poor will cheat her. But what of you? Have you been comfortable out there at Two Forks? Not too cold?"

"Oh, very," says Esther. "But Pick—that is, I think you know I've taken the Miller claim near Half-a-Mind. And who knows how cold that will be." She feels a little disloyal, for certainly Vincent will have done his best at the cabin.

"Ah," says Jane Fremont, nodding. Her brow is smooth, but Esther feels she is not saying something she is thinking. "Yes. The Millers gave it up, finally."

"I'm not sure I can stay on it—all that time," Esther says. "But you do it, don't you? You have a claim."

"Yes—but I have plenty to do when I'm there. Pick suggested you take the claim, did he?"

Esther is on her guard. "He said that the Millers had left and that there was water . . ."

". . . and it was a property worth staking for," Jane says. "I see. I see. Excellent. And that mare outside. Has the riding been coming along?"

"Yes, though I don't feel quite easy on the sidesaddle. At home some ladies wear bloomers to ride bicycles, but I think bloomers would look awful on a horse."

"Oh, I think they probably look awful on anybody. But it's much easier to go astride. This is my secret. I have split some of my dresses into a sort of trouser, and I ride to town in the most scandalously bifurcated garment that ever shamed a dance hall. To teach, I change at school. Otherwise I just mind my posture."

"Perhaps I should split a dress. I have some old ones."

"Come to my claim some Saturday, and we'll sew. One of the benefits of the West is that though we are forced to make certain adaptations, there are only a handful of folks around to be witness. You could wear striped trousers and a cardboard box out here and no one in Chicago would ever know!"

It is a blessing, this joke. The warmth she remembers from the night of the dance flows over her again. Jane is a blend of austerity and kindness, both remote and suddenly, warmly near. She can laugh like a girl, and Esther is grateful to laugh with her, a friend, someone who is not a buckaroo likely to mumble or spit. "I hope to see you again soon," she says to Jane, and Jane says, "You may depend upon it. I will come and pry you out of that old ranch if I must."

Joe Peaslee has still not appeared, so when Jane Fremont has taken her leave, Esther creeps back and pulls aside the curtain a bit with one tentative finger. Then she forgets herself and pulls it wider.

Books. Books heaped on board shelves, bowing the wood and bending the brackets, books filling tall cases on either side of a small glass window, books in wooden crates stacked beside the back door. So many books that the smell of paper, glue, and leather perfumes the air. The gold on the bindings is dazzling. A sweet sort of relief surges through her. She has not been among books since the day those belonging to her mother were crated and stored in Chicago. The Flemings had few books, she couldn't afford to buy one often in the train stations on her journey, and at Two Forks there are only volumes on animal husbandry. Perhaps Joe Peaslee would lend her some of these. When her joy subsides, she sees other things in the room: a cot and store-bought blankets, a coffeepot. There are bunches of limp, drying plants, bowls of rocks, bowls of water, glass bells and curved glass disks, loose wires, a door key hung on a string, and stacks of papers and magazines. A machine of some kind covered with a burlap sack sits on an old saloon table. She lifts the edge of the burlap. A typewriter. At one side of the room, a steep stairway, almost a ladder, rises through a hole in the ceiling.

She calls up the ladder. "Hello?"

A man speaks from above, but not, apparently, to her. "What is it? Where are they?"

She watches, but no face appears, so she climbs. As her eyes reach the level of the second floor, she sees a long, narrow room—not a room, really, but an atticky box in which one cannot stand up. A thin-faced man, gangly, probably tall, and attired in a greasy buffalo coat against the cold of the attic, is bunched against the front wall in an attitude of childlike, rapturous concentration. He holds to his eye a long black telescope, annulated with brass, the wide end of which is lodged in a hole in the wall that faces the street. There is a series of holes, like poked-out knotholes, progressing across the wall at different heights. These are the holes that puncture the false front of the store. When his lamp is lighted, the holes become the stars she saw. He is peering out from among the letters of his sign.

He pops the telescope from the wall and collapses it with a neat gesture. "False alarm my back gave me," he says. His face is delicate and fretful and droops forward, like a camel's. Under his eyes are broad charcoal grooves that cut into the freckled flesh of his nose and cheeks. Hours spent squinting into the spyglass must have formed the wrinkles that crenellate his temples and disappear into his corn-gray hair.

"I'm beginning not to trust my spine," he says, walking toward her on his knees. "My vertebrae have in the past foretold all sorts of dangers. Frauds. Treacheries. It feels as if the bones are singing, a . . . a *harp* of harbinger, a *piano* of precaution, and the worse the threat, the farther down it reaches. But I've been looking out all morning and have seen nothing."

Esther retreats a few rungs on the ladder. "Are you expecting someone?"

He crunches his long, old body and turns. Esther descends to the floor, and he comes creaking down after her, his flat feet splayed. Then he turns to her. "Not precisely. I just mean not to be caught unaware."

"By whom?"

"Whoever it might be who is coming."

"But you must have some idea what you're looking for."

"Must I? Do you?" Seeing Esther's discomfiture, he says, "My spine, you see, got its peculiar injury, its gift, while I served in the army. It tingles, it suggests developments, and because I'm incurably curious, I come up here to see what they will be." He rubs the small of his back. "You're Pickett's orphan girl, aren't you? Lately I happen to have been reading about orphans. Many a penniless governess sitting at someone's feet before the fire. Pecking at her breakfast, you know. Painting and drawing, praying a good deal. I gather that they often do well, but only after numerous trials. There's one who goes poking around in an attic and has trouble from it, and one who loses her beauty to the pox, and so on. Do you know the little gray one who goes into the attic?"

She thinks for a moment he is asking whether she is actually acquainted with a fictional orphan. "I don't think so."

He pats his palm with the spyglass, bemused. "They undergo trials, and then they marry. Do you plan to marry?"

Before her mother became ill, Esther had thought about what she might do in life, and that included occasional daydreams about a . . . a person . . . who saw her feeding ducks or window-shopping or reading a book on a streetcar and was passionately drawn to her despite her big, raw shoulders and her skirt that most certainly needed letting down again. A kind fellow, confident and educated, surprised by his own love. Even on the train coming here, looking out at the towns that appeared, swelled, and slipped past, she thought about such a person. But since she has seen the real Oregon and knows it to be scarce of men of any kind she recognizes, this vision has shrunk, winked out. She says slowly, "I don't know. There's no one I plan now to marry, if that's what you mean." Not unless he has elegant bachelors hidden in the tobacco jars in the store. "But I'm not an orphaned orphan," she says, "not the kind you mean. I'm grown, you see, and I had my mother until last August. I hope I'm not so bedraggled as most of them. And I can't draw even a straight line, much less paint. What happens in books doesn't always happen in life."

"True. I don't dispute that." He stalks past her like a crane through water, goes to his front window, and presses the lens of the spyglass against it. "No sign yet," he murmurs. "But, oh, ho! What will come marauding when I turn my back?"

He might almost be joking but isn't, quite. He is taut, he is stringy with nerves.

She remembers that Pick will be waiting. "Mr. Peaslee, Pick sent me to get chloroform, baking soda, and bullets."

He brightens. He swings away from the window, deposits his spyglass on the counter, and goes to a shelf, where he begins laying his hand on a series of unmarked amber bottles stopped with corks. "Chloroform. Hum-dee-dee." He takes one off the shelf, uncorks and sniffs it. "The very one."

"Why don't you label them?"

"I don't like how they look, labels."

"What if you make a mistake? I've heard of people being poisoned."

"Never." He gives her a look of gleeful challenge.

"But what if you have a cold?"

He affects being insulted. "Rarely."

"It's dangerous, your method."

"I suppose so." Undisturbed, he pours out the liquid into a smaller bottle and stops it with a tiny, grubby cork. He takes a box of baking soda from a shelf and places it next to the bottle. "Now for bullets. Rifle or pistol?"

She pauses. "Pick said Winchester seventy-three."

Joe Peaslee opens a drawer and begins moving boxes here and there, as though solving a Chinese puzzle. "Rifle, is what. Rifle. And what's the point of it, I'd like to know." He contracts his face in thought. "What does one need bullets for? To warn marauders? Succeed in an argument? Abbreviate the gasping of a sick beast? Oh, there's no helping anything. No changing it."

"But I thought you were curious."

"To be curious merely means I like to stay informed. In me it is not a quality that in the least implies *action*. Everything's already been decided. The dice are already tumbling, you see. They've left the hand!" He shakes the box of bullets. One falls and glitters at his feet.

Esther bends and picks it up. It is quite small. Its polished dome doesn't look lethal at all. "Don't *you* have a gun? I thought everyone did, in the West."

"Of course I do. Right there behind the cash register. But it is a mere reference to action."

"You wouldn't shoot it? Even if there were bandits?"

"Well, if you must pester and demand—I suppose I would." He sighs. "I would dislike myself for it. You say you can neither draw nor paint?"

"Not a bit. I'm dreadful at it."

"No diary? Nor other essay?"

She hesitates. "Not really. Not to speak of."

He sighs, as if frustrated. "Really, it's strange how infrequently some people are the authors of satire. Orphans, for instance, may have great cause to pass judgment, but they are loath to judge. That is a power which, exercised, will land the orphan on the street." He hands her the box of bullets, which she puts in her pocket. Some people have strange manners, she thinks, but such manners are like a briar of thorns, within which something magical may dwell.

He stands behind his counter, tall and frail among the parti-color goods and bottles. "I hope I haven't frightened you," he says. "It's just that my brain takes over."

"Oh," she says. "Mine does, too."

8

WHEN SHE ARRIVES back at Two Forks and carries her purchases into the house, she is surprised to find Pick in the parlor. But she understands when the strange man sitting with him stands, bows, and introduces himself: Mr. Elliot, of the Far West Navigation and Railway. They are discussing the potential "spur line" from Peterson to Century and points south.

A train to Century—that *would* be something. How easily one could go to Peterson—just for the day. Other people, shops, excursions, and, in easy reach, rivers, trees. Century will boom, with the train. But Esther won't be here then, she remembers. No, she will have gone home long before this line is built.

"I can have a steer as fat as I like here, but by the time I trail him to Winnemucca, he's lost twenty percent. A line through would save us no counting how much. And I don't think I need to say that the more the main folk here prosper, the more commerce the town will attract. Century's like to give Peterson a run for its money one day, because we've got all these other towns to the south and they'd rather come to us than Peterson—they do already, for groceries and the hotel. Route through Century, and you'll get your expenses back in a year."

"Yes . . ." says Mr. Elliot, drawing out the word with great thoughtfulness. "I think we are interested in determining the prospects of the *various* communities here on the high desert. Century certainly has much to recommend it, much to recommend it. But there is Failing, to your east. And Jack-Straw—"

"Jack-High," Esther murmurs.

"Only a wide spot in the trail," Pick says.

"Though it may not always *be*," says Mr. Elliot with gleaming patience. He crosses his legs and bounces a foot. The toes of his peculiar yellow boots are capped in lustrous silver. "Of course, I'm not sure we want to commit ourselves to putting a town called Jack-High at the end of the line, for people would certainly think it was invented."

"An old Bannock beat a bunch of big cardplayers in an expensive game," says Pick. "That was the story. They were pretty sure of themselves, and they all bluffed, and the Indian beat them with a hand that was only jack high. Took all their money. Later they went to where he was camped and took it all back. But the town got its name."

Mr. Elliot rubs his hands together and blows on them, though the room seems quite warm to Esther. "Yes. This is the variety of question—not the identical question, but the variety of question—that it is my charge to answer about the towns. Our representative in Portland has had reports, anecdotal reports, of difficulties in this region. Conflicts. We hope and expect that the towns here, the township areas, will have ironed away these wrinkles by the time we must make our decision, for it is the experience of ourselves at the Far West Navigation and Railway and of those, including myself, who have forwarded the rail enterprise in other regions that instability is the enemy of business, and the enemy of business is the enemy of the railroad. This land, for example. Clearly, it can support some good number of animals—I saw many on the way down from Peterson—but what is the capacity? And should competition or limitation arise, in the form of drought, for example, or federal interference—" Mr. Elliot licks his thumb and rubs out a mark on a boot cap. "I think I make the position in which we at the FWNR find ourselves adequately clear?"

Esther is still hovering in the parlor doorway. Pick looks up at her. "Would you mind getting us a cup of tea? Elliot, will you take a bit of whiskey, too? Or some other spirit?"

"Brandy, if you keep it. And tea. I'm always cold out here."

When she returns some time later with tea and brandy on a tin tray, Pick and Mr. Elliot are deep in quiet conversation. Elliot is leaning forward over his crossed knees, listening to Pick, who is explaining something with spread fingers. Esther stands holding the tray, very still.

". . . outstayed their welcome, well then, that's what'll happen. They're a bit discouraged right now, and we might get them to come in with us—on our terms, of course."

Mr. Elliot suddenly laughs—Esther thinks he is unused to it, he haws excessively—and says, "A sort of benevolent assimilation, like they used on the Tagalogs over there in the jungle?"

"With a little less back talk, I hope." Pick sees Esther. "There we are. Thank you, Blackbird."

"The lady's health," says Mr. Elliot, lifting the tiny glass toward Esther, and Pick does the same.

She is embarrassed. She has not made herself a cup of tea, but she smooths her skirt and sits next to Pick on the sofa.

"Pickett," Mr. Elliot says. "I'm going to be circulating around the state for the next six months, to which I'm not looking forward, because I expect to freeze or swelter the entire time, but I won't be back to write up my recommendations for this area until, perhaps, September. There's time enough for whatever arrangements you and your neighbors would like to come to. I'll see how things lie then."

"Fair enough." Pick offers his little glass of brandy to Esther, and she shakes her head. But she is pleased. There is respect in the gesture, the assumption that she is not a child, but a young woman who may decide for herself whether she will choose brandy. Sitting on the velvet sofa in the parlor, gazing at the little figures in the blue toile wallpaper, she suddenly imagines that she is the lady of this house, its mistress. She brings the brandy on the tray with grace and aplomb and takes a bit herself. She has made the cake she serves. She wears a hat adorned with cherries and a feather, and a white dress, tight in the waist and heavy with applied silk flowers.

Pick is holding the tiny glass in his blunt brown fingers. When Mr. Elliot stands to assume his buffalo coat, Pick hands the glass to Esther, who puts it on the tray. Before she follows them out, she puts her finger in the golden syrup left in the glass and touches it to her tongue.

9

THAT EVENING, she goes up to the spare room and gathers a few belongings—underclothes, her hairbrush—and packs them in her valise. Her trunk has already been taken to the claim cabin. It is probably sitting there by itself, near the hard bed where she will soon sleep, miles from any town.

Teddy, Enrique, and Noggin Koerner have gathered in the kitchen to play checkers, Pick is reading some papers that came in the mail. Vincent gets out his harmonica and applies it to his beard. At the first notes, Esther's throat closes, as if over a large pebble. She sees children running out onto a breakwater and laughing, and the lights of a hotel at night. She feels heat hanging around her, hears fans turning, smells lake water, lilacs, hot limestone.

But it is no Chicago song Vincent plays. Mournfully, Teddy sings,

> "It's just a little bloodstained book
> That a bullet has torn in two
> It tells the fate of Nick and Nate
> Which is known to all of you
> Nick had the nerve to write it down
> While bullets fell like rain
> At your request, I'll do my best
> To tell his tale again."

Mad with thirst, this Nate tries to crawl to the well for water, but his opponents are relentless and shoot him to death. Though lying on the floor of a shack surrounded by assassins, Nick apparently provides himself with pen and paper and begins his memoirs. When the last note has sounded over the bleeding and fading pair, Esther asks Vincent, "Why were those men trying to kill Nick and Nate?"

"Well, you would ask that. I can't say I know. That information ain't in the song."

Teddy is braiding a rope—no, a *riata*—out of hide. He dips the braided portion in a bucket of water and says, "Now, now, let me recall. I heard once. They were small-time ranchers, and a big cattle boss wanted their land, so he hired these strongmen from Texas to take it from them."

"That wasn't it," says Noggin Koerner. "That's some other story." He rubs the blue bulb of his head with a pallid hand. "I worked in Wyoming, and everybody knew this one. Them two boys were rustlers. They had no spread to call home and nothing of their own, and they just stole and stole until they got caught."

Pick looks up from his papers. "You boys are all fools. Those stories are so old there's nothing of the truth left in them, if there ever was any. I don't know how I'm ever going to get a modern operation going around here if my hands don't know a nursery rhyme when they hear it." He shakes his head in comic dismay.

Vincent blows into his harmonica. "You can see Nate Champion's grave if you care to, out east."

"And that wouldn't tell you anything, either."

"But someone must know," Esther says in consternation. "Is any of it true?"

"The truth is, they're both dead," Noggin says.

She thinks of Joe Peaslee shaking the bullet out onto the floor. "I forgot to ask you earlier. Is Joe Peaslee mad?"

The men laugh. "No. Crazy, you mean?" says Pick. "I don't think so. Not yet, anyway."

"Tell her about the plume buyers," Vincent suggests.

Teddy sucks his teeth and shakes his head.

Pick pulls on his ear and considers. "Peaslee was in the army for a while—fought the Bannock and the Paiute way back when, and it broke him down a bit. Every once in a while the evils get hold of him and he puts a sign on that door and disappears for a few days. But he's an old soldier, and people make allowances. That's how he got away with the business with the plume buyers. In ninety-two we had ourselves a winter, a real equalizer. Most stock died off. Nobody came out of that with much to speak of. But Half-a-Mind was full of ice, and when it melted that spring, the egrets came, hundreds of 'em."

"Oh—*egret* plumes. I love them." One of Esther's teachers had a famous hat that trembled with those glamorous pale feathers.

"The lake was like an eiderdown," Vincent says. "An acre of it."

"That was when Miller had your claim, Esther. He sold licenses to people to harvest birds. A lot of people were counting on that, and it was every man after his own profit. One morning a bunch of them go out to make their harvest. There are the egrets in the nests and on the shore, dipping for grub. Snowy egrets, should have been white."

Vincent can't restrain himself. "Blue!" he tells Esther. "Blue as your copybook!"

"Somebody went and took printing ink from the office of the *Century Intelligence*, whole tins of it, and poured it all along the shore. Half of the birds were blue, and their plumes were ruined. Some people were for killing them anyway, hoping there'd be a market for blue feathers. But the plume buyers, who had come down as far as Peterson, got back on the stage and went home."

"Was it Joe Peaslee?"

"He was the only one of us in church with blue hands. He was shooting himself in the foot, if he did do it, because no one had any money to spend in his store that spring. But he's a fellow who might put a whim or a sympathy first. Like I said, people forgive and forget. And now, Esther, it's getting black outside. You don't want Wilbur Grist to come down here from the land office and sic that dog on you for failure to occupy!" He tilts his head and clicks his cheek at her, as if at a pony.

"That's a monster of a little dog," Vincent says. He looks uncomfortable.

"But how would he know?" she asks. "I expect he trusts you."

"Hah!" says Pick. "You expect wrong. But we're clever devils, aren't we, you and I? We can keep that dog away for a while."

"Three months," she says. "That's what you said. That it would take three months."

"Some folks owe me money. I'll look in on them and let them know there's a good, faithful girl freezing her nose off to hold down a claim and they'd better pay me back so I can redeem her. But you might get to like it out there. Plenty do."

Doubtful.

Enrique coughs. He is the mill rider at Two Forks, charged with visiting the windmills all over the ranch and seeing that they're drawing up water as they should. From him a question often sounds like a surly statement, as if he's already gotten an answer and doesn't like its nature. Now he says, "She going on her own to that claim."

"Aw," says Vincent. He gets up and stretches. "Darn, I'm creaky. Maybe she needs an escort."

"You want company?" Pick asks. There is still that teasing in his voice, and the challenge. She has been to the claim cabin several times, once even by herself, to measure the little window for a curtain she then made and put up. Duniway was biddable enough then, and they'd encountered neither soul nor antelope on the way. But now it's dark outside, and looking like snow. A peculiar heat begins under her ribs, the commingling of desolate protest with the determination to bear up and do what is required, required by Pick, who looks at her steadily. It boils there ineffectually, down under the self that knows words and can speak. She shrugs, and she goes and takes her coat off the coat tree by the kitchen door.

"Good girl," says Pick.

Vincent says, "Be careful with that stove. Don't get out of hand with that coal, and watch your damper. Don't kill yourself on your first night!" He hands her a cloth bag, and she peeks in: roast beef and corn bread with raisins. "And here's your key. I put a lock on the door for you. There's plenty for your breakfast there unless you give in and share with Duniway."

"I thought I might come back for breakfast."

"Sure, if you want to."

As she goes to the door, she calls back, "I never heard of a horse that ate bread."

Vincent shrugs. "You never heard of Duniway, then. And if you try to take something away from her once she's got it, you'll catch a face full of hooves."

It is indeed night, and it is large all around her, but strangely bright. Above her the moon examines the desert, and the sprawled junipers cast precise silhouettes. I am a scout in a new country, she tells herself. I will have to file a detailed report. Once they are well away from Two Forks, Duniway goes willingly. It is as if in that great bone the mare calls a head she carries a chart showing where the nearest grain is to be found. Once, when Esther, uncertain of the path, hauls back on the reins, the mare bounces her chin and tears her head forward.

The shadows are flattening, and it is darker. A flake of snow strikes Esther's glove, and a few more follow. Duniway's sallow mane begins to whiten. By the time they come upon Half-a-Mind, its ice thinly frosted, and turn north, the snow is rushing down in fat millions. Behind them Duniway's tracks are dark and wet. The locks of Esther's hair that have fallen out of her hat are white and frozen on her scarf. She is longing to reach shelter, but when she sees the dark shapes of the cabin and its little outbuildings looming through the snow's gauze, she considers turning the mare around. The cabin is like a chicken house or a corncrib. Surely it can't really be meant for people. For a person.

She dismounts onto numbed feet and leads Duniway into the dark stable. She unsaddles and unbridles her. In the blackness she throws a blanket over the mare's high back and lugs the tack into the corner and lays it on a pile of hay. She puts her fingers into the mare's water bucket—Vincent has apparently filled it, thank goodness, for she doesn't fancy stumbling down to the lakeshore and breaking through the crust, even with a lantern. She puts double handfuls of grain into the feedbox bolted to the wall. Then she hurries through the collecting snow toward the cabin and fumbles for the key Vincent has given her. For a moment she thinks she has lost it, but then her fingers find its slim, icy shape deep in the lining of her pocket. The lock is new. It clicks open, a city sound.

A few coals gleam in the stove, and by their light she puts a match to the lamp that stands on the table. Vincent has indeed been hard at work here. The room is now patched with all sorts of materials. Old sawn boards, a few rough planks that look to have been chipped and smoothed with a hatchet, black tar paper, and thick sheaves of newsprint busy with old words—all are nailed, pegged, and in some places plastered against the walls. The dignified banner titles of the *Century Intelligence*, the *Peterson Argus*, and the *Prineville Review* are to be seen at all latitudes and longitudes around the room, even on the ceiling. In a couple of places, including the wall at the foot of the bed, she recognizes forlorn scraps of the blue toile wallpaper that adorns the Two Forks parlor and office, here to much less elegant effect. The bed is now dressed in a ticking-stripe quilt, and her trunk, open, is at the foot. She pokes up the fire and adds more coal. Then, still in her coat, she sits and waits until the fire begins to have some effect on the cold.

When she can no longer see her breath, she takes off her dress and puts on her nightdress over her woolens. In her valise she has a bottle of ink, which she puts on the table near the stove to warm. She takes out her pocket watch. She had it set right at the ranch, but it has run down. What is the exact time? Was it perhaps six o'clock when she left Two Forks, and is it a quarter past seven now? Near enough will have to do. She winds it up and places it, too, on the table, for there is nothing at the bedside.

Now with pen and paper she sits at the table and draws a little calendar. Today is the sixteenth of January. She marks the sixteenths of February, of March, and of April. There is enough in her purse to buy a ticket back, and she may wire for what else she may need. But she won't be able to keep herself for long in Chicago. She will have to find some work to do. And she finds it difficult to admit that, having arrived at a place after a long journey, she would like nothing so much as to return home. She would like to retract the gesture, roll time back up like a length of ribbon, and find herself standing again at a window in Union Station, waiting to push the heavy coins across the counter to the ticket agent, his face tinted pale green by his eyeshade.

But here she is, now. She crosses today off the calendar and hangs it on one of Vincent's new nails. Then she turns to a small collection of papers in her own hand. She began them the month after her mother died, and now and then she adds a bit. "Dear Ma. Dear Ma." The snow whispers and scrapes on the boards outside. She dips the pen again and begins to write.

Dear Ma. It may surprise you to hear that I am homesteading a claim in Oregon. I'm writing this on a piece of bark with a lump of charcoal, sitting on a hewn stump. Well—nearly, at least.

She describes everything that has happened and all the people she has met. Pick and Vincent, Noggin Koerner of the gray smile. Strange, droll Jane Fremont and Violet Fowler, postmistress, desperate for influence; the earnest, loud cattleman Carey Stoop; the burly, coiled Cruff brothers up in the grass on the bluff. Two women, Delight and Delores, who apparently share a child, and the child herself, Marguerite. Esther spends some sentences on the episode of the stewed corn.

The account covers three pages, back and front. Even with the blots and cross-outs, she likes the look of her own writing. It is solid. She herself weighs more, having written it. Thoreau was alone in the woods for a time, and look what he made of his solitude. She will turn over a new leaf during this sojourn; she will be industrious and independent. When she is older, she will be able to say that these privations have tested her and made her the woman of character she has become. She adds a few words to this effect, blows on the ink to dry it, and sits back for a moment in her chair, listening for any sound. There is only the snow scrubbing the roof, ticktacking on the window.

The newspapers on the wall in front of her tell of other times, other people. Births from years ago: Stoop and Duncan and Jacob, paired with Christian names she doesn't recognize. The railroad coming to Peterson. An election campaign in Portland. Somewhere else, a fight that led to a murder. An account of the fall of Manila, back when Americans were allies of the Filipinos and not enemies.

It is odd to think of all that time has wrought, and will wreak, on the people she described tonight, on everyone. Someone certainly will dig a cellar, run for office, bring forth children, fall victim to evil, perpetrate a war. She wonders, briefly, what will happen to her. What some newspaper, placed for warmth in the wall of some other room, may say of Esther Chambers.

It is warm enough now to stand right by the window and look out. She scrapes a little frost off the glass and makes a peephole. At the end of the path lies the pale field of Half-a-Mind. In the heavy storm the snow seems to fall upward, like white birds escaping off the water.

10

PICK, TOO, SITS DOWN with pen in hand after the girl has gone. He peruses his ledger, considers his business in a number of particulars, and is pleased. Because Esther has been willing and has understood the essential points of the situation, Pick finds himself with free access to water that others must go without.

He likes to plan for his cattle and his ranch and the lands that surround and support them. He is alert and peaceful in the contemplation of them; they are his home. And he is familiar with beef. Since he was a boy, he has driven it before him and led it behind him, has dug water holes for it in the heat of the day with crisping hands, has dosed it with quinine and supplied it with salt. He has steamed great lots of corn over fires for its food, has brought it in heat to be bred, upended it in the womb, delivered it into daylight, washed its eyes, and given it his finger to suck. He has dragged its young away while it bawled. He has stitched its wounds with thread and applied salves of axle grease and carbolic acid to them. He has burned its hide with an iron, notched its ear with a knife, and severed its testicles with a razor. He has kicked mounds of fresh manure looking for evidence of disease.

He makes a few sketches in his ledger, of particular promising cows. He dislikes a coarse creature with a thick hide, joints full of ligament, and long horns that curl: all that is waste, for it cannot be sold or eaten. Density of the bone makes a good animal, also a lean shank and a muscled rib and some length in the juncture of the thighs called the twist. He seeks a neat, strong little animal whose eating goes directly to the point of fleshing it out, and he most prefers one that matures for the market early, for breeding such animals is how a cowman gets ahead. That, and nourishing them well, which takes forage, a great deal of it, and water.

Noggin Koerner walks into the study, grazing the doorframe with his knuckles by way of a knock.

"I did what you said. Duncan's down one farm wagon. You ought to have seen it catch fire. Whoof! That'll put a crimp in him getting his wool to Peterson," he says. "I guess all those sheep yahoos will keep their slingshots in their pockets for a while after they hear about this. Maybe I should take my matchbook to some other of them."

"I don't want to come back at somebody who's done me no wrong. It's only Duncan I know for sure did the windows, anyway. I saw his fat yellow head as they hightailed it back toward Peterson."

"Those Cruffs are wrong enough."

"Not wrong in the legal sense. Those bluffs are open range. Got to be careful, there. They know the law, and they aren't scared."

"Mouthy."

"I won't argue with that."

Noggin doesn't seem inclined to go. "I thought about tying one of Duncan's dogs to the wagon before I put the match to it. They wouldn't soon forget that."

Pick has begun to work on his books again, but he looks up. "I told you to leave the cussed dogs out of it."

"Little son of a bitch tried to bite me."

"I mean it. Rein that crap in."

"Yeah, all right. By the way, Elijah's foreman says Elijah and Carey are thinking about hitting up Peaslee for some of the cash for Elliot."

"That's a dumb idea. For all he's half cracked, Peaslee doesn't do what's downright against the law. He won't go for that."

"He dyed those birds."

"Wild birds, so no crime."

"You want me to provide him some encouragement on this Elliot thing?"

"Let Peaslee do as he pleases. And I don't want you cutting any shines on that front, either. I'll make the decisions."

Noggins nods. "That's why I call you the boss."

Now into his ledger Pick copies a passage from a book on ranching that he has found useful.

> Nothing but sheer ignorance, or obstinacy, can be an apology for adhering to a bad practice in anything; and when only a common diligence and foresight is necessary to acquire the good, he who doggedly persists in the bad deserves little sympathy, either for his want of success or his absolute losses.

Common diligence and foresight. Yes, and discipline. He has these in plenty, and the future, therefore, is his friend.

PART TWO

THE LIBERTY AND THE RING

11

EACH MORNING, Esther escapes the cold cabin as soon as it is seemly and rides to Two Forks for breakfast. It is a grumpy and busy meal among the buckaroos, who don't like waking up any more than anybody else and are all elbows in their pursuit of coffee and ham. Eventually, though, everyone is astride and gone to ride a fence line or mend a windmill, and the house is quiet except for Vincent going about his tasks with an air of merry duty. She peels potatoes for him, she minds the corn bread as it bakes, and she greases rows of boots. These are all things she's done before, though not on so large a scale, and Vincent tells her stories and she tells him some of hers. Sometimes, though, Vincent's "not much for talking," and she will take any excuse to ride to Century and, putting Duniway in at Schmidt's Livery Stable, distract herself in what passes for a town.

The wagon that caught fire out at Brookie Duncan's sheep ranch a couple of weeks earlier was much discussed among the women she has met. Mornings, they often congregate for a time in the church or in Delight Endicott's front room, and Esther joins them there. "Brookie says it was arson," says one woman. "He could smell the kerosene." Mrs. Fowler, the postmistress who looks like a puppet, says, "Well, he'd smell kerosene anyway if he was drunk and toppled a lamp and burned his own wagon." Ida Schmidt of the livery says this isn't fair, that Brookie wasn't even at home that evening, and Jane Fremont says with some impatience that it looks like more of that tit-for-tat rumpus in the world of the stockmen. Phelia Jacob says she doesn't put it past a good-for-nothing like Brookie to burn his own wagon and then blame a cattleman.

"Is it a lot of trouble to get another wagon?" Esther asks. The responses come thick and fast: wagons are expensive, Brookie has lost a lot of lambs to coyotes and other accidents in the last couple of years, and even should he manage to afford it, a new one would have to be ordered and built. Meanwhile, everybody else's wagons will be in spring use, and he'll be hard-pressed to borrow one. "It'll take him twice as long to get his wool to Peterson, so he'll lose money," Jane says, "and it'll leave his wife with only a couple of mules to ride while he's gone. We can pitch in to help her, though. Can't we?" She looks at the other women, whose remarks "Of course" and "Indeed we shall" cascade over one another in a flow of sincerity.

In the afternoons Esther visits Joe Peaslee, whom she finds perusing the newspapers. He predicts that rose water will soon be hard to come by, or that belt buckles are plentiful and therefore as cheap as chalk—which indicates how he should order and price his goods. "I'm lucky to be out of soldiering," he tells her. "I didn't like it."

"Why did you ever go in?"

"That's a good question. Because I was young and feisty. Because I ran out of money. Because I thought I'd learn something." His face dims a moment, then brightens. "Now, storekeeping I'm suited for. I believe I have a talent."

But since his formula for prediction depends not only on his devoted reading of congressional speeches on the subject of gold but also on the subtle half steps of pain playing up his back, his store is frequently stocked with strange items that he cannot for the moment sell. At the beginning of February, for example, he gets a great lading of ready-made shirts, not white nor blue, but orange, which fill his upper shelves and nourish cowboy jokes for weeks, until a large family of Swedes, pausing in Century while scouting land, carts them all off. Thereafter the buckaroos note that you can't be snuck up on anymore by a Swede, as you'd have to be blind not to see those shirts coming.

Joe sometimes prices common items very low in order to make way for something special he plans to bring on: a velvet case full of astronomical instruments or a book on the cookery of India. People are accustomed to asking, "What are you trying to get rid of, Joe?" and leaving loaded with three bolts of dress goods, a case of canned beans, and a year's worth of tooth powder. Many of his predictions work against him, but often he makes a killing. There are numbers of stories about this luck. At the livery stable, when Esther is putting up Duniway so she won't have to stand in the cold, Odie Underwood the saloonkeeper tells Esther about a time last spring when the district attorney came down from Peterson and bought three brand-new Singers to give to his three maiden daughters. The sewing machines had been languishing in Peaslee's window since Christmas, but he wouldn't hear a word about discounting them, and when the district attorney, who had never been to Century before as far as anyone knew, rode up and tied his horse, Joe Peaslee waved him in as though he'd been expecting him. So, though he is sport for cowboys, Joe never quite goes bankrupt, and he and the district attorney got to be friendly over their transaction. The sewing machines had the desired effect, and the daughters got sudden strings of beaux.

Joe doesn't say much more about fighting the Indians, but Esther learns something about his earlier life. He came from the East long ago and has never gone back. He was a homely, lively boy, she gathers, thin and squinty, with an interest in classifications and taxonomies, in conjugations and genealogies; he was sent to Baltimore for schooling, and his lapels were forever being groomed by one or another elderly aunt. But he was dissatisfied and restless. This was in '59, before the war. He was ashamed to admit that war did not interest him, he did not care for honor much, and he thought others were better qualified to defend the Union.

One morning he went out to say goodbye to a cousin who was

leaving for the West. His cousin asked him to hop up into the buggy and ride a little way. At the edge of town Joe thought he might as well go as far as Harrisburg, where he had left his watch to be repaired. By Harrisburg he was emancipated. He had only a little money and the magnifying glass in his trouser pocket, but he had passed, still sleepy, through some membrane, and he could not go home.

In the West he began trapping and trading, and hiring out to cut trees. Had he stayed in the East, he muses aloud to Esther, he would have perhaps become an expert in banks, or clocks, or in cutting silhouettes, but here there was nothing made by people worth studying. Here there were just giant chunks of beauty and disaster, ridged with the odd flora of the cool, wild, windy, and wet. Joe developed an interest in plants and discovered one or two varieties that were to be found in no books. He shows Esther the colored sketches he made of them all those years ago. One is a penstemon, of intense lavender blue with a stripe of white in the throat, like the silk skirt of a French doll, which he found growing on a rocky slope recently denuded of snow. The other is a pyrola—wintergreen—that sprang up from a cloak of hemlock needles around the base of a tree. It was leafless and sulphur yellow. "Like the crook of an elfin shepherd," he says. "But alight. As if it were made of fireflies."

He writes a letter now and then to the national organization of botanists but has never received a reply, so *Pyrola peasleii* has gone unlogged and unnoted. Still, sometimes he closes his store in the middle of the day and goes out in the desert botanizing and zoologizing, He takes his spyglass and looks through the wrong end at little dry gray plants, little piles of rock.

Esther puts on two scarves and goes with him. She tries to learn what it is he is looking at: bitterbrush, rabbitbrush, big sage—but when she has memorized a name, she can't remember what the thing looks like. She is used to bright colors and actual flowers, a dahlia, a gladiolus. Who can tell one gray thing from another, and why should one? She is beginning to know the birds, though.

There is the turkey vulture, who flies in a wobbly drunken way, and the desert magpie, who looks just like any magpie but nests on the ground and backs into her nest, keeping everything in sight until she is well in. The jackrabbits are thin and long, and so fast one's eyes can't follow their zagging bolts through the brush.

Often Joe doesn't stay out long. He gets a message from his spine and becomes cross or puzzled and has to go home. He smokes cigarettes then, which he rolls himself. Since his back has need of recovery from its bouts of prophecy, he often conducts business lying supine on his front counter. Customers help themselves and make their own change at the drawer, looking down into his face and asking after his health. Tucked under a plaid blanket, his head on a bag of flour, he converses with them about the weather, the railroad, and politics in Peterson. The store is also home to an odorous yellow cat whose long fur is matted here and there into hard lumps and whose long tail, dragging along the ground, picks up bits of straw and smears of mud. This cat often lurches up onto the counter and lays itself across Joe's neck.

During those times Esther does chores for him or peruses the bookshelves for something to take back to the claim to read in those hours after dark and before bed, when she needs to be transported. Among the books somewhere, he claims, is the one about the orphan who explored the attic. Esther browses the shelves and looks in boxes but has not found it.

Near the bookshelves, hanging down from the molding in the back room, a little askew, is an oil portrait of a man with a head as large, pocked, and blond as a prize cheese. While she looks for the orphan book, this fellow regards her with cockeyed censure. "Who is he?" she finally asks resentfully.

Joe answers from the counter. He holds up a forefinger, which the cat stands up on his chest to inspect before lying down again. "Larsson Jacob, do you mean? Esther, Lars is our forefather! Lars in his genius saw the future of Century, and—hoping to give Peterson a run for its money—platted us way down here in the scrub. He subscribed to the belief that *rain follows* where the *plow leads*. The desert would be made green if the farmer would just assert himself. Human activity woos the land, he theorized, convinces it to give up its harsh ways and become hospitable. Lars put up windmills on the townsite, over solid earth where no well had yet been dug, that the desert might grasp his intentions and acquiesce!" He nods at the ceiling, murmuring, "Lars is a joy to me."

The industrious Lars also caused a telegraph line to be strung from Peterson to Century as soon as Main Street was graded, though there was no telegraph office to attach it to, only a tented wagon where the line workers lived. When it was in time connected, he is reported to have said, "There is a field of power along the line, and by—a process—it disperses obstacles, even the rabbits." The mechanism of the process was unclear, but it was his observation that the marauding of hard-won gardens by jackrabbits had diminished in the second year of the town, and this relief the homesteaders could attribute directly to his prescience with the windmills and the telegraph. There was rain in the wintertime—Lars Jacob believed the telegraph poles combed the wind and caused it to give up moisture—and the first settlers grew decent crops of rye, which in later years were recalled as splendidly abundant. For four more seasons Century was lush; then dry years lined up like debt collectors. The rabbits returned in droves and the windmills spun uselessly over their boggy well shafts and the farms dried up and Larsson Jacob had a stroke.

His children, an unconvinced brood who had spent their playtime grubbing sage and praying for rain, did not farm, but bought cattle and prospered, and they now live all over the desert, from Peterson down to Lakeview. In time the presence of Lars comes to seem comforting to Esther rather than censorious. *That's it. Read, think, and speculate,* he seems to say as she pages through her French or history or grammar, *and don't go too long in the sun.* And she does read, for when she returns to Chicago in April, she means to sit for her examinations. Then she will be graduated, and getting somewhere.

12

ONE AFTERNOON, a little sleepy over the moods of verbs, she lets her gaze fall idly on the typewriter under the potato sack at Peaslee's. Her mother typed for Mr. Fleming, and Esther had learned a little when she visited that office. She lifts the sack. "Does this work?"

"That high-quality sack will hold dozens of potatoes," says Joe Peaslee to the ceiling.

"The typewriter!"

"Oh, the typewriter? Yes. I bought it nearly new. The previous owner was a young lady who was the amanuensis to a railroad bigwig but left that occupation for domestic pursuits. It hasn't had much use this winter." Interested, as though he's never seen the typewriter himself, he gets down off the counter and winces his way over to her.

The machine is lacquer black, with rows of keys curved and descending like seats in a theater. She rubs the dust off the nameplate: LIBERTY MACHINES. She presses down on a key: *I*. A thin metal arm flings itself up from the machine's insides and pauses, just shy of the platen.

"Do you use it?"

"Not much now. Maddening—too slow. Now when I complain to McKinley, I use ink."

"Your handwriting is very elegant," Esther says. "I'm sure the President has noticed."

"I know it is. Not all of us old soldiers scratch like hens."

She reaches out and presses the keys again: *E. S. T.*

"Here." He picks up an old handbill and slips it into the machine with some clever manipulation of his fingers around the black roller.

What shall she say? Anything. The first words in her mind. She glances at her grammar.

THE INFI

"Does it only do the uppercase?"
"You shift up and down. Here's the key."

THE INFI TheInfinitive mood isthat fsrm of the verb,which xpresses thebeing, acti

Two of the little arms rise at once and collide and cling. Joe Peaslee reaches in and disentangles them.

At this moment several men come into the store. She leans back in the chair to look at them through the curtain. They are the spry Elijah Jacob—descendant of Lars, she realizes—handsome Carey Stoop, and Noggin Koerner. She looks back at her typing.

which xpresses thebeing, action or passion,
in an unlimited manner, and without person or number; as
To read, to speak.

She works with the thumb and first two fingers of each hand, gazing at the *H* in the middle of the keyboard, her mouth open, eyelids heavy, glancing now and then at her grammar, which is held open by a large bar of Jaxon soap she has pinched from a shelf.

The men seem to be discussing something rather serious. Joe has shaded his eyes with one hand as he listens, and he pats the counter with the other one. Occasionally Elijah Jacob laughs. They are speaking of Mr. Elliot, the train representative. Elijah says, "You have to see how everybody will benefit if we get that spur line down here, Joe."

Carey shifts energetically from one foot to the other. "Why, you'd sell out everything here three times a month, Peaslee! What would you do with all that cash?"

"I know what I'd do," says Elijah. He bounces up tall in his boots and speaks slyly. "Holiday in San Francisco. Twenty hotel dinners, twenty boat trips around the bay, a diamond bracelet for Phelia, and a Chinese girl to tell my fortune."

The men lower their voices, and all Esther can hear now is the shortness of Joe's answers. The others lean in. She is leaning, too, trying to hear, when suddenly Noggin Koerner's face appears right in front of her at the curtain.

"What're you doing there?" he says.

"Oh, I'm just practicing." It always startles her that he is really quite young. He has some condition, she supposes, that prevents him from growing hair. Too ornery to grow it, says Vincent.

"Huh. Those your books?"

"Joe's, mostly. This grammar is mine."

"Huh. There's a lot of 'em."

In the front room, voices get louder. Carey Stoop sounds vexed. "I don't know about you, Peaslee, but I'm sick of starving to death out here while these outfits closer to the train make all the money. A lot of 'em are bad ranchers, they don't run things tight or keep their buckaroos in line, but they get their beef to Chicago fast, and that's what counts. Why shouldn't we join that party, I want to know. Why should I only get paid for a bunch of skin and bones when he was a fattie coming out of my corral?"

"I've no objection to you earning, Carey. But I won't bribe an official of the railroad. Much too complicated."

Elijah Jacob tips up and back in his boots, shaking his head. "He means not to pitch in, Carey. Look at him. The train will come and he'll turn the profit whether he contributes now or not. Well, Peaslee, if you're a man who can stand to reap the benefits of some-body else's work, then so be it."

"Work—is that what you call gathering money for Elliot's nest egg? I don't have to subscribe to every campaign somebody dreams up, particularly those on the shady side of the statutes. I have neither the energy nor the liquidity to do so. But I don't presume to tell you what you should do, Jacob, or anyone else. So let us not have hard feelings."

"Fair enough." Elijah chunks the heel of his boot on the floor. His tone changes, darkens a little, becomes both warning and sentimental. "I know you understand what's at stake here, Joe. This town is always a little too close to the edge, business-wise. We have a duty to assure our future."

"The future. Ah." Joe doesn't seem persuaded by this appeal.

Esther has been listening closely, and now Noggin Koerner waves his hand in front of her face. She is again startled. He shows her his gray-gummed smile, and seeing the yellow cat passing his feet, he gives a little kick at its hind end, knocking it awry.

"Don't do that," she says.

"Do what?" He tosses his hat in his hands, then flips it and puts it onto his head as he goes, saying over his shoulder, "Don't work too hard. It'll curdle you up like that teacher."

When they've gone, Joe comes back with a cigarette in his hand. His mouth works a bit. He sits down at his desk and looks at his pen.

"What is it? Have you a letter to write?"

"Oh, why should I?" He is cross. "It seems the Far West Railway's Oregon and Washington representative—"

"Mr. Elliot, with the silver boots?"

"Yes. Mr. Elliot is not all that he should be. Friendlier with Century's finer citizens than other towns would think proper, given that they are all competing for the same prize. I suppose someone should explain the situation to Elliot's superiors, that they may take steps to correct him if they choose. But my philosophy is: Why interfere with Elliot or anyone else? All of it is already what it's going to be."

"Do you mean the railroad? Or the—the world?"

Joe says nothing, but examines the burning end of his cigarette.

"One can't sit back if one knows there is injustice. That's disgraceful," Esther says.

He smokes and looks extremely diverted. "Disgraceful?"

"One *should* interfere. One can't just sit and let it unfold."

"An orphan repudiates Providence? Look what blasphemies the twentieth century wreaks! You may be injuring your own cause, you know, if you think Elliot should be discouraged."

I can see it might disturb you not to follow the letter of the law, Pick had said. But he couldn't have meant that one must ignore all the law always. "I don't know what my own cause is," she says. "But you're not talking about Providence, anyway. You don't believe in a divine plan. You mean that it's all just one thing pushing and another falling, and that one pushing something else. A machine, and you think we should just let it work."

"Perhaps the world *is* a machine. And we're watching it wind down."

"It isn't! It has people in it, and they do things, they act. Machines don't make anything new, and now so much is happening that never happened before. You must not read the papers."

"I do read the papers. But it all seems the same to me."

How could he say so? She remembers sitting heavyhearted in the Flemings' spare room those last days in December before she left for the West. She looked often at her ticket then, reading the date on it. December 31, December 31, it said, as if a bird in a cage had not been cloaked for the night in the dark house of her mind. But outside her window, Chicago was delirious with anticipation for the turning of the century. Great events were expected, great progress heralded, and much in the century then passing into history was deplored. Fused together by a merriment so colossal it mimicked the effects of drink, the people of Chicago—architects, butchers, coal carriers, schoolgirls—went arm in arm about the town like crabs, tipping sideways, making a dance-hall step of their lost balance. In the big houses, fine clocks ticked toward midnight; sherry and champagne plashed; women enjoyed the liquid drag of silk dresses on stairs. There was a lively world for someone to join when she was finished being sad.

With some stubbornness she says, "I don't think the world is just a repeating machine. No more are we. There is an unknown future."

"So you are a free person who can make her destiny?"

"Why shouldn't I be?"

"It may be an illusion."

"Then it's one I like."

Joe laughs. He puts out his cigarette and stores the butt carefully in a cigar box. His eyes are glazy and soft. "All right. Elijah wouldn't want me to talk about his activities, but for your sake, free orphan, I will inform the railroad that Mr. Elliot appears to have discretionary income incommensurate with his station, that he is cozy with our local cattle lords, and that they may draw their own conclusions from these facts. But it is purely symbolic that I write. Don't expect the railroad or anyone else to thank me, and don't expect the world to change." He takes up the pen and dips it. She is disturbed that he is so cynical, but she is surprised and pleased that she has even momentarily prevailed over so dark an attitude.

She has an affinity for typewriting, she finds. She never suspected she'd be good at it, but her hands seem to have been waiting to learn. *Amanuensis to a railroad bigwig.* As she becomes more practiced, she can lift a whole lesson from the grammar at once, four lines with examples and roman numerals, and reproduce it with only a few glances back at the book. If she makes an error, she cuts a small piece of paper, licks it so it will stick to the page, and inks in the proper letter. Soon she decides to recapitulate in type the letter to her mother she has been writing, and to go forward from there.

This project stretches out before her and gives her a feeling of secret purpose. No one knows she writes this letter; she doesn't want anyone to know. They would think it perhaps sweet and pitiable, orphanish. This is not the truth. She is not confused. Her mother is gone and cannot hear her. But still she writes.

13

ONE MORNING IT OCCURS to Esther that even though she means to give it up, she might as well see the land she has signed her name to, and she takes up the plat map given her by Pick and looks at the marked section.

One hundred and sixty acres. It sounds like a great deal, but each side is only a quarter mile long. The cabin lies where Pick has marked it, just inside the western boundary of the claim about halfway up. The lake is shown by a few hatch lines just southeast of the cabin. She takes a pencil and draws the bluff where it lies out there, running down the east side of Half-a-Mind. But this is all she knows about it. She means to ride the whole perimeter and so starts south along the lake.

A few birds have begun to assemble at Half-a-Mind, and there is an oblong of green water showing in the middle. One of her walks with Joe Peaslee took them to the lake, and during a fit of his mumbling and note taking she learned the names of some birds: grebe, avocet, the thin little phalaropes stamping around on the clouded, crisp ice near the shore. "Grebe. Avocet. Phalarope," she recites, and then, as she turns from the lake to strike out north through the brush, she sings the names in ascending steps, do-mi-so.

The buckaroos often sing, and she knows why. The unpeopled distance and the careless cold weigh upon a person, compressing the spirit into a chunk without movement. Any two notes sung together press back and make a space for the tiny soul to warm up and swirl about.

" 'I've got a mule, her name is Sal,' " she sings. " 'Fifteen miles on the Erie Canal.' " It is a lovely song, plaintive but vigorous, its minor key turning major on the pivotal little *oh*. As if resenting being compared to a mule, or simply listening, Duniway swivels her ears back toward Esther.

"We've hauled some barges in our day
filled with lumber, coal, and hay
and we know every inch of the way
from Albany to Buffalo, oh,
Low bridge, everybody down,
low bridge, because we're coming to a—"

A whistle—*whee-ee? whee-ee?*—floats up from the water behind. "Curlew," she says aloud.

After ten minutes' mare walk south along the property line past the lake, she reaches a writhing juniper of unusual breadth. *That's your corner*, Pick had told her. Now she goes east, toward the rocky heaps where the bluff diminishes into the plain. She wishes her old papa could see her ride. He would nod and purse his lips in mock criticism under his mustache: *Very bad, I'm afraid. Very bad indeed.* He would call her by the Indian names he had invented for her. These were "Catfoot," because she was a quiet little girl, and, when she knew something that surprised him, "Listens-at-Doors." He used to claim that Catfoot knew several languages, including Swahili, and that Listens-at-Doors had swindled him out of his best fountain pen. Catfoot was organizing an African expedition and had not invited him to join the party, and Listens-at-Doors wore a false beard. Catfoot never ate, and Listens-at-Doors never slept. It was a good thing for him that there was usually only Esther, he said, for he was no match for the three of them in cahoots. He's been gone now for so many years.

She makes the turn to go below the bluff, and Duniway picks her way with care along that short slope. Above her the cliff's edge marks where her land becomes rangeland. Just ahead is the path that switchbacks up across the orange face, which extends up dozens and dozens of feet, not quite so high as the Marshall Field store at home, but certainly more intimidating, with its flakes of rock and cracks and hanging roots. She is in deep shadow here, cold, so she's glad when she comes to her final turn. At the northeast corner, Pick had told her, look for the surveyors' stake. She finds it easily, and beyond that another post with a metal plaque affixed: FAR WEST NAVIGATION AND RAILWAY. Well. It certainly looks as if they mean to come. Pick will be happy about that. She turns toward town and clicks the mare into a trot.

When she dismounts in front of Joe's and ties Duniway to the rail, she sees a movement under the board sidewalk near her feet. It is the cat. Usually one can't keep the cat away; it cannot seem to keep its own blood warm without pressing up against a human. But now it will not come out. It wears an evil, thirsty expression, eyes narrowed.

"Puss-puss," she says, and reaches under and pulls it out.

The head. The poor head. There is a cut in the skin between the ears, and a dark flap of bloodied fur is loose there, as though someone has meant to peel a potato and stopped partway. There is blood on the neck and wet blood on Esther's hands. She gathers up the cat and takes him inside, where Joe is consulting with Violet Fowler over a pile of dress goods.

Mute, she brings the cat before them.

"Mercy on us," murmurs Violet. "Scalped." She reaches out. The cat exhales a ghastly breath of warning.

Esther storms, "It was done on purpose. Look at how straight the cut is."

"A cat gets into all kinds of trouble," Violet says. "This is probably barbed wire. Squeezing under some fence where he ought not to be. Some old nail."

"Perhaps," says Joe. He bends the cat's ears forward to examine the wound. "But that is not comfortable. No, that is uncomfortable. We shall fix you up, old friend. Clean you up and put in a stitch." He gets a piece of cloth and doses it from one of his bottles, then wipes the wound clean. The cat huddles on his lap.

"I don't suppose it would have been an Indian," says Violet. "Not in the twentieth century. Every last baby of them was sent up to Yakima twenty years ago."

"Whoever it was—why must people be such dreadful bullies?" Esther asks. "What has a cat ever done to them?"

Joe strokes the cat. "Perhaps they mean it for me."

"You, Joe? Why?"

He is silent, threading a needle. Esther feels a flash of cold. "Not—not that letter."

"Probably not. How would anyone know what I wrote in a letter?"

"I'm sure I couldn't say," says Violet, flushing. "I handle the mail with care."

"Someone at the railroad may have told Elliot. That would explain it. And as Violet says, it could be some old nail. Why do people bully?" Joe puts a knot on the thread. "I'd ask—given what people are—why do they ever leave off?"

14

JANE, HOLDING A RIFLE, is standing in the small snowy field beside her claim cabin. She prods something with the barrel, then bends and picks it up. It is long and dark and leggy. A jackrabbit. Esther wriggles her cold feet to warm them before dismounting to examine the rabbit. It's been shot in the shoulder. Its fur ruffles a little in the wind. Esther is glad she herself doesn't have to kill rabbits, and in Jane's lonely figure she senses both revulsion and determination. What is it, really? Penance? She shivers.

"Does it disturb you?"

Esther explains what has just passed at Joe's.

Jane frowns. "That is very—well, I hope it's nothing. An accident."

"In Chicago, people thought the small towns were calm places. Safe."

"But in Century, animals get hurt."

"And windows broken and wagons burned. It's like a wayward boy running wild."

"Yes. Well, but we can't give such boys up for lost. They must be taught what is right."

"But who can teach a whole town?"

"I don't know. Not me, certainly. But I want better for Century."

Esther agrees. Sturdy, striving, half built, gripped down on its austere and spicy earth. A place worthy of the work of love. "I hope the cat heals quickly."

"Yes. Let us hope for that." Jane wraps a string around the

rabbit's ankles and carries it over to hang it upside down on a hook beside the door. She looks at Esther in apology. "One doesn't like to kill them, but in the summer they're a true plague. One day radishes, the next, holes. Would you like to see the place?" she asks wryly. "It won't take long."

They look at the snowy clods of last year's rye field and regard a tiny pumpkin, amber with decay, that lies still connected to its blackened vine in the handkerchief square of the kitchen garden. The lower walls of the stable are made of desert rocks slabbed together with clay. "It'll hold until that clay crumbles," Jane says.

"Did you build all of this?"

"Only a bit. I haven't much time to learn how to do it, with teaching school. But I'm paid for teaching, and so I'm able to hire hands. I may get ahead, one day."

This is another difference from Chicago, that so many people seem to be alone. Of course there were those without families in cities, but they seemed to have had them, or to be going to have them. Here are Joe, Jane Fremont, Pick, Vincent. Forming friendships the way one would lean three sticks together to make a fire. But otherwise thinking and planning and living inside the one, the only, the lonely mind. Well, that isn't exactly true. All of them hold conversation with another thing, at least—Pick with the range, Vincent with Pick, Joe Peaslee with his books and his oracular spine. She herself with her departed. Jane with what? Something, Esther thinks.

The stable comprises three stalls. In one stands Jane's short black gelding, the Vicar, in the next a milk cow with flappy, defeated-looking haunches. In the third is a half-grown copper Hereford with large ears.

"What's her name?"

"She hasn't got one. She's just the maverick. She was a gift."

"From whom?"

"That I don't know. I came home one day, and here she was. You see the *J* brand? It's supposed to be for Jane, it seems. The brand was new, just healing. Probably she was wild last fall—born late, never branded—and someone found her and claimed her on my behalf. Very kind! So I am a rancher now, as well as farmer and teacher."

"If you kept a sheep, you would be everybody," says Esther.

"Yes. Well, perhaps Santa Claus will bring a fat little merino instead of the usual coal."

"But you would never get coal! You're very good!"

Jane Fremont laughs the sort of laugh that comes out as a puff of disdain through the nose. "Bless you for thinking so," she says. "I don't know who brought the maverick, but I begin to have an idea. It's a buckaroo's business, catching a wild calf."

That silver hairbrush from Joe Peaslee's, and now this little cow. There were ranchers enough, Esther knows, and their sons and relations, to make the narrowing down a task. One of Jane's students, besotted? Or someone who had seen her in passing, who liked to assist from a distance and not be thanked. Pick might do something like that, Esther thinks. Pick, who is not married, has not yet married. She sees herself again at Two Forks, giving instructions, making beds. She thinks of Pick's mischievous lupine smile. She hasn't seen him single out Jane for attention. But she'd be a match for him. Esther's not sure how she feels about that prospect.

The cabin is large and clean, and the flames in the stove are orange and green. Esther sits down in a rocking chair with the Sears, Roebuck catalogue in her lap, warms her feet, and tries not to fall asleep. From an open shelf Jane takes a sterling coffeepot with a sinuous neck. She boils water, makes coffee and sieves it, and pours it into china cups that sit high on their pedestaled bases. On the cups Japanese birds fan their tails with feathers like flared threads. Hungry for details, Esther caresses the cup, draws the shape of the bird's head with her fingertip. There is a glossy loaf of braided bread, which Jane cuts and hands across.

The musty smell off the voluminous pages of Sears, Roebuck is as comforting as the hearth. Jane Fremont is burrowing about in her sewing basket while Esther peruses fancy hats and dishware and machinery and seeds and garden tools and needles and other notions, as well as more intimate elixirs and salves that promise plumping and whitening and blushing for less than a penny a day. Esther thinks with resentment of her own bumps and rashes, her protruding pins and laddered stockings, the griminess that collects on the ribbon lining of her corsets and has to be rubbed out again and again with a soapy finger. Jane appears complete. *She* is not still growing. Her clothes are old but elegant, and they fit like paint.

Perhaps her family was rich once. But who are they? She never speaks of them, and if they are dead, like Esther's, she would surely speak of them, would be unable to stop herself. It is sad if her family has become poor or suffered illness. Jane Fremont ought to be the toast of Boston. She has been to college, she plays the piano and reads Latin and even some Greek. In Chicago, anyway, she would be among the affianced young ladies in pleated white frocks, laughing on the streetcars, pouring into the parks for picnics with successful young men in their shirtsleeves and vests, everyone free and joyous and accomplished. None of them need ever call roll in a desert schoolhouse. "Do you miss your home?" Esther asks.

Jane Fremont holds several pins between her lips. She spreads a dress over her lap, removes the pins, and says, "Some days I do. But I'm a lady of the West now. I'll just have to hitch up my pants and get used to it."

"Doesn't your mother miss you?"

Jane puts the pins one by one into a tiny pincushion shaped like a strawberry. "I don't know if she does. I suppose she may. No, that's wrong of me. I'm sure she must."

A living mother, then. "Will you stay always?"

"Why not?"

"But—forgive me—did something . . . happen at home?"

"Oh, well, yes. Various things." She is silent. "Here I stay and try to work and be pleasant to my neighbors. And who knows— I may shock the world and get married one day."

"Some of the buckaroos at Two Forks think you're pretty."

"Some? Whatever is the matter with the rest of those fellows?"

"Why, I believe they prefer Mrs. Fowler!" Esther says with an air of innocence.

"Well!" says Jane. "And they may have her for a yodel, I daresay. I never saw a woman set her cap as she does when cowboys are circulating."

Esther scoffs. "I wouldn't want a cowboy. He would be on the range, or going to Nevada, or on his way back. He'd never be at home, isn't that so?"

"Just my sort of man. Salaried, yet invisible."

"You don't mean it. Do you? I would want someone to stay by me forever." Her words tumble out. "If I were ever to marry, that is."

"Why shouldn't you?"

She remembers a freckled and amusing boy, the cousin of a school friend, whose transparent friendliness had made her laugh every few moments when she was with him. He worked at a suburban ice-cream shop, and she persuaded her friend to ride the streetcar out to visit him, and then once, she went alone. But that day he seemed preoccupied, too busy or unwilling to talk with her. She felt ashamed, found wanting, and she did not go again. She thought of that boy at night for weeks. There is still no evidence that she will ever be acceptable to one of those rough, compelling creatures who can be so kind, or not, according to an insoluble code. But it would be wonderful to be sought. If she were the favorite of a man, she could go about and still draw attention and love; she could never step out of that lamp glow, for the light would travel with her.

"Listen," says Jane. "If you don't want the cowboys rattling away to Nevada, then you'd best hope for the train. When the train can take the cattle, you'll have cowboys stacked up on the porch like cordwood, with nothing to do but shell peas for you and shine your shoes. Changes are afoot, I daresay. And 'in the spring the wanton lapwing gets himself another crest.'"

Pick. How he stands, how he puts his hand over the muzzle of his horse for no reason she can see, and the horse stands there breathing into his still, rounded hand. She thinks of the boy from the ice-cream shop rubbing her shoe with a cloth. The thought is intimate, ticklish. She slaps both hands down on Sears, Roebuck in embarrassment.

Jane laughs, too. "You're not twenty-one, are you, Esther?"

This is unexpected, and she doesn't know what to say. She bends down to the sack at her feet and takes one of her mother's dresses out of it, cradling the bodice in her lap. She smooths it, her mind roving. Ah—she has it. "Could you—would you give me my examinations? I haven't been graduated, and I thought I'd— well, never mind. I just don't want to wait anymore."

Jane regards her with kindness, and nods. "I'd be honored to have you sit for your examinations in my school. Let us say in a month or so? You will have time to prepare. After we have our crops in the ground, but before the rabbits are at them." She hands Esther a pair of shears, handles first. "Find the center seam and cut the skirt there," she says. "It will be much more comfortable. And don't mind my questions. Let's just agree you're not a day over twenty. I'll bet a four-dollar dog on that."

15

PICK HAS MADE LOVE to three women in his life. The first was Minnie Dial, the wife of his first foreman Cody Dial, a genial girl with a gap between her front teeth and a ferocious talent with a cookstove. He was a dour kid then, barely able to raise a beard, riding around his ranch daydreaming about how to be a good man, strong and well thought of, a rich man who could be free when it was warranted and tight when it wasn't. Such a man was said to be square—nothing off about a fellow, his corners met, his sides aligned, and no quality in ascendancy over any other. A man of judgment. Out from the ranch in the morning, he thought about what to attempt and what to defer, whom to speak to and whom to let alone. On the way back, though, he thought about Minnie Dial.

She was older, twenty-six or -seven, and mad for Cody, and since the couple lived that first year with Pick in the new pine-scented house at Two Forks, her giggles and sighs and occasional short cries often kept Pick awake and burning into the night. Sometimes he came up softly to look in the kitchen window when she was rubbing the laundry on the washboard in her underclothes, so as to see her with her plump arms bare and a patch of milky skin quivering and surging inside the armhole of her chemise. She had a crude way of talking, said *damn* like any buckaroo, and he disliked a crude mouth on a woman, but still she weakened him. This grudging fascination made him sharp with her, and he couldn't be playful or lighthearted in her presence. She just shrugged when he was cold, shot a laughing glance at her husband, and with one hand—the other usually held spoon or spatula—tucked her shirtwaist more firmly into the band of her gaudy green skirt. Cody was a decent fellow. He never said much, never said Minnie's name. Called her "she": a boat, a mare, a divinity.

But Minnie was an energetic girl, and adventurous, and she liked Pick. One day he came in early, too tired, cold, his throat a little sore, and she was getting lunch on the stove, leaning over, her heavy bosom nearly skating on the hot griddle. It was quiet in the house. He could hear the tick of the clock, the wind hitting the house with its puff and blow. She turned her head, not far enough to look at him but enough to see him out of the corner of her eye, and she dropped her round chin to her shoulder, as though shy. Then she lifted her skirt in the back, lifted it as if unconscious, and tucked the hem into her waistband. The leaves of it, on either side of her white petticoat, swooped up to her waist like draped calico curtains on either side of a veiled stage. As she reached to stir something, he could see her body under the petticoat, lush and mobile, and he went to her in silence and picked up the petticoat by its ruffled, embroidered cambric hem. The female excess of those ruffles, the obscuring pages of cotton, and the quiet, dark place made underneath. His head ached and his throat crawled with fever. He crushed the ruffles in his hand, smelled them, and then with some awkwardness at touching the small of her back, he tucked the whole mess into that accommodating waistband.

It was autumn, cold out, but she had not yet put on winter woolens. Bleached cambric again, the drawers, closed with a white drawstring and, where they ended at her knees, a beguiling pink stitch like that around the edge of a blanket. He took an end of the drawstring and tugged it. Placidly she stirred the soup. Loosed, the waist of the drawers was huge. They fell easily down her hips, and she put her free hand around and with a pretty, thoughtless, ordinary gesture she pushed the cloth low on her pale thighs and to her knees, and then they fell to her feet. Neatly she stepped out of one side and put her feet apart, precisely, like a dance-hall girl.

The bottom of her, framed by cloth, engendered in him a

sweet wince: its roundness, pallor, and weight; its few little freckles. He placed his thumbs in the fuzzed dimples at the curve of her back and held her and squeezed. She stopped stirring; she arched her back. He pushed her forward until her hips braced against the stove top; her free hand dropped to the hot iron, and she jerked it back, having scorched the heel of her thumb. He took the burned hand and pressed the hot place to his cold cheek.

She had put her spoon down and was unbuttoning the placket of her shirtwaist. He took over this operation, wormed the heel of his hand into her corset, and lifted her breasts roughly as he pulled at his belt. He put his forehead against the back of her neck and looked down and strove to undo the strained buttons of his trousers. She tilted her head back to rest it against him. With a little toe-heel motion of one foot, she separated her legs a little farther. He was still for a moment. Miles away, his throat was killing him.

She turned her head and again without meeting his eyes said, "Pick, honey. Come on." And he went on.

It was just the one or two times, and since Cody never knew, Pick didn't think about it too much. It was a relief, though, when they got their own place and moved out of the county. Later there was a girl in Klamath Falls, Winifred something, who kept a boardinghouse with her mother—an airy, educated girl with a sly glance and silky brown hair who entertained other wealthy young cattlemen in cleanliness and delicacy, but was not for marrying because she pined exclusively for an actor she had met ages earlier in Rapid City.

And then some years ago he met Delores, who had been cooking for three bachelor homesteaders but decided to leave after the predictable drunken rivalries broke out. He had asked her to come by if she wanted to help Vincent cook, but from the first he knew he couldn't have her in the house as a servant. She was too much, too crackling in her speech, too clever for that. He didn't hire her, but he asked her to come back. She was drawn to him, he knew, but independent and wary, for good enough reason. Her mother had been a drinker, and Delores had taken care of her through ugly times. Delores was one of those girls who had gotten very pretty very young and had attracted the interest of those who didn't know a child when they saw one, and because of that she was scornful toward most men. Not to Pick, though. She unknotted herself for him.

Her own father had depended on her, and she had been his hope. He expected the rest of the world to honor her, and so Delores expected it herself. She didn't see any reason why she shouldn't marry Pick, be mistress of Two Forks. She was astonished when the man she loved balked about her Indian grandmother.

Well. Now he is astonished himself, when he remembers. He teased her until she got silent and then kept teasing her and got a little mean, and one day she just went away like any Indian. He looked for her, but she wouldn't be found, wouldn't turn a hair in forgiveness. A year later she turned up married to Fred Green and living in Jack-High. Which one of them had been more the fool, Pick was unable to say. Good luck to her, because with that sad case for a husband she'd need it.

This was how he thought about Delores. He had walled her off, like a corpse in a story. For a while his heart jerked and hissed as if he'd walled it up with her. Now he can hardly remember what it was like to kiss her. But when she comes to bring eggs to the ranch and stops her wagon out on the road and he can see her figure sitting there remote on the high seat, he feels he has failed at something. It is a feeling he cannot tolerate.

So he begins to notice Esther. He is getting used to having her around. He likes it. It makes spring feel real, somehow. He can feel it down in the deep, cold ground, gathering its buds, its gay troops of all colors preparing a sweet, reluctant, stealthy invasion. His very limbs feel different, as if they know that sometime soon there might be a little softness, a little love to spend like money, and the body's whole business won't be to keep itself alive on skinflint rations. Yes, she is a pleasant girl, intelligent. And under him, or inside him, spring is banging its little green drum.

16

THE MYSTERY of Jane Fremont's past intrigues Esther enough that she forgets to worry about burned wagons and the hurt cat. And her curiosity is soon rewarded by an unusual incident. One afternoon a woman passes on the sidewalk outside of Peaslee's Century Emporium. Before Esther's eyes can adjust from near to far, she thinks, Why is Jane wearing a hat at this hour? But then she sees she's wrong; the woman is a stranger in a stylish green traveling coat, shorter and plumper than Jane Fremont, and the hat is plumed and a bit blowsy, not in Jane's style. Esther returns to her history, where she is trying to remember precisely how James I and his mother were related to Elizabeth Tudor. Elizabeth: now that was a name. An imperious queen, four syllables, and that exotic *z* amidships. *Esther* is plain. When she reads it in a book, she is ill disposed toward the character that bears it; it makes her think of someone scrubbing a floor. At school, boys pointed out that it rhymed with things like *pester* and *fester*.

The bell on the door rings. This time it is indeed Jane, vivacious and distracted. "I had hoped to find you here," she says. "Would you be willing to stay with the scholars for an hour? The sixth-reader class is parsing. The others will take care of themselves. If you could come over shortly, I would be most obliged."

Esther promises, and marks her place in her book.

Joe Peaslee is in the back room, talking to himself. This habit startled her at first. He has been reading the eastern newspapers on the subject of the hostilities in the Philippines, finding many items that incense him, and he disputes with these as he goes about his chores. She goes in to explain that she'll be leaving shortly, and does he want any help with shelving before she does? He doesn't.

"What is happening in the war?" she asks him. What she knows about it, sadly, is mostly what she has read on the wall of the cabin next to her mirror, where the newspaper leaves Vincent applied for insulation are most recent. The war started a long time ago in Cuba—she remembers making a felt flag in school—and she knows that it's moved on to other islands and that there's someone named Aguinaldo who is held to be either foolish and arrogant or vicious and wily. "Oh," says Joe unhelpfully, "they just found themselves there, and having chased off the Spanish, thought they'd stay. They don't like to give up something once they've got it."

"They—you mean—"

"Oh, Mr. McKinley's generals. They're all great friends, you know, and they like to travel among the smaller-statured peoples and see if they can grind them a little shorter."

Esther is not shocked by his casual reference to the President, for she has heard it from him before. It's not just the politicians and generals who come in for Joe Peaslee's abuse. He dislikes a good deal of poetry and reads an enormous amount of it in order to revile it. He is at present going through the oeuvre of Walt Whitman—"for the second time," he tells her, because apparently the first time around it did not burn sufficiently under the coals of his scorn and continued to get itself reprinted in commemorative editions. What didn't he like about it? Oh, the high spirits. The man had refused to be discouraged. If he'd ever truly been discouraged, he couldn't have always written so lavishly, with such sweetness. Joe doesn't like the piling up of the words into great heaps. He tells Esther that reading Whitman is like watching someone glut on a large meal and then pick the debris out of his beard. Esther herself likes the poems, and privately she thinks that someone who keeps his store the way Joe Peaslee does should think twice before objecting to someone else's debris. Once, as he mumbled and gestured over some volume, Esther asked, "Do you remember the emperor Caligula, who disputed with Neptune?" and Joe Peaslee's dromedarial nose drew downward in sardonic appreciation.

"I'm going to the school now, Joe. I'm leaving my English history. Don't let anybody buy it."

The sixth-reader class comprises several small spry Jacob children—descendants of the redoubtable Lars in Joe Peaslee's portrait—a couple of antsy Stoops, Gerald Schmidt from the livery, and the well-matured redheaded Duncan girls, daughters of the burly blond sheepman Brookie.

"'The earth is a round body.'" Esther reads, facing the circle of children and youths. "Lenore?"

Lenore Duncan, exhausted with boredom, has pulled one lavish ginger curl from the broad red-gold plait she wears down her neck and is now examining it as if it were a rose and she a bemused Gibson girl on a picnic. Esther urges her, "Come now. What is the subject of the sentence 'The earth is a round body'?"

"*Thuh. Thuh* earth," says Gerald Schmidt, a solid boy who, like his father Alfred at the livery, always seems to be losing a suspender.

"Oh, well, that's very close indeed, but not quite the thing. Lenore?"

Lenore has a head cold. She attempts to sniff, but instead her mouth pops open and a look of misery passes over her face. Esther casts a desperate glance toward the door, but Jane Fremont is gone, in the company of the plump lady. The lady smiled politely at Esther, but Jane did not introduce them.

Nearby, Marguerite Green, supposed to be looking at her primer, has twisted around in her seat and is kicking her feet, which are clad in pretty black boots with patent toes that Delight ordered from Sears, Roebuck. She stage-whispers, "*Gerald* is a round body."

"Say!" complains Gerald, a stripe of red unrolling on each of his plump cheeks.

"Shame, Marguerite," says Esther rather perfunctorily. Violet Fowler had once said that the child might just as well have been christened Shame, since she heard it nearly as often as her given name. "Read your book. Here, Lenore. Let's try another. 'Hark! the trumpet sounds.' What is the subject?"

"The soldier."

"I beg your pardon?"

"The soldier," says Lenore, dreamy, "who blew the trumpet. He did the action. He's the subject."

"Oh, but the idea is not to—to reach beyond the sentence for a soldier who's not there. The subject must be—"

Lenore looks hurt and then righteous. "Who blew it, then?"

"It's the trumpet. The *trumpet* sounds," says one of the other children.

Esther hurries on. "Yes—and what, Lenore, do we call the word *hark*?"

Marguerite twists around in her seat again, then gets up on her knees and leans against the high back. Before Lenore can speak, she suggests, "An . . . infection? An inspection?" She is gambling.

"*Say!*" Gerald puts in again.

"Inter . . . fliction?" Marguerite looks at Esther, her black eyes bright, and when Esther makes an effort and looks stern, Marguerite looks stern, too, and draws her brown braid across her lip like a mustache.

One of the Stoop children says, "Inter*jec*tion. And why doesn't the second-reader class keep its nose out of our parsing."

Gerald says, "I'll parse her face, the dirty Indian."

"Gerald!" Esther takes his collar and jerks it a little. "What in the world—"

"Her mother's an Indian," Gerald insists. "I'll hit her for what she said."

Marguerite has dropped her braid. She places her hands together as though to pray. "Try it, Gerald. Please try it."

"It's some way back in the family," says Jane wearily when she has returned alone and the children have gone, circling and pushing one another, clustering and trudging across the yard toward Main Street. "Delores Green's grandmother was—oh, Walpapi, I think, some kind of Paiute. I suppose one can see it, looking at her. I can't think how Gerald Schmidt would know that; it's not something Ida would make a point of talking about. But the other children—May and Maudie Fowler—I'm sure Violet has told them." Jane goes and sits at her desk and puts her hands over her eyes.

"That's what Phelia Jacob meant that day," Esther says, "when she said she knew Delores was a Christian. Delores was angry about that."

"As she should have been, seeing as she's got a far better understanding of what *Christian* means than Phelia ever did."

"Pick told me nobody around here cared if a person was an Indian or an orphan. I guess it's not true."

"It's mostly true. How can we bother with fine distinctions about grandmothers when we have so few neighbors to begin with? When they're angry, the children simply drag out whatever they can use. But I suppose in Chicago it is different."

"It . . . it depended. I think most people married people who were like them. And then there were people who just didn't look this way or that way, and no one particularly bothered them and they could do and marry as they pleased. Now and then someone said something. My mother had friends, Mr. and Mrs. Joliette, who were musicians. They used to come over and play with her."

"Did your mother play?"

"Yes. The flute and the clarinet. The sweet one and the sleepy one, she called them. I play a little, but badly. I like better to listen. When the Joliettes came over, I used to sit on the stairs when I was supposed to be asleep. Then Mrs. Joliette died—they were older than my mother. Mr. Joliette used to come over still, and they would play. And then someone at school said my mother kept company with niggers. I shouldn't have told her, but I did tell her because I was surprised that anybody thought he was a colored man. And she said no, it was true, he was light skinned but a colored man, that was his family and his upbringing. After that he didn't come to our house anymore, though sometimes she met him at other people's houses. I asked her why he didn't come, and she said it was because it was all the same to her and I might as well not have any trouble at school."

Jane shakes her head and presses her fingers to her eyes. "Yes. A mother wants one simply not to have too much trouble. The sweet one and the sleepy one. I think I would have liked her."

"Oh, you would have! And she would have liked you. But what about your visitor? Is she a friend of yours?"

Jane Fremont looks at the door. "Yes, a dear friend."

"Has she come to stay, then?"

Jane lays her hands flat on her desk. "No. Well, she will stay the night in the hotel. She is on her way to San Francisco for a visit. The truth is that her name is Clara Linstrom, and she is my sister. She has asked me to come home, but I don't wish to go. So there is nothing more to talk about, and she is leaving." Her brow wrinkles and then smooths. She stands up. "Will you keep my secret? Will you forget she was here?"

"I understand. It's private."

Jane goes to the window and with a bit of struggle raises the sash. She bends down and puts her face out into the damp. Esther joins her and looks out.

Jane wipes her face. "All winter one can't really smell the air. Now it's got the dirt on it, and the junipers and those big pines over there across the plain. You'll need that plow soon."

Esther sniffs. "Yes. That will be a picture. I've not yet broken the news to the mare that she is wanted to pull a plow." She picks up her coat and turns to go and then comes back. "Jane—Mr. Joliette, of whom I was speaking?"

"Yes, of course."

It's a strange thing to say, and she isn't sure what she means by it, but she wants to. "He wasn't a nigger."

Jane raises her eyebrows. "Of course not. No one is. Not even Phelia Jacob."

1 7

ESTHER has marked off all but a few days on her handmade calendar, but Pick has said nothing about buying the claim. She puts off asking him, though. Calves have started to come, and he is busy on the range. She is preparing for her examinations, and then there is the planting to do. She never thought, three months ago, that she would stay here a day longer than she had to. But now she has in her shed the little plow brought over from Jane's in the wagon, and it is more real in her mind than Damen Avenue or a streetcar or a playbill on a brick wall. It has two arms and two teeth for biting the earth, and Esther means to tame it. She wants to leave something growing, some mark that she has been here.

Rain scuds hard on the roof one night, and when Esther rises, she sees that much of the snow has melted and washed away. The gray land she is used to is, in a few days, suffused with a delicate, sharp green, like the taste of tea. The green clearing in the middle of Half-a-Mind widens, and what was once her water hole in the ice becomes just water, a little muddy, so that she has to step out on a rock to get a clear dip for her bucket. A legion of dark ducks falls out of the clouds, pulls back above the water, and alights, honking. In the shallows and on the olive sand revealed by the thaw, avocets tipple with their teaspoon beaks. All day, like swoops of speckled bunting, swallows drape the lime-blue sky.

In the cabin, Esther is able to fold up one of her stiff quilts and lay it across the end of the bed. Duniway has gone delirious on a diet of grasses and buds, which she nips on the fly while Esther strives to control her head. In her stall she rattles and blows greetings to her kin in sheds on other claims out of sight across the desert.

When Esther drags the mare out of her stall and hitches her to the plow, she thrusts out her large gray hip in aggrieved disbelief and attempts to nip Esther's oilskin coat. But when Esther flaps the long, long traces and grasps the handles of the plow, miraculously, the mare starts forward a little. The plow wheel turns, and the teeth turn the soil. It takes a long time, and Esther's hands are sore and her stockings wet to the knee. But a little field, a patch, a postage stamp, is made. She turns in horse manure and straw from the shed, and gypsum from Joe Peaslee's, all according to Vincent's instructions. Then, after watching Jane, she trades the plow for a spidery wheelbarrow seeder and sows five pounds of alfalfa seed.

At Two Forks, Pick hires more hands, soft-eyed and deliberate Mexican men who smile at the gambits of the buckaroos but never laugh, being too shy. They all mount up early in the mornings and bring in ponderous groups of expectant cows and their disturbed yearlings. When the band reaches the juniper fence line and the wide gates, the riders whip into action, their horses crunching and whirling as they cut between the cows and the half-grown calves. The yearlings startle and trot in circles, the mothers emitting a fatigued lowing, but the zagging of the cow ponies and the snaps of the riatas force the animals to enter separate enclosures. Once inside, the yearlings gather at the fence and protest. The mothers lie down on the turf and rest their great bellies. The prize bulls Knock-Knock and Waterloo, in their own pens, brace themselves against the rails and bawl, their great white polls and chests muddy and their tiny eyes confused. They will be fathers again soon, though they know nothing about it.

Esther rides by them when, after a long afternoon driving the seeder, she goes over to Two Forks in the early evening to have a bath. The bathroom is off the kitchen, and the bath itself is an elegant affair, porcelain over cast iron, with copper fittings. Vincent can never look at it without mentioning how heavy the cotton-picking thing was, how it nearly buckled four oxen and made them lame to pull the wagon. But Esther is glad for it. The water is heated with a little stove there in the corner of the room, and it flows down from a suspended tank through copper fittings to gush from a faucet shaped like the head of a dragon. The porcelain is silky, and the iron preserves the heat. Pick has admitted to her, almost in shame, that though he didn't think much of living in town when he was younger, he did like things to look handsome, and he brought back with him a few fancy tastes.

Underwater, her skin looks pale, almost green. She stretches, rounds her back, and rolls her shoulders, for she is sore from struggling to guide the plow. The tub is so long, made for a man, that when she's at full length, her toes just nudge up over the waterline. She has fine feet, at least; they look well in shoes. She skates the soap over her belly, thighs, and the backs of her legs. The soap is pink and fragrant. At the claim she washes in a china bowl and rubs fiercely with a towel that is usually in need of washing itself. She has had trouble keeping up with what must be done over there. She sometimes wakes to a sordid pan of old beans still sitting on the stove. But it is spring, and she has planted the alfalfa, and now she thinks of the place a little differently. She wants to see the plants come up. How long will it take? Perhaps she could stay a little longer. She has heard nothing from anyone in Chicago for a little while, and it is harder to imagine that place than she ever thought it would be. And what will she do there besides type? As she thinks, she washes her face and neck, and the feel of the washcloth is at once silky and rough. Her body has been well worked in the field, but she feels alert, warm, and restless even after she has emerged and dressed.

Pick has gone to town with a prospectus from the Far West Navigation and Railway in his pocket, bound for a meeting at Underwood's. Esther trails down the hall toward the front of the quiet house, where Pick's bedroom gives onto the widow's walk. A spring slant of afternoon sun reddens the floorboards of the room and the simple iron railings of the bedstead. The quilt is a thin white nine-patch with blocks of slate blue and black. She lifts herself up on it and lies down. The room is papered with a pattern of golden diamonds and sheaves, and on the wall hang the smoky oval tintypes of Pick's parents, like two reflective brown eyes. This is what Pick sees at night after he has undressed. It's hard to imagine what it's like to be him.

Suddenly afraid of being found out, she gets down. On top of the highboy is a small mirrored stand with two drawers. Though she is tall, it is too high—she can see only the top half of her face, and even that is half in shadow. She regrets, for the thousandth time, her pale, sparse eyelashes. She tugs open the stiff door and steps onto the narrow little balcony. Out here the wind is whipping and puffing off the desert. Its smell is sharp and granular. In the distance, Half-a-Mind glints like the edge of a coin among a softening blur of reeds.

At the south end, where the aspens make a spindly grove, there is a gathering of gray and white. It thickens and spreads along the shore. Then there is a box she recognizes as a sheepherder's camp wagon, bumping up toward the water. Two men wearing long mackintoshes are sitting up on the high seat. She can't recognize them at this distance. But the sheep are watering at her lake. *Trespass.* And where will they walk with their sharp feet? No doubt into her alfalfa field. Her stomach leaps, partly in indignation, partly in the pleasure of having an excuse for an errand.

Having had a rest after her exertions, Duniway exits the Two Forks stable with an air of business, as if she understands Esther's urgency. When Esther switches her, she bestirs herself, for a quarter of a mile, to canter. Esther clings and then relaxes. Whether from experience or the comfort of the new split skirt, she finds she is now a rider.

The meeting, it turns out, is in the saloon. There is no companion nearby, and it is a lingering lesson of her childhood that girls do not go into drinking establishments, especially not alone. Esther can see the men gathered at the back curve of the bar, talking, and she can see her cousin's blue shirt among the coats and woolen jackets, but the proceedings must be compelling, for no one gets up to go about his business, and the bartender, a Jacob cousin of some sort, keeps an interested vigil near them and does not come up toward the window.

She's about to walk up the street to the livery, to knock on the Schmidts' door and ask Alfred to go in after Pick, when Noggin Koerner walks up and says, "Where you going?"

"I was just hoping to speak with Pick. Are you going into the meeting?"

He squints into the saloon. "I guess I am."

"Would you please tell him that someone is watering sheep at Half-a-Mind? The south end, nearest Two Forks."

"How many? Who are they?"

"I don't know the men. Numbers of sheep—perhaps a hundred?"

Noggin goes in at once and nudges through several men to deliver the message. Pick slaps the table and questions Noggin, who shrugs. Pick puts his head in his hands and broods a moment. Then he rises and comes out to Esther.

"Who did you see? Was it Brookie?"

"I don't think so. They didn't have blond hair, I don't think. But they had hats."

"And Duncan's only got the one wagon now," said Noggin.

Pick gives him a narrow, cautionary glance. "Well, if it's Brookie, it doesn't seem to have slowed him down much. Maybe it's Cruffs or somebody else altogether. There's a couple outfits been by lately."

"I'll bet it's Cruffs," says Noggin. "Showing off."

"All right, Blackbird, I've got to get back in there."

Now she is preoccupied. No doubt those *are* Cruffs out there. Having come down off the bluff, they mean to add insult to injury by drinking up the lake. She thinks again of that boy, with his dark, glowering eyes and bold speech. He wore a blue sweater, cabled and dense. Strangely, for the first time, she recalls a few seeds that clung to the blue wool near the collar.

Burning with a new kind of excitement, she leads Duniway down to Joe Peaslee's, so urgent in her steps and careless of the mud that she leaps across puddles instead of going around them. As she approaches the door, it swings open toward her and she catches and holds it. Large, awkward shoulders in overalls, rosy cheekbones, a dark glance under a cap—a boy is coming out carrying a parcel, and it is that very Cruff she has been remembering. He is right here in front of her, not driving sheep out at Half-a-Mind, and there on the sidewalk is his brother. They are innocent. But instead of feeling ashamed at maligning them unfairly in her mind, she simply resents them, especially the boy. He pushes the door open wide and turns to the side so that she can pass him. She is conscious of a scent of animals, mud, peppermint, and smoke, and she can't help but look up.

He gestures with his parcel toward the back room. "He's not in the best shape. You might leave him alone."

"Is he ill?"

"You could say that. I don't think you ought to see him." He's worried; he looks back over his shoulder.

"I can help him."

His smile is doubtful. "Well, suit yourself." He lets the door close behind her.

She hurries in. "Joe?" He is neither lying on the counter nor in the back room fussing among his trinkets. Pushing her scarf back, she climbs the ladder. He is crouched against the wall, wrapped in a blanket, in an attitude combining the longing for rest with a visceral alertness. His face perspires, and his spyglass lies in front of him. At her emergence at the top of the ladder he opens his eyes and shifts his foot in fear. The spyglass rolls a half circle and stops.

"Someone," he said, and closes his eyes.

He doesn't seem to understand who she is. Esther clings to the ladder post, pressing her face against the wood. "What are you doing, Joe?"

He opens his eyes again. This time he sees her, as if he has forced his mind into action. He yawns, and then again, wide enough that his jaw makes a cracking sound. "What?"

"What are you doing?"

"An experiment."

"It's made you ill; you should leave off. Did you make a mistake with the bottles?"

"No. No." His voice breaks. He is pale and, around his eyes, sulfurous. "That is—yes. I'll have a try at it another time. Will you bring me a bottle of Welsh Oats Essence? There's a crate on the shelf near the till."

She rushes down the ladder, finds the medicine, and returns. He tries to shake the bottle, but his arm is weak. She takes it from him, shakes and opens it, and helps him to drink. When his head falls back, she smells the elixir: strong, like camphor. "What is it for?"

"For what ails me."

"What does ail you?"

Under his yellow eyelids, his eyes move. "The evils."

She sits still a moment. In Chicago, several times, a heavyset, mournful-looking colored man fell asleep against the railing on their shady front steps. Each time, Esther's mother let him sleep for a time, then, while Esther watched from the window, went out and shook his shoulder gently, gave him some money, and sent him away. *Is he drunk?* Esther asked. *No. Not drunk,* her mother said. *I think he has the misfortune to want morphine.*

She kneels there, holding the open bottle. There is a doctor in Peterson—Dr. Bloucher. "Do you want the doctor? Let me call for him."

"No."

"You prefer to be ill?"

"I prefer to be ill. And I don't want water. And I don't want soup."

She descends the ladder and stands at the Liberty. There is a page in it that she typed the last time she was here, a lesson on making plurals: *beef, thief, self, wife; beefs, thieves, selves, wives* . . .

She wrenches the platen handle to bring up a blank part of the page and types out in a rush

the evils the evils the evils

Her face in her hands, she feels tears coming. Oh, poor Joe. It is degrading for him. He has the misfortune to want it, and, as her mother said, *When you want something like that, it is hard to want anything else.* If only her mother were here. She would know what to do for him, how to soothe him and give him courage. But Esther is nothing, nobody. She cannot help.

As she pulls these tears off her face with her hand and wipes the hand on her skirt, there is a shout on the street, then a few other loud voices. She runs to the door and, as the din does not subside, down to the post office, where Violet Fowler has come out to stand on the sidewalk.

"There you go." Mrs. Fowler's creased chin works with satisfaction. "As if there's no work to do, it being spring, they've got to get drunk and fight."

Two men are grappling in the street. The taller is Noggin Koerner. He throws punches so slow it seems he is merely extending his fists, until they strike flesh with a solid thump or miss and are slowly retracted. The sometime receptor of these blows is the Cruff boy. He is quick of foot, though his aim is corrupted a bit by what looks like sheer rage. He claps Koerner twice on the side of the head and pushes him away. Koerner regains his balance, and Pick, who is standing nearby with his hat in one hand, calls out to him. For a moment that quick bark distracts the Cruff boy, who looks that way, and Koerner leaps at his opponent and clouts him full in the jaw. The boy lurches sideways, falls hard on one knee, and collapses onto his elbow. Noggin would be after him, on him, but the older brother, Michael, steps forward. Several other buckaroos hold Noggin back. Michael kneels and then holds up his hand so that someone in the crowd can toss him a cloth, which he puts to the boy's face. Noggin stands like a stopped clock, biting his tongue, one limp hand cradled in the other.

Esther is cringing, horrified. How did it happen? Noggin must know it was not the Cruffs at the lake. But she is ashamed. Her partisanship and tale-telling, her self-importance. And now she has left Joe ill.

"If only Jane employed my programs more vigorously," says Violet in an injured, fretful voice. "There would be much less of this carousing."

Esther shouldn't answer, but in her present state of dismay it seems the most ridiculous sanctimony she's ever heard. "Don't you dare. Was Noggin ever a student of Jane's? I don't think he was, nor was any Cruff. Don't speak against Jane Fremont just because men happen to fight."

"I'm sure you know I spoke generally, Esther. There's no call to be rude."

"And there's no call to be insulting."

She turns back up the street. It's her first quarrel in Century. Her mother used to say that one's home was the place where there were people one didn't want to meet on the street. What was a place where one not only met them but raised one's voice?

With a dose of Welsh Oats Essence and one of his cigarettes, Joe Peaslee has recovered a bit. He has roused himself and managed the ladder and is standing in his doorway, smoking, wrapped in the blanket like an Indian brave. "A fight?"

"Yes." Still shaky, she feels shy, and she sees his lined face a bit differently: less old, more ravaged.

But he is lucid and dignified. "My backbone was singing all morning like Jenny Lind. I thought something worse than a fight was coming."

"It's Noggin Koerner and that Cruff boy who was here earlier."

"Benjamin, who wanted three penny comics and some overalls."

"I met him once."

"You don't like him?"

"Maybe not him. It's the sheep. They range all over, you know, and they eat everything." She gets a little more indignant as she speaks, recalling the conversations she's heard at the ranch. "But the sheepherders cut fences for them. And sheepherders broke the windows at Two Forks. Pick says if the sheep would stay high in the rock and let the cattle have the lowlands, then all would be well, but the sheep go where they please, and no one stops them. Except for Pick. He tries to keep them in order."

Joe frowns. "You are a quick study, obviously. You are as persuasive as the man himself. Well, the world gets smaller and smaller. It was only a matter of time."

"What was?"

"That we should crowd one another. Jostle and push like forty-niners. And worse." The fight seems to be over. Men are standing around in the street talking, and the Cruff boy is standing up. Joe goes inside, and Esther follows.

"What do you mean?"

He climbs up onto his counter and lies back. "Suppose there is a meadow near a stream, where the bunchgrass grows tall." His hands aren't shaking now. He indicates the tallness of the grass by extending long fingers, grasslike, off his chest.

"Yes."

"There's an Indian trapping rabbits. There's a farmer growing beans. There's a sheep drinking water. There's a cow eating grass. And under the ground Uncle Sam is mining for gold. Each is sure he has a right to be there. They insist on their rights with hoof, arrow, rifle, and pickax. They fall together into the pit they've made. Everyone is right, everybody ends up in a mess. Chaos, Esther."

"But is there nothing to be done? They should have met and made a treaty."

"Tell that to a cow. Oh, well, perhaps someday one will emerge victorious from the ruin and be dusted off and congratulated by the railroad."

Esther is dubious. "Is the railroad to be the judge of who's right, then? That's not fair. A railroad is just a—a thing."

"*Corporation* is the word."

"So then, not a person. It isn't reasonable. It's meant to build things and make money. How can it know what's fair?"

"It doesn't know anything. It doesn't have to. It just rolls along and knocks down what's in the way and takes money from those who can afford to pay."

"That's not justice."

"The railroad thinks it is. Like the army, like a ravisher of women. Like any bully. If it can overpower something, and wants to, then it may." His hand falls weak against his chest. In a moment he has fallen asleep.

Esther takes the cigarette out of his fingers, wets and pinches it out, and restores it to the cigar box. She walks around the store thinking, until she puts the idea together. Back when she first met him, he resisted involving himself in Century affairs. He was an observer only. Now she understands his cynicism. When a white man first drove an Indian off a bit of land, it was guaranteed that someday Noggin Koerner would beat a shepherd in the street. Without fail, domination begets domination.

There is tramping outside on the boards, and Pick is coming in with several men, including Noggin Koerner, still holding one hand in the other, his scalp purple with exercise and irritation, and the Cruff boy, Benjamin.

"Hello, Esther. We need a splint and a roll of bandage." Pick is wry. "Young Mr. Cruff here has seen fit to break Noggin's hand with his skull. Since that puts me out one wrangler in calf season, the Cruffs have consented to reimburse us with work."

"But—it wasn't them at the lake. They're here. It must have been—"

"Be that as it may. Michael has agreed that Ben threw the first punch."

"After that fellow opened his dirty mouth!" Benjamin Cruff says. Michael puts a hand on his arm. Ben has retrieved his parcel and is holding it carefully. But what a transformation. The parcel is torn and shows the dusty denim and buckle of an overall. His cheek is bruised and his mouth swollen, with blood at the corner. "Nice to see you again," he says to Esther. "A real pleasure." His brown eyes are furious.

Pick says, "Noggin's loss is your gain, Esther. Ben here is going to dig you a well."

18

SHE WANTS TO put that awful day out of her mind. But the fight lingers like a taste she can find on the roof of her mouth. She has been waiting, she realizes, for that explosion into spring one can expect in Illinois. The return of heat and softness. The change of tree, narrow and brown and crouching in ice, into a dancing girl, the overnight decision by the redbud to turn itself inside out and display its brilliant crimson underclothes. But no such thing here. Only the wettening, the greening of what was gray, the gray having ascended into the sky, where it dyes the atmosphere. One knows it is spring only because one sees men fighting.

At dinner at Two Forks the men are lively with discussion. The details of the fight have been conveyed to all those who were not present, and now there is discussion of other fights. Esther is pouring out pancakes. She has had some practice, since the buckaroos have pancakes three times a week for breakfast and once a week for supper. She tries to make them neat, golden and uniform, so they will stack beautifully. It means something to her to see the men eat what she has made. They do it with a species of determination she has never seen at table.

Noggin Koerner has to eat with his left hand, and this reminds them to chide him about his choice of opponent. "Say, Koerner, I hear they got a couple little girls over at Failing that are tough customers."

"Yeah, buckaroo, you know that baby Delores Green's got? He's been running his mouth something awful. You better get out there and thrash him."

Noggin is imperturbable. "That Cruff boy's old enough. He's long since old enough. All those Cruffs need thrashing. Thieves and squatters, micks with big mouths. I don't like these outfits that move around without a home ranch."

Teddy ruminates. "They got one, though, don't they?"

Someone supplies, "It's up in Morrow County."

"Well, they don't go there enough. Down here all they got's a little pile of rotten potato skins to roll around in. They don't got a ranch they can be proud of, so they want to take ours, crawl all over it with their vermin." His head is sweating, glossy. "I feel sorry for them and all their nothing. But the fact they're too shiftless to make their way ain't my problem. If they want to come on this property, they'll deal with us, won't they."

The men are eating. They only murmur a little in agreement. Esther eats a pancake with her fingers. This whole situation is unfair. Why should Ben Cruff pay for what Brookie Duncan has almost certainly done? And why can't someone like Noggin see it's wrong? But she learned from her mother, who disliked lawyers but still had them to supper, that one's own antipathies deserve the closest questioning. So in her mind she tries out defenses of Koerner. It is good and proper that he should be attached to Two Forks and should defend it against sheep and other trespassers. If buckaroos weren't loyal, why, they might get tired in the middle of a drive and drop away to find another spread; they might steal cattle or fail to put themselves out to protect them. But she cannot persuade herself. A startling thought flashes across her mind: I hate Noggin Koerner.

When Pick comes into the kitchen to get a plate to take back to his study, she regards him. He is familiar now, his blue shirts and tense shoulders, his dark boots, shorn blond hair, and light eyes. The men wouldn't think of crossing him or letting him down. Not because he'd suffer from it, but because he'd be disappointed. Oh, not disappointed in you, the way a father might be, but disappointed in himself, that he failed to anticipate your weakness. That is a strange strength for him to have—that people would sooner knock themselves unconscious on a rock than allow him to feel his own judgment is flawed.

The buckaroos have left the table, sighing and groaning. Vincent has wrapped Koerner's broken hand in a tight cloth. He and Esther and Teddy have washed most of the dishes. Esther eats slowly. She is thinking about the ride back to the claim in the dark, never as bad as she thinks it will be, but never easy. She blows out the lamp and sits at the table. A slim line of light shows under the door of Vincent's room, and through the kitchen door the red wallpaper of the hall glows in reflected light from Pick's study. Now the light is blotted as Pick appears in silhouette.

"Esther, is that you? Come on in a moment."

She follows him to the large, deep desk. He is in stocking feet. Out of the boots he is a little shorter. He gestures to the rolling chair in front of the desk. There are papers on the desk with figures on them. It hasn't yet been three months, but perhaps he is ready to bring up the subject of the claim himself. Perhaps the fight has made him hurry. As he turns away to poke at the fire, there is a flare of muscle up his back, under his shirt. The room is deliciously warm. She sits down and stretches her arms toward the heat.

As he picks up a rag and wipes his hands, he nods at her. "I had a question about that ring of yours."

It is inside the collar of her waist, and she takes it out.

"You like pearls?"

She has never considered it. It is a pearl ring that she has been given. It would do her no good to prefer rubies. "I do like it."

"I once heard a lady say pearls were spit up by fish," he says, rubbing the back of his neck. "She didn't care for them."

"Oh, yes?" She wonders what lady that would have been.

"We could take that to Peterson and have it sized for you. Then you could wear it on your hand."

"I'd be afraid I'd lose it."

"Oh, you wouldn't lose it, I daresay." With a relaxed and casual motion he sits down on the footstool near her and reaches up and takes her hand. She is surprised. Her hand is limp, like a paw. He covers it with his other hand. "Listen, Esther, I've been thinking. I like you, and I feel you suit me. When you came here, you didn't know a horse from a hammer handle, but you're learning fast. Since it seems to me you're going to be a fine woman, I thought I'd ask you something. I know you're young yet, but I'm not in a hurry. I'd like for us to have an understanding. What do you say to that?"

She hears the words and understands that he has made a request of her, a serious one. Beyond him the blue toile wallpaper, with its strange French fairy-tale people, seems animated, alive. Lions ramp and wolves course down a hill. The old man stands repeatedly in the mouth of a cave. Again and again a maid turns away from a youth who carries yoked buckets across his shoulders. A queen holds a baby to the light.

Pick is still waiting, holding her hand.

She says, "An understanding, between you and me."

"Yes. About the future. Yours and mine."

She can't find what to say. She gropes around in her feelings, in her language, but there is nothing there, the trunk is empty. She doesn't know what she thinks or feels. Yet he is waiting. She falls back on her determination to do what he asks of her, which has served her well enough so far.

"All right," she says shyly.

He looks pleased, relieved. "You like me, then."

It is not that she doesn't like him. Of course she likes him. More than likes him. "Oh, yes. I do."

"Good. And you don't have to tell anybody until you feel like it." He uncovers her hand and caresses her ring finger. Her skin prickles. She touches the back of his hand with her fingers. He leans forward and kisses her. The feeling of the soft whiskered mouth remains there. This is her first kiss since childhood. He has kissed her. She touches her lips, and he smiles.

"So you want to give me that ring and have me send it up to Peterson?"

"Oh. Not now," she says.

He looks as if he understands this. "When you're ready," he says. He stands up, and she stands up, too, confused. He puts his hands on her shoulders and, with an air of focus and formality, kisses her cheek. Her hand comes up and clasps his upper arm, which is hard under his shirt. He leaves his hand on the back of her neck and speaks against her ear. "I had a disappointment years ago. I got proud, and no one would suit me. But someone who can make my interests her own, someone with no falseness—that person's word I will trust."

This night he rides with her to the cabin. He hangs up the bridle for her and puts the saddle on the hay bale and curries Duniway and puts on her blanket. Esther stands by, peaceful, her chores simply lifted away. He escorts her to her door, sees her in, and departs. As the door closes behind him, another door, in her mind, opens. It is heavy, oaken, bound with brass, but it swings wide in silence and there is a lovely garden. Scarlet lamps of roses, the curving horns of white-green lilacs. Abundant water pours into a carved vessel. The king kneels, the queen holds the baby to the light. Her dress is not black. It is white, exquisite white.

Before she lies down to sleep, Esther takes the calendar she made from its nail. She turns it over and hangs it up that way. Through the paper she can see the faint traces of the days she has marked off. But this side is unwritten, and clean.

PART THREE

THE WELL. THE PICNIC.
THE NIGHT RIDERS.

19

THE WINDLASS GROANS as she cranks it, and Esther's hands are sore. She strains to push the handle through the top of its circuit. A little further—and over. Now she can draw it toward her. Below, the laden bucket of rock and dirt climbs with the turning. But she has neglected to even the rope, and the knots tied in it have crowded upon one another, building up a clot on the cross-piece as it turns. The last knot is damp from resting in the mud at the bottom of the hole, and it slips sideways off the coil and smacks tight to the bare wood. The handle of the windlass jerks away from her and scrapes the insides of her wrist. The bucket drops a foot, hard. It swings and bangs against the side of the well, and debris slides off it and falls.

"Rocks!" she calls out. But the rocks have a head start on her puny warning. She pictures her voice chasing down into the shaft, ten feet, twenty, and hears a faint showering sound at the bottom. She sets the windlass with the bar and kneels on the platform.

"Hello?" No answer. "Hello?"

She was instructed by Pick. Keep the rope even, bring the bucket up smoothly. But she is tired, and the fact that Ben Cruff has been six days on her claim, rarely meeting her glance, tires her further. She offered her help because she didn't like the idea of lolling about the place talking to the rabbits while Ben Cruff worked for her benefit. But he often overloads the big bucket with the stone he has pickaxed out of the well bottom, and there are times when she does not feel she can get the windlass to turn an inch further, and those times she does not even the rope.

Now she has poured rocks on him and he is probably killed.

They have had only one real conversation. Each noontime he takes his dinner and goes and sits on a rock to eat cold rabbit and canned tomatoes and read a comic serial in a grubby penny dreadful. When she asked what story he is following, he brought himself to explain, with great seriousness. The hero, Grant Goodwell, was a student at Yale College, an excellent athlete and friend, and full of common sense. Though young, he was often consulted on matters of importance by the powerful friends of his father, the statesman John Goodwell of New York. The thing was, Ben explained to Esther slowly, any man could break up a smuggling ring or win a footrace against stuck-up fellows from Dartmouth, provided he just set himself to it, but it is Grant Goodwell's sportsmanship that sets him apart. "Wins and loses with a smile," Ben told her. "Will rather lose everything than cheat." Ben has cousins in the East whom he has never met, who send their old magazines out, but sometimes they forget, and often it takes a long time to get the mail. It is a sore point with Ben that he receives word of Grant Goodwell's accomplishments when they are six months old. Esther has never met someone like Ben. He is both dignified and innocent, sometimes eager and sometimes surly. Perhaps it is because she herself is ill at ease. When they look right at each other, they are wary, and Ben often contents himself with training his glittering gaze on her ear or her shoulder.

"I used to read about Grant Goodwell sometimes in school," said Esther. "It *was* exciting."

"In school?"

"No, no, I mean—there was a girl, and she had a brother, and sometime she brought the magazine to school."

"What was he doing then?"

"Her brother?"

"Grant Goodwell."

"I think he was in the army. Yes, for a while he went into the army. Or the navy. There was something about hiding the flag, the ship's flag, so it wouldn't be stolen."

Ben Cruff took off his hat and wiped his head and put the hat back on. He nodded, his dark eyes alive with energy. "I'm not surprised. He wouldn't hold with tyranny. Was he injured?"

Esther thought. She imagined the elaborate story she could invent for Grant Goodwell—shot all over, abducted by pirates. But if Ben ever did find out that she had made something up and misled him, well, she wouldn't like that.

"I think so. He had to wear a sling."

"And I'll wager he never complained of it!"

"I never saw the rest of it. The continued part."

"They never finish it. I understand that, it's business. They have to keep us coming back. It's hard to wait, though."

"I think so, too."

"Maybe I should draw my own comic. *Adventures of a Youngest Brother in a Freezing Camp Wagon.* But I guess nobody would buy it." After this long loquacity he fell silent.

Now she looks down into the well and for the first time uses his name. "Ben! Ben! Are you hurt?"

The lamp hangs on an iron spike in the well wall and casts a sickly light. He is small, foreshortened into a shadowed bump, and his hands clasp his head. Has he been wearing the cookpot stuffed with rags on his head? Or has he laid it aside as too much bother? His voice wafts up. "Don't know. Let that rope down without the bucket, will you?"

Having lost half its burden, the bucket is light now. She pulls up the last few feet of the rope by hand and heaves it onto the platform. It is nearly full of mothball-colored chips, which she imagines to be salty. She unbars the windlass. "Rope coming," she calls.

She is sorry to have made such a mistake. He spends the days down there in the black and cold, where it is still winter, while she has the softened spring wind to dry her perspiration, the purple ladders of the lupine to gaze at, and Duniway, who puts her great bone of a nose out of the shed to catch the sun, for company.

He comes up hand over hand into the sunlight, ears sticking out and backlit, pausing just at the rim to rest his feet on a knot in the rope and shake the pain from his wrists. A few more reaches and he hugs the windlass and hangs there. Esther watches his hands—which have a peculiar squareness where the thumb joins on—to be sure he has a good grasp. But if he hasn't, what can she do? If he falls or keels over from gas below, she can only saddle Duniway and ride to Two Forks for assistance.

When he has walked his feet onto the platform and rolled up-right, he rubs his shoulder and pinches it, giving her an impassive look. She wants to apologize for her failure, but the fact that he means to stand there and be scornful hardens her.

"I suppose in Chicago you've got machines to dig the wells," he says. "They don't mind if you're careless and drop rocks."

"In Chicago the wells are already dug," she says. "And of course in Chicago we have a feature of weather you are unacquainted with. We call it rain."

"That so."

"Yes, it is."

"Why'd you leave there, then? So's you can come out here and decorate a shack with rocks and bones?"

To alleviate the bareness of the cabin, she has collected pretty rocks and put them on her windowsill. She realizes now that they aren't pretty. They're just rocks. "I can't see that it's any of your business. You shouldn't be looking inside anyway."

"If you don't draw the curtain, then why not?"

"Because it's rude. You're a hired hand."

"No one's paying me."

"Then what are you?"

He considers, rubbing at his shoulder. "I'm not a cheat. I'm not a thief nor a truckler."

"How very admirable."

His collarbone and neck are flushed, and he looks away. A dark line draws itself in the outer whorl of his ear, and a black bead collects on his earlobe.

"Oh, no," she says. "Look."

He puts his hand up and looks at the blood on his fingers. "I guess I ought to wash it."

"I have water. Come inside."

He tilts over so the ear will drip in the dust and not on his shirt and overalls strap. "The busybodies aren't going to like me coming in there."

"Who's to know?"

"No one, unless you go crying." He cups his hand under his ear, follows her, and sits down in the chair. He keeps his eyes on the table. She gives him a rag and a bowl of water. He pinches at the ear with the cloth for a moment. "Aw, it's on my shirt."

"If you tilt over as you were before, then . . . here's a bit of newspaper. That'll catch the drips." She pauses, then says in a rush, "This is my fault. I wasn't careful enough."

He doesn't look up. "That's all right."

She spreads the paper on the floor and watches him try to wash behind his ear. "May I do it?" She takes the cloth out of his hand and wipes the wounds. There is a short cut crowning a bump at the back of his head, and a tiny split in the ear's top curve. "Is this bump from a rock or is it just you?"

"Where?"

"Here."

"That there's my bump of etiquette. Goes with the bump of conversation on the other side."

Perhaps he won't hold it against her forever. "This ear's got a little notch in it," she says. "I suppose it'll grow back together."

"Scarred for life."

"Grow your hair long over it, like Joe Peaslee. Nobody will see it."

With the cloth pressed to his ear, he looks at the stack of pages, weighted by the ink bottle, that sits on a corner of the table. "What's that you're writing? Did you write all those pages?"

"It's a letter."

"Who to?"

She could name anyone. A friend, an old teacher, William McKinley, Nellie Bly. But she'd rather tell the truth. "It's to my mother."

"I thought she was dead."

"She is." She should be feeling horribly awkward, but she is just standing there looking at the pages she has made, one after another, day after day. Like the hole he has dug and made into a well.

"I guess having them die doesn't stop you having things to say to them."

That's right, she thinks. That's exactly right. You just go on talking to them and having them talk back to you. She stands there smiling a little, with tears in her throat. She coughs.

He looks up. "Well, what's wrong now?"

"Nothing."

"You're crying."

"Not really."

"Yes, you are. I'm the one that's hurt, if you don't mind. You and Koerner seem determined to kill me off."

She laughs and says, "You've still got blood on your neck."

He wipes his neck and looks at the cloth. "I feel a little poorly," he says. He goes back out into the yard, bends over, and puts his hands on his knees.

Esther follows. "I *am* sorry," she says again.

From the other direction comes the jingling of rigging and the squeak of a wagon axle and a sound of someone singing. In a moment Violet Fowler, the postmistress, drives into the yard. She stands to haul back on the lines, and with the tiny hat she wears tilted forward on her hair and the white WCTU ribbon that flutters at her breast, she looks like a doll come to life. She has her daughters with her, May and Maudie, who wear matching purple calico frocks. Maudie sits up straight next to her mother, but May lies on her back on the rear wagon seat, kicking up her feet and singing "Sipping Cider from a Straw."

Violet sits again with the reins in her lap. "Hello, Esther. Hello, Ben. Pick told me he was getting a well dug out on Miller's old place."

"It's me who's digging it," says Ben. "Not Pickett."

"He's got blood on him!" says May, squirming.

"Let me see it. Now, that's a good cut, Ben. Shall I fetch you to the doctor?"

"I'll just pour some liquor on it."

Violet smiles frostily. "Some around here will call that a waste, but far be it from me. Is that your alfalfa, Esther? What are you going to do here with all these improvements—run cows like Pick? Or are you going to be our schoolteacher when Jane Fremont gets married?"

"Is she going to get married?"

"She's a young woman—why not? But maybe she wants to keep to her nunnery on that claim. In any case, I do have an errand, Esther. We're on our way back from Two Forks—we helped Vincent with a baking—and Pick asked us to look in on you because of something he heard. It concerns . . . the unaccompanied young ladies of the area. It seems the two Duncan girls were on their way home from Peterson and met up with some buckaroos. I suppose the men had been drinking."

· "Lenore and—"

"Patsy," says Maudie.

Esther knows them, and remembers Lenore from that day at the school: she of the stuffy nose and strawberry French braid, and Patsy, very like her, both indifferent students but playful and interested in the boys.

"But what happened?"

Maudie says in a raw voice, "They cut Lenore's hair."

Esther recoils. Ben is silent.

Violet spreads her hands. "It appears that a couple of Jacob hands had been in town and they'd been talking about those broken windows at Two Forks and how far they had to drive cattle this winter to find range not bitten down by sheep. And when they saw Brookie Duncan at Odell's, they challenged him with it, and he told them to mind their own business, bosses should discuss these matters and buckaroos should keep quiet."

"I'll be he didn't say 'keep quiet,'" says Ben. He laughs warily. "He's a good sheepman but not much for manners."

"Then it was just by chance that on the way back from town the buckaroos crossed the path of the girls coming home from shopping."

When her mother pauses, perhaps trying to choose the right language, Maudie takes up the story. "They told Lenore that her dad owed them money and that he'd offered them her braid instead—you know that turned-in braid she wears at the back. They were joshing and teasing. Lenore knows the foreman. He bought the box lunch she made at the last box social. So when he took hold of her hair, she thought he was joking."

Young May puts her hand up to one of her own braids. "And then one of the others just took out his knife and cut it. There were three of the Jacob buckaroos and Teddy Ray."

"Teddy? Our Teddy?" Esther sits down on the steps in shock. This is horrible.

"He was well ahead on the road. Maybe he didn't know what was happening. But Lenore said he could have come back, and he didn't."

Violet lowers her voice. "I don't mean to run you down, Ben, of course I don't, but when girls from a sheep family have this kind of trouble, it's just wise to keep an eye on the cattle girls."

"I think you know the Cruffs well enough to know how safe a girl is around one of us."

Esther is uncertain and embarrassed. "There isn't any problem here," she says. "I'll tell Pick."

Maudie says, soft, "They threw her braid on the road." They are all silent a moment.

Violet says, "Well, Esther, I've got to get back and spread the mail around. Joe Peaslee's in for a shock, I think, as he's got another letter from *Pacific* magazine. They don't want his plant drawings, I venture. I hate to see him disappointed." She says this with her eyes a little closed, her eyelids purple and shrunk. You don't hate it at all, thinks Esther.

"Cold water to take out that blood," says Violet. "Hup! Go on, Soupy." She drives out of the yard and creaks away.

Esther sits. She pictures Teddy Ray, the jovial and methodical ranch foreman for whom she has made pancakes a dozen times, pictures him standing on the road while Jacob's buckaroo cuts off Lenore's hair and throws it down. Would Teddy let something like that happen while he was watching? Oh, there must have been something else. Her mind arranges, mitigates the details. Lenore was flirting. The foreman courting. But she feels deep dismay. The Duncan children came home distraught. This was not a game. It is worse than broken glass or burned wagons. Wherever it started, it ended in a place from which there might be no return.

Ben is watching the retreating Fowler family. "Gone to tell stories on me," he says. "Get me in dutch with Pickett."

"About what?"

"She'll find some excuse to make trouble for a Cruff. Especially now."

"Why are you concerned with Pick? He didn't do this. You can be mad at the Jacob buckaroos if you care to. And anyway, Pick's very fair. All the buckaroos say so."

"It's not fair that I'm here, is it, when Koerner started that fight? Anyhow, people wouldn't say anything else to you, would they? You act like you've got your head in the clouds, but listen—nobody's fooled. Everyone knows he paid you to come out here and squat. You're not even kin to him."

She feels like crying. Everything is so horrible. "I *am* kin to him. He is my cousin on my father's side."

"Well, your father's dead, and Pickett never saw you in his life before New Year's. That's not much. And no one believes you're twenty-one. You're cheating."

"I don't think I have to satisfy you on that count," says Esther stiffly. "Mr. Grist at the land office knows how old I am."

"Grist's as crooked as a snake. Or he must not have looked at you."

She folds her arms.

"That won't help," he says cruelly.

She remembers this from school. There were boys who wouldn't speak to a girl who wasn't pretty. They didn't mean anything by it, really. Just that a girl earned the right to be listened to and believed by her prettiness, and other girls might as well be ghosts.

"I think you're jealous of people with real homes," she says. "You wish everybody had to follow a bunch of dirty sheep around and sleep in an old wagon."

"If you call this a real home, you must be short a few cards. My real home up in Morrow County puts this little wreck to shame. And sheep are no dirtier than cows," he says.

"Sheep—"

"Sheep are no dirtier than cows. I call stealing land dirtier than anything a sheep ever did. You think Miller left his claim 'cause he just felt like it? Pickett routed him and then stole his water. And anyway, I'm not always going to be in sheep. I'm going to build things."

"Such as?"

"Such as buildings. And bridges."

"You're a . . . mutton puncher."

"That's pretty language on you. Did he teach you that? While I'm picking my way to hell in that hole, our bands are lambing and my brothers need me. Michael says we've lost three bummer lambs that should have lived—because I wasn't there to feed them."

"Is there any reason in the world why I should know what a bummer lamb is?"

"I guess people who've spent their life at garden parties don't know much. It's a lamb without a mother. And it has to be nursed."

"You didn't have to be here. You had to pick a fight with Noggin Koerner, or you'd be up there nursing all the lambs you wanted."

"I didn't start that fight. He came barreling out of Odie Underwood's looking for one."

"You didn't have to join in. You're not Grant Goodwell. He's a character in a comic magazine. He's not real." Her heart is full and stinging. She can't stop herself. "Besides—he's a Yale man, and you never saw the inside of a school. You aren't expected to uphold his standards."

White with hurt, his face looks suddenly childlike. She is on the verge of feeling sorry again, but he checks her with a thrust chin and says, "Why don't you stop talking and start working. Or else go back where you came from."

Each of the next three days he comes a little earlier, as if longing to be finished with his servitude. He puts his horse away in the shed and goes to the well and lets himself down the rope without knocking for her. She pushes aside her blankets and flies into her clothes, scowling between yawns, and goes out without eating, still pinning her hair. One morning she wakes in blackness and turns her head to look out the window—there is no light at all. But she has heard a knocking. She gets up and lights the lamp, puts on her wrapper, and goes to the door.

Ben's old horse Sugar stands near the well, a shadow in the dark. It is very cold, still. "Is that you?" she says softly. Another shadow bulges out from behind Sugar and separates. He's been sitting against the well platform. He comes toward her, into the lamplight, sees that she is not dressed, and stops. He looks back toward the well and keeps his face averted as he speaks. "We're done."

"What?" She is so sleepy.

"The well's dug."

She comes out. Last night he put a few boards over the well

mouth to keep out animals, but he has pulled them aside and tied his own lantern to the rope. He lowers it in. Far down, the light makes a glint on a flat black circle.

"The water came up overnight," he says. He begins hauling the lantern up. "It was coming in the walls around me yesterday. It takes a while to seep up and get started."

"I can't believe it."

"Thought I'd never get there?"

"I suppose I never thought there was really water down there."

"What's that mean?"

"Just that it's a desert."

"So we were doing all this work for our health."

"I won't have to carry water from the lake," she says. "What-ever will I do with all my leisure?"

"Write your dead mama, I reckon."

She stares at him. Her passions collide and make her momen-tarily mute. She picks up her lamp and turns away. The oil sloshes and the light flares.

"Careful now," he says. He sounds chastened.

It gives her courage. She turns back. "Do you mean to insult me every chance you get?" she says. "Do you sleep up there among the sheep and think of what will pain me?"

He looks impassive. The sun is coming now, and the kerosene glow is cheapened. It is yellow and limited where it still lights the dirt, the well platform, and Esther's bare feet.

"That's not so. I don't mind if you write to your mother. If my mother was dead, I might do it."

"It's not for you to mind or not mind. Nothing about me is your business."

"Listen. Why don't you go put on your shoes."

"My feet aren't your business, either. If the well is finished, you needn't come here anymore, is that right? I'll tell my cousin it's all over, that you've paid your debt."

"More than paid it, I think. He ought to owe me."

"That's between him and you, then."

He goes to Sugar, steps up on the well rim, and settles himself on the horse's bare back. "He'll need to build you a well cover. So's you don't wander out here mooning, and fall in and drown."

"Goodbye."

"Don't act so high. In that getup you're hardly decent." He clicks the corner of his cheek, taps Sugar, and rides away.

A cold rose-colored dawn is unfolding behind the bluffs. The work is done. She will be able to have a bath and go to town. But she feels strangely unfree.

20

UNLIKE THE BREAKING OF THE WINDOWS at Two Forks and the burning of the Duncan wagon, Lenore's stolen hair does not earn mention in the *Century Intelligence*. Gordon Cecil is heard to say that outright violations must be reported, but an incident such as this—peculiar, disputed, and touching on the humiliation of a girl— is best left out of the printed discourse.

But the confusion and anger the situation generates is considerable. Violet Fowler insists on the drunkenness of the buckaroos, but she doesn't sway many minds. As one homesteader wife says, "A man don't *do* drunk what he don't *want* to do sober." "It's disgusting," says Delight Endicott. "I don't care what Brookie did to any cow or cowman." Ida Schmidt says, "Is it this kind of a place, Century? Where girls are not safe from their neighbors? Ach, no, *schrecklich*." Her husband is more sanguine. "Foolery. Those boys just got themselves out of hand."

Others say Lenore is a self-regarding flirt or bored out on that ranch and angling for attention in town. Everyone is talking about it. One evening Esther happens to be at Two Forks when Delores Green arrives with the eggs. She can't find Vincent, and she goes reluctantly out with the cart to meet the wagon. Every time she has met Delores in the past month, she has gotten the same impression she did that first time: something about her is unpleasant to Delores, no matter how she tries to cover up the fact with ordinary conversation. So Esther is ready to have a quick exchange with her and let her get away at once, but as Delores hands down crates of eggs, she says to Esther gravely, "You've heard about the Duncan girl and the buckaroos, haven't you? What do you think of it?"

"Yes, it's shocking. I never was so surprised that they would do something like that. But perhaps I don't know enough about it."

Delores stands tall in the wagon, hands on her hips. "Not me. I'm not surprised."

"Because of what goes on between sheep and cattle people? Between Brookie and the rest of them? Is it a feud? Would you call it a feud?"

"Because . . ." Delores kneels down in the wagon bed so she's closer to Esther. "Because not everyone is worth trusting. Not everyone knows that other people are real and have rights and claims. Or they may know it, but at the crucial moment they forget. So one might as well be ready, Miss Chambers."

"I? I should be ready? But please call me Esther."

"I mean—anyone." Her lovely face, gilded by moonlight, closes over. She seems cross, as if she's spoken too freely. "Here's Vincent coming, but I must go," she says, cold and bright. "Tell him I'll collect the egg money next week."

The Jacob buckaroo who cut Lenore's hair is marched off to apologize to the girl and her family. Thereafter, whenever he comes to town, he looks neither this way nor that, but ties his horse at the rear of the saloon and enters by the back door. The foreman, Osterhaus, blusters about how he was misunderstood, then assumes an air of martyrdom. Elijah sends him out with two or three others to ride fence for a couple of days. Lenore returns to school, a noticeable switch of hair, too brown to be her own, patching the cut place at the nape of her neck and secured with a defiant black velvet bow. But Jebby Stoop, a cattle boy and best friends with Osterhaus's young brother, leans forward in his seat that first day, whispers to Lenore that she is a liar, yanks the bow away, and tosses it to another boy, who throws it out the window. One of the other girls captures the hairpiece before it slides off weeping Lenore's neck, but Jane Fremont takes Jebby Stoop out on the schoolhouse steps and thrashes him with a stick ten times. "I've whipped other children like that who deserved it much less," she says later with dry anger. "I believe I'll have to raise the price of admission for a whipping on the stairs." In a few days the children seem to have forgotten. But no one else has.

Esther can't bring herself to ask Teddy what exactly happened, but at dinnertime a day or so later, Noggin does it for her. "You going to tell us what you did to those Duncan girls, Ted?" There's something playful in his tone, and he glances around the room as though looking for companions in his mirth. Only a dozen men are present, the others being occupied elsewhere on the ranch and eating their dinners on the hoof, and none of those present seem inclined to encourage Koerner with their attention. Teddy barely looks up from his beef and peas, and he very particularly doesn't look at Esther. He is ashamed, yes. But there are other feelings: impatience, anger. He is not wholly sorry.

Esther is disappointed that the newspaper seems to have done no more investigation of the incident than she herself has in third-hand conversations. Now she notices that Lenore's travail is not the only omission in the *Intelligence*. The national news, for instance, comes down from Portland via Peterson in the form of sheets of printed steel plate. Esther has seen the pieces unloaded from the stage, wrapped in an old blanket, and felt the heat of curiosity. Anything might be written there: assassination, a new war, a crisis in the banks, and all taking place perhaps days ago while the local citizenry went about their business unknowing. The whole issue is printed every Friday morning and read through by most of the county, including Esther, before supper. And so that very week she is perturbed to see in the bottom right-hand corner of the national page a small inky block of nothing—no words, not even an advertisement. Like a night window in the news or a hole in it, the blackened square draws the eye. Esther turns the page back and forth, trying to understand what isn't there.

Later she takes it in to Joe, and shows it to him. As they are reading, Gordon himself comes into the store.

Joe holds up the paper. "Ahoy, Cecil! An imp has got loose in your press and blotted something out."

With his pinkie finger Gordon traces the little trench in his bowed upper lip. "An inflammatory cartoon. It was misleading on the matter of the peace in the Philippines. The editors in Portland erred in running it."

"Standards," supplies Joe. "Objectivity."

"Yes—"

"Harmony. Decency."

"If there is no loss of—"

"Actual information."

"You understand my position, Joe. And the shaving soap I ordered? With the verbena scent?"

"On top of the box by the door." Joe gives the newspaper a pat. "There's nothing about your position, Cecil, that I fail to understand."

The fact of the matter, as Esther later understands from Pick, is that Elijah Jacob happened to be up in Peterson the day before and saw a copy of the *Peterson Argus*. The cartoon showed President McKinley sitting under a palm tree reading a leather-bound book labeled TAKING IT ALL, his crossed legs propped comfortably on the back of a dark-skinned young woman labeled DEMOCRACY.

Elijah Jacob thought as much of democracy as the next fellow, but he had a cousin from Medford who had lost a foot to gangrene over there outside of Manila, and he did not think much of aspersions cast on the motives of the President. How was the nation to be protected if there was such rank-and-file dissension?

When he got back to Century, he dropped by the *Intelligence* office, two doors down from the livery, to let Cecil know what was coming by boilerplate. When Pick came in, Elijah was sharing the worst story he'd heard from his cousin: the Filipinos buried Spanish prisoners up to their necks in the sand and coated their faces with sugar. "Huge meat-eating ants did the rest," said Elijah with lurid enthusiasm.

"Foul," said Gordon Cecil. He grimaced. "This is what happens when you mix the black blood with the yellow blood. I ask you, do such people deserve to run their own affairs?"

Ferris Pickett rubbed his neck. "Meat-eating ants?"

"Think about it. The man can't move. His mouth is propped open with a stick." Elijah bounced up in his boots. "Those goo-goo babies are cute, but look what they grow up into."

"I don't mean to doubt your cousin, Elijah," Pick said, "but I've heard that story before. About the ants. They used to say the Bannock around here did that same thing. With honey, as I recall."

Gordon said, "There is probably a species of cunning common to those who don't have guns and swords. They must make do with what they have."

"Maybe," said Pick. "Or maybe somebody likes to make up stories. But it's your concern, Cecil. You do the paper, so you put in it what you like."

Hearing this later, Esther says to Pick, "But what sort of a newspaper is it, then, if he just blots out what he doesn't like? Is it a watercolor, where you wash away the bad stroke?"

Pick laughs and says, "I couldn't say. I've never made a watercolor. Or a newspaper."

When Esther reports on these events later, Joe Peaslee says, "Yes, and if the Filipinos had bayonets to fight with, the stories would have them skewering Spanish babies. One's enemy is always particularly unkind to infants, you see."

"You mean it's made up?"

"I don't say that. Atrocities are real. I have seen them. Propaganda is also real."

"But Joe, people either do things or they don't. Someone knows what happened, and the newspaper should find it out!"

Joe waves his hand, cynical. "Some paper, perhaps, but not Cecil's. Ah, well. It's a faraway war and the short men will lose it."

After that, when Esther reads the paper, she wonders whether something has been left out. Whether Aguinaldo's daughter has been caught on a road. Whether someone has cut off a girl's black hair.

21

THAT NIGHT in her bed, though she curls close in a ball and puts her hands on her head, she is too cold to sleep. In Chicago such a feeling would have passed. Her mother would have put another blanket on her and put more coal in the heater, and she would have drifted down again into her balmy dreams. But tonight there is no such blanket. When she turns in bed, shivering her way up out of some distress about a dinner table too vast to be set in time for a meal, she recalls that she has almost no coal left in the cabin. She lies there for some time, feeling brittle and exhausted. Finally she gets up, puts on her coat and shoes, and goes out, under ice-blue stars, to the shed. Duniway is lying down, her front legs folded as neat as a deer's. The mare raises her head, her eyes rolling white and suspicious in the darkness, but when Esther comes forward and kneels against her, she puts her head down again and blows out a great sigh. Esther thinks of Ben Cruff dragging sheep-skins closer as the wind blows under his wagon, and then of Pick's room, heated by the parlor chimney, its rug lush carved velvet. She adjusts herself against Duniway and inhales her smoky, salty smell. Against the mare's bulk she finally grows warm, though she is privy all night to the purl and gulp of horse digestion.

In the morning, picking bits of chaff from her hair, she goes to the alfalfa patch. A month ago the blue-green plants sprouted, and now, in May, they are higher than her shoe tops. This morning their fibrous green tendrils are livid with frost. Oh, what should she do? The early sun is pouring down on them, and she has heard that sun is dangerous after frost. In the grip of an unfamiliar panic, she goes inside the fence and begins to warm the stalks in her hands. The frost melts, but her hands become stiff and clumsy, and she breaks some of the tendrils. She blows on her hands, puts them into her armpits, then clasps the plants again. When she has finished all the rows, she goes out and shuts the gate. Delight Endicott is having a tea party this morning, at which the women will sew shirts for unfortunate children, and Esther will ask what the procedure is for frost.

The ladies gather. They are tardy, out of spirits, gloomy and enervated. The farmers among them have suffered serious losses, ones that destroy the chance for a prosperous year. Esther learns that there is nothing to be done but wait, to see which plants will succumb and which will survive. Jane Fremont has lost most of her vegetables. She takes coffee today, not tea. What an unpleasant accumulation of events, thinks Esther. The yellow cat, cut; Lenore's shearing. Burned things, frozen things.

"I begin to think Century is under a curse," she says to Jane.

"I don't blame you."

Delight joins them and puts some sugar on a plate. "That's what Delores Green said. They've probably lost most of their rye and some of the alfalfa. They have the chickens, but it's not enough to get them ahead."

"She works hard," Jane says. "Fred, too, but Delores never stops."

"It's only May. Isn't there time to plant again?" asks Esther.

"There is time," Jane says. "But new seed must be bought, at some expense. And there is no room for another disaster. That is an uncomfortable position for us farmers to be in."

But Delight explains that Fred and the reverend have reached an agreement already that morning. Mr. Endicott will fund the Greens' new planting of rye, to be repaid in time. A whisper of pleasure mixes with Esther's embarrassment and uncertainy. Perhaps the world is going better than she thought. When people break down the wall of pride to seek help, help is given.

"That's very generous, Delight," says Phelia Jacob. "You've done right by that family from the beginning. But homesteading isn't easy. What do you plan to do with that quarter section of yours, Esther?" Phelia is wearing a particularly elaborate mantelet jacket of peacock blue today, the wrists choked with ivory lace. Nothing could indicate more clearly that she rarely washes a dish.

"I have some alfalfa—well, whatever's left. I don't have any other plan yet."

"Well, I have one for you. You live on a ranch stocked with bachelors. Snap your fingers—go on!"

All the women laugh, and Phelia continues. "Someone's got to get Ferris Pickett one of these days—don't tell us you haven't considered it."

"Aren't you cousins?" asks Violet. "I thought you were cousins."

"Yes, barely. Third—or fourth?—and once removed."

"I see," says Violet. "I didn't understand."

Phelia shrugs. "I don't care whose cousin he is, he's been tormenting the girls for years now, and we're all a bit tired. Let somebody settle him down for good is what I say."

How far had Pick's "torment" gone? Had another woman stood in his office with her hand in his and made an understanding? No. No one else would have been so convenient as she, so mild. There would have been less talking, less fireside. Less chastity. Dusk and wind, sudden visits, hard embraces. She could ask him. She has the right.

"You can't say Pick needs settling," says Violet. "He's as steady as they come." Her tone is cross. But she seems to be purposely obscuring some feeling there, and as she opens her marionette's jaw to drink tea, Esther understands that the feeling is passionate devotion. Not just to Pick's cause, but to his person. Oh, Violet. She must be only eight or nine years older than he, a difference that may feel just possible to traverse. They are friendly colleagues in the affairs of Century and of similar turns of mind. Such relations often change their nature, deepen. Unless someone else stumbles into the picture. No wonder Violet always chews Esther over, unable to swallow.

Phelia's impatient. "Certainly he's steady, Violet. All the more reason he should raise some boys. Who'll he leave all that to when he goes, Noggin Koerner? No, it's time he got a family. Or if you don't want *him*, Esther, one or two of those buckaroos might make a husband. You can have them build you a gazebo out there on Half-a-Mind. I sent Elijah here, there, and the moon that first year!"

"You can see people might wonder," says Violet with a tinny laugh. "Your having spent the winter out there."

"Oh, Violet, must you know *everyone's* business?" Jane sounds weary.

Esther wants to change the subject from love, from Pick and buckaroos. "I have been learning to type on Joe Peaslee's Liberty," she puts in. "Perhaps I may write letters for a businessman or put down someone's memoirs. I'm much faster than I was at first. Now I can write a letter. I can think and type at the same time."

Delight sits on the arm of Esther's chair and pats her shoulder. "Leave her alone, all of you. A girl gets her plans from her people, and Pick is all the people she's got. She's just lost her mother."

"Lots of us have lost mothers," says Violet. "I don't see it's ever prevented a girl from setting her cap. It even helps. A man likes an orphan." She puts her teacup down on its saucer and both on the table. Her eyes are shining with dread and eagerness. "By the way, Esther. That chain you wear. What's on that chain?"

When Reverend Endicott and the doe-eyed Fred Green come into the room to beg for coffee, they encounter uproar. The reverend holds up his white hands, palms toward the noise. "Delight, what is this?"

"This Miss Chambers is the sliest of boots," Delight says. "All this while she has worn Ferris Pickett's ring around her neck, and never a word! Bravo for Violet!"

"I *do* have eyes in my head," Violet says with an air of martyred pride.

"The ring is just from the family," says Esther.

"I don't know a young man who passes out pearl rings without any thought," Delight says. "I believe he's spoken for you."

Fred Green gives her a thoughtful look and, oddly, kindly, shakes her hand. "I wish you happiness, and I'm sure Delores does, too."

"No, no," says Esther. "You misunderstand. It's not decided."

Jane whispers, "They want something that's not ugly to talk about. Just shrug and smile and they'll leave you alone."

But they are delighted with their discovery, and they are planning her wedding. She will live with Pick forever as mistress of Two Forks.

That night Esther lies in bed for a long time before she begins to feels sleepy. The stars beyond the tiny window are not so icy. They swing and swim in the dark out there. The window becomes the window of a train, and she feels she is being pulled forward by some unseen motor. She is breathless, she wants to slide down and hold on, but she knows she must sit upright because she is holding something in her lap. She peers down. It is a little chicken whose shell has shattered. The down is still soupy on its back, its tiny tri-claws are tender. Its soft beak opens in protest. She is exhausted, but she begins the obvious chore. She picks up flecks of shell on her licked finger and puts the egg together again, chip by chip, until the chick is closed again in darkness.

22

IT IS JUNE. The church windows are open, and Reverend Endicott stands at the pulpit. "We have suffered ill luck and ill humor this spring, my friends, and it has been suggested to me that we delay our traditional picnic. I think not." He does not spread his usual calm unction over the words. He is querulous and nervy. "It is important in times like these to maintain our precious unity."

Brookie Duncan's wife, Eileen, stands up at the very end of one of the rear pews. Her pink-gold bangs—usually stylishly curled—are damp and flat. "I'm taking my girls to Medford to visit their grandmother. Have your picnic without us." The congregation waits in astonishment for her to continue. Eileen looks as if she is wavering on her feet, but instead of sitting, she leaves the pew and strides out of the church, trailed by Lenore and Patsy, their eyes downcast in confusion. After a moment Brookie stands up, too. While all watch, he covers his head with his hat and follows his family. The church is quiet enough that they can hear his heavy tread going down the steps outside.

Reverend Endicott smacks the pulpit. But he says, "We will do it. And I expect to see this whole congregation there."

Therefore, the next Saturday, a procession of conveyances wheel up amber clouds of dust along the road around Half-a-Mind, bound for the ice caves just south of the lake. Elijah and Phelia Jacob, as befitting cattle gentry, come along smartly, each driving a black buggy full of daughters-in-law and grandchildren, and their sons and buckaroos spread out around them in the green and luscious rabbitbrush. Wagons trundle along behind, piloted by storekeeper or hired boy or fresh no-name homesteader and a big-eyed mail-order wife. Mrs. Fowler and her daughters ride with Carey Stoop, whose occasional laugh is the only sound the desert stillness can't reduce to mere tinkling; Jane Fremont comes with the Endicotts and Marguerite, who is discovered to be hanging upside down from the back of the wagon, exposing her underclothes and lifting her head just in time to miss the rocks that pass underneath.

Joe Peaslee walks, circling back to bend over some florescence or animal business that interests him, making notes in the little book he keeps in the pocket of his blue military coat, which he has put on for this special occasion.

And people come from the south, too, up out of the desert, and from the east, skirting the Peterson Bluffs. Delores and Fred and the baby all come together on one horse; Delores balances a pan of something on the pommel in front of her, while the baby, wrapped up on Fred's back, drums on his head.

To Esther everyone looks thin and fatigued, pale, shaggy. They ride as though stiff and aching. Not many people talk. But they are bravely turned out for spring in cream or pink or blue calico, in fresh Levi's and brushed cowboy hats, in battered straw boaters whitened with chalk.

In honor of Esther's recent sitting for and passing her examinations, Jane Fremont has given her a lavender skirt and striped waist, and together they have taken it in at the bosom and let down the hem. Esther has been wearing a black skirt and white waist for some time now, but this is the first color she has worn since last August. Her black clothes won't last much longer, anyway. They have been washed so much that they are turning from black into something like the ash color of her hair. The new clothes refresh her spirit. While dressing, she opened her trunk and found the ribbons she used to wear on her long plait, a red and a blue, and these she has tied to Duniway's headband, which—combined with the blind white eye and the bony aristocracy of the nose—make the mare look like an old madwoman dressed up in her maiden finery.

On the wall she has pinned her diploma. Jane Fremont inscribed it in her lean, delicate hand: "Esther Chambers, on this day, twentieth May of the year nineteen hundred, in the county of Peterson, state of Oregon." Esther is happy and relieved to have passed her subjects in the nineties, except for geography, in which she made an eighty-one. And Pick has been in a pleasant mood since the calving has yielded more surviving young than usual and he has lost not a single cow of complications. He takes Esther's hand now and then, and often he asks her over to Two Forks to take supper in the parlor. He holds her on his knee and kisses her carefully. She likes it, but she is shy and a little cold. Perhaps she is still more nervous around him, less compelled than she should be, but there is time. Whatever her other uncertainties, she does have a few rows of healthy plants, new clothes, a graduation, and an understanding. And as her neighbors pass by her cabin, past her alfalfa patch and her lake, she feels the pride of ownership, as though it is a party she herself is giving.

The ice cave is not in the bluffs themselves, but under an ordinary hump of land to the south, covered with the flat, downy bushes of the yellow desert primrose. It lies just beyond the boundary of Esther's claim, on open range. There, against the few junipers that lie between the lake and the cave, men set up tables and ladies weigh them down with food.

The mouth of the cave is wider than it is tall, like the space under the porch of a farmhouse, but apparently the hole goes deep. Child after child armed with burlap sack and chisel slips into the aperture. Somewhere inside are salty stores of ice. It is hard to dig a cellar in the desert, or at least hard to dig it deep enough to preserve the ice one might harvest off a lake, but here the desert keeps a cool perverse secret all summer, containing its freezing opposite inside it. After a time the first children begin appearing again, lugging or dragging their treasure, and women begin packing the ice around the pails of cooked custard that stand in the washtubs. Baskets are opened and cloths spread. It is a bright day but a bit cool, and the wind occasionally whips up and takes a napkin from the hand of a diner and flings it against a bush.

Half-a-Mind, ringed with rich lemon-green grasses, is a rippling blue, much denser than the light, inconsequential sky. The water has drawn in, leaving a cakey brown strip at the edge that clings to shoes. Children wander up to play there, dragging sticks and chasing one another and throwing rocks into the water. There are few rocks flat enough to skip, and most attempts—no matter how one leans to the side and cocks the arm—end in ignoble plonks. Buckaroos try, too, then turn back to rejoin their comrades, who are loitering near where cold baked chicken and corn bread and tiny pinkish Summer Lake strawberries are being put out on tables made of sawhorses. Phelia Jacob and her hired girls have brought a rainbow of pickles: cucumbers, beets, tomatoes. "These'll go well with that chicken," says Phelia. "My word—would you look yonder. There's Brookie Duncan."

Esther squints. "Did he come alone? I guess so."

"Look," Phelia points out. "He's brought meat. That's not mutton, either. Maybe Eileen and the girls don't yet feel like mixing with cowboys, but that looks like peacemaking—Brookie doesn't let a dime go easily. What is it? Did he get an elk?"

Brookie is indeed opening paper packages of fresh meat and putting it on spits to be roasted. He is unexpectedly cheerful: smiling, flushed, perhaps having drunk something strong. When Pick passes and speaks, Brookie gives him a giddy look and laughs.

Michael Cruff is here, Esther sees, and she feels a tingle in her chest as she looks for Ben. There he is, in his cap, new dungarees, and an ivory-colored shirt. He looks older. She has only ever seen him in his overalls.

The buckaroos are lined up politely now, holding hats and plates in hands. "I know, I know—you're hungry. That'll hush you up," says Mrs. Fowler to Carey Stoop, returning a full plate to him.

He pretends to see something amiss. "Did you put paprika in my potatoes again?" he says loudly. "Violet, you know that'll just parch me!"

Enrique, the blushing Two Forks mill rider, takes up the joke. "Good for me I brought whiskey!"

Violet aims her wooden spoon as though to rap him with it, and he cowers and puts his neckerchief over his face. These hijinks are a relief to Esther. People are recovering. The winter has not ruined them.

Not far away, the Endicotts and the Greens sit together on a blanket. Esther would like to catch Delores's eye. She has not seen her since the day she came to deliver eggs. But Delores seems always to be engaged, with the baby Westie, with food, with Marguerite's cutlery.

Esther sits down between Pick and Vincent. When Pick hands her a napkin and their fingers touch, he smiles at her, and in smiling back, she sees Violet and Phelia exchanging glances. She has new stature. No longer an orphaned outsider, a city mouse with an unusual vocabulary. She is reintroduced, in fact, at the side of the man they most respect, and it makes her feel both significant and unnerved.

She is browsing the last of the food on her plate, waiting for her turn to churn the ice cream, when a little dog comes toward her through the standing people. Its short tail is sprung to one side; its eyes bug out like grapes. It waggles its piggy body, puts its nose to the ground and inhales, raises its head and looks at Esther's plate, and sneezes.

"Nick! Nicky!" she hears. Through the crowd she can see a little man turning here and there, looking. A chill descends into her belly. It is Mr. Grist, the land officer from up in Peterson. She has not seen him since that day she pretended she was twenty-one. She puts her plate on the ground, stands, and hurries back behind the women at the ice-cream tubs. The dog is now rummaging through the chicken bones on her plate, and its owner is advancing toward it, scolding.

In memory she hears Ben Cruff say, *No one believes you're twenty-one.* She touches her hair, smooths her dress. Suppose Mr. Grist should realize his error. He would denounce her, would he not?

But he took her signature, he blotted it and filed it. She will not lose the claim, nor his watering hole. It is the large frauds that come in for scrutiny and disapprobation, while the industrious individual, the rancher, is often praised. Still, she does not want to speak to Mr. Grist. She does not like to think about that day when she lied.

As she passes a wagon, she catches a lantern hanging off the front seat. She tries to make her back look calm and unremarkable as she glides toward the mouth of the cave. Crouching, she gathers her skirt in one hand, kneels, and crawls in.

It is dark. She feels her way along until the ceiling opens up and she can just stand. In the dish under the lamp chimney, her fingers find a match. She scrapes it on a rock and watches it flare.

The floor of the cave—though it can hardly be called that, so uneven and rocky and rifted is it—slopes down and makes a curve, and a drift of dark sand has piled up at the far side. The tracks of the children who came for ice earlier are wet and elongated in the sand. Esther balances with one hand on the rocks and with the other holds the lamp high.

It is eerier than she expected, more earthy and strange. The ice hangs in cones overhead and spreads out below in shallow, cloudy ponds, yellow with the earth's mineral seep. In several places water has dripped and frozen over banks of rocks and collected in layers, so there are smooth benches of ice marked with yellow whorls. Chips grate under her feet where the boys knocked off icicles to haul aboveground. She takes off her apron and lays it on one of the benches and sits down on it. It is cold. What can she do? Even if she stays for an hour, Mr. Grist is sure to see her when she emerges. He may hear her name called and be watching.

It is so silent in here. The buzz and chatter of the picnic are muted to nothing. Nervous, she hums a little.

"I've got a mule, her name is Sal
Fifteen miles on the Erie Canal
She's a good old worker and . . ."

A figure stands above her on the path. Her hands fling themselves one to each side and she topples the lamp and then catches
it. The intruder makes crazy shadows, like a crowd of people
leaping and moving. He advances toward her, and she sees that it
is Ben Cruff. His new jeans are rolled up, but they still hang over
his heels like sailor pants.

"Quick catch with that lamp," he says. "I'm sorry if I scared
you." He runs his hand over an icicle. "What're you doing down
here? Don't you like ice cream?"

"I do like it."

"So do I. They made it with strawberries, did you know that?
Somebody brought up ten quarts from Summer Lake. That's a
day's ride." He hooks his thumbs in his jeans pockets, then removes
them and folds his arms. "Aren't you cold down here?"

"Yes," she says, and laughs a little. "Frozen!"

"Come back up a little and I'll show you something."

She shakes out the apron and reties it. When he nears the
mouth of the cave, he goes to one side, to a cleft in the wall she
hadn't seen before. He clambers over some rocks and reaches back
for the lantern. He holds out his hand and she takes it and climbs
after him.

"Careful for your dress here. Now look up."

On the low ceiling is a patch of gray, mottled with black, the
size of a big dishpan. It stirs. The lantern light shimmers on—
skin? Fur. "Bats?"

"Yes. You scared? Oh, that's right," he says over her protest.
"That's right. You don't get scared. You're as cool as those icicles."

"Look at them sleeping."

"Cozy as they might be."

Ranks of pale bodies; folded soft-skin wings; quiet, dark mouse
faces. An occasional shiver, a stirring passes through them.

He reaches up his hand and nestles it among the bats, who
make a sleepy shift to accommodate it. Ben smiles, looking at her
but also into the dark, concentrating. "If you're very calm, you
can feel them breathing."

"They don't bite?"

"They've never bitten me."

"But what if one is mad?"

"Hasn't been so far."

"You're as foolish as Joe Peaslee."

"I suppose."

She reaches up her own hand. "Soft."

"It's a little like being with sheep," he says. "They stick together at night. You can hear them breathing and making their sounds."

"I suppose most animals do. Cattle, even."

"I s'pose."

"One night on my claim—" she says. "Oh, I don't know."

"Which night?"

"Just one night. The night of the frost. I was cold. I went out and slept in Duniway's stall with her."

"Well, horses smell better than other animals. It's a pleasure to have a horse breathe on you."

"Yes. Have you done with shearing?"

"Oh, sure. Last week. We earmarked our lambs, and then we sheared. We had a heck of a clip this year. Three thousand pounds of wool. We mule-trained it up to Peterson and sent it to Shaniko to sell. That's good money to take to our ma and pa up in Morrow. If our other bands at home did as well, we'll be sitting pretty for two years." He confides, "It may be that I'll get a new horse. I've got my eye on a good-looking scamp Carey Stoop raised, if he doesn't sell him from under me just to spite a sheepman. I could use a better horse than Sugar. He can hardly get the wagon up to the camp on the bluffs anymore. Did you know I can see your lamp from up there?"

Shy, she tilts her head back again and puts her hand among the bats so she won't have to look at him. "I can see your fire, some nights."

A bat detaches itself from the sleeping group and flutters wildly toward the cave mouth. "It must be coming on to sunset," says Ben. "Listen. I'm sorry I was so mean."

"You weren't mean."

"I wasn't sweet, either."

"I'm afraid to take back my hand," says Esther. "I might wake them all up."

"Here." He reaches and nudges away the creatures. He closes his hand over hers and draws it down. A chittering sigh goes through the bats. A flare of wings here and there.

Esther nods toward him. "Is your ear healed?"

"Except for the scar. I'm marked. Now nobody can poach me out of your band."

She wrinkles her nose. "Who'd want to poach the likes of you?"

"You greenies don't know how dangerous this country can be. There's hundreds of rustlers out there in skirts."

She smiles down at the rocks. "We should go out. But I don't want to talk to Mr. Grist."

"You aren't twenty-one, are you?"

"You knew that already."

"I wasn't sure."

"I'm only eighteen!" she cries, half laughing. It feels so good to say so, and safe here in the cave.

"That's younger than me," he says. "I'm nineteen."

"You won't tell anyone?"

"No."

"On your word."

"Yes. Look, don't worry about Grist. I'll take care of him. I'll stand in his line of sight."

But when they emerge from the cave—faces screwed up and blinking even in the mellow orange light of evening—there is no need for subterfuge. Bowls of ice cream tilt and leak onto the blankets, a piece of beef smokes to a crisp on a spit—and all the picnic guests are clustered up near the lakeshore, rumbling with comment and standing on tiptoe. Some are jogging farther up the waterline to get a better view.

"What is it?" she whispers.

He nods down at two men who stand knee-deep in the lake. There is a bobbing white thing in the lake—a large white face and red-brown neck. Esther recognizes Knock-Knock, Pick's younger bull, his eyes half closed. He's escaped, and swimming. Then he turns his head, turns it, and the head keeps turning. It lolls, floats, and upends to show the gray tissue of amputation, the sawed bone and ratted fur. Beheaded. This precious animal.

A prolonged intake of breath, gasps from all those who can see the bull's head.

"Oh, no. Oh, no."

"My Lord."

"God al*mighty*," says Teddy the foreman.

Men cast about for long sticks and use them and the tips of their gun barrels to pull the sad, loathsome head into the shallows. Teddy purses his lips and hauls it up on the mud by the ears. Pick bends over it. "That's my bull Knock-Knock. He's got my earmark."

"You sheepers are devils," Phelia Jacob cries out. "Pure devils!"

At this, a torrent of protests erupt, and then other voices demand silence. "Shut up. What's Pickett say?"

"God damn it to hell," says Teddy again, wiping his hands on his pants.

"Ted Ray, stop that swearing," says Delight Endicott, almost in tears. "Just stop it. I can't stand it."

Michael and Ben Cruff push forward. "What the hell—"

"Somebody killed my prize bull. Do you know anything about this?"

Michael chooses his words carefully. "Pick, I have never seen that bull in my life, and if I had, I would not have touched a hair of him."

"Well, somebody touched him. Somebody butchered him."

"Devils and rustlers," Phelia says.

"Hold your tongue," Jane tells her.

"Are you taking their side, Jane Fremont? Is that what you're doing?"

"Phelia, be *still*."

Brookie Duncan, his round face red with heat and sunset, has moved a little way along the shore and is standing by himself. It is clear now that he is drunk, maybe very drunk. He calls out, "That bull is for all you cattle boys. Who want to shame my family and ruin my livelihood."

"Brookie, that's not fair," says Carey Stoop.

"Hah! Fair! That's rich from you, Stoop, you blasted fraud. And I hope you enjoyed your beef, everybody. It cost Pickett some eagles to have it shipped here from Chicago on the hoof."

Carey Stoop's handsome face is flaming. "I'm going to thrash that son of a bitch."

Michael Cruff says to Pick, "He's had a hard time of it. You know he has. That lost wagon crippled his season."

"I don't give a shit about his hard time," says Pick.

In fear Esther looks for Jane, who comes to her and takes her hand. "He doesn't mean it."

"I think he does mean it," Esther says. She can see Ben up there, shoulder to shoulder with his brother. Will he ever speak to her again?

A voice raises a shout then, at the edge of the crowd. It is Joe Peaslee. His hair is now rumpled, his blue coat open, and his vest dirty. He strides back and forth along the lakeshore. "To the fort!" he calls. "Send for reinforcements!" He is lurching, stumbling along in the shallows.

Pick has been under tight control when facing the disaster. But when he sees Joe Peaslee, his contempt bursts forth. "Why doesn't somebody put that old man away? He's an embarrassment."

Joe doesn't seem to hear, but goes on stalking through the mud, gesturing.

Reverend Endicott says, "Friends, I beg you. Let calm characterize our—"

"Put it in the wagon," Pick tells Teddy and Noggin. They heave the bull's head onto a tablecloth, wrap it, and carry it between them. Noggin shoulders Reverend Endicott out of the way, and the minister stands to one side, angry and helpless. Over near the food, women are slapping plates willy-nilly into baskets and putting platters uncovered into the wagon beds. Napkins blow against the bushes and stick there. Men light lanterns. It is getting dark, and everyone is in a hurry to get home.

As Esther bridles Duniway, Ben Cruff passes by. He is too far away for her to read his expression. "I'll be seeing you," he says, and goes on.

Does it mean he will or he won't? Duniway tosses her head, and the red and blue ribbons whip Esther's hands. She has trouble getting the pin into the cheek strap of the bridle.

A few boys begin to sing.

"One night dark
When bed we all were in
Lady O'Leary left the shed the lantern in."

Their mothers tell them to be quiet, stop fooling, and help. The boys carry boxes and baskets to the wagons. But they continue to sing softly,

"One night dark
When bed we all were in
Lady O'Leary left the shed the lantern in
And when the kick cowed it over
She eyed her wink and said
There'll be a time hot
In the town old
Tonight."

23

HALF-A-MIND draws in its borders. It looks as if a different body of water has sneaked in and occupied the marshy footprint of the winter lake. The minerals natural to the soil rise to the surface and crust like chalk. At Esther's end of the lake the wind is razored by the parched grass, and at the south end the aspens, twisted and salty, rattle their coins. The cattle are distressed when they come to the windmills for water. They clamber over one another to get to the troughs, where they sometimes relieve themselves, looking around dumb-eyed, the hollows over their brow bones cupped and deep.

Unhappy buckaroos from Two Forks cut hay on the southern edge of Esther's claim, where it dries in an hour. They build a shed and stack the hay inside it and then move to another field along a wash two miles east, on open range. There they build another shed. When they come into the ranch at night, their hands look as if they've been dipped in walnut oil, sweating and as dark as wood. They itch from the hay, and they complain: it's not fit work for a good hand, Ferris should hire more Mexicans. They fill their hats under the pump and turn them over their heads. Sometimes after supper they come over to swim in the shrinking silk murk of the lake. From her cabin Esther cannot see them, but she can hear their deep shouts and laughing.

She folds most of her bedclothes and puts them away in her trunk. Still she is not cool enough. She drags her bed into the center of the cabin. She drops her nightgown to her waist, ties its arms there, and, half naked, lies down with her head toward the open door.

The episode of the beheaded bull has been taken by different parties each in his way. In large groups the buckaroos guard the deadlines up in the summer pasturages with their Winchesters resting crosswise in front of the saddle horn rather than sheathed at the knee. Brookie Duncan sits up on his porch at night, sometimes alone, sometimes with friends, and always with a loaded rifle.

Most of the itinerant sheep have melted from the country, trailed by night to higher pasture to the north, outside of Peterson County. One band of Cruff sheep remains: two hundred head, an afterthought, recaptured strays and ewes that gave birth late. For a time this band grazes out of sight west of town, but one evening Esther sees a tiny light in the bluffs. It can't matter to anyone that they are there, for Pick's cows have already eaten it down and moved on. It can't matter to anyone but her.

She takes her own lamp to the doorway and passes her slate in front of it a few times. There is no answering signal. Again. No response. By and by she puts the slate down and extinguishes the lamp. She lies down on her bed and gazes at the light until its shape is emblazoned on her brain.

After seeing Joe Peaslee in such a state at the picnic, Pick tells Esther to stay away from him. "He's a fiend for dope, and that's what he'll always be. I don't know if he's dangerous, but I don't want to find out too late. I mean it. Stay away."

Could it be true that Joe is dangerous? She doesn't think so, since his cigarettes generally make him only distant and sleepy. But she doesn't know how to convince Pick of this, and in any case he's been in a black mood. Thus she has disregarded his injunction only once—to tap at the glass of the store and wave at Joe—and he didn't seem to recognize her. How he must think of her now: one of those whose movements must be tracked by spyglass. Not to speak to him, not to ask him questions, not to hear him moving about as she picks her way among the keys of the

Liberty. How alone he is, and perhaps sick, with no one to tell him he's drunk enough Welsh Oats Essence. She must check up on him, if only from afar.

In order to provide herself with a reason to pass the store, she takes to stopping in at the newspaper office, two doors down Second Street. The air there is pungent with the smells of hot metal and ink and oil and the sharp waft of the benzene Gordon Cecil uses to clean his type. He moves about quickly—his large, polished body light on his small feet, like a beetle—a damp rag in one hand and a tiny pair of calipers in the other. "Point ought two ought five," he declares to himself. "Point ought eleven. Ought ought three." He calculates the widths of the paper, muslin, and thin cardboard packing the cylinder so that each line of type will come squarely into contact with the paper in the bed without any relative movement. "*Pressure without slur.* These are my watchwords," he tells Esther.

He will not let her take measurements, but when the press is not running, he lets her oil it. Contacting surfaces must be oiled where they rub. Much harm can be done to the machinery, he tells her, for want of a single drop of oil. At first Esther just searches for oil holes, fills them with her can, and presses in a little piece of felt. After several visits, though, she begins to see the press as groups of parts with particular functions, and she begins to look for the holes where they should be. She is pleased when Gordon trusts her to oil the press alone. And one slow afternoon he shows her how to set type on the cylinders. She comes to recognize at a glance the reversed look of common words like *Portland, railroad, social,* and *beef.* When there is a fire at a ranch up in Browning, Gordon writes the notice and Esther sets the type. She errs only by indicating that there has been

no loss of life excebt for boultry.

She's still fascinated by the heavy boilerplate stamped with the state and national news. Before it is clamped and inked, she runs her fingers over the type and reads backward to herself the words written by reporters as far away as Chicago or Boston.

"I find the press a rich source of philosophy," says Gordon. "In order for it to run smoothly, the type must fall in line—no word must obtrude—and the mechanism must be oiled where it is likely to chafe. This is true of people, you must agree. When a collective goal is sought, everyone must fall into line, despite their differences, and present a united front. Pressure without slur! That's what makes a newspaper. Certain individualists with no thought of the common enterprise put their heads up and tear the paper. That's not civil."

Today Violet Fowler comes into the shop with a notice to be printed regarding postal rates. Esther has just unwrapped the plates, and she looks at them. She runs her hands across the letters, gazing down with her head cocked, reversing them in her mind.

Governor has declared that the west hills of Peterson County will be closed to grazing from the first of September pursuant to an agreement with the Bureau of

Her heart quickens. She skates her fingers farther along the greasy type. There is perhaps copper in the hills, the article states, and the grazing cattle will be driven off or confiscated.

"What is it?" asks Violet. "Bad news?"

"They've closed the west hills to grazing."

Gordon and Violet look at each other. "Well, well," says Violet. "The camel is going to be awfully swaybacked now."

"Violet."

"Oh, Gordon, a great girl like this? She knows the way of things. Think of who she is." She turns to Esther. "He thinks that it's some kind of a secret that there's not enough rangeland to go around anymore. Not enough good land. Fewer animals to go to market—"

"Mrs. Fowler is rash," says Gordon. "This is news we've been expecting. There's no reason this should materially—"

"Less profit for the train," Esther says. "It's like a game of musical chairs. They took out a chair, and someone will have nowhere to sit."

"You see? She does understand. Anything that keeps cattle from foraging affects the railroad deal," says Violet. "The government! They may not mine that copper for years, and meanwhile they'll hobble this township."

Gordon rubs his pursed lips with a finger. "Perhaps more encouragement to Elliot, to overlook—"

Violet's wrinkles deepen. "Elliot is gathering his encouragement wherever he can find it, I don't doubt, and that includes from those cattlemen down Jack-High way." She turns to Esther. "I must run out and inform Pick. This news won't please him, but he'll know what to do."

"I'll do it," Esther says.

"I'm happy to tell him," says Violet.

"I said I will tell him," Esther says. "I'm going that way."

Joe sees Esther Chambers as he sits cross-legged in his attic, the telescope on the floor beside him. She hasn't come to visit him lately, and he assumes he has crossed some line and become a suspicious personage. It has happened before, that friends have gone, affinities have dissolved in the face of his difficulties. But it is probably for the best, as he is not at present good company for anyone, even a dear girl sympathetic with his struggling.

Because, after years of mild alarms and apprehensions, his spine is now in spasm. He cannot lie down at night without smoking his special cigarettes, and even then, adoze, he finds his mind hung with memories, like curtains he has to push through to reach sleep. Here he sees himself walking through a pine forest, through the dry needles, his ears inside out with listening, and then from above his head a single harsh Bannock word spoken at a conversational volume. He cannot bear to look up at his own death, and he moves on until he is in the open and circling around to his horse, bowels weak with relief. Here, after a skirmish, lie a pair of dead Walpapi in plaid flannel shirts, arms flung wide in the dust. Here a woman and two little girls make water beside a trail, the three black heads bowed, balanced over straw sandals. Here is a raid on a winter evening, a narrow chest leaping to meet a bullet and women scattering like water on hot grease. Here in the dawn light is a lodge made of mats, a husky brown fruit that peels open under his fire and spills out the pulp of children.

They are gone now, dispersed to reservation and religious school. They cannot fight anymore. He himself is a merchant, not a soldier anymore, and the desert has been quiet for a decade.

But all around him, the will to dominate is surging again. He recognizes it. He himself once dragged people behind his saddle and twisted to shoot and leaned down to ply his knife, and he knows the smell of righteous evil in the sweat of a man, because he has smelled it on himself. But it isn't Walpapi or Bannock or Paiute who are dragged—it is the next enemy, the next obstacle to primacy. For so long he has watched, retired from the fray, suffused in numbing smoke. Now he wants to fight. He must get up. He must get up and man his lookout.

24

IN THE EVENING sometimes, when Ben's sweat has cooled on his back and he has made himself a plateful of canned beans and tomato pickles pieced out with hunks of bread, he wanders toward the edge of the bluff where there is no sheep dung and sits down cross-legged on the short grass. A few prickles of light float on the violet lake of air before him; a cluster to the southwest marks Two Forks, and when he sees them, he eats with more gusto, though he isn't sure what the Pickett ranch, which he has never visited, really means to him. He has heard from others what the house looks like, and how those large, costly windows cracked like sugar candy, and how the buckaroos are not so quick to jeer and spit when rolled out of their bunks at two o'clock in the morning. But the other, nearer light, the claim cabin, makes him feel gentle, and it is not to be denied that the cabin is a satellite of the ranch, like a little moon circling in its gravity, and that its inhabitant is under the protection of his enemy. He chews the hot beans and nudges up the broth with his bread as he thinks of her coming out that last morning in her dressing gown with the string untied, just the two leaves wrapped around her, and her usual alertness replaced by the myopia of sleep. But her body moved as always, that antelope startle-and-freeze before acting. Anything physical she begins with an effort, as if she has to command her body to do it, as though her natural state is one of stillness, of floating, perhaps. He imagines her on her back, floating on the oiled green of Half-a-Mind, and her hair, that indeterminate silk, going green in the water as well and clinging to her face, neck, shoulders, to the long, pale arms he has seen but not quite yet seen. White islands break the surface, the green water sliding and the rest of her surfacing as she turns on her front and slips with a quick flush of kicking deeper into the water.

His face is hot, and he can feel his pulse beating in his ear where the cut has nearly healed. He sets his plate aside and puts his hands carefully on his thighs. He once saw a drawing of a woman without clothes; their old hand up in Morrow, Tom Jeff, sketched a woman for him in the clay near a stream, and he pretended only a mild interest, but later stole back and lined the drawing with pebbles so it could not be washed away, and he visited it until there was no need to visit; it was drawn in his mind. So he has an idea of what is in front, but the backside is a mystery, one it hurts him not to know the solution to. At home there is a priest who has instructed him on what it is godly to know and do, and he has so far done his best, but now what he wants to know overcomes him, and shocks pass through his body.

It is past time to take these lambs and start up to Morrow. He ought to move before Pickett catches wind he's here. But he can't leave. His mind always returns to Esther: ivory and wet, green and near. He'll stay another day. Perhaps he'll go down and see her. His brothers can wait a bit. He's waited for them before. One day, or maybe two.

25

BY MIDMORNING every day, the sun has heated most surfaces to burning. The pail must descend far into the well to find the water, but when Esther hauls it up, the water is still clear and smells of soda, of stones. She lugs the buckets to the furrows in the alfalfa patch. As she tips each bucket, she puts her hand into its gush of coolness. She hopes these plants are grateful. They are at her knee now, and putting out a rough, sweet purple flower, like a pea but flatter, a little peacock in mauve mourning dress. It smells wonderful. Perhaps Larsson Jacob was right, that it was possible to garden this desert.

Duniway stands in her stall with her head hanging down and her muzzle bubbling in her bucket. "Come on out," says Esther. She heaves up one more pail of water and pours it down Duniway's back and neck, leaving the last bit to cascade over her eyes and nose. The mare sighs and switches her wet tail. Her lips hang loose, and her long brown teeth show. Esther slaps the wet neck with her hand. "You are such an old thing. Such an old thing."

She is damp herself now, and her dress clings to her legs. But still she is restless and hot. She fetches the bridle, slips it on the dozing mare, who accepts the bit with unusual docility and begins slurping it with her large tongue. Esther looses the halter rope, then gets up on the well cover and boosts herself onto the mare's bare back. This dress is not split and the skirt bunches at her knees. Her bare heels bounce on Duniway's ribs. There is no sign of sheep or wagon up on the bluff, but she can see only the edge of it. That she doesn't see them doesn't mean they aren't there.

They go south around the lake until they reach the hummock over the ice cave. She ties Duniway to some rocks in a sliver of shade, then edges into the cave. It is cold and still, with a strange freshness, as if dawn is hiding here.

She has no lamp today. But a bit of earth has fallen in, and a thick beam of sunlight, solid with motes, lights the path. She goes down and looks at the ice, which is diminished, and chips off a piece with a stone. The shard is as big as a book and smooth on one side. This she rubs gratefully on her neck and face. The group of bats is smaller, too, and the gray-white fur makes the animals a little ghastly. She feels the creep of dread, but at the same moment, nearly, as though fear has flushed out other feelings, she thinks of Ben Cruff saying, *Nobody can poach me.*

She has thought of venturing up onto the bluff to see him, but she has shrunk from encountering one of his brothers, or a stranger, who would have nothing better to do than mull on her excuses. If he would just flash his lamp so that she would know it is he up there. Soon it will be too late, for the grass will be grazed to dirt and he will have to move the band home to Morrow County. If she wants to meet him, she will have to go up there.

She comes out of the cave into the heat and wanders up the lakeshore, closer to the bluff, Duniway trailing. Near a large, pitted boulder, she ties Duniway again and sits down in the boulder's shade. She rubs the ice on her feet. It is foolish not to have worn shoes. She sets the ice down on a patch of straw-stiff grass and takes half a boiled potato out of her apron pocket and eats it. It is good, but its mealiness makes her thirsty. She could go down to the lake for a drink, but just now she feels too drowsy, almost too drowsy to move. With a last gleam of will she unties her apron and bunches it under her ear. A scrim of music hangs over the still land around her. The thin desert bees keening, the clink of Duniway's huge shod toenails as she forages among the rocks, the hollow flap of a waterbird in ascent. These sounds that are barely sounds weave an enclosure about Esther, like a veil around an Arabian bed.

Her sleep is long and short. Part of her mind reckons the ticking past of small events: shadow moving up her foot, the settling of the birds into the reeds, a brief sunset succeeded in another quarter of the sky by the moon. Another part lays out dreams like a long game of patience, matching a figure of the well and windlass with one of a busy Chicago avenue, so that in her sleep she wonders if she will be strong enough to winch up water for everyone who is thirsty. When she wakes, it is almost night. Her hand lies on damp earth, for the ice has melted and made mud, and that in turn has nearly dried.

A gray thing, substantial, drops from the bluff some distance up the shore and strikes the earth. She is not sure that she has really seen something; she is still waking. Then something else falls. There are cries. The cries converge with the falling.

The last mortal sound of a sheep is the worse for its awkwardness. The poor voice that is so repetitious and comic in the field is inadequate to speak of the cruelty and confusion of death's approach. The face of a sheep is all nose, and now the voices are moist and dull, supremely nasal as they blare and crack and fail. One gray clot strikes the rocky apron only a few horse lengths from where Esther now huddles over her knees. The sound is the thud of a bag of grain fused with a grunt of great effort. She cannot hear the neck splinter, but she feels it.

More and more fall. It is not a snow, for snow never fell with such force. The bawling of creatures is unendurable. She covers her ears, digs the heels of her hands in.

Then she uncovers them. Far above, there are gay, distant shouts of *hi* and *hoop*. The sheep are not stampeding out of idiocy. They are being rounded up and driven over the brink.

Now the fallen sheep form a gray berm, and those falling hit it and slide off, thick and inert. This sound is quieter; it is like a lull. She rises and darts through the rocks to Duniway, who is rigid at the end of her picket rope, her eyes insane and white. Esther, using all her weight on the rope, tries to pull the mare close to calm her. But the Duniway stamps and foams, her hind end clattering back and forth in desperation. In her flailing she strikes Esther's jaw with her nose. Esther lets go of the rope and the mare runs down through the rocks, the motion of her great pale haunches and long head visible until she reaches the south end of the lake and hides herself in the aspens.

At last they have all fallen. There are hundreds. They lie piled and scattered from the base of the bluff down to within a few yards of the lake. From them comes the odor of dirt, and of injury. The tender complexities that animals enclose in their skins are exposed, and the fumes of blood and water and oil make an aromatic colloid that in daylight would have pinkened the air. Some of the sheep are still living, and so with the smell rises a sigh of complaint, a last irritability. Esther kneels and leans against a large, cool boulder and spits a little blood, for when Duniway hit her, she bit her tongue.

Voices and hoofbeats, not above but near and unmuted. With some hope, she lifts her head and looks. Then she ducks it again and curls small against the rock.

The riders come in among the sheep. The horses look large and black in the near darkness, and the men astride them are headless—that is, they wear sacks, feed sacks, over their heads with holes torn out for their eyes, and the broad sacks look like weak, headless shoulders. They waste no time but go in among the sheep and begin to shoot and to club and to cut. Esther watches through a cleft between rocks. A sheep near her labors to its feet, but one hind leg gives like a folding rule and the sheep lurches. A rider is on it in a moment. It is someone tall. Osterhaus, the Jacob foreman? With a rifle held in an arm's casual cradle he shoots it dead. The bullet passes entirely through the flesh, strikes rock, and makes a high, stinging sound. The sheep's muzzle plows the dust, and Esther is near enough to see the dirt cake up in the dull, sorrowful eye. The tall man wheels and trots back to the loose group of comrades. One of them removes his hood, shakes it, and puts it back on. His head looks white in the starlight. Noggin Koerner, maybe. Or maybe not.

It takes a long time for them to find all the live ones, but at last they seem satisfied. The riders are tired; they sit relaxed on their mounts. They call to one another, low and insinuating. Then they begin to move north along the shore, and after some time she can no longer hear the footfalls of the horses.

She unfolds from her hiding place. It feels very strange to stand and walk on two legs, uncertain and risky. She passes a few lambs that lie pinched in crevices like bundles of woolly sticks. A salty grit fills her mouth, and she wets her lips again and again. Most of the sheep are twisted and collapsed, with calm, sleeping faces. These died in the fall. Others show the gory crater of a shot, fretted with white bone, in the customary location of an eye or ear. Some have a spongy depression at the back of the skull where a club has struck, and the noses of these are thrust forward, as though, when the blow fell, they tried to flatten themselves to avoid it. Others wear a clotted, glistening kerchief where blood rushed from a whitened flap of throat. In the moonlight the blood gleams violet, as if these were rare sheep of tropical plumage.

Though she will later be haunted by these details, she is at the moment consumed with another thought. Stumbling, treading on thorns, she limps toward the soft, hoof-ringed dust of the path that leads up the bluff. When she reaches it, she begins to run. For if this is the fate of the sheep, what of the shepherd?

PART FOUR

THE EVILS

26

IN THE PEACHY LIGHT of early morning, carrying a halter and rope, Esther walks the mile and a half to Two Forks. She can see the house a long way off, sitting up above its dust like a white cake on a table. Dawn shines off the windows and blinds her, and she keeps her eyes on her own cool shadow as she walks. The desert is still fresh, austere, expectant, the sagebrush flushing out scent in waves, now and then a rabbit grazing, a little wind feathering its fur. All loveliness ahead of her. Behind, horrible. The house stands there, waiting.

Near the corral, as Esther expected, Duniway is loitering with her nose against an upright. When she looks at Esther, there is unknowing in her gaze. There are no other sounds. The buckaroos are still sleeping.

As she is putting Duniway's nose into the halter, the kitchen door opens and Pick comes out. He smiles. Is he innocent? He must be—he shows no discomfiture at all. He says, "Lose your mare again? Didn't you jump on that picket stake with both feet?"

"I believe I know how to stake a horse by now. It wasn't that. She was frightened."

"Frightened?"

It is hard to meet his eyes. What will she see there? But he seems the same as ever. "Don't you know? They ran the Cruffs' sheep off the bluff. The sheep were almost all gone. Oh, why didn't you let them go?"

Pick puts his arms around her and looks over her head toward the unseen bluffs. "God damn it. Of all the—"

"You sent them. Because of the calves and the deadlines."

"What do you mean, ran them off the bluff?"

"Drove them off, rode behind them, yelling. And they *shot* them. And they *cut* them with *knives*." She is choking now. She pushes back from him.

"Esther. Wait. Somebody got drunk and scratchy. Did you see anyone? Anyone see you?"

She is sick in her stomach. She wants to say, *I think I know*—but for now, for once, she will keep her cards close. Catfoot. Listens-at-Doors.

"I was asleep," she says. "But I heard it. I went and saw what it was. Whoever did it was gone."

"So you're sure they didn't see you? We're going to keep you out of this. Understand?"

"We have to get the police."

"Sheriff, you mean. He's up in Peterson—we'll get him. Who was tending that camp? Ben Cruff?"

She knows perfectly well who was there, but she lies boldly. "I don't know. There was no one at his camp."

"Esther. You shouldn't have gone up there. Well, he's cleared out, I guess. I don't blame him," says Pick.

Bitterly Esther says, "Violet will be thrilled to hear about this."

"Oh, yeah. Anything rotten. She's like to pop a couple of buttons over this one."

27

THE RIDE TO TOWN IS DIFFICULT. Away from Two Forks, Duni-way recovers her fear. When a rabbit starts up from a clutch of brush, Duniway goes up with it and lands several feet to one side, with Esther grabbing desperately at the pommel. Spying a large, benign rock, which she has passed a hundred times before, Duniway becomes a stone mare, heavy and still. Even the sound of her own hooves striking the ground seems to frighten her.

At the livery, Jane, Ida, Odell, and Violet are gathered, and when Esther and Pick ride up, everyone turns to them and waits with anxious faces. As Esther dismounts, Jane runs to her. She takes Esther's upper arms in her hands and looks into her face. "You're well?"

The touch brings Esther almost to tears. "I saw them."

"I know. Vincent telegraphed ahead of you from Two Forks, and now the sheriff is coming from Peterson."

Pick is still on his horse. "When's he coming?"

"Right away. The deputy telegraphed back. He must be on the road now."

"I'll go up there and meet him coming." He turns Lobo and goes down the street at a canter.

Why? Esther is resentful. So you can tell him what to think, whom to pursue? She drops her head against Duniway.

The sheriff spends two days in Century. Walking through the charnel ground, he wears a smear of citronella on his upper lip, which he reapplies several times from a tin in his pocket. Pick and other citizens have rubbed their kerchiefs with camphor and wear them over their noses. Asked what she saw, Esther says only, "I could see horses, but I didn't get there in time."

The sheriff trudges up, looks over Ben Cruff's abandoned campsite, and then returns to town to send telegrams. In an undertone, Violet reports on this: there was one to the Cruffs, explaining that Ben is still missing, and one to the federal marshal in Prineville, saying that since the sheep fell off federal land but hit ground belonging to the state, he reckons jurisdiction belongs to him, Willie Fromm.

Fromm looks tired, and no wonder. To Pick he says, "I've got a pile of dead woollies, a bunch of cowboys who won't say anything, and forty thousand acres to cover. I don't have a lot of help to do it. But I'm not stupid, and I won't turn a blind eye to anything I find, Pickett. I don't know if you are aware of it, but there's a reporter from Salem asking questions around Peterson."

Pick seems perplexed. "Salem? What's he doing out here?"

"I don't know. But it would be foolish to think, anymore, that nobody's watching what happens in the high desert. The state woolgrowers association is already taking an interest in this case. Hasn't got into the Century paper yet, but in Peterson they're saying the woolgrowers want to hang somebody for this. North of here, the Cruffs are somebody. And the governor's not keen on sending ever more sheriffs out here to bird-dog the local disputes—he doesn't have the salaries to burn. He might choose an incident one of these days to come down on."

Pick is as exercised as Esther has ever seen him. He raises his voice, not quite to a shout, but loud enough to make Willie Fromm take a step back. "That bow-tied bastard's never set foot in this county. These are local matters, and if they aren't, they're federal. He should complain to his friends in Washington, D.C., if he doesn't like what he sees out here."

"You want I tell him that, Pickett? Because that's what I'll do."

"You don't dare, Fromm."

"I do dare."

"Go ahead, then. And then go to hell."

When Esther goes back to the cabin late in the day, she is carrying the *Peterson Argus*, copies of which were ridden down to Century in haste that morning. She takes it into the quiet cabin, where Ben Cruff is lying on the bed. The side of his face is blue with bruise, and he winces as he sits up. He holds one arm close to his body.

"There's something in here from the ones who did it," she says, spreading the paper across both their knees. "They sent it to the *Argus* last week, and the publisher put it in his editorial. I don't think he guessed they meant to act at once." Together they read, Ben moving his finger down the page.

> We have organized in secrecy and we will act in secrecy, not out of shame but in order to protect ourselves, who find our liveli-hood beset by an ignorant government and the lawless foreigners and Californians who pasture their sheep on our lands. If in the accomplishment of a mission—the killing of sheep—it becomes necessary for the group to shoot a herder or camp tender, we will do it and bury him where he falls. Should one of our own fall, he shall be buried and nothing said about the manner of his death. We have been forced to these exigencies but we will pur-sue them until these vermin have learned to respect traditional boundaries or have cleared out altogether.
>
> Peterson County Sheep Shooters

She waits until he finishes it and looks at her. "They're mad," she says. "I didn't credit how very much."

"Vermin. Like something you can step on and not notice."

Esther remembers Elijah Jacob laughing about burning a bag of spiders. "Vermin," she says. "What a terrible word."

"I'll say one thing. They didn't sound so educated when they were tying my hands."

She had found him like that, that night, hands bound, eyes masked with a rag, lashed to the wheel of his wagon. At her approach, he became alert, listening without turning his head, like a man who'd been blind for years instead of a single night. "It's just me," she said. "It's Esther."

Under the blindfold his mouth drew back for a moment in the grimace of tears and then straightened itself. Once, Esther had cut her finger at a picnic, and she had not cried then, nor all the way home in the carriage, but when she saw her mother standing at the top of the steps, her silence broke and she wept into her mother's hip. This was like that—tears in the anticipation of comfort—and Esther's own throat choked as she worked the tight dew-swelled rope at his wrists. His blocky hands were whitened and cold.

"I've got a knife somewhere," he said.

"No, it's just coming. Wait a minute."

When he was loose, he drew his hands around to his lap, rested a moment, then rubbed each shoulder, giving short hisses of pain.

"I saw it," she said. "I saw them coming down."

He looked bleak. "They all dead?"

She looked toward the precipice, where the velvety gray grass looked bleached in the moonlight. Feeling the need to be heavy and close to the ground, she crouched next to him. "Some didn't go over. Some little ones. But most of the big ones. They shot them if they didn't die." She ducked her face into her knees.

"What?"

"One of the dogs, too."

"Yes. The dogs were crazy. I heard them crying."

He whistled. A white flag appeared and seemed to advance across the flat meadow, and it became the breast of a slinking border collie. The dog lay flat at Ben's feet, like a pelt. Ben said, "He'll round up whichever's left. I've got to get us to the other side of town before it gets too light."

"But the wagon?"

"Leave it. I've got no horse to pull it, anyway. They took Sugar with them. I was supposed to go over and get my new gelding from Carey Stoop this week. Good thing I didn't pay in advance. That fellow'd be laughing even harder than he is now."

"But it's getting light already, and you'll have to testify."

"Testify? *Yes, sir, after they beat me, they shook my hand and I knew every man by his grip. Just arrest any cowpunch who's standing around looking shocked.* No. I price my skin a little dearer than that."

"Would they hurt you?"

"I won't give them the opportunity."

"Sheep are one thing. Murder's another."

"It's all the same to them. They're felons already and due for hanging."

"But they could have and they didn't."

"No. They didn't." He rubbed his shoulder again. "I thought they were going to. When they were hitting me."

She stood up. "Come to my place. You can wait there until dark."

He laughed and then winced as he got to his feet. "Pickett will turn you out."

"How will he know? He wouldn't anyway, in spite of what you think."

"His men were among them."

"That doesn't mean he was."

His brown eyes had lost some of their burning quality, and his face was bloodless with fatigue and pain. "You have a lot of trust."

She put her hand on his shoulder. They were nearly the same height. "I'm twenty-one years old, you remember," she told him. "I do as I please."

"I'd be obliged for a little sleep," he said.

When they reached Esther's yard, Ben went and stood at the head of the path and looked across the lake at his still, still flock.

"It's the ugliest thing I ever saw done," he said. "I hope I never see worse."

28

PICK SETS HIS BUCKAROOS to dragging the carcasses south of the lake and putting them into a shallow pit, for if they lie where they fell, their rottenness will poison the water. In the drafts above the bluff, vultures circle with their wing tips lifted, as though flirting. On the ground they waddle and hunch and fill their red beaks with tufts of dead wool.

Violet Fowler tacks back and forth behind her counter, propelled by gusts of rumor: the letter is a hoax by those meaning to discredit the cattlemen, the vanished Ben Cruff killed the sheep himself in the madness of drink—the Irish in their cups are troubled, it goes without saying—or, alternately, the lackeys of California cattle barons are roaming the country, destroying sheep to clear the land for a large invasion of their drought-starved cows. There have been sheep killings in other places, Violet points out. Crook and Lake counties nearby, and as far north as Wallowa.

Jane Fremont is forced to glower at some of her scholars and comfort others as a game springs up in the schoolyard that involves driving the primary class over an imaginary cliff. Marguerite Green allows herself to be pushed over the line, where she falls to the ground in a heap. But soon she rallies her fellows, and the sheep are raised from the dead to become sheep warriors who drive the oppressors back to the schoolhouse steps, brandishing hooves and emitting unsheeplike roars.

All this Esther reports to Ben. He is still not well enough to go, and they are not sure it is safe for him to cross so much open country and so much Jacob and Stoop acreage.

"Not a nice skin to be in, the skin of a witness," says Ben.

He won't let her put him in the bed, but insists on a pallet of blankets on the floor. The dog sleeps near him. In the warm night she hears him stirring, and once, a word, whined: "No."

On the second night, she says, "You must take the bed. You're hurt. You need to rest more than I do."

"Oh, it's who needs it more, not whose bed it is?"

"Indeed!"

"I guess we could both be on the floor, but it seems like a waste of a mattress."

He agrees to share. They sleep—or perhaps he sleeps, for Esther doesn't—head to toe, with a rolled-up quilt between them. In the morning he eases her embarrassment by complaining about her feet. "Too bad I didn't get beat up in the winter; at least I'd have a set of stockings between me and all those toes." They both jump at every noise. It would be like Violet Fowler—"right smack in her repertory," says Ben—to come out and look around. For of course there is only one room, and she might not believe that Ben has been housing in the shed, even if he puts straw in his hair, as he suggests. But no one else ever visits Esther here. During the burial of the sheep the occasional buckaroo comes through the yard to draw water, but mostly she and Ben are safe from scrutiny.

She has to handle Pick, though. Immediately after the event he says to her, "Well, that's it. You'd better pack up your stuff and come back to Two Forks."

"But the claim—"

"You can finish your months later, in the autumn."

"I want to stay."

"Why? Oh—are you being delicate about you and me? Go and stay with Jane, then. I'm sure she'll have you."

"It's my claim and I'm staying on it. Especially now."

"It's going to start to smell pretty bad, even though we buried them."

"That doesn't bother me. At least not yet."

Pick is surprised, and not entirely pleased. But he is preoccupied, also, and doesn't press the matter.

She feels guilty, deceitful, but not completely, for even if there were no Ben Cruff to care for, she would not let herself be cowed and driven by people like those sheep killers. Whenever she meets a cattleman in the street or on the road now, she feels a combination of fear and defiance. Was it you?

On the third night, she tells Ben, "I heard in town that Noggin Koerner and Osterhaus and some other buckaroos were at a dance that night, all the way over in Failing."

"Well, Koerner wasn't, at least. He was knocking the hell out of me up on that bluff."

"You're sure it was him?"

"He was one of the only ones I did see. And when I struck out, I grazed him. I felt his bald head."

"Then how could he be at a dance?"

"Alibi dance. It's only twelve miles. They get somebody to throw it, they act all public, then they hightail it over here. Big enough dance, people circulating, nobody knows who's there or not there or out on the porch spooning. Koerner. Now we're even, I guess."

"Did you really break his hand that time?"

"Doubt it. Shamming, probably."

"What did he say to make you fight?"

"It's a dirty thing, not for women."

"But tell me."

"He just said that when I outgrew ewes, he had a heifer I might like."

She knows what that means. "I hate him."

"You're not the only one. That fellow hasn't got a friend on this earth, except maybe Pickett."

"Pick should dismiss him. He would, if I told him what he'd said."

"Maybe he would. But he needs somebody like Koerner around to keep his own hands clean. I know, I know. I'm too ready to run him down."

"Was he there last night? He wasn't, was he?"

"Doesn't mean he didn't have a hand in it. And why do you take up for him? He's nothing to you."

She is silent a moment. "Not nothing. He knew my father. And I know he's not—he tries to be good. And he didn't have to take me when I had nowhere to go. You have your brothers, you have your parents up in Morrow. He gave me a home."

Ben works his cheek, considering this. "Still," he says, "he made you sign your name. I think this home is a black square on his checkerboard. And you're the checker."

Esther is hunched over, drawing in the dust with her finger. "There's more, though. It wasn't like this at first, but now we— have an understanding." It is surprisingly easy to tell him this. Perhaps she could tell him anything.

"He *is* paying you."

"No. An understanding."

He gets that look to his jaw, as if he is holding an egg on his tongue and has to make room for it. "So you're in love with him."

She tries to call up a sustaining vision: herself, in white, chosen. "It's not for a long time."

"I don't see how a grown man has any business noticing a schoolgirl."

"I haven't been to school in a year."

"Oh, my mistake."

"I'm the only one he trusts." Pick is unclaimed. A little wild, promising, full of powers. These qualities have made her covetous, she realizes. "At least he doesn't trust many people."

"That's his own fault. And he's not so nice to women. Maybe he's nice to you now, but wait. He wasn't to Delores Nash."

"Who?"

"Delores Green, now. He wouldn't marry an Indian girl, though I'm about as Indian as she is. So she married Fred."

She turns to him and draws back a bit, trying to see his whole face. Pick wanted to marry her? No. Didn't want to. That was the point.

"Was that too ugly?" Ben asks.

Esther says, "I have been thinking it was Jane who disappointed him."

"Jane Fremont? I doubt she'd have the President, let alone a cattleman. Don't keep them from trying, though."

"It wasn't Pick who left her the maverick?"

"Pick? Naw. Who's always got himself worked up? Who's always watching the girls?"

"You don't mean Carey Stoop? He must be years younger than she is."

"Not so many. He's loved her a long time. Sometimes it seems she likes him, but she can't quite say yes to him." He goes to the doorway again and looks out. "I thought maybe you weren't spoken for, either. Well, go ahead. Get to the other side of the checkerboard and let him queen you." His voice warbles a little.

"Are you . . . are you crying?"

He doesn't answer.

"Ben." She pulls on his arm and turns him a little toward her. He brushes his hand down, once under each eye.

"I cry too easy," he says. "I always have. My brothers used to tease me until I cried, because it was so easy."

"That was wrong of them. You're so much younger! What did they say?"

"Oh, they told me my head was too big."

"Your head!"

"Once, I got a new pony. She was pretty and fast, but she had a little deer's legs. My brothers Sean and Michael looked her all over, and they came up to me all serious. I thought there was something wrong with her. Sean says, 'You can saddle her and go for a ride, but if you don't want to break her back, your head's going to have to stay home.' I beat on them for a while, and then I cried. They called me Salty Sue."

"Salty Sue." She can't help herself, she is laughing.

"Well, all right. Don't make me wish I hadn't told you." He shakes his head, but he is smiling, too, through his air of injury.

The kettle is whistling. She runs to it, brings it out, and pours it into her washbasin, which is already partly filled with cold water. She sits down on the step.

"Listen," he says. "Don't let on what you saw up there."

"That's what Pick said. But if no one tells, it's just not fair."

"Doesn't matter, when there's worse in the balance. I don't trust any of those boys when they've got their ginger up. Buckaroos are buckaroos for a reason. They're not bankers and they don't drive trains and they don't farm. They like riding around on their own, thrashing the bejesus out of a steer now and then, and mending their gear and getting drunk."

"That's what they say about you. The getting drunk."

"Well, some do. I don't. Anyway—"

"I shouldn't say who I saw."

"You shouldn't say you saw at all."

She tests the water in the basin with her fingers. "May I wash my feet? Would that be too dangerous?"

Ben looks away from her bare feet and fidgets with the pocket of his dungarees. "Hand me that pail. I'll water that nag of yours." He goes off toward the well.

She unlaces her shoes and takes them off. The scratches and bruises she suffered the other night have now swollen and darkened. The soles of both feet are pricked and sore, and one ankle is burned, from where she slept in the sun. Wincing, she puts them in the water, sloshes them slowly, and stares down at them. She can hear Ben talking to Duniway and the shed door creaking. She takes up her washcloth. He is coming back. She puts the cloth over her ankles.

He draws near to her and puts the pail down. Then he kneels

and takes the cloth away. He makes a sound that is almost a whistle. "Did you do all this running up onto the bluff?"

She doesn't answer, for now he holds one foot in his hand, his palm cupped around the heel. He turns it this way and that, looking at the wounds. Then he takes the cloth and washes the ball of the foot, which is tough and polished, the shrinking arch, the brown instep with a few gold hairs. He concentrates as though he is carving the foot out of wood. Then, hooding his fingertip with the cloth, he washes each of her toes and in between them. He catches a little water in his hand and pours it high on her ankle. His heavy cheek is flushed, and his stubbly eyelashes cast a faint darkness, a shadow on his cheek. The scar on his ear is just beginning to turn white.

Her head rolls against the doorframe, and she looks out past him at the sky. Its space flows into her, as though they are the same size. It contains her, but she contains it, also. She is bigger than it is, though she moves around in it and her body is at its mercy.

He raises his gaze to her—as amber as horehound, though his cheekbones are certainly Irish. "Did I hurt you?" he asks.

"No," she says. "It's just that my feet are so dirty."

"That's why you have me."

He keeps his head down until her feet are dry and booted again and it is time to make supper.

Later, she is sitting at the table with her letter in front of her. It is thick now, tied crossways with a string to keep it from losing pages. But she is unable to write tonight. Ben sits on the bed, reading the newspaper again. When he shakes it and it cracks, a damp flush comes out all over her. She straightens her page and then spends a little time looking at her hands: weird, enchanted instruments. Her heartbeats seem the resonant sum of many minor beats, tiny drummings in her flesh.

At length she steals a look at him. He has put the newspaper down and is examining the photograph of her mother and father, still gray and glassy and remote. He holds it up. "No offense, I hope. I'm curious."

"No." She gets up and comes over to sit next to him. "That was years ago, when I was a baby."

"How long since she died?"

"Almost a year. It'll be a year in a few days."

"Sorry about that."

"It makes me hate August," she says. "Did you ever lose someone?"

"Our old hand Tom Jeff. He got thrown and didn't light right. And my little cousin, who got sick. That was in the winter, though. Well, she got sick in the winter and died in the spring. I can't hate half the year, so I don't hate any of it."

"Do you remember her?"

"Oh, yes. She was only two, but she had a curly head like me. Say—you look like your mother."

"Do I? I didn't think I did."

"What happened to her?"

Esther takes the picture and holds it. "She'd had flu."

He hitches his knee up on the bed. "But it wasn't that?"

"No. It was—it was very hot that day. And completely still. No one was outside except men who were working. The heat is different there. It feels like wet clothes on you, that you just have to keep wearing, and there's no way you can move that will make a breeze or a cool place. But my mother was feeling better, she was sleeping. The doctor said the danger was past. We'd given her an alcohol bath, and her fever was gone. It was almost time for school again. I was to get a new dress. She was sleeping."

Ben takes hold of a piece of her skirt and rubs it between his fingers.

Below her mother's window in the next yard that day, a child was quarreling with a dog. *Drop that, Gypsy! Drop it!* Esther went to her mother's door and listened but heard no stirring. She went back to the kitchen—where she had been writing a letter to a friend who had left school to get married—and picked at some cold lamb and vegetables with her fingers. When she finished the letter, she went down to the back garden and picked a handful of blueberries, then went back and lay down on the sofa with *Kidnapped*. She was cross. She wanted new books and hadn't been to the library, having misplaced a copy of *Huckleberry Finn* and delaying the inevitable confession of it to the librarian. But the dress was supposed to come that day. When the doorbell rang, she jumped up and ran in her stocking feet to answer it.

At first there seemed to be no one on the stoop, and she looked out only onto the hot, quiet street, stiff red marigolds in the window boxes, a maid in the building opposite shaking a mop out the window. She had the sudden feeling that behind her in the house or in front of her in the city there was nothing that could make her happy, and the doorbell had been rung by her future, to bring her down the stairs to taunt her. But then a man stood up from where he had bent to rest a parcel, and the feeling passed. "Muster and Lowe, delivery," he said, and Esther took a little money from an enamel bowl near the door and exchanged it for the parcel.

The dress was beautiful. Light wool, apple red, the bodice simple and elegant, not cumbered with any childish wide collar. Esther set up the ironing board on the kitchen table and heated the iron. Making tiny movements with the black nose, she pressed the crumpled shoulders and went panel by panel around the skirt. Then she wiped her sweating face with a towel, took off her shirt-waist and skirt, and pulled the new dress over her head. In the hall mirror she could see that her hair was disheveled and her shoes wanted blacking, and the dress seemed a little big in the bosom, but it suited her. She put back her shoulders and raised her chin. She would eat a great lot and become more round, but if she preserved a good posture, the dress would still fit. She couldn't quite manage the tiny hooks at the back of her neck, so she went and listened at her mother's bedroom door, then pushed it open and went in. The curtains were open and the light was streaming in. Surely it was too light to sleep.

The dog's barking drifted up from the yard. Esther bent and

picked up the linen bedcover that had slid off the bed. The oval in the middle was embroidered with her mother's initials, the married ones. Esther had lain on it so often and dreamed. As she stood there at the foot of the bed, she touched the dense, silky *C* in the center. She didn't want to raise her head and look at her mother.

But she did raise it. Long enough to see her mother's face slid low on the pillow, the cheek soft with illness. One eye open, but the eye not looking. There was no iris, no pupil flaring with warmth. Only the sticky white curve of blindness.

After a little silence Ben asks, "Do you still have that dress?"

Esther has risen to find her handkerchief, and she turns to him, wiping her nose. "That red dress? Yes."

"Do you have it here? Would you put it on?"

"After I've just told you such a sad story?"

He shrugs. "Your mama bought it for you, and she wanted you to wear it. Not all that black. Anyway, don't you think you ought to do right by the living?"

"Oh, is it doing right by you to put on a red dress?"

"Well, let's see it, then I'll tell you." He faces away from her.

She takes the dress from the trunk, turns away, sheds her blouse and skirt. The dress fits closely now. She can feel it at her waist, across her chest and shoulders.

"Can I see it now?"

"First you must do the hooks in back for me. There are some I can't reach." She backs up to him. His fingers at her neck, blunt and gentle. She turns around and steps back so he can see her.

He raises his eyebrows, whistles a bit. But he has lost a bit of his exuberance. "You look different, in colors."

"You don't like it." She holds out the skirt and looks down at it. What can be wrong with this dress?

"I do like it. That's maybe the prettiest dress I've ever seen."

"But what's wrong?"

He shrugs.

"What?"

"I guess I'm the dirty one now."

"You—"

"I said I guess I'm the dirty one."

She moves toward him, stumbles, and almost falls. He catches her wrist and lifts her to her feet.

She lifts her eyes to his brown face. "You aren't dirty. You are not dirty."

The homemade buttonholes of his shirt are crimped and difficult. As she works them, she thinks what care he has to take each day to save his shirt and not lose a button through carelessness. He isn't careless, he is careful and solid, but still so soft, with such a tenderness in his boy's heart. He stands still as she works down—the button over his chest, the rib button, the button over the belly. When she bends to the last one, it is bound with a bit of wool from the shirt, and in fury she bites the wool with her teeth. His belly contracts, and he puts his hands on her arms. She pushes the shirttails to either side—there!—revealing an undershirt that has indeed seen cleaner days. She places her hands, together, on his chest and hooks her thumbs over the shirt, draws it down, and makes a fence with her fingers. Inside it is her captured patch of sweet skin, marked with a freckle and a few wild, curling red-black hairs, and at the center of that acre there is the place that must be kissed, a little cup holding a drop of sweat, a drop trembling with the passing of his precious nearby blood.

29

ONE MORNING a few days after the slaughter, Joe Peaslee puts on his military coat and sergeant's hat and produces from the rubbish in his back room a gold-headed cane. Thus attired, he walks out of town toward Half-a-Mind. Esther learns this later, for he doesn't stop to see her. When he returns, his face is red with heat and his whiskers are damp. He has a glass of gin in the saloon, pays with a whole half a dollar, and then goes out into the street and begins to speak earnestly, emphasizing his words with taps of the cane on the ground. He speaks to passing children, as if not recognizing their youth. "Soldiers!" he says. "I campaigned and maneuvered and carried the bayonet, and long was my journey home. Now the bodies lie again on the field. Listen!"

"Poor man," says Reverend Endicott. "He's got his wars crossed. He thinks the woollies are men." He shakes his head and goes on toward the church, where there is to be a special afternoon service regarding the recent events at Half-a-Mind.

Joe puts his hand on the breast of his jacket, as proud as a man of historical importance. His voice is sly and threaded with mirth, and it carries to those shaking their heads in the doorways. "They will have bullets," he says, sweeping wide his open hands. "I cannot deny them."

Delight Endicott feels something ought to be done. She takes his arm. "Joe, you're not well, and it's much too hot. Go home."

With his cane he makes an X in the dirt in front of her. "I know who you are," he says. "I know what you are doing. And I know you know better."

Her face crumples. She withdraws to the dry goods store, where other ladies are shocked on her behalf. Mrs. Endicott! Who's never been other than kind to Joe or anyone else! They mop her face and take her by each arm and escort her down to the church, where she sits trembling in the front pew next to Marguerite. By and by the pews behind her begin to fill. Mr. Endicott is to deliver a reassuring message, calling for order and peace. Most of the town is here, and a few cowboys lounge at the rear. Esther, arriving late, her thoughts full of Ben, cannot reach Jane Fremont in a forward pew and has to stand in a corner and make way for people squeezing by.

Mr. Endicott is in his anteroom preparing his remarks when Joe Peaslee makes his way up the center aisle. He goes to the pulpit and fixes the congregation with a haunted, merry expression. They look back at him in puzzlement, unease.

"My fellow Centurians," he says. "As you may know, I have for some time been confined to home by the suffering of my spine. I tried to ignore it, for it has misled me before. But it persisted, however I applied cordials and medications, hoping for my relief. The sensation was orchestral. It was—*chromatic*. It seemed to want me to know something. I couldn't understand what." He places both hands on the pulpit and whispers. "*I am iridescent under my coat.*"

Violet Fowler covers May's ears. May bats at her hands. The rest of the people are transfixed.

Joe resumes his public voice. "This morning the pain drove me from town and out along the road and to the scene of butchery. You know to what shameful field I refer, what hell's garden. I wanted to see it, but I was afraid to be tainted by that cruelty. So I fled. And as I came slowly home, I felt something surging up my spine again. Oh, no, I thought. Not that pain again. But I realized this was different. It was not pain. It bubbled up, it spilled into my heart, and when it spilled, I understood. It was pain no longer. It was joy. It was transport. Not prophecy, but realized truth. I brimmed, like a fountain—"

"Joe," says Mr. Endicott. He is at one side, pulling his fingers and indulging the hunch in his back. The congregation gapes at him. "Joe, I think—"

"Like a great fountain of *knowledge*," Joe insists. "What do I know? I know that in my position as merchant I sell eggs and blankets, I sell bullets and powder, and sometimes I gather from such sales what my fellow men are planning."

In the pew in front of Esther, Elijah Jacob looks over at his buckaroo Osterhaus, and both look at Pick, where he leans against a window frame. Pick is frowning. Watchful. He moves forward, just to the next window.

"But this knowledge is only paper, only chaff. Citizens, the true knowledge is this: we dispute over fences. We adore our territory, but in seizing our land, we give away our souls. You yourselves—are you fenced? Do you feel your acre contracting? Do you fight it?"

Some people are staring at their laps, still. Others are murmuring. "Upon my honor, this is the most absurd use of a pulpit I've ever seen," says Phelia Jacob. "Are we to be subjected further—"

Joe slaps the pulpit with his hand. "Are you parched? Do you starve? Citizens, take heart! You yourself cannot be fenced! Your soul is at liberty. I call on you to relinquish your boundaries—"

Elijah Jacob has his hand on Phelia's knee, holding her in her place, but now he jeers openly. "Spoken like a merchant, Peaslee— are you going to forswear locks on your door?"

Joe's eyes flash at him, at all of them. "Let go your fences, let the dust take them. I entreat you, pass across every border, giving here and taking there with the soul's genius for hospitality." He holds his hand up, half open, its wrist tender with prominent veins. It trembles, and his face is shining. "Citizens!"

Marguerite Green pipes, "What fountain? Where is it?"

Joe looks down at her, smiles, clasps a hand to his chest. "The fountain is here."

Pick has stepped up beside him and removed his hat. Joe looks at him and falters. His voice softens. "Ferris—take heart." He puts both hands on Pick's arm and looks at him in supplication. For the first time, he seems bleary, confused. Old.

Pick leads him away, and Esther makes her way out of the pew. Reverend Endicott tweaks down his own coat sleeves and moves to the pulpit. "We will—let us go on, my friends," he says.

Esther escapes. Outside, seeing Joe and Pick standing together, she hesitates. What if Joe speaks to her as he did to Delight?

"So you had a long walk today, Joe?" Pick's tone is gentle, but grave and probing.

Joe remembers, and his face registers amazed grief. "I did. I saw what was done. You would not believe it. They've all just been struck down, just struck down by something speeding."

"Struck down? I don't think it was a train that killed those sheep."

"Oh, no, no. Not the train. History, you see, has stalked them and run them down." He takes Esther's hand. Pick moves a little closer. But Joe only says seriously, "Remember, at my place I have plenty of ink and also the Liberty."

"Do you need me to write something, Joe?"

"Don't forget anything." He turns his head a little so he can eye her aslant, conspiratorial. He whisper-sings,

"Nick had the nerve to write it down
while bullets fell like rain.
At your request, I'll do my best,
to tell that tale again."

She doesn't understand what he wants her to say, or to whom. But she grasps his idea about the sheep killing. The past of this Oregon—settlers duped, children abandoned, Indians deported and murdered—this past guaranteed that someday this band of sheep would be destroyed. Domination begets domination. How can it end? Only justice can pacify history. And justice is hard to come by. She wishes there were something she *could* write for him. But she can only love him. "Joe," she says tenderly, "won't you go home and rest?"

He ceases muttering and gesturing and says with his lost clarity, "My lamb, it's an excellent suggestion. But my home is in the great state of Pennsylvania. You must see that I am old. I'd never make it."

"Your home at the store, Joe," says Pick. He is soothing, but he presses Joe's back firmly. He has cut him out from the group and is corralling him.

Perhaps he fears that more will be said about bullets. "I'll go with you," Esther says.

They settle Joe on his cot, with the yellow cat on his chest. He rubs the white tracks of scarring on its head. "I will come back in the morning," Esther promises, and Pick doesn't contradict her.

On the way out to the junction she will turn off toward Half-a-Mind, Pick tells her that a telegram has come to the Duncans, who are keeping the remaining Cruff lambs. Apparently Michael Cruff is coming. He is on the warpath. Not only about the loss of his stock, but because he hasn't heard from his little brother.

In the thin starlight, Ben breaks from kissing her. "Look after Joe," he says. "Write if you need help. I'll meet Michael and we'll get those lambs north and then I'll write to you. Remember what I said. Don't tell anyone anything." He takes hold of Duniway's reins and gives the mare a doubtful look.

"She's really very good. Her trot is easy; you won't get tired."

"She'll be very good at leaving me crying in a thornbush. What's Pickett going to say?"

"I'll say she ran away again."

"All right. But you'll have to come up to Morrow County to get her. My pa isn't going to want to feed an engine like this all winter. Listen, if you get lost on the way, ask anyone in Morrow for the Cruffs. We're easy to find up there. We stay put in a house and everything. This mare will be lonesome, and she'll eat like a bear."

"I'll try."

"Esther. I'll be waiting. Come as soon as you can."

30

ONCE, STAYING WITH THE FLEMINGS after her mother died, Esther had made herself drunk. She lay in bed that night restless with loneliness, unable to stand the polish of the bedclothes. She sat up and said, aloud, "Mama. Come back." She wasn't sure how she could pass the night. If only one could change bodies, be someone else for a time while one's own body curled up and suffered.

In her nightgown she crept down into the Flemings' parlor and opened the decanter of sherry. The decanter was etched with white flowers and reinforced with a rococo silver binding, and the liquid inside glowed orange. She drank three goblets in succession, replaced the carved stopper, and went upstairs to lie on her bed again. After a little while she found herself looking with curiosity and fondness at the gas fixture, with its neat little flame and glass bell. It seemed alive; it seemed to intend to be itself. Its warmth and truth suffused her. And what it meant was even more than what it was. It communicated to her its thoughts about fire. How strange it was that she had never noticed before.

After Ben leaves, she is again in that state. Anything she looks at—a sprawled stalk of grass, a bird on a roof—burns with self. A horse tied in front of the church is a specific horse, belonging to Odell Underwood and having a short neck and a swayed back, but it is also the emblem of a horse, referring to the ancient grace of horses. Head down, tail switching, the horse means to suggest its own infinitude. And hers. And that of the creature, the marvelous creature that calls itself Ben Cruff.

When Esther tells Pick that Duniway is gone, he does not

scold her. He puts his hand on her shoulder and rubs her neck and brushes the hair along her temple. "Likely she'll turn up," he says. "The smell of blood can madden a horse. She just needs to settle down."

She does not flinch from the caress, because she feels very strong. She walks everywhere she goes but is never tired.

31

WHEN HER GIRLS ARE IN BED, Violet Fowler goes downstairs into the darkened post office. She does not need to put on a light, navigating between the counter and the boxes behind her with perfect practice. When she reaches the box for outgoing mail at the end of the counter, she kneels and takes her key from around her neck and opens the panel at the side. She feels over the pile of mail in the dark with her hand and scoops letters out into her cupped apron. When the pile has been diminished by half, she pauses, but she can't see why she should deprive herself of the whole lot, and she goes on gathering until she has emptied the box and her apron is heavy. With one expert hand she wields the key, locks the panel, and hangs the key around her neck.

Under the lamp, she examines the letters. Mr. Paul Endicott to a reverend in Klamath Falls, the latest in a series; Carey Stoop to his mother in Prineville; Ferris Pickett to Jasper Pursell, a cattleman on the Winslow Ranch in Hermiston. Jane Fremont to a Clara Linstrom—that was the sister—in Boston. The Schmidts to their married daughter in St. Louis. Delight Endicott to Sears, Roebuck. Odell Underwood to Sears, Roebuck. Odell Underwood to John Deere. Joe Peaslee to *Pacific* magazine. Something with no return address, to Grant Goodwell on the Cruff ranch in Morrow. Joe Peaslee to the district attorney.

On the stove the kettle has been boiling and pouring steam through its bent spout, and Violet makes a few choices and carries them over and goes to work. Her face becomes damp and her hair curls as she eases open the flaps; she trembles a little. When one of the girls turns over in bed in the other room and sighs, she looks up, catches her own reflection in the glass, and flushes.

My dear Reverend Gillespie,

The house you describe will suit us admirably, I am sure, for I feel confident in your knowledge of the town and your taste in things domestic. Among ministers this is no slur, I am sure you understand, but a compliment, for all needs to be domestically harmonious if the pastor is to devote himself to his flock, domestically and civically, and while I don't complain of the former, my wife being the kindest and most industrious of women, but the latter sort of harmony is in short supply here in Century. We feel called to move on, and we aren't sorry to leave this tangle behind.

We hope to join you the first of September or thereabouts. We have as you may imagine a number of affairs to wind up here, certain debts being owed us, and certain arrangements to be made. The one thing my wife has lacked to complete her contentment may be in reach.

Well. She has guessed that the Endicotts were planning to leave Century. Paul has always been restless, being trained in the East and accustomed to a wider sphere of influence. And he dislikes the developments in Century because he is a weakling and a coward and no one listens to him. As for the completion of Delight's happiness—how could that be? Surely Delight Endicott is as barren as Sinai.

She picks up the letter addressed to the Cruff ranch and turns it over. The sender has not written her name. Violet applies steam.

I hope that wretched mare has behaved herself. I find as I walk that I remember more and more of her tricks. Perhaps she won't dare employ them, as you are not the novice I was.

When she finishes it, Violet folds the letter and replaces it in the envelope. Well, this is a development. Not that she hasn't suspected. But she thought it would have fallen away by now, a meager attachment between children. Shouldn't Pick know of this? Violet taps the envelope with her fingertip and then pushes it, still with one finger, toward a corner of the table. This one will not be sent at once.

Now for Joe Peaslee. There is a package addressed to him, just a small box in brown paper, badly fastened. That's easy enough. One end is loose already, and the box slides out almost without a crackle. The top lifts off. Coiled there in the box is a bit of rope, and in the center of the coil is a box of matches.

Anonymous threats are uncivilized, in Violet's opinion, and childish. But Joe is not the soul of discretion, and it's certainly possible that he might make things uncomfortable for some individuals. Still—rope? Was that really necessary? She replaces the top of the box and reseals the package. Now she hefts the letter from Joe himself to the district attorney and holds it to the light. What does poor Joe Peaslee want to be bothering the district attorney about? It's known that they were friendly over the matter of the sewing machines, but can he even string together a sentence in his current state?

She did tell Ferris Pickett, last winter, that Joe Peaslee had sent a letter to the railroad, back when Mr. Elliot was in town, but she didn't read the letter itself. She never has opened any important— that is to say, *business*—correspondence, for she believes that as long as she restricts her surveillance to the personal sphere, her inquiries are a facet of her Christian duty: the knowledge she gleans from private letters just confirms what her intuition has already told her, and she is made better able to administer to the moral health of her neighbors. Occasionally she reads no good of herself and, stinging, resolves to give up her nighttime vice, but always, after the sun goes down and she has a string of hours to fill with washing or ironing or reading the newspaper, she returns to the box with her key, a corrupt thrill sparkling inside her. She is adept at opening letters sealed with gum or with wax, and usually she returns them to the box the very evening she examines them, so they are not delayed in reaching their destinations.

In the letters, she has found, people are more impassioned than they seem when you speak to them. They have desperate plans for their own lives but little consciousness of the desperation of others. Something always comes along to thwart their designs for themselves, though, or the planners just forget what end they intended to pursue. When they remember, well, years have passed.

But now something is happening. The separate illusions and desires—the powerful illusions and hearty desires she has been partaking of all this time—have begun to interlock. Century has never been a city. It has not known many causes with multiple effects, nor effects with multiple causes. But now sensitive factions are developing. Principles are in play, and money lies on the table. The cowboys are restless and blue. The sheep riffraff are provoked. Everyone is drinking. She can feel them out there drinking, turning into beasts. And when the Endicotts move to Klamath Falls, there will be only Violet to govern them. She will choose the new minister to suit herself, and she will prevail in Century. She may even venture into the saloon.

Through the paper of Joe Peaslee's envelope she can see the large, looping writing he has recently affected. "Bluff," she can read. "Empor—. —unition." Perhaps this is something that should be . . . known. To herself first, but of course only that she may inform the interested parties. The interested parties are sometimes grateful. The kettle is giving off no steam now, and its iron bottom is discoloring with heat. Violet moves it to the back of the stove with a cloth. After a moment she lifts its lid and leans down to dip a ladleful of fresh water from the bucket on the floor.

32

IT IS UNDERSTANDABLE that no letter comes at once from Ben. He will have had to reach Peterson, find Michael, go to the Duncans' ranch to reclaim the surviving lambs, and ride at a lamb's pace up to Morrow County. Esther asks Vincent how far it is to Morrow. "It must be a couple hundred miles," he says. "Why?"

Then he will have to greet his family and tell them the story. They will decide whether to press their case with Peterson County. Perhaps then he will receive her letter and sit to write. Some letters take a little while to compose. And then of course the letter must travel. Esther dare not hope for it for perhaps weeks. At least two, maybe three, maybe four. She mustn't allow any secret hope to grow, the hope that he might long for her as she for him, and write at night by the campfire, and detour, against prudence, into Prineville, Browning, or Nelsonia to send it.

Instead Esther returns to helping Mr. Cecil with the *Intelligence*. She sets the type for the notice he has written.

A great loss to Century is coming, as our Reverend Mr. Endicott has been wooed and won by the congregation of Klamath Falls Methodist. The Rev. and Mrs. Endicott will leave for the west in about three weeks' time and beg that all baptisms and other ceremonies be planned at once. Century will miss our kind shepherd and his talented lady and will be no doubt long in finding any suitable replacement. Some citizens have agreed sadly to this task, and position seekers may apply either to Alfred

Schmidt of Schmidt's Livery, Odell Underwood of Underwood's Tavern and Spirits, or Mrs. Violet Fowler at the post office.

When Esther has finished with this and washed her hands, she goes down to the schoolhouse to look for Jane. Though school is not in session, children are playing in the yard. Marguerite Green is jumping a rope turned by May Fowler and a thin, reedy Stoop girl. Marguerite's brown braids lift and fall.

"My arm, my arm," moans May. Marguerite, too breathless to warn May aloud, just points her finger at her: *keep turning.*

The other girls chant, "Hundred sixty. Hundred sixty-one. Hundred sixty-two."

"My arm is falling off!"

Jane Fremont has approached from the other side, and she understands the situation at once. She and Esther move to stand behind May and the Stoop girl and reach over their heads to grasp the rope near their hands. All four turn together, two, three times. Then the girls duck away and Jane and Esther turn the rope for Marguerite.

A few of the boys have come over to watch. "Uh-oh. Don't miss! Thirty-six! Forty million!"

Marguerite places her hands over her ears. When she clears her two hundredth jump, she watches the rope come around and emphatically jumps again: two hundred and one, putting her claim on the next five score. Then she stops, and Jane and Esther catch the rope so it will not whip her. Breathing hard, she reaches up and tightens her braids.

"That's wonderful, Marguerite!" Esther says. The child smiles. She has lost both teeth in front, but there is nothing modest in her. She feels joy and victory, and there is no veiling it.

As the girls take the rope and race toward the schoolhouse, Esther sees Pick standing near the steps, batting his leg with his hat. It is Jane, apparently, whom Pick wants, for he accompanies her into the schoolhouse. Uncertainly, Esther follows. Her neck is damp from exertion, and the chain rubs the nape. She must tell him. In dread, she follows them up the stairs.

Inside, standing near her desk, Jane is looking into an envelope that appears to be full of money.

"Oh, excuse me."

"No. Come in, of course," Jane says. "This is—"

"Nothing you can't know." Pick points to the envelope. "There's a situation in town."

"What situation?"

Jane says, "Esther, you know Delight Endicott has suffered a great deal being without children. And she has come to love Marguerite. And it has led her and the reverend to ask the Greens if they may have her for always. Adopt her and take her with them to Klamath Falls. He has taken a church there."

"Take her? But would Delores—"

"No. She asked, first, if I could board Marguerite."

"That would be wonderful."

"Yes," Jane says. "Well, it's not so very easy as that. You may remember that the Greens are in the Endicotts' debt."

"For the rye seed."

"Exactly. And the Endicotts have suggested that Fred and Delores should pay the money back. In order to show, as it were, that they can provide for Marguerite."

"My God."

"Exactly."

Pick says, "Endicott knows legal talk. He knows how to make a man jump when he wants to. Fred's not much match for that kind of thing. But he was smart enough to lay it all out for Delores. Delores told Jane and Jane told me."

Now Esther understands, and she puts her hand on Pick's arm. "And this money—you mean to pay the debt."

He puts the arm around her waist. "The little girl wants to stay with her mother."

Esther is happy, not only at Marguerite being saved. He *is* what she hopes him to be. "I am sorry for Delight."

"Yes," Jane says soberly. "She will feel it the death of her hopes."

"I can't imagine the Endicotts gone away. How different it will be."

"Will you miss church so much, Blackbird?"

His playfulness gives Esther a twinge. She is touched and irritated at once.

Jane laughs. "We plan to borrow a minister to keep us together until we can find someone for good. Carey Stoop is inquiring in Jack-High, and Gordon is drafting an advertisement for the eastern papers."

"I never thought Carey Stoop much interested in church affairs."

Jane is pink. "Nor is he. But I am a dreadful Borgia. I made some use of his gentlemanly instincts."

Esther walks out with Pick to his horse. He looses the reins from under a rock, but doesn't mount. "Esther, one thing about the Endicotts going. We could sneak in a wedding beforehand if we were light on our feet. I don't need something fancy if you don't."

Her bones turn to string. "But—I haven't even made the six months on the claim. And this is only the first year."

"Yes. I see. Did you think when we spoke before that I meant we should wait five years? I didn't. We've had a letter from Elliot. It looks like the train is going to come, and they mean to take the claim. They'll pay for it, and they'll give us—you—a water easement on the south side so we won't lose the use of the lake. But the train is planned to come right down the west side."

"Take the claim?"

"Yes."

"But can they do that? Isn't it mine?"

"You'll just sell it to them. Why, Esther, we've wanted this for months, haven't we?"

Those acres of hot dirt, the crevices sprouting flowers. The glitter across the lake in the morning. The alfalfa's sea-foam rustle when she hoes in horse manure. A hawk on a fence post, a coil of rusted barbed wire. The well she and Ben made, and the bed they lay in together. And now, down through the middle of it, the great black roar of the train.

She exerts herself. "Will they knock down the cabin?"

"Maybe. It might be in their way. In any case, now that I have the prospect of some company, I find myself a little impatient. Aren't you tired of sitting out there playing cat's cradle?" His expression is light and fond, alert to her. She feels, all at once, her power to disappoint him. Hurt him, even. It is frightening. She touches the ring around her neck. Tell him. Reach your hands to the back of your neck and unclasp the chain.

But her nerves are jerked, her heart tossed by all these developments, and she is wretched with fear. She pictures him recoiling from her, his face going cold and closed, his gay expectancy extinguished. His disapproval of her will be final. His attention and respect, conferred on her—her!—will be canceled. All her coming and goings, her thoughts and her feelings, her future life—the empty future—will become invisible to him. He will cease to care at all, and at once.

When she can speak, she says, "I miss my mother."

He pulls her to him, and she listens for a moment to his heart, beating like anybody else's. "I can see how you might. Listen. I won't be a backwoodsman whose bride brings her dolls to the altar. Think about it, but there's no reason to rush just because of the Endicotts. Other folks can do the job."

This generosity moves her. The memory of Ben, of bathing in his touching, fades back. As Pick mounts and rides away, she turns toward the school, all those strings inside pulling this way and that.

As she reenters the schoolroom through the cloakroom, she is rubbing her face with both hands. Jane says, "What is it?"

Her old impulse is to dissemble. But her body is too real, too glowing, to raise any kind of mask. She sits down on one of the primary benches. "Pick wants for us to marry. Much sooner than

I had thought." She pulls the pearl ring out of her shirtwaist. The pearl in its tiny gold landscape is dense and milky. It casts a faint ivory glow on the skin of her fingertips.

"Then you must have some things to think about."

"He says he didn't have a hand in the sheep killing."

"Well, then."

"You don't think he'd lie?"

Jane takes this question seriously. "He might not lie himself. He'd try to avoid it. But I do know, I think, of a time he asked someone to perjure herself for his profit."

"Did he?"

"You know he did. And he did it when he had no right to ask."

"Yes. The claim still isn't really mine. But I can see how someone comes to think the land she lives on is hers."

"And when you are married, it will be his, too."

"It will be neither of ours. We will be equally wrong."

"But the most important thing, Esther, is not even whether he's of good character. The first question is whether you want to be with him always."

"I don't know. I don't think so."

"I can see you're thinking of something else."

"Not something."

"Aha. Someone, then."

"It is Ben Cruff. He did not run away. He was staying with me. They beat him, and he had to recover. He left just a week ago."

"And he did recover?"

"Mostly."

"And he . . . has responded?"

His glowering, lush glance, the dampness of the curls above his forehead, his blunt and silken body. It is too much. Esther drops her face into her hands.

Jane laughs. "As Delight would say, oh, my stars!"

"Yes! My absurd stars!"

"Well, don't malign them. But I see your position."

"I don't want Pick to be angry. I agreed to an understanding—and everyone knows. And I like the house at Two Forks, and I like Vincent and the buckaroos. And I also don't know—what there is for me in Morrow County. If I were to go there. Another new place."

"Yes, and those who keep sheep are away more often than the cowboys you have already dismissed. And you are an educated young woman. Morrow is no metropolis."

"Ben says he doesn't always mean to keep sheep."

"Well, he's a serious fellow, and I trust what he says, even about himself. I think very well of Ben. As for Pick being angry—I'm not sure you have much choice about that. He probably will be angry. Some people, and Pick is one of them, have very strong opinions."

"I often think I don't have any. At least not about the things he cares about."

"It takes a woman longer to have them, because there are so many other people to take into account. But opinions are useless, anyway. We're guided by something previous to them. Believe me on this point. They go obsolete quickly. Then they just lie around in the mind, romantic, getting in the way."

"Yes. Like ruined statuary in a lithograph."

The schoolroom is warm. Jane goes to her window and opens it wide. The desert summer smells—dirt and sage, whiffs of the schoolyard privy, and distant baked pine—float in. She turns back. "I was going to say, *Unfortunately, yes*, and then I thought, perhaps not so unfortunately. Perhaps we should be grateful to find ourselves littered with toppled convictions. Because we must all make our mistakes, even the terrible ones."

"Must we? I don't want to!"

Jane sits down on one of the primary class benches and presses back her hair. There is a little feather of gray strands in the autumn-leaf brown, where she puts it behind her ear. "Well. I'll tell you something. I've told you very little about myself, and you've been good enough not to pry, even when you had reason.

I still don't know—well, perhaps I do. I can call it what it was. Will you believe me when I say I was a thief? I was. I stole."

Jane, large-eyed, ragged, taking a loaf of bread off a window-sill? Picking a pocket, perhaps? Any other scenario is impossible. But her grave demeanor, elegant posture, high white forehead—are these the attributes of the urchin?

Jane says, "Before I was a teacher, I was a thief. And before that, I was a nurse. No, perhaps I was never a nurse, really. I nursed people, but I stood by while they were robbed. So any good I may have done them . . ."

Esther sits down beside her. "Stood by?"

"Yes. I was trained at a school in Philadelphia just after leaving college. One of the teachers at the school, a doctor, took an interest in me. A strong interest. And I was delighted. Overwhelmed. He seemed wonderful to me. But he was engaged to be married. I thought perhaps . . . well, but he didn't. He told me he didn't feel he could break it off. I thought that was terribly honorable. And it would have been honorable if he had not continued to press his suit with me. And when my training was done, he asked me to come to work for him as a visiting nurse who would see to his patients when he could not. He was married by then. Even so, I would have done anything to be near him. And I did do it. Those who were old, alone, dying. And wealthy. He forged their names on papers."

"Oh, no."

"I knew he was doing it. I think I told myself that no one would miss the money, that he deserved to be compensated be-cause he worked at all hours and read every new book so he could give the best care. Oh, you should have seen it. Imagine me at the bedside, with an old woman looking up at me from her bed-clothes. Shaking with pain. And me, soothing her while he rus-tled at the little boudoir writing desk. I might as well have put a blade to her throat." She looks at Esther. "Yes. You have the tears I don't anymore. Well, then he was caught at it, and charged. He would not implicate me. I gave evidence against him. He went to prison."

Outside, there are the squeaks and jingles of harnesses passing on First Street, a shout of greeting. A bird comes to rest on the sill of the open window of the schoolroom but immediately pitches away again.

"And you came out here."

"Yes."

"And your mother, and your sister—"

"Yes. And two brothers. And they have children I have never seen."

"Can't you go back?"

Jane lifts her shoulders and drops them. She is silent for a moment. "I used to long to go home. This desert seemed awful, the horrible opposite of everything I loved. Now . . ."

"Yes."

"It's the place where I have seen myself plainly."

Yes. Esther thinks again of her claim section, is flooded with its details. Her own place. Not hers. But hers.

"And now of course there are friends here."

Esther is emboldened. "Is Carey Stoop a friend?"

Jane laughs. "Yes. Have you seen that? Did you guess about the maverick?"

"Ben told me."

"Ben Cruff! Well, yes. He and Carey have crossed paths now and then, and it hasn't always been unfriendly. I do care for Carey, I truly do. But he is still—he thinks he must fight, that everything requires fighting."

"Does *anything* require it? I can't think of anything."

"There are things that I can imagine," Jane says. "I'm sorry I can imagine them. But none of those things has ever happened— nor probably will—to Carey."

Esther reaches back, unclasps her chain, unthreads the ring, and rubs it on her skirt.

"It's very pretty," Jane says.

"Yes."

"The doctor I told you of—he once said that a pearl was like a person. Like a person's mind, I mean to say." Jane takes the ring from Esther and holds it up. "You know how it grows, don't you? A little sand, a little milk. Layer by layer. It takes so long to grow a mind, even to know that one has one, and then to . . . to protect it while it becomes substantial. And at what cost to the creature? Always to be irritated, always troubled by something caught in the throat. The creature wonders what all this pain is leading to. After what happened later, I wondered if I had given up on that work and let him make my mind for me."

Esther understands. She rises, resolute. "I have let Pick keep me from Joe. I must see him."

"I hope you will find him in. I tried this morning. He wasn't at home."

When Jane offers it, Esther takes the ring back and rethreads it around her neck. She puts her hand over it where it lies on her breastbone. "Why does a mind have to grow so slowly? Why can't it be easier?"

33

ONCE, DURING THE WEEK Ben was with her at Half-a-Mind, they caught Duniway rolling in the alfalfa. It didn't appear that she had eaten any of it; she had just waded in—it was only a foot high then—and lain down. With surprising litheness and joy she wriggled her large bottom and kicked her legs. When she saw them coming for her, she regained her feet and ambled off, just out of reach, threatening to disappear into the desert evening. Ben circled round, caught her, and led her—her white eye blinking, all innocence—into the shed. Esther had left the stall door open. She'd just walked away and left the stall open, and the shed door, too.

"I don't blame you," Ben said. "How's a lady supposed to keep house when she's got a puppy like me pulling on her skirt all the time. No wonder she can't keep her mind on her mare."

Esther knew she was flushed. She didn't like to admit that she was entranced by him. "I've got more on my mind than you, puppy. Will the alfalfa grow back? Look at it, it's all mashed down."

"It'll spring up. Grass likes to grow. Don't tell me you're a farmer now."

"I just want it to come back."

They did not go to the other side of the lakeshore, though they could smell its condition, for anyone could be poking around, and often they saw figures of people who were drawn to the catastrophe, to see and inhale and disparage or affirm it. Instead they sat inside, bare armed in the heat, and talked. Esther described

Chicago, and Ben asked many questions. He wanted to know how this and that worked, how large the buildings were and how they were built. Esther was chagrined, for she knew almost nothing. There were beams, there were girders. One saw slow trains chugging, carrying stones, and cranes standing against the sky. "Well, darn it," Ben said, "what good are you?"

"I know where to buy good ice cream."

"I guess that's something."

She told him about her journey, how strange it was to wake after the fitful sleep of the traveler to an unknown landscape, an alien river of syrupy brown, a stony slope rising into fog. A town, a town, another town, where strangers lived and died, and wildness, wildness, wildness that had a history no one would ever know. And one met people on a train and made little friendships that ended forever in a gathering of belongings when the train stopped here or there. There was a droll, kind conductor who had been with her for a day and a night out of Chicago but had descended the train at Julesburg on the Nebraska-Colorado border. He was returning home, and he was happy about it. He said he was a city man. He didn't care if it was jailhouse or courthouse, he liked a big building made of stone. "You can't lure me," he admonished Esther one evening in Nebraska. "You can't lure me with your apples and your corn, your pigs and your squashes. You go on and grow a great big squash. You wash it, bring it to town, cut it up, cook it, and serve it to me with a white napkin on LaSalle Street. Then I'll make the acquaintance of your almighty squash!"

Ben watched her imitate this conductor. He considered for a minute. "I think *you're* an almighty squash."

At other times she read to him. She lay on the bed and held the book open over her face while he sat on the floor and reclined against the frame.

"When the centuries behind me like a fruitful land reposed;
When I clung to all the present for the promise that it closed:
When I dip't into the future far as human eye could see;
Saw the Vision of the world and all the wonder that would
        be.—"

Ben dropped his head back to look at her. "So after all that clinging and visioning, then what? What'd he get for it?"

"Oh, it doesn't end well. The girl—she's his cousin—she marries somebody else."

"About what I'd expect. Maybe he offered her a homestead."

"Maybe he did. I like this homestead, you know."

"Even when it's a sheep graveyard?"

"I don't like that part. I still can't believe it. You took care of them. They were yours. And then they were just killed."

"Well, it's over," he said. "That's not bad poetry, you know."

"It's Tennyson, you imbecile!" She tapped his head with the book. He caught it in his hand and placed it in his lap. He held his hands out wide from his body like an actor and said, distinctly,

"And she turned—her bosom shaken with a sudden storm
    of sighs—
All the spirit deeply dawning in the dark of hazel eyes."

Esther sat up.

He put his hands behind his head. "Didn't think I knew that, huh? Thought I'd never been to school?"

"I thought you said you hadn't."

"Well, not much, but some. And I've been years at the school of Ma, and that's a pretty good one."

"What else do you know?"

"Try me."

"Browning."

"Which?"

"Oh, don't tell me you know both!"

"Well, I won't make you listen to everything I know. What do you like?"

"Mr. Stevenson."

"From *Treasure Island*?"

"Yes, but this was poems. My mother gave me the book when I turned fifteen. I was too grown up for it, she said, but that had never stopped her from liking something, so she supposed I might."

"How'd it go?"

"Let's see. 'Go, little book.' Wait. What is it?"

"Go, little book, and wish to all
flowers in the garden, meat in the hall."

She paused to think.

"A bin of wine, a spice of wit
A house with lawns enclosing it
A living river by the door
A nightingale in the sycamore!"

He looked out the open door at the dusty yard. "Not much of a garden, Mr. Stevenson."

"Nor much of a hall."

"And I haven't seen any wine around here. I expect you're holding out on me."

That night they lay bare to the waist, nose to nose, on top of the quilt. He put one hand under one of her breasts, his thumb nestled between. "Do you know what to do about—about not—well, about babies?" He gave her a humble look.

"I know about the safe and the unsafe times. My mother told me."

"And that's all right."

"I think so."

He dragged his thumb down to her belly and stroked her there. "What kind of river was that, in the poem?"

"A living river."

"I just don't want you to have to marry me unless you want to. You might not be sure yet."

She put her arms around him and pulled him close and said into his curls a few helpless and insufficient words. "I think you are the best person in the world."

34

Dear Ben,

Joe Peaslee has gone. He has not opened the store for business for two days. The yellow cat was found putting its paw out under the back door. His horses are still at the livery. There was no note, no sign of anything. Jane says she saw him night before last with his glass, going out at dusk to zoologize, or she assumed so. You may guess what they are saying, given his illness. That he has become tired of life. But would he have done it?

People have been searching. They divided the valley—some to cover the road to Peterson, some the claims toward Jane Fremont's and the Calhouns' as far as Failing and Wagontire. And Half-a-Mind seems empty, except of birds. They found no sign he'd been anywhere. You have not heard from him? I thought perhaps he might have taken it into his head to visit your family, as his audience here had grown impatient.

There must be some explanation. For if he wanted to make away with himself, I cannot believe he would have left the yellow cat locked inside.

I wish you were here. Every evening I look up, but whatever lamp you burn or fire you light is days away, in Morrow.

She closes the ink bottle and takes it and the pen back to Pick's desk; she has used all her own ink and has yet to get more. Then she returns to the long table in the kitchen and takes up the week's *Century Intelligence* and carefully tears out the notice of Joe's disappearance. She herself set the type for it, and for the first time, she made no mistakes. She folds it and puts it into the envelope with the letter. Ben has not yet written. Has he, in this handful of days, forgotten her? Regretted her? Is he at home among people who despise cattlemen or among girls he used to know? Her loneliness was a stone casing that Ben smashed and scattered. She is free, but she is so tender. A mere breath could injure her newborn skin.

She must mail the letter at once. She will seek out Vincent, to borrow Lester for the trip.

Though it is the middle of the afternoon and he would usually be rolling out a sheet of biscuit the size of a door, in preparation for supper, Vincent lies on his back on his bed, which is propped against the wall where paint and plaster have chipped away to show lath. Strange that this house, practically new, should be chipping at all, but the heat of the day and the cold of evening stretch and contract most things, houses not excepted. Beside him, between him and the wall, is a flat, checkered bundle. He moves to place his hand on it when she enters.

"Vincent? You're not well?"

"Sorry old sack of dung. Sick all over." When he turns to look at her, she sees that he has cut his beard. It's a ragged square now, like a dog-chewed, yellowed handkerchief. It looks as if he has sawed at it with a knife.

He has been as kind to her as anyone else in Century, kind and constant, and she should be able to ask him what he has done with his beard, but he looks old and small and curled, and her dread bounds forth and guards him from her question. Instead she gestures toward the bag. "What is it?"

He appears to consider. Then he sits up, reaches under his bed, and pulls out a frying pan. He puts it on the bed and picks up the bag and upturns it gently. Tiny sulfur-colored pebbles and little flakes and fragment of brighter yellow slide out, making high clinks on the iron. There are five or six fistfuls of them.

Esther puts her hand over her mouth. "What is it—is it gold?" He looks at the door, and she lowers her voice. "Vincent, wherever did you get all that?"

"Panned it. I'm old, you know. I did a bunch of things back when, and I fetched up in Alaska one time, up in Juneau it was, and I was Johnny-on-the-spot. Best pay I ever got."

"Didn't you want to stay and get rich?"

"No! Too dang cold. And I could see things were going to get crazy, with all those dudes pouring in. Well, that was twenty years ago, and I never had a call to spend it on anything. Ferris takes good care of us buckaroos. It's for a rainy day. But I like to look at it sometimes. Makes me feel better."

"My goodness." She recalls her errand. "Vincent, if you don't want him, may I take Lester to town? I'll have him back by supper."

"What're you going to do there?"

"Mail this letter. And see if there is news of Joe."

"What news?"

"Well, any."

"I doubt there's going to be some."

She melts a little in anxiety. "Do you know something?"

He scrapes the gold back into the bag and carefully wipes the pan with his finger. "Just what I feel."

"What do you feel?"

He pauses, his finger dusted with gold, like an idol. "That this is all a trap, a trap we've got into by foolishness. I don't know how we're going to climb out."

He seems to be talking about the whole range, not Joe alone. He must be discouraged by the fighting, the disarray, the horrible surprises. She kneels beside him. "Vincent, don't worry. We'll find him. There may yet be many reasons to celebrate."

"You ought to go home. This place isn't right anymore."

She thinks of Chicago: furniture covered in cloths, scudding leaves, and cold iron railings. "I don't know that any place is."

He wraps the blanket closer around his shoulders. "Why'd you go and lose your mare? She's probably et by coyotes by now. I thought you would have taken better care of an animal that trusted you like that!"

She stands. "I have some reason to believe that she is in good hands."

He flicks his eyes at her. "That so?"

"You don't have to worry about absolutely everybody."

His face softens, and he sighs and reaches up for her hand. "This century's not even a year old, and already it's wearing me out."

As she rides, she is absorbed in thought. Agreement, partnership— the handclasps that served for contracts—all obviated, broken. She, too, has changed her mind. "I've changed my mind." Strange, strange expression. Perhaps it means to exchange one mind for another, the way one changes one's hat. Perhaps to determine to alter it, as a navigator does the heading of the ship. But Esther's mind has *been* changed, by forces outside her.

No, not even that. Her mind is like a tulip in a bank of tulips that have come up red year after year, and in bud it looked like any other—slim, furrowed, and green—and even began to rosify like all the others, and then, finally, it opens. In the sea of red, this one's petals alone are dappled with orange and the stamens are black. So the mind has not changed at all, really. It was called red too early, before it ripened into its final character.

Violet is not in the post office when Esther enters. May takes Esther's letter and puts it in the box. She has heard nothing more about Joe Peaslee. He is still missing. "I heard he's been taken up by God," May says, her eyes wide and dramatic. "He went out in the desert and God heard him talking and knew he was mad, and took him right up."

"Who told you that?"

"Marguerite Green. She says God won't leave a mad person to die, but just scoops him up and keeps him."

"Like a jack, or a marble?"

"That's it. My, wouldn't that be a ride!"

At Joe Peaslee's, there is, of course, no answer to her knock.

She goes around to the back and knocks again. Then she brings out her key and goes inside. It is warm and silent and dim. She brushes her hand across the Liberty as she passes it. Dust. The yellow cat is curled on the chair. It lifts its head and begins to wash. Someone has put a bowl of meat scraps on the floor, which accounts for a faint oily smell in the air. She touches the cat's head, and it transfers its washing to the back of her hand. Fear and melancholy and the sweetness of the cat play in her, a chord.

Where is he? Why has he gone? She has hardly seen him in weeks, since Pick forbade it after the picnic. Why did she obey, even when she saw that he was alone in his madness? When it was most crucial that his friends gather around, she abandoned him. This debit cancels all her previous affection. The cat rubs against her, and she picks it up and lays it against her shoulder and rubs the ridge of scar on its head. She has loved someone and done nothing for him. She might as well have been ironing a dress while someone went finally to sleep.

She goes to Joe's desk, a narrow affair piled with papers, and sits with the cat on her lap and surveys them. Perhaps there is something here, but what, and how deep in the pile? The papers are pulled back a bit, though, in front of one of the tiny pen drawers. As if he'd needed to put something there. She pulls the drawer open, just the couple of inches it will come.

There is a letter here. Without hesitation she opens it.

There is nobody but you to witness for us, Joe. I know they bought that ammunition from you, though of course no one knew what they'd do with it. But none of the rest of them will ever talk. There's only you.

This letter is from Michael Cruff. Did Joe respond? Has he gone to witness, or run away? And what is this, in this little box? A piece of knotted rope. She's heard of this sort of message. A rope, poison, matches. Crude coward's threats.

In the front room, just then, she hears a faint clink. A rustle. A clink again. The cat digs in its claws to push off Esther's legs. It must be Joe, for isn't that the sound of him measuring out the contents of his amber apothecary bottles, the ones with no labels?

But it is Marguerite Green who stands there, holding a bottle in both hands. Two other bottles sit on the counter, their stoppers lying willy-nilly beside them. She notes Esther's presence, hears her gasp, but raises the bottle to her lips and drinks.

"Stop." Fierceness comes easily into Esther's voice. "Marguerite." In a moment she is beside her and taking the bottle. She looks at the others. "Did you drink from these?"

Marguerite points to one of them. "That one."

Esther sniffs it. Only wintergreen oil. And the one she holds now in her hand: spirits of alcohol. "How much did you drink of this?"

"Not much. It's nasty."

Good. She'll have a stomachache, perhaps, and a little dizziness. Esther grasps her again and says, "This is so dangerous, Marguerite. What could you have been thinking? And where is Mrs. Endicott?"

Marguerite pulls away. "I'm too sick to go with them. I'm so sick." She wipes her knit brow with her golden little hand.

"Were you trying to doctor yourself?" Esther drops her chin and crouches a little to look into the child's face. "Oh—are you *making* yourself sick? Marguerite?"

A stillness in the little body shocks her, a stillness that suggests there is yet a secret in the child's mind, and looking at the long row of bottles, Esther understands. If she had drunk from all of them, Marguerite would, perhaps, have gone nowhere ever again. She takes the child by both arms in order to tell her that this is never, never the way—and then drops them. For wouldn't she herself have been tempted had she anything like this child's reasons and this child's ingenuity?

Finally she asks, "How did you ever get in here, anyway?"

Marguerite shows a chain around her neck, upon which— Esther might have guessed—Joe Peaslee has strung a key. For someone who needs a refuge, a key is provided. Esther goes to the front door and locks it—to forestall anyone else.

Marguerite says, "Klamath Falls. There's not even a falls there, Gerald Schmidt told me. He went last Christmas."

"Miss Fremont is going to help you. And I'll help you. You shan't go if you don't want to."

"Reverend Endicott will come and get me."

"We won't let him."

Marguerite is silent for a moment. "But I'd better hide anyway, until they've gone."

"When do they go?"

"Tomorrow."

Esther isn't sure what to say. But surely the matter will be resolved soon. Jane must have gone to the Endicotts with the money by now. But keep the child away for a little while, let the dust settle.

"I like these books," says Marguerite.

"So do I. Look—there are secret books behind the front ones. It's two rows deep."

"Twice as many." The child gloats. Without her front teeth she looks vulnerable, literally without defenses.

"Come and choose one."

"Won't Mr. Peaslee be mad?"

"No, no. When he comes back, he'll be glad as anything that you have a book of his. Come choose."

They peruse the books for some time while the sun lowers outside. Esther doesn't light a lamp. The child's eye lands on a blue cloth book up near the ceiling. Esther stands on a chair and hands it down. "*Birds of England*," Marguerite reads with disappointment. "What else is there?"

Esther looks through the gap and sees something back there—*Autobiography*—in three slim purplish brown volumes, lettered in gold. "Well—"

The handle of the front door in the other room is jiggled. They look at each other. Esther silently descends from the ladder and motions Marguerite to be quiet.

The hours Esther has spent here have made the contents of this store and their sounds familiar to her, so that without a glimpse of the visitor she can tell what is happening. Flap—a gunnysack is shaken open. The glass case opened, something soft—tobacco?—scooped and wrapped in paper. A box of buttons is taken or moved, cans of beans, too. A clinking sound on the glass—a razor? The gunnysack thumps now when it's rested on the floor. A sound of breath, as if exerting, and the little bell of the cash register pinging as the register is moved. A little whistle comes: *It tells the fate of Nick and Nate that is known to all of you.* Tap, tap, the tattoo of boots, the door inquiring and expressing disappointment again as it is closed and locked. Locked, with a key. Could it be Joe himself?

Esther rushes to look into the front room, with Marguerite behind her, then to the window. Across the street, in the light from the back of Schmidt's Livery, she sees Noggin Koerner, his hat between his knees and a sack at his feet, filling a pipe with tobacco. As he packs it, he looks back at the place he's looted, and though the light must be shining against the darkened windows, hiding her somewhat, he looks straight at her. He packs his pipe, then puts his hat on and picks up the sack. He is about to turn away, his shoulders are turning, when he whips back and makes a horrible face, all teeth and tongue. His burdened hands jerk toward her, half jesting, half murderous. Then he winks and saunters away.

Esther's heart is thundering.

Marguerite says, "Let's go away. He has the key. He can open the door whenever he wants to."

He has the key. Could he, too, have had some arrangement with Joe? Or did he steal it sometime, and now that he knows Joe is gone, he loots the store. She will watch him. She will see if he tries to do it again.

"Yes, let's go." She remembers the money Pick means to offer Delores. "How are you feeling? All right in the stomach? It may be that things have changed at the reverend's."

35

BUT WHEN ESTHER ARRIVES in the morning to see the Endicotts off, Marguerite is sitting in the Endicotts' open buggy and her mother is standing beside her. Fred and the baby aren't there—they must have stayed away. But what can be wrong? Have they not redeemed the debt and taken Marguerite home? Esther approaches shyly. Delores gives no sign of welcome, but she is not unfriendly. She is only preoccupied, and where she usually masks her feelings in expressionless stillness, today silent waves of interior pain—anger? desperation?—burn across her face. She pats Marguerite's shoe and traces the laces with her fingers.

But the child speaks in a businesslike manner. "My mother will come for me in one month," she tells Esther. "It's all settled. They are going to cut the alfalfa and sell it, and then they will come for me. And I will have a holiday in Klamath Falls."

Delores bestirs herself. "Miss Chambers. Esther. May I speak with you a moment in private?"

Esther accompanies her a little way along the street, out of earshot of Marguerite but well within sight of her little figure, sitting dutifully on the buggy seat.

"I think I must beg your pardon," says Delores. "That is—I understand from Jane Fremont and from Mrs. Endicott how you helped my daughter. How you—saved her."

"Oh, but perhaps there was not much danger, really—"

Delores gives her a glimmering, melting look. "But there was. There was a great deal of danger. She told me what she meant by it."

"And yet—oh, forgive me, but yet, you will let her go?"

"Marguerite has promised me that she will never do something so foolish again." She sees Esther's consternation and worry. "Oh, bless you, truly, for caring for her so. She is lucky to have friends like you and Jane. I know she will triumph, my little girl, because she has the gift of making herself loved. I cannot tell you why I let her go today, but it is something that I must, must do, and if—if you were me, I suspect you would do the same. I suspect you would understand." Her black eyes are swimming with fortitude and loss.

They walk back to the wagon, and Esther stands back as Delores balances on the buggy step, touches foreheads with Marguerite, and kisses her. Within a minute afterward, Delores has stridden to her wagon, clucked up her horses, and departed. Marguerite watches her drive away. She has accepted this wrinkle in the fabric of her little life, as children must. The world is what grown people say it is, and to argue it is to suffer even further.

Delight is supervising the swaddling of her piano, where it now stands in the far wagon, and Jane is with her. Reverend Endicott has used what looks like Marguerite's jump rope to lash a blanket around the piano stool. "So she is going with you, after all?" Esther asks.

Delight looks conscious. "Yes. Well, we were unable to settle on a course of action that would be best for Marguerite, so we have determined to take her, and revisit the subject shortly."

"Then you'll come back to Century soon? The Greens' alfalfa must be almost ready."

"Yes . . ." says Delight. Esther has trespassed, apparently. To speak of money, of the debt, is to suggest its leverage, which Delight cannot countenance. "Excuse me a moment, Esther. Just a moment." She hurries to her husband and begins to speak with him. He puts his hand on her shoulder.

"She knows it's wrong," Jane Fremont says.

"I told them last night what Marguerite had been doing at the store," Esther tells her. "Surely they understand that she is too melancholy to be parted from her parents?"

"They have merely determined to watch her more closely. That drink of wintergreen was the end of her freedom. I'm surprised they've tied the piano stool with that jump rope—they might as well have tied the child herself."

"But there is no more debt, so on what grounds do they take her?"

"The debt has not yet been repaid."

Esther is shocked. "You don't mean to say Pick changed his mind?"

"Not at all. Merely that Delores would not accept help from him. She refused."

Esther looks over at Marguerite and breathes, "But that's obstinate."

"She seems to have determined that Pick is no one to her, and she cannot be beholden to him. I know. I could have shaken her, I was so angry."

"If Joe were here, he would think of something."

"I wonder why he has gone."

"He left the yellow cat."

Jane takes Esther's hand and squeezes it in both of hers. "Then surely he will come back."

The Endicotts had been packing the wagons for two days, and now there is only the sweeping of the apartment behind the church to be done. The other women go in to help.

In an instant, Esther's urge to comfort Marguerite develops into a plan. It takes only a few moments for her to run down the street to Joe's store, to use her key, step up on the ladder, and find the book she and Marguerite were looking at—*Jane Eyre: An Autobiography*, in three small purple volumes. She takes a length of ribbon and ties them this way and that and jogs back to the wagons with this parcel under her arm. Marguerite is still alone in the wagon box, playing with her skirt.

Esther holds the bundle up. "Something to keep you company and help you think of us until you come back. If it's too hard to read, just remember there are lots of others, here and everywhere.

When Joe Peaslee comes back, perhaps he will order some books especially for little girls."

Marguerite has a look of thrilled greed. "Tell him to get lots of them."

"Lots and lots! Every book for little girls that there is! We'll have to build a great big wagon to bring them from Peterson."

Marguerite clutches the books. "Be sure to put an oilcloth over them. Because the rain might get on them and make the pages stick together."

"You may depend on that. If I must, I'll take an oilskin right off the back of a buckaroo."

Esther and Jane have stopped at the crossing of the Peterson and Jack-High roads, where Jane will walk west to her claim and Esther east to hers, when Pick rides up to them. They are both feeling not only worry for Marguerite, but also the depression that enters the heart when one is left behind and must take up one's life again in a diminished place. They shield their eyes to look up at him. Seeing their faces, he dismounts.

"They've taken her," he says.

"Delores would not accept the money," Jane admits.

He hits his leg with his hat. "But why tell her? You should have just—"

"I tried. Paul Endicott—" Jane's eyebrows arch as high as Esther has ever seen them, in caustic disdain. "Paul opined that since Fred had entered into the contract, only he could cancel the debt. And of course, taking the money from you doesn't speak at all well for Fred's capacity to provide for that family. The reverend made a point of that."

"What business is it of Endicott's?"

"He thinks love makes it his business."

Esther clenches her fists. "That's not love. It's stealing."

"Ah, but they don't *know* it's stealing. They are absolutely persuaded that they are in the right. That they can take care of

Marguerite best. And they won't say so, but the real reason they think Delores and Fred not fit for Marguerite is not because they're poor. It's because Delores is a part-blood Indian. Marguerite doesn't have to suffer that fate, they think. They think they can raise her as a white girl and save her from the misfortune of her birth."

At this, Pick shrugs. He's silent for a moment. "I suppose you know about me and Delores, Esther."

"Yes. Some."

"It's been seven years, though. A long time for her still to be mad at me. I'd have thought she'd have given it up by now. Though maybe she's not still mad. Just being her fool-proud self. In any case, I guess, this is the chickens coming home to roost."

Only seven years? Not as long ago as she had thought. She had imagined them like herself and Ben, barely grown. So they were a little older, and Pick had built his house, and—

Her heart floods. She makes herself look at him. "Seven years means that Marguerite is your little girl."

Jane says, "I must go."

"No need. I guess you could say she's my little girl. I helped make her, but I've never done much for her."

Of course. Of course. The child is like him, square in the shoulder, gold in the eyes—but she is like her mother, too, with the dark, flyaway hair, long waist, and shrewd concentration.

Pick goes on. "You see what kind of woman she is. You don't insist much to her, or you're liable to find her gone without a word. I imagine you're disgusted with me now."

Disgust is not the feeling. Esther has understood for many years that women who have children without being married are woeful, that the men who have assisted them, while not so dreadfully compromised, have embarrassed themselves and put their children in a marked condition. But what have Pick and Delores done that she and Ben have not? Not much separates Pick from Ben and her from Delores. She has no stone to throw, though

Pick of course doesn't know that. Esther's head is aching. She wants Marguerite back. She wants this little child of Century restored to them all. "We must go after them! Let us go to the livery and get a buggy. Make them take the money. Make them take it!"

"I don't think so, Blackbird. I'd probably have to make a scene that'd scare her. Let's see what Fred and Delores can work out. But it makes me mad that they won't put their pride in their pocket. They should think what's best for the girl."

"Perhaps," Jane says, "what's best for Marguerite is that her mother act according to her conscience."

Pick shrugs. "Maybe."

Esther must ask him now, for she may not have the courage to open the topic again. "Someone told me you wouldn't marry Delores because she's part Indian. Did you know she was when you—you took up together?"

Pick is silent for a moment. "I won't ask you where you got that, because I suppose a few folks know about it. I did know who her grandma was when I met her. And I don't know if that's why we didn't marry—I can't recall all of what I was thinking, because I was young and it was a long time ago. But let me ask you. Would you marry an Indian?"

"I don't know," she says, hot but even. "And I don't *have* to know."

"Well, I balked at it. It didn't fit my idea of me, somehow. I did go looking for her back then, if that means anything to you, Esther, and you, Jane. I knew I'd been a cad, and I asked all around for her. But she was gone down to Lakeview, and she was going to have the baby, and she did what she thought she had to and married Fred Green. Though the truth is, she might not have come back to me even if she wasn't already married. I'm sure she doesn't like scratching to get ahead, but otherwise she seems happy with Fred. That was my first chance for a good woman. I wrecked it."

"Oh, Ferris, stop it," says Jane. "There will always be more chances for someone like you."

This is true. He is handsome, strong, intelligent, wealthy, and of generally sound judgment. He will always lead, even when he is not elected. People will look to him, especially women.

But he looks as if he's been slapped with a glove. "No wonder you can't love anybody, Jane. You wouldn't forgive a drowned dog his smell."

She laughs, but she is also tearful. "That's not so. I can forgive anything, but people have to admit what they've done. They can't just go on and on making things simpler than they are, or easier— they can't sit up at night arranging a story that satisfies themselves and no one else. I'm not righteous. I have my own past, and it is not one to be proud of. But at least I have never imagined a fellow human being my inferior."

They are all quiet for a moment. Pick says, "All right. I don't think of myself the way you describe me, but I don't suppose most people know themselves all that well. That's how they get them-selves—" He pauses, as if searching for words, as if trying to de-cide whether to speak at all. "Just forget I said it."

Esther thinks that his hands may be shaking.

But the next moment she is washed over with realization, and she forgets everything else for the moment. She says to Jane, in wonder, "Your name's not really Fremont, is it?"

Jane wipes her face with both hands. "How could you possibly know that?"

"You—I knew it!—you passed through the town of Fremont on the way here on the train. I did, too. And when I first heard your name, I wondered if you were from that town. But you saw the same sign I did, didn't you, and you changed your name. And Jane. Is that even real?"

"It's Jeanette."

"'Jeanette'?" Pick says. He has calmed, and he gives a mild, teasing smile. "Sounds foreign to me."

"Yes. My father's parents were French. Jeanette Alice Martin.

It's strange to say. It used to be my name, and now it sounds like someone else's."

Once, Esther had complained to Joe Peaslee about being called Esther.

"No? She who saved her people?"

"But I haven't any people," she said, "not anymore."

"You have them," he told her. "You will know them when you meet them. And I'll wager they will still need their Esther."

Pick accompanies Esther to the cabin turnoff. There he polishes the pommel of his saddle with his thumb. "I don't have any explanation. I used to think, She's doing this because she's an Indian, she's doing that because she's an Indian. Sometimes she looked strange to me. Once, when she was sleeping, I measured her face with my finger. Maybe it was too wide, or her nose too short. Of course I couldn't tell anything by it. It was wrong of me."

She waits to see if he will say more, but he has exhausted his willingness to reveal himself, at least for now. She is soft toward his distress and glad he has come to know what he should have known before. She wishes to speak to him with the same frankness. But without Ben or Joe by her, she is awash in feelings, bobbing here and there. Ben must write, or Joe must come home. She needs one of them to anchor her, to remind her that she is Esther Chambers and her decisions are her own.

36

IT IS ONLY THE NEXT DAY that Fred Green rides into Esther's yard while she is examining her remaining alfalfa plants. He doesn't speak until he's off his horse. Like some other men, he thinks it rude to talk to a woman from above her head. He scratches his mustache and says, "I think you've been busy here, Miss Chambers. I saw this place when Miller had it, and it wasn't much."

"Thank you. I do have the well now. But I'm worried about this alfalfa. I lost some of it in the frost, and now what's left—the stems are yellow. What do you—but you didn't come to talk about alfalfa, I suppose."

He fingers a stalk. "No. I've actually brought you a gift. Marguerite made it, and she wanted you to have it."

"Really?"

He reaches inside his shirt and brings out a couple of sheets of paper bound with a cross-stitching of black yarn. On the first is written in regular though shaky penmanship "Being the Town Century Oregon yr. 1900." In an upper corner is a child's drawing of a woman in an inky dark skirt and etched blouse, her hair a dense scrub of lead pencil.

"That's you," Fred says. "She said she didn't know how to spell Esther."

The second page is a map of Century and its environs, done in ink and patches of colored chalk. It is apparently a project for school. Here is the church, the hotel, the post office, the livery, the newspaper office, and other establishments; here are the Peterson,

Failing, and Jack-High roads, and here is a green blotch that is Half-a-Mind. But Marguerite has decorated her assignment with more personal notations. Fred explains: a dark oval nicked with pale chalk is the ice cave. Something that looks like a canoe with a sun above it is a large, well-known watering trough and its tall windmill, north of town on the Peterson road. Just south of Century are two precise little bows, like tied shoelaces, next to the tiny figure of a girl with her arms raised straight up above her head.

"That's where she lost a pair of hair ribbons Mrs. Endicott gave her. It really put her dander up. But she didn't tell me what this is." Fred points to a small drawing of a face with an oversize, blackened mouth, near the post office in town. "Near Peaslee's place, from the look of it."

Esther remembers Noggin Koerner, the grimace he made that day. "I might know what that is," she says. "But this?" Down to one side, in what is unvisited, unknown rangeland to anybody but a shepherd or a buckaroo, is a patch of little ovals clustered together.

"I couldn't tell, either. But Delores recognized it. Marguerite overheard Delores telling me a story once. A family story. Not a happy one."

The story of her parentage? No. Much further back. Delores had a great-uncle, Fred says, an old Paiute fighter with only one foot, who in his old age remembered his childhood with much greater precision than anything that had happened afterward. When he was a boy and his family had never known a settler and only seen a white man from a distance, it was rumored that the big-eyed strangers were predators who meant to eat children if they could get them. The mothers were sure of it. So one day, when they heard the settlers were coming, they took the children into the desert and dug holes for them and made them lie down and buried them with just their faces showing. They put rabbit brush and other things all around their faces, and they left them there all day and all night. The children couldn't move, and they had to wet in their clothes, and every sound they heard they thought was the giants with the big white eyes coming to cook and eat them.

Esther puts a hand over her mouth and shakes her head. "And these ovals are the children's faces?"

He gives her a wincing grin and shrugs. "I don't know all of it. You can have Delores tell you sometime. If you'd like."

"I'd like to. I'd like to know her more."

"She didn't know if you'd want to."

"I do want to."

"I'll let her know that." He says it simply, but with kind feeling.

Gordon Cecil told her all those months ago at the dance that Fred Green wasn't much of a farmer. Perhaps not. But she can see why Delores might have loved him and cleaved to him. His quietude has a richness to it. Whenever she has seen him with the baby or Marguerite, the children are pulling on handfuls of his clothes, playing with his hands, chattering to him. Many—not only men—would find it exasperating, but he is at ease, in a proper place, engaged in a joyful duty. Not a farmer, but a father. She is glad, glad that Marguerite has him to love her, since Pick has not seen his way to fathering her. Looking at Fred's face, Esther longs for her own parents. She knows why a woman might choose a poor man despite what it means in work and grief.

Yet farmer enough, apparently: Fred takes up a spade and goes to the end of the field and there digs a small, deep hole. Then he turns the spade over and scratches the bottom of the hole with the tip of the blade. "Ah, well."

"What is it?"

"Can't tell if it's rock or hardpan soil, but it's darned stiff. Alfalfa likes to put down a deep root."

"Does it?"

"I think you've got a whole layer under there. And the root can't get down past it, and the water fetches up there and rots the roots. You can grow something shallower here next year. Peas, maybe. But try your deep-root plant, your perennial, somewhere else."

That night she pins Marguerite's map to the wall over some columns of the *Century Intelligence*, the little girl's private pen-and-ink Century over Gordon Cecil's typeset public one.

She dips her finger into her water glass and paints a little "BC" on the map where Ben's camp used to be. In the warm evening the initials begin to dry and fade at once.

Can't he write to tell her why he does not write?

37

SEARCH FOR PEASLEE OVER: BODY DISCOVERED

The body of Joseph Peaslee, merchant, was found last Monday by Patrick Hadley, a homesteader, about one and a quarter miles from Peaslee's residence and establishment in Century. The body was lying in brush on Hadley's land about two hundred yards from the Peterson-Century road.

For more than two weeks, since the evening of August 19 of this year, Joe Peaslee has been missing, and every effort has been put forth to ferret out the mystery of his sudden and unaccountable disappearance. The story is a familiar one to readers of the *Intelligence*, and the matter has been one of extreme interest to every resident of Peterson County. All kinds of theories have been advanced, but the one his friends most adhered to was that in a moment of aberration he had put an end to his own life. His health of mind had been of some concern to his associates in recent days, though his financial affairs appear to have been in good order.

Mr. Peaslee was a well-known merchant of Century and had not an enemy in the world. When the body was found last Monday, the fact was at once made known, and it was soon discovered that it was the body of Joseph Peaslee and the news flashed over the county by wire. Leading citizens were summoned, also the district attorney and county physician. The body was carefully guarded on the spot until the arrival of these gentlemen. Upon examination, two bullet holes were found, one in the right shoulder and one in the palate, and by the side of the dead man was found a .38 caliber revolver, thought to belong to the deceased, with two empty chambers. The bullet that caused the shoulder wound, .38 caliber, lodged in the bone and was recovered. The other bullet passed through the throat and spine and was not found.

An inquest will be held, pending arrival of the coroner from Peterson.

It's a special issue of the *Intelligence*, only the one page long. Gordon refrains from placing advertisements. But after some consideration he has Esther add a final paragraph. Though it may look like unseemly haste, it assures Gordon that his next issue will be as popular as this one.

The last will and testament of the deceased, kept at the bank in Peterson, requires an auction of all his goods, the proceeds to go to distant family in the East. Watch this space for an announcement of the public auction.

By now Esther's fingers feel numb. A few times she drops the type on the table and floor.

That afternoon, she puts one of the special issues into an envelope and takes it to the post office. But what is the use? There is no word, and there may never be. Ben has forgotten her or been persuaded against her. Something she said or did, or the way she moved or looked has disappointed him. He does not want her anymore. That is easy to understand. But how can it be that he doesn't care for Joe? If that affection could be jettisoned, then the world, and people, are much different than she ever thought them. Everyone has begun to look uncanny—like a person, but not really a person—now that Ben appears to have abandoned his friend.

When she reaches the post office, the mail carriers are just getting down from their buggy, disentangling themselves from bags and rifles. One of them, a stocky fellow with a red, leathery face, sees the letter in her hand. "Is that going out?" He takes it and looks at it. "Esther Chambers? Is that you?"

"Yes, it's me."

"I think I've got one for you, too. No, look! It's your lucky day." He hands her two letters.

One is from Ben. His handwriting, finally. But she must be prepared for its contents. The other—she knows this writing, too, but from some other time. My word—Mr. Fleming, her mother's employer, back in Chicago. She has not thought of him, really, for months. She opens it first.

> . . . and since the lease on the warehouse space is coming due for renewal, I thought I'd see if you wanted to take it for another year. We have not heard from you for some time, and we would like to know that you are well and happy.

The warehouse is where her mother's furniture is stored. It is not many pieces, nor is it valuable. But certain things, things that made her turn away in pain a year earlier, now seem poignant, desirable. There is a desk, bulky and absurd, and the bedspread, the one that slipped off her mother's bed the afternoon she died. Well, Esther will think of what she must do, but not now. Not when there is Ben's letter to read. She opens it.

> After all this time I have to think you regret . . .

She reads on, one hand clasping her forehead. When she has finished the page, she hurries up onto the sidewalk and bangs open the door of the post office. At the counter Violet Fowler is sorting mail and visiting with the mail carrier. Esther puts the letter down in front of her.

"I've just had this letter from Ben Cruff," she says.

"Oh? Yes?" Violet blinks.

"I'm—I understand from what he writes that there must have

been other letters, but I never received them. Where could they have gone?"

Violet gives the letter a blank, level look, and her hand flies to her temperance ribbon. "It's a long way from Morrow County. Anything might have happened to a letter or even two. Sometimes they blow away . . ."

"Blow away?" says the mail carrier. He puts his large sunburned hands on his hips. "If they blow, I get down and chase them! Well, I know there were more. Not that much comes to Century. Violet, we even spoke of Miss Chambers's letters the one time. You said—"

Violet slaps a bundle of envelopes down. "What? What did I say, John?"

"Now, don't get mad—"

Violet says, "Why were you writing to him? I don't know what you'd have to say to a Cruff, under the present circumstances. But I suppose I have an idea." The whites of her eyes are pink with disgusted tears.

Esther's stomach turns. The letters have been stolen, and read. Violet has read them and thought them evil. Then a worse thought occurs. "But—did you send them, after all? Has he not—does he think—"

"Here." Violet plucks a key from her waist, opens a drawer, and takes out a little bundle. She throws it down in front of Esther. She grimaces. "I expected more from a white girl. But you waltz in and—when there's any number who—just *decent*—and you waltzing in. Right in, where we've already been forever!" The skin under her eyes is dry, puckered with anguish. She has her own secret thirst. For things that are a burden to Esther.

"I'm going outside," says the mail carrier. "Because I didn't hear this, and I don't know about it. I'm deaf and dumb." He shakes his head in slow surprise and dismay. "Aw, Violet. Damn it."

Esther sits right down on the sidewalk in front of the post office. There are four letters from Ben. Four—and he thinking she has not written at all. She is wretched. The first letters tell of his re-union with his brother Michael and their subsequent journey and plans.

The sheriff up here in Morrow says that unfortunately it's not his business who kills sheep in Peterson County, he isn't allowed to put his oar in even if the Peterson sheriff is a coward. Michael has written to Joe Peaslee about telling what he knows but hasn't heard back, so he has gone on and written to the governor's office. Michael's slow to the boil, but look out after!

The later letters are softer, more uncertain, and she sees his mind going back over their times together, reassuring himself that it was real, that she did love him.

Do you remember that day I first saw you? You came walking along among the sheep in a black dress and you had that almighty fair hair, and the dog went around and around you. I thought you looked like somebody who'd just raised up out of the lake on a sea horse. I wasn't very pleasant, I know. Michael told me later that I'd have to ratchet down the flattery if I didn't want all the city girls bothering me for more. I saw you a few other times when you didn't see me. I didn't have much to talk about, so I didn't come after you. Maybe when I was mad was the only time I could get over being shy. Anyhow these fool lambs are jostling and I'm late to bed. The lambs say good night and want you to write soon, as they are dreadful dull now that nobody's trying to kill them. And I wouldn't mind it, either, a letter from you.

She wheels away and then looks at the letter again. She is des-perate to tell him she has not been inconstant. Why has she been patient? She could have telegraphed long since.

With the letters in her pocket she goes into the hotel, where the clerk—Odell Underwood's younger brother, recently arrived from Baltimore—looks at her expectantly. She takes up a telegraph form and checks her pocketbook for money. She will have to be brief. And Odell Underwood's younger brother will read her words. Well, let him do it, and let him tell whom he will. After a moment she writes:

Benjamin Cruff, Cruff Station, Morrow, Oregon.
Be sure of me.

PART FIVE

A DISCOVERY. A FIRE.

38

THE INQUEST is held in the school, and the children are much perturbed at being kept out while the most bloody business ever to
enliven that room transpires. Attendance for adults is apparently
mandatory, and if Esther didn't have her own peculiar role to play,
she would have to knock Mrs. Phelia Jacob down to get a seat. In
Chicago, ladies would claim to be repelled by such topics as gore
and madness, but here there was no pretense. Whether possessed
by affection, unease, fascination, or righteousness, everyone seems
eager to see which official description will be attached to the
death of Joseph Peaslee.

Yesterday Esther was approached by Gordon Cecil and asked
to take down the transcript of the inquiry on the typewriter; the
coroner's court reporter, who usually travels with him, has broken his wrist. And so she is near the front of the room, the Liberty
gleaming its grin in front of her. Most people she knows are here,
and there are strangers, too, witnesses and visitors. The coroner,
as plump and glossy as a fish, whoops it up in the front row with
a well-dressed stranger—no, not a stranger. Mr. Elliot, from the
Far West Navigation and Railway. Esther recognizes the shining
boots. He said he would be back in the fall, and here he is. Perhaps rumors have reached him. Perhaps he has come to assess the
situation for himself.

The coroner consults with Esther. "Do you think you'll be
able to keep up with the testimony?"

"I hope so."

"I'll stop the proceedings now and then so you can catch up.

And really—the essence. That's what we need. Not every hem and haw."

Gordon Cecil appears with a narrow spool of paper, which he places in front of the Liberty and feeds the raw end under the platen. "This way you don't change pages. You just keep on going."

Pick is here, too. He doesn't touch her, but stands with one hand in his back pocket and surveys the room. With some diffidence he says, "You sure you want to do this? It's not pretty, what they'll have to testify about."

"I can do it. Thank you."

"I know you can. I just didn't know if you wanted to."

The coroner raps his pencil on Jane Fremont's desk, and conversation subsides. "Let's start this proceeding. I've a got a witness list here, and I'll just call you in order. Is the jury settled? All right."

The coroner's jury have taken their places. There are six, and three of them are familiar. The farrier from Failing, who orders his shoes and nails and files from Joe. One of the Jacob ranch hands, who sits forward in his chair with an air of studious importance. Carey Stoop. He stands now and takes off his hat. "If you don't mind, Mr. Lovejoy, I'd ask to be excused on account of I knew the deceased well and perhaps might not give a proper evaluation of the evidence."

"You Carey Stoop?"

"Yes, sir."

"I knew your dad. No, I can't excuse you, I've got no alternates. Your number came up, Carey. Time to do your duty."

Crestfallen, Carey takes his seat. Jane Fremont watches him, pulling on her fingers.

People on the threshold, who stand crowded shoulder to shoulder, rustle and shuffle a bit and part to let Vincent into the room. He's got a blanket wrapped around him, and he moves slowly. So many people seem to be ailing. Not just the old men—it's also Carey Stoop, whose cheeks are sallow under their pink stripes, and Violet Fowler, dark around the eyes. Jane Fremont, who keeps pressing her lips in on themselves and brushing at the corners of her eyes as though at cobwebs. Even Pick, whose light eyes and golden mustache and silence always give him the look of a mountain lion—even he seems older, encumbered. His wide chest and shoulders are stiff, as if he were wearing a breastplate of iron. Esther thinks, That is the man I am supposed to marry.

Since the revelation that he is Marguerite's father, he has been a little cool to Esther. She understands this. He expects her to be injured, to remonstrate with him about his failures. But she won't. Nothing about the way men and women are together is surprising to her now. Her mother had told her that it was the nature of people to find themselves in trouble now and then, even principled people, especially principled people. Folly is everywhere. But honest conduct after folly is rare. Pick is waiting for her disapproval, but the fact that he waits for her to decry his having loved a woman, rather than his having ignored a child, makes her think he doesn't know her at all. He judges, and expects others to judge also. He doesn't know the difference between himself and other people. When he looks at them, he sees only himself.

The first witness, Alfred Schmidt of Schmidt's Livery Stable, comes to the stand and gives brief testimony about Joe Peaslee's movements the day before he disappeared. Esther begins to type. Very soon she is in a haze of transcription, staring neither at the witness nor at her fingers, but at the paper, where the thin black arms spider out and strike it. The coroner asks questions, shuffles papers, and sniffs.

The witnesses succeed one another, but the audience hears little it doesn't already know. Just before midday, when Esther is taking every opportunity to shake her hands at the wrists and press her fingers backward and forward, Noggin Koerner is called to the stand. Those members of the audience who are not from Century examine him with curiosity; it can well be believed that they have never seen a man with such a blue head. Koerner's gaze trolls the room, coming to rest on Esther.

The coroner says playfully, "We'll start, unless the witness has a question for the court reporter."

Koerner doesn't flicker an eyelash. He turns his whole body toward the coroner, and he looks like a thighbone dangling from a string. "I was wondering how come she had on that red dress."

"Well, nothing like a red dress . . ."

"What she means by it."

". . . and you can take up sartorial questions outside the court's time. All right. What's your name and how old are you?"

His name is Arthur Robert Koerner, and he is twenty-eight years old, born in Billings, Montana, or so he's told. He has crewed for Ferris Pickett for fifteen months and is in good standing with his boss as far as he knows. On the evening of the nineteenth of August he was riding into Century from the ranch and saw Joe Peaslee walking in the brush aimlessly, carrying an old army-issue Colt revolver. Koerner can't say for sure, but it looked like the one Peaslee kept behind his cash register. He thinks so because he liked to rib Peaslee about it, why keep an old thing like that around, he'd have thought Peaslee could afford a better gun.

Esther stops typing and looks up at him. He meets her gaze and scratches his neck. Suddenly he, and the coroner next to him, appear to elongate on the diagonal, to waver there like a mirage and then snap back into their ordinary shapes. She remembers a certain combination of sounds, a groping, a clanking, from that day at the store. Noggin Koerner never saw Joe Peaslee walking with the gun that day, because Noggin himself stole it from behind the cash register later. And Esther was there. She should have known it. At least she should have told someone what she'd seen. But she'd been too overwhelmed thinking of Marguerite, of Ben. And Koerner now comes into court and swears to lies, and she herself writes the lies into the official record.

The testimony continues. No, they didn't speak that day. He

waved at Peaslee, but Joe didn't wave back, and Koerner thought, Well, he's an old man and he doesn't see that well. Koerner didn't think anything of it. It was a Sunday, and Peaslee often didn't open his store on Sunday, everybody knew that.

One more thing. Has Mr. Koerner any information regarding the slaughter of a large band of sheep belonging to the Cruff and Duncan outfits, at Half-a-Mind south of Century back in early August? No, he has no information other than what is general. He went to a dance that night at Failing and stayed quite late on account of a young lady.

The coroner lays a finger on the side of his plump, waxy nose. "I won't ask you to name the young lady," he says. "I don't want to hurt the court reporter's feelings!" The people in the court room, unamused, take the opportunity to shift.

Hurt the court reporter's feelings, Esther types, doggedly.

The final witness before lunch is the doctor from Peterson. His name is Virgil Bloucher, and he has come now and again to Century, once when a buckaroo broke his leg and again when Odie Underwood the saloonkeeper was laid low with kidney trouble. With his wavy hair and lush, drooping mustache, he looks like a languid, resentful dog. His speech is delayed by considering pauses, into which the coroner is likely to leap with further questions, prompting a further bowing of Dr. Bloucher's resentful shoulders. He's wearing a silk tie of a peculiar pea green, the silk disturbed in a way that suggests he tied it several times to get it right.

The coroner asks if, when summoned to the place where Joe Peaslee lay, Dr. Bloucher had formed any opinion about what had transpired there. The doctor says there wasn't much he could tell for sure. Probably Mr. Peaslee had died where he lay. Any possibility he died elsewhere and was moved? Possible, but no way to tell. Rain, animals . . . evidence had been carried away. The two wounds were perhaps made by the same gun, the one found with him, though the unfound second bullet leaves it a bit in doubt. Yes, the wounds are consistent with suicide, if one imagines a right-handed man meaning to shoot himself in the heart and faltering toward the shoulder, then resituating the gun for better effect in his mouth.

Better effect in the mouth, types Esther. She hears Joe's voice. *I hope I haven't frightened you.* But the voice is not quite right even in her mind. It is thinned; there is no breath behind it. She stops typing for a moment in order to chase that dear sound.

"So," Lovejoy says. "Not an accident, possibly suicide. Any chance of homicide?"

There is silence in the room. "I can't really say," says Dr. Bloucher. "The shoulder wound did not bleed much. You can see it on the coat."

Joe Peaslee's military coat, wrapped in canvas, is brought forward and laid upon the front table, where it is exposed in its wretched blue. It smells only faintly of death. The shoulder, the collar are destroyed. The jury is allowed to get up and file past. Carey Stoop is the only one who touches it. He puts a finger into a cuff and lifts it slightly.

The shoulder wound did not bleed much, says Dr. Bloucher again. Thus it was possibly inflicted postmortem. But such a retardation of the flow might have been caused by the bullet striking mostly bone instead of the softer tissue.

The coroner, apprised of Joe's habits, asks if the blood question might be explained by the use of opium or other narcotic. The doctor's collar appears to be savaging his chin. "I suppose it might." Suppose? The doctor heaves a sigh. Yes. The quieting of all the systems, the slowing of the beat of the heart. Yes. Certainly.

At noon the coroner calls for a recess, and the cramped audience rustles and stretches and flees into the yard, where lunches are retrieved from wagons and saddlebags, and all the nearby privies are centers of activity. In the empty room, Esther finishes her notes and reads over them. Then she goes to the front table, where the jacket still lies, and uncovers it. Thick blue wool, heavy buttons. She lifts one sleeve, slides it over her hand, and strokes the wool. As she does so, she allows herself to look at the burned and torn shoulder, the horrible collar and back. Then she drops the sleeve and touches the cloth near the shoulder and scratches it with her fingernail. The doctor has not been precise. It's not that the shoulder wound bled little. It seems to Esther that it didn't bleed at all.

By three o'clock all the witnesses have testified. Esther's arms ache to the elbow, and her spine foretells calamity. The coroner commits the jury to its task, and everyone emerges into a warm though strangely blue afternoon, the melancholy surprise of October. By suppertime the verdict has not come back. Carey Stoop is seen eating a ham sandwich in the back room at Odie Underwood's, but he doesn't speak to anyone. Many of the crowd who came into town for the inquest are staying for the funeral the next day. The hotel's four rooms are full of the coroner and the doctor and Elijah and Phelia Jacob and kin, and there are lots of bachelors camped under their wagons in the schoolyard, moving one into another's lamplight to crouch and go through the day's events over whiskey, water, chicken, and beans.

While Pick talks "business" with Elijah, Esther takes her supper with Jane and the Schmidts in the office at the livery. Once, Jane says, "Two shots," and Alfred Schmidt says quietly, "Twice, he did it."

Ida Schmidt says to Esther, "He has done it, do you think? He would hide, all this time, and then do this?"

Esther shakes her head. His mind was haunted, confused by sorrow and blood. Who could know what he might have done?

The coroner's jury do not trouble themselves for long. Esther has drunk some strong coffee with the Schmidts and is listening to Ida sing Gerald, Johann, and Louisa to sleep when the street outside erupts with loud discussion. The verdict has come in. Joseph Peaslee, storekeeper of Century, is legally a suicide.

Esther doesn't want to talk anymore, so she slips out and wanders along the street toward Joe's. She passes Noggin Koerner and

Teddy and Enrique sitting on the edge of the sidewalk in front of Odie Underwood's, and Koerner is tossing playing cards into his upended hat. He looks up at her and, preparing to toss the next card, turns it instead toward her and wiggles it in his fingers. It is the ace of hearts, and somehow its red flutter unnerves her. She thinks she has never hated anyone before, but she does hate him. Teddy and Enrique lift their hands, and she lifts hers, then curls her fingers and hurries on.

When she goes into Joe's, she wishes she had not come. The store and the back room are full of things, individual and specific items that crowd the shelves with cold, inert ardor. The books are aromatic in their leathery bindings, each with its pages, its multiple pages that require turning. Cornmeal and flour in large coarse bags, axle grease in a box, satin ribbon on spools. Scissors, needles, and thread in the glass case; soda, soap, and tooth powder. Shirts in white boxes. Hoes and rakes and saws. Everything with its distinctive outline, insufferably real. Waiting with dumb readiness to be used again, to be moved and sorted and employed without knowledge of whose living hand provided the impetus. What belongs to a dead person should become softened and glazed, poised to transubstantiate. And then it should go, and the chambers be swept clean.

She climbs the ladder and, hunching, goes to the spyholes. The spyglass isn't here. He must have taken it with him. But why no note? Why no provision for the care of the yellow cat? She looks out through a hole, then another. By craning her neck, she can see where Noggin and Teddy and Enrique were sitting, but they seem to be gone now.

Her neck aches from the typing she did at the inquest. My poor spine, she thinks as she descends the ladder.

Up on a shelf is the wooden box where Joe kept his cigarettes. She takes it down and opens it. One cigarette only remains, rolled into the crack at the back of the box. She takes it out and smells it. Then she takes up a box of matches, scratches one on the side of the cash register, and lights the cigarette. She has never smoked anything in her life, but she dearly wishes to smell that smell again.

A cough convulses her on the first breath, and the noise of it is startling. She inhales again, lightly. This time she does not cough, though her eyes burn. Once more. She puts the cigarette on the top of the cash register, where its ashes will fall on the floor. At the end of the counter is the folded blanket Joe always rested his head upon. There are some gray and brown hairs there, and a drift of pale cat fuzz. Without much thought she lifts herself up and lies back.

Was this what Joe saw when he closed his eyes? Washes of blue and black, like inky waves pouring across space, withdrawing to reveal a line of tiny figures toiling along a path. A chair like the coroner's witness chair, and in it a man with a beard—Vincent— no, no, it is Walt Whitman, speaking poetry. She smiles, or feels she is smiling, perceiving that she has somehow entered the mind of Joe Peaslee, and she is so relieved, so relieved. Now little cabinets, like those on a ship, begin to click open, and she becomes absorbed in noting their contents even though the contents are sad: a bolt of cloth eaten by moths, with light showing through the holes, a dog shaking its head, Noggin Koerner's hat upside down in the dirt. From one cabinet, letters fall, slicing and toppling end over end, and she reaches to catch them but finds she is too far away. She is ashamed—there are miles of land between her and those cabinets, which she sees now are merely caves with doors hung on them, imperfect doors with stretched leather hinges.

She is concentrating hard, and it seems natural, therefore, that she should find herself walking backward along a railroad track, feeling behind her with her foot for the broad safety of the tie. Soon she will be at home in her infancy, and she will do everything again without loneliness or fear. But between the ties are black bars of space, slots of darkness into which she might slip. What is down there? Careful. Careful.

In the closed store the pink twilight comes through the blinds, and she has a headache. Those cigarette dreams still drag the floor of her mind. But presently they begin to melt away.

She has woken knowing things of which she went to sleep unsure. If he did not kill himself, which she is certain he did not, then somewhere the lost bullet is waiting to be found. He would not have been held captive before his death—who would risk that, it would be ridiculous. So his body must have been secreted, preserved, before being put in Hadley's field. And of course there was only one place that would have sufficed for that purpose. She doesn't know what happened, exactly, or why, exactly. But she does know where, and if she is clever, that one fact will lever loose the rest of the story. Then she will see—well, what she will see.

39

GORDON CECIL doesn't mind standing in for the departed Reverend Endicott at Peaslee's funeral. He doesn't need to prepare; he'll just read from the book and say a few words about Joe—whom he'll miss, a good fellow, though compromised in the mind, as soldiers sometimes are—and Gordon will summon his aplomb so that no one will guess what he knows about the passing of the man lying there, dried out and still.

He surveys himself in his chestnut suit with its gray pinstripes. It is rather new, snug in the shoulders and buttoning nicely across that avoirdupois that gives a man the look of success. But he must prepare his type frames for inking, and so over the suit he puts on a large white apron. As he ties it around his waist, he notices that white flatters him now that he's gotten a little silvery on the sides. He might look well in a clerical collar. How easy it would be, here in the desert, to go to another place, another town, a hundred, two hundred miles away, and take up a new life. Who would question him? He could make up testimonials on his handpress, and certainly he is used to composition under the pressure of time, so sermons would present no problem. A newspaperman gets less respect than he used to, especially out here where half the folk don't read very well, and what is the point of blackening his hands every day and ruining his eyesight and making that whistling cold ride up to Peterson to carry back the boilerplate every week? Why shouldn't he be paid more attention? And why shouldn't a widow or two nestle up to him for comfort?

But the press, the press itself. That big, odorous presence, his comrade, his busy ox. It cost him a good deal of money to bring the press to Century and assemble it in the room he had built for it. What will he do with it now? Perhaps he may induce someone to buy it, to take over the whole operation. If there is no local interest, he will run an advertisement in the eastern papers: *For the adventurous man of letters and talents, an opportunity.* Someone always wants a change, a new field of play. And though the century has turned, there are plenty of those who haven't noticed it and still imagine that something is to be won out here merely for the claiming, or by application of earnest ideals. Then Gordon will be free to roam, a mysterious visitor who needs never carry paper and pencil—sleek, sleek will be his pockets, and his entire figure will improve.

Yes, he must leave Century. If only because he knows something he would prefer not to. In fact, it could be construed that he is a participant in recent unpleasant events, rather than a commentator, and he finds it uncomfortable to have committed himself in this way. Elliot of the Far West Navigation and Railway is in town again, apparently alarmed by the recent instability, though he has not made his final report and may yet be ripe for the final persuasion. So the cattle party may yet prevail, of course, and the whole threat of exposure fade away. But Gordon is nothing if not prudent. He will shed his possessions and depart for other pastures.

After the funeral he goes to Odie Underwood's, and when he returns to the printing office the better for several whiskeys, he finds Esther Chambers putting the tray of set type into the press. "Violet came by with the verdict," she says. "I finished the notice for you." Gordon is extremely satisfied. He runs the papers and stacks them and distributes them around town. Then he saddles his horse and puts a bundle of papers behind his saddle and goes up by twilight to Peterson, where he will scoop his competitors by distributing the *Intelligence* in the saloon and hotel.

So this is how the people of Century come to read in their newspaper not the inquest account they anticipated, but a letter penned by a ghost.

My neighbors, I never took my own life. It was you who took me, bound me, shot me, pronounced over me, and at last buried me. You, my friends, my fellows, my comrades and patrons. The coroner's jury said suicide. This was convenient for you. Perhaps there was insufficient evidence to attach blame to other parties, but it is as sorrowful a failure to malign the innocent dead as to arraign the innocent living. I who have been buried, however, my mouth is unstopped. Since no one has the courage to speak for me, I speak.

For why should a man who means to kill himself leave no note, why a storekeeper no instructions for the disposition of his property? If he longs to die, why shoot first in the shoulder? Why should such a wound never bleed at all? If he died where he was found, why should the papers in his pocket be unsullied by blood, damp, heat, or dew, why the body undisturbed by animals, why a man of over six feet and dressed in military blue and brass lie in an open meadow for days, undiscovered?

Mysteries of nature or climate, or my madness, or the will of God—any might bear the attribution. There is plenty of sand about, affording ample opportunity to stop the eyes and ears, if one is so inclined.

Others might consider a different story. A neighbor walking his usual path in the evening, taken and hidden and shot in the mouth, the bullet passing into whatever lay below. His own gun retrieved later, and the second shot fired from it to decorate the corpse for the murderer's convenience. Who would kill and then desecrate in this way? Only the most ruthless, whose own skin is at stake.

Therefore there will be no confession from the guilty. What then can prove the truth? The first bullet, which came from the murderer's gun. This bullet exists. Who will find it first?

40

CAREY STOOP reads the mysterious article while walking out to his kitchen garden. "Well, I'll be a—" he says aloud. "Damn it, Cecil. Damn it."

Pick reads it while drinking coffee at Two Forks. He drinks steadily, reading with one eye over the edge of the cup.

Phelia Jacob is putting up her buggy at the livery stable, and she leans in to read over Ida Schmidt's shoulder. Ida takes off her pince-nez and gazes out the door. Phelia says, "Well, what will they do when they see this?"

"But who was making this?" asks Ida. "Not Mr. Cecil. And some of it is true, maybe? Or all of it true?"

Phelia shakes her head. "The inquest is over, and he is buried. Let anyone write what he will."

All afternoon—it is Saturday—Jane Fremont reads compositions in the schoolroom. She doesn't see the letter in the newspaper. If she did see it, she would be frightened.

Within the hour Carey Stoop rides up to the kitchen door of Two Forks, gets down, and knocks. Pick is cooking a pancake. He nods for Carey to come in. "Put up your mare out back."

"She'll stand." He sits down. "Pick, I haven't been sleeping."

"You didn't do it. I didn't either."

"I sat on that jury, and I didn't say a thing. I felt I couldn't. The others made the decision and I just said it was all right by me. But I still can't sleep. I wake up and I find I'm— We put him in harm's way."

"We were goaded to it."

"By that old man?"

Pick traps Carey's wrist against the table. "I never killed anyone. Don't you forget that."

Carey looks down. "Let go my hand. Let it go."

Pick releases him.

"Who is Koerner, anyway? He works for you. You pay him."

"I'm not his father. I don't tell him what to do."

"I guess you don't."

"Carey, you've known me a long time. I'd never kill a man. Those days are behind us."

"To me it looks more like they're ahead. We barely get it together out here and then it starts coming apart."

"Well, what are you going to do about it?"

Stoop takes a letter out of his vest and tosses it on the table. "This is from that fellow I know in Crook County. They've had trouble there, too. He's getting a stockmen's meeting together."

"Stockmen's meeting?"

"He's getting everybody together. Cattle, sheep, homesteaders."

"Carey, you were born here. You want to sit down with those lamblickers and give this land away?"

Carey slaps the table. "We get out of blood, and now we're right the hell back into it. I didn't sign up for this. I want the law. I want it on my side, not on my back. Maybe what's done is done, but we can't let this go on."

"It won't go on. It'll die out. I don't get all this shift and bend in you, Carey. Let's hold fast. When they see they can't move us, they'll go somewhere else."

"And when that's used up, they'll come back."

Pick pushes back from the table, clasps his hands between his spread knees, and looks at them, then at Carey. "Is this because you want to be a good boy and cozy up to Teacher?"

Carey shrugs. "Look to your own girl, is my advice."

"What do you mean?"

"You know, don't you, that she's Joe Peaslee? She's the ghost-writer."

"She's just a kid."

"Not anymore, I guess."

"What makes you think it's her?"

"Cecil says."

"Is that all?"

"I think he knows."

Pick says quickly, "Who else knows? Has he told anybody?" He thinks of Koerner. Noggin hasn't ever said so, but he doesn't care for Esther. Jealous, somehow.

"I don't know why he would. He doesn't want anybody to know he was outwitted by a girl. Listen. There's profit in sheep, Pickett."

Pick stands up. "Yeah, well, there's profit in whores, but you don't see me building a cathouse."

"All I'm saying is, there's going to be a meeting."

"Fine."

"Everybody's getting together."

"I guess that'll be everybody except me."

"All right, then."

"All right."

41

KOERNER IS DUE TO LEAVE with the Pickett drive to Winnemucca directly after the auction of Peaslee's stuff. By way of preparing for the drive, he goes to town and buys two ready-made shirts and three black neckerchiefs from Odie Underwood, who has developed a sideline since Joe Peaslee's store has been closed. In the saloon Koerner reads the mysterious letter. He puts his purchases under his arm and goes down the street to have a look at Gordon Cecil.

When Cecil sees him standing in the doorway, he takes a few steps away and then goes behind the press and begins running his hands over it in a preoccupied way. Koerner steps to the side so he can see the man.

"What can I do for you, Koerner?"

Koerner blinks.

Cecil lowers his voice. "I'm not sure it's the wisest thing for you to be here. I'm speaking as a friend."

Koerner moves to scratch his chin, and Cecil grips the press in fear. He says, "I didn't write it. You know that. For God's sake, why would I?"

Koerner turns his head and looks behind him. The street is empty.

"I've forgotten that night, is what I want to say," Cecil adds. "I can't remember a thing about it. I was drinking. And my family's amnesiac, you know. Any shock will set us right off our memory." He places his hand on the press and says, "Who's going to get that bullet?"

Koerner doesn't move.

"I hope you're not looking at me. I have no memory of that night. I don't think I could even find the damn thing. I'm not saying a word, Koerner, but damn me if I get in any deeper. Koerner. I don't mind getting sheep out, and Lord knows I want the train. But damn me for an imbecile if I get in any deeper."

When Koerner sees that Cecil means to hide behind the press and talk about reasons for things, and plans, he looks around the room. He's never been in the printing office. He picks up a type stick and hefts it a couple of times. It is made of lead.

"Pickett's girl."

Koerner looks up.

Between the metal uprights of the press carriage, Cecil says, "Pickett's girl wrote it. I told her what I thought of her. She gained my trust and then she trespassed. But what more can I do? What law will help me? We can't have an investigation."

Koerner sucks a tooth as he thinks about this. He puts down the type stick, picks up his shirts, and leaves the shop, whistling.

Gordon Cecil sits right down on the floor of his shop and tilts his head back against the wall. He puts his hand inside his vest and feels his heart, then takes out his watch and consults it. The watch is heavy and solid, and the gold warms in his hand, and the whole thing ticks. He presses it against his forehead.

Koerner rides back to Two Forks and joins a group of hands who have their horses out for shoeing prior to the drive. Teddy is counting a stack of shoes. "Ten men, five horses. Enrique, how many horses you got? Five? Five horses each. Four feet each. Kits, cats, sacks, and wives. How many going to Winnemucca?"

"I got four horses," says Koerner. "I ought to get one more to round out my string."

"Elijah Jacob's looking to sell his paint mare."

"I don't want that mare. Her trot's like a punch in the butt." Koerner takes his buckskin saddle horse around the side of the corral and commences to pare his hooves and to shoe him. This buckskin is a biter. As Koerner pulls the forefoot between his legs and fits the shoe to it, the horse takes hold of his sleeve and worries it. Koerner jerks his elbow back and catches the animal in the lip. It puts back its ears and bobs its head. "That's right," Koerner says. "Do your damnedest." He strikes ten neat blows, one for each nail and one to bend the nail back where it comes out the top of the hoof. He moves on to the hind foot, rasps off the nailheads, and pries off the old shoe.

When he finishes with the buckskin, he turns it loose in the corral, puts away his tools, tacks up his bay gelding, and mounts.

"Where you going?" asks Teddy. "You're not leaving me your whole string to shoe, are you?"

"I'll shoe 'em tomorrow. I'm going to get something I left."

42

WHEN PICK GETS TO HALF-A-MIND, he sees that it is almost dry, three small ponds connected by ridged white mud and colonies of clicking reeds. But the sky is gray, and the thick surface of the water is ruffled by wind. Rain will be coming back one of these days.

Esther is not at her cabin. He goes on, and passes the place where the sheep are buried. The earth has revealed some of the carcasses, testifying to the quick and shallow interments. The sheep are mostly bone now, though here and there gray curls cling to a spread-jawed skull, and sleeves of skin bind the shards of legs together.

The terrain is rough, and Pick gets off his horse and leads him among the stones. The swallows are darting out from the bluff and over the desert, confused, flying in irregular patterns. One comes down out of the air, lands near him, and struggles to fly again. It is not a bird, though. It is a bat. The cave's white bats are flying in the daytime, stubborn and lost.

In perplexity, he looks down toward the hummock of the cave and sees two things. A stream of smoke rising from the hidden entrance to the cave, and a man approaching on horseback at speed, kicking up puffs of dust. Before he wholly understands what these things signify, Pick drops Lobo's reins and runs.

Esther gathered a skirtful of the paltry wood the desert affords, relying on the aspen fall at the south end of the lake. With the cave's intermittent cold breath, she feared the fire she built just inside the mouth would not catch, but it leaped up and then burned low and rich. She poked it flat and laid two green sticks across it and put her teakettle on to heat.

As she guessed, the bullet is buried in the ice. When she rubs away the dark, hard blood, she can see its shadow deep in the layers.

She will melt away the ice and prove that Joe Peaslee did not die by his own hand. That is, unless someone comes to stop her. And then she will know what she wants to.

Pick's feet ache in his boots after his rough sprint over rocky soil, and he has difficulty calming his breath. He is aware that Lobo is following slowly along the lakeshore, but his attention is all on Koerner, who has stopped in front of the cave but remains in the saddle.

"What's that smoke?" Koerner says.

"I don't know." What is she doing? He doesn't care, just so long as she keeps doing it and doesn't come out of the cave.

Koerner takes his rifle out of the scabbard by his knee and lays it across the saddle. "There's something in there I want, boss."

"I'll get it. You don't have to worry about it."

"Well, I don't want to go off to Winnemucca and leave a mess."

"I'll clean up the mess."

"But even if it's cleaned up, there's somebody who's got it in her head. She can talk about it. Cecil doesn't like somebody knowing, either."

"Cecil can go screw."

"Well . . . I don't like to know there's somebody got it in her head and can talk. I just don't like that. It bothers me. I never looked through a noose, and I don't aim to."

"You won't. I say so."

Koerner gives his gray-gummed smile. "I kind of feel like seeing to things myself."

A few yards away, Lobo is picking around in the rocks, looking for forage. Pick's rifle is there. He shouldn't have left it. He feels the danger in Koerner—not the excitable kind that killed Peaslee, but a density, a tendency toward self-preservation. Like a boulder poised to roll. Stay down there, Esther. Don't come out.

Koerner sees Pick looking at the rifle. "I got a knife, too," he says. "It won't make a lot of noise."

"A knife?"

Koerner pats his boot. "Want to see?"

No," Pick says. The rejection is involuntary, but it's a misstep.

Koerner smiles again. "Scared?"

Pick doesn't answer right away.

"Boss? You scared of this knife?"

Pick clears his throat. He musters his coldest tone and chips off the words. "Koerner. You're a good hand. You've been a lot of use to me, and you've been loyal to the spread. But I'm telling you to stay on top of the buckskin there and go on about your business. Don't follow the drive, and don't come back."

"You're cutting me out?" Koerner looks bleached. He picks something off the neck of the buckskin.

Pick's voice sounds false in his own ears, but he maintains the brutal diamond edge. "I don't have a lot of room here, after what you did."

"What about my pay?"

Pick is about to open his vest pocket, to pay Koerner any sum to get him to go, but he stops himself and arranges his face in a sneer. As he does it, actual disgust pours through him. He nearly spits. "You want me to pay you? After the trouble you've caused me? That's nerve."

Koerner sucks his tooth. "I gotta get somewhere. Find a new spread."

Now Pick makes a show of taking out a couple of double eagles. He looks at them and chooses the older, dirtier one. "Take it." He flips it up.

Koerner lifts his hand. The coin is in the smoke, but he catches it. He rubs at the raised girlish profile of Liberty on the coin. Every few years, he reflects, he finds himself looking at a dead man, and then people get all excited. He is always surprised when it happens again. "Where should I go?"

Pick thinks, Anywhere but here. But Koerner wants a last direction from the boss.

"Texas," Pick says.

"How you going to keep her quiet?"

"Let me worry about that."

She pours the hot water on the ice and sweeps it off with her hand. The watery blood is rusty pink and soaks the forearm of her dress. Later she will find black rimmings of blood, like successive shorelines, ringing the sleeve. She pours the water and wipes it, pours and wipes. A well is forming in the ice, a smooth pocket cupping a draught of pink. Her fingers find a lump at the bottom of the cup, and the lump becomes the squat, burst shape she seeks. She wiggles it, and it comes free. She holds it up.

"Forty-five caliber," says Pick.

He's standing above her on the rocks, holding his hat in one hand. A sweat comes out on her back. She drops her face into her fists. The bullet slug is bulky in her fingers. "Pick. I didn't think it was you. How could you? Why would you ever do it?"

Pick descends. He seems very tired. "Listen. I'll tell you. It wasn't me."

"But you're here."

"There are others that could have been here."

"Oh, no." Joe, surrounded.

"You were right, you know. That bullet didn't come from his gun."

"What happened?"

He passes his palm over his handsome face, touching his mouth as people do when they mean to lie. Then he crouches, and his hands hang limp off his knees.

"It was to be a warning," he says. "Just a warning. After that talk he made in church, those who'd bought the bullets that week started saying he had to be warned. Cecil tried to tell him to keep quiet. Somebody sent him a bit of rope and a box of matches. Did he tell you that? But Peaslee kept talking. I don't know if you knew he was drinking, too. He'd go into Odie Underwood's and roll out that philosophy and always make some mention of bullets. Those sheep that died added up to a big crime, and nobody wanted to hang for a bunch of mutton. I wasn't there that night, but I knew what they were going to do. I agreed with them that the sheep had to go.

"But Peaslee was too crazy to take the hints. He just kept on, kept on. And so we thought—yes, I thought, too—we'll just take him aside one day when he's out botanizing and scare him, and maybe that'll get through. Cecil was for doing nothing, saying he was loco and nobody'd believe him now anyway, but none of the rest of us wanted to depend on that. He had that friend up in Peterson, the district attorney, and Violet told me he'd written to him. She kept that letter back. But that fellow knew Peaslee, and he'd believe him, and that's all it would have taken to put the lot of us in the dock. Well, taking somebody aside for a warning is hard. We left it to Koerner and Osterhaus, and they were rough. They blindfolded him and brought him here. We all got here as soon as it was dark that night, and we had Clark, a new hire from Stoop's outfit, to tell Joe what we wanted from him—somebody whose voice Joe wouldn't know, was the idea—and this young Clark was going to give him the message and we were going to take him back to his place and let him go. God damn it. Peaslee was raving by then. And Clark steps up to give the message—he's supposed to say that the store building could burn and everybody would blame a spark from Peaslee's cigarette—and Peaslee's lying there with the blindfold over his eyes, and I can see his face clear, and there's, you know, his mind comes back to him and he looks . . . hopeful. And he says . . . he says . . . ." He breaks off and fits the heel of his hand between his eyes. "He says, 'Ferris? Is that you?'"

She clasps herself with her arms and rocks back and forth. Tears run down and catch the hard bend of Pick's jaw and cling there.

"'Is that you?' he says. I can't do anything, and no one else is moving. Except for Koerner. He takes out his gun and puts it in Peaslee's mouth. We could hear his teeth click on the metal. It was a harsh way to scare a fellow. I pointed at Clark. This was all done in silence, you know, for fear we could be called out later. And when Clark's opening his mouth to speak, there's a . . . a sound, as if he's shouted, a huge shout, and he stumbles back, and then I see Peaslee's jaw put to one side. Koerner rubs his gun on his leg. He's sort of smiling, I guess, and he says, 'No more talking.' And Carey Stoop says, 'You stupid fucker, why'd you do that?' and he keeps saying it, 'Why'd you do that?' Vincent was crying. We saw that we should untie his hands and that we'd have to get his gun from the store and make out he'd done it himself. So Cecil got his keys, and later Koerner went in and got the gun. And later Jacob shot the body and Carey and Osterhaus put it in Hadley's field. Before we left the cave, Vincent said, 'He's dead, ain't he? We're not leaving him hurt?' So I went back and looked at him. *Ferris, is that you?* I was thinking. But he was long gone. When I got outside, Carey had gone after Koerner. We stood around and watched. I never saw anything like Koerner just then. He let Carey beat him, and he just kept smiling and his teeth were all outlined in blood. I never saw anything like that son of a bitch."

43

WHEN ESTHER STOOD in front of the type flat the evening of Joe's funeral—Gordon Cecil away and celebratory in the saloon—gathering and setting the letters, she felt deliberate and exhilarated. Her mind was alive. The evidence she had acquired was fresh, and her ire and grief and passion were fresh. Her words flowed to her from somewhere, delicious and unstinting; her eyes and her hands, seizing and fitting the type into the sticks, were so obedient they seemed not to be mere dumb tools, but to have their own knowledge. She was not concerned that Cecil would return. She was speaking with her hands, and the inevitability of her speech was such that the world would understand and would dare not produce a Cecil or any other impediment.

But when Pick tells her of the murder of Joe Peaslee, in greed, in fear, impulse, she is crippled. Her hand is cramped around the lead evidence of treachery, so stiff she might have to break her bones to open it.

Together they clamber out of the cave. The desert is still gray with mist. There is no sign of Noggin Koerner. Pick carries the kettle and stamps out the fire. He pours the remaining water over the coals. Esther sits down on a rock, and Pick crouches beside her.

"I never would have hurt him," he says. "Do you know that? He was always good to me. There aren't that many of the old men left. Vincent won't talk to me now, after what happened."

"He's been sick."

"Won't talk to me. I told him I never meant to harm Joe. He doesn't listen. There's nobody anymore to show me what to do."

"But you knew what kind of person Noggin Koerner is. Or you ought to have known, if you were the boss. You shouldn't have let him near."

"I guess I shouldn't. But something had to be done. We needed the railroad, and for that we needed the sheep out. This range was meant for cattle, they grow well here, and we saw that and we came here and made it a place for raising them. And it hasn't been easy, but we've learned how to do it. And when we're about to get a little help, to get our burdens eased by the railroad, then the sheep come in and ruin our range? I wouldn't have been much of a man if I just gave it up like that."

"Did you kill Ben's sheep?"

"No. I was supposed to go, but when I got to the lake, I thought better of it and went home. I thought if I didn't show, they'd all turn back. But Koerner wanted to thrash the Cruff kid, and so he went ahead. I didn't mean that anyone should die, least of all Joe Peaslee. But I have been in a fight where everything runs against me, the weather, the government, that Duncan son of a bitch." He reaches out and grasps a handful of dirt and lets it spill out of his fist. "I kept up my end of the bargain, and still nothing's right. That's how I know someone welshed."

"But you have everything. You have money and guns, and Gordon Cecil prints what you like in the newspaper, and Noggin Koerner runs around without a brain in his head, and there's nobody to tell you anything or stop you. But you still think you all are injured parties. That's what makes this fight so stupid. Everyone thinks he's an underdog and the other fellow's powerful and wicked and a cheater. The worst person in the world is the one who feels wronged and righteous."

"Well. I don't know about how people feel, only what they do. And that's what I act on. Anyway, it doesn't matter anymore. After the inquest Elliot let us know that the FWNR thinks Century too unstable. It's going to put the line way over the other side of the bluffs, through Failing. That's the end, you know. It's over in Century." He rises from his crouch.

"How can you—that train is nothing, that stupid, stupid train. It was already over, Pick. It was over when you—when Joe—"

She is standing now, too, swinging away and back again in rage. For all his decency, he has been unable to avoid malefaction. His strength and diligence have made him hard, ringing, and hollow. A supple self, a humble and grassy and windproof self is required in these times, and he doesn't have it. He doesn't even know there is such a way to be—he would see it as a deficiency, a baseness from which silver is worn away.

"I know it's not right. We should have turned Koerner in. We should have explained. But after Joe was dead, we all felt so bad. There didn't seem to be anything to gain by confessing."

"You left him here, lying alone in the cold. Until the time came to drag him up and throw him in a field and call him a suicide."

"Esther," he says, "we can leave here. We can go to Idaho. It's not shut down yet, it's still free."

She presses the fist that holds the bullet against her forehead. "But won't you do the same thing there?"

"It wasn't my fault." He continues, gravely, as if he understands her anger but believes that if she is sensible, she will see the point. "Idaho, Esther. Unless you'd rather marry into mutton."

She looks at him in astonishment.

"Yes, I know all about it. I'm not blind, and even if I were, other people aren't. I'll admit I was angry, but I know I'm not perfect myself. Jane doesn't think much of me putting you out here on the claim and then falling for you. *Esther is not twenty-one*, she said, *and you mustn't think she is.* She set me back on my heels a little, and I'm still setting there. But remember. You have to choose sometime. If you're going to love someone, you've got to shoulder his cause. It's one party or the other." He stands up, knees crackling. "I don't know what you plan to do with that bullet. But I'm asking you to be a woman to me. Forgive me."

Forgive him. And then what?

As she thinks, there is a sound, an arid chime. They both look to the north. It comes again and grows rounder, *dan-din-dang, dan-din-dang.* The school bell?

"Fire," says Pick. "Something's burning."

44

ESTHER PUTS THE BULLET INTO HER SHOE TOP, under the stocking. In the same moment Pick has mounted Lobo and is offering her his hand, and in the next moment she is lifted up. She hasn't sat here—holding on to Pick's waist and the edge of the saddle—for months, and it's like visiting a house one knew as a child, everything smaller, everything slightly the wrong color, not how one remembered. She holds tight as they round the lake past the yellow alfalfa and canter out toward the Century road. As they turn toward town, they see the fire wagons coming, three of them, two pump-boilers and a water tank. There aren't many places out this way that might burn, Esther thinks. Is it Jane's? Let it not be Jane's, over there in the dry grass against the small, hot juniper hills.

The wagons rattle and thunder past them, and Lobo dances sideways. On the second wagon, Odell Underwood is standing, waving his hat at Pick and pointing down the road toward Two Forks.

The cattle gathered for the drive have escaped their corrals. They circle and swirl around the Two Forks buildings, and from a distance the house looks like it's floating on brown floodwater. "What the hell is this?" says Pick. "What are all those cows doing in the yard? Where the hell are the buckaroos?" He dismounts and gives the reins to Esther, who moves forward into the saddle. The cows are lowing. Distress, inquiry, dumb energy, the baritone spectrum in colors, simultaneous and ridiculous. They are everywhere, loose and confused. The men on the fire wagons have to lash at the cattle to clear a path toward the house. A steer stands on the veranda.

Yes, the first-floor windows, though still closed, are emitting veils of smoke, and there is a sick, improper light behind them. The fire wagons, manned by Alfred Schmidt and other citizens, are hauled into position and the boilers lighted and stoked with coal. A fire on a ranch this far from town is usually a disaster. But the wagons are here already. Esther thinks, Surely, surely, they will save it. Despite the flames, the house looks like itself, cool and frosted, all white paint and glass and iron, a bridal cake at a prison wedding.

But inside the house something explodes. Esther feels split by the hard, rude sound. Lobo skitters sideways, sawing his head up and down against the bit, and Esther must ride him in a circle to steady him. His sides bellow in, out, and the corners of his mouth are sore and foaming.

The sound has also disturbed the cattle. A stuttering, a shiver runs through them, and some that are closest to the open desert peel away from the main herd at a trot. Others follow, and their agitation increases, communicates itself, and then all of them are pouring southward, cleaving around the house at a heavy, dangerous canter, the horns of young steers clacking and tangling. They pound the dry earth with their hooves, they bay operatically, they make an escape into country so barren it might as well be unmapped. Goodbye, goodbye. The steer on the veranda, finding himself alone, braves the steps, heaving breath out through his shining wet nostrils. Goodbye, goodbye.

In another window, rags of orange run up the balustrade of the staircase like pennants being jerked up a pole. The fire subsides, wavers, and pulls itself upward again, and there is a flash and a soft roaring, as though ghosts of fire are coursing in victory into the upper story. A tattoo of hard pops as the doors of unseen rooms are breached. Esther imagines the fire rifling down the

hallway, bursting into closets, curling the wallpaper, and blister-
ing the molding. She thinks suddenly of her own little place.
Could the fire travel there? Could a fatal cinder be falling on her
roof at this moment? No—the wind is from the north, and all the
debris will blow south into the unbuilt desert. Still, she must steel
herself against the urge to wrench Lobo around and ride home.

In front of the house, Michael Cruff stands, backed by a couple
of brothers and other sheepmen. Pick has gone to him, his face
as still as death but for his mouth. He asks Michael a question.
Michael shrugs.

"God damn it," Pick says, or she thinks he says, for the fire is
louder now and he is some yards away. "God damn it."

Around her, people and horses are gathering. Folks have heard
the bell and followed the wagons out. Esther slides off Lobo and
loops the reins over the saddle horn. She runs to Pick. Michael is
saying, "I know you'll have a sight of trouble getting them back.
But we didn't shoot one of them, and in fairness we could've. We
could've kicked the Jesus out of somebody you love and killed
your animals and put all of you in the dock."

"You couldn't put anybody anywhere." Pick is terse and dis-
missive, but he is afraid. Esther can tell. He isn't sure what to do.

"I could, Pickett. I know more than you think about what
happened to Joe Peaslee."

Pick looks at Esther, and she shakes her head. She hasn't told
anyone; she only just found out herself. How could Michael Cruff
know? Pick looks around at the gathered men. "Where is Stoop?
Where is he?" he demands.

Michael doesn't change his expression, but Esther knows Pick's
guess is right. It is Carey who, in remorse, has betrayed him.

Pick says, "Word of this will get back to the railroad, you
know. I guess you Cruffs don't mind breaking up a town. What're
you going to do, tell the law?" There is a note Esther doesn't recognize in his voice: Hurt? Self-pity?

In the light's fluctuation, Michael's face lights up pink and
orange, darkens, lights, darkens. His voice lifts over the flames.

"Not yet. I don't want to sit around for a year while lawyers talk, waiting for justice that might not come. I want you to own right now that you've been a villain and pay right now for villainy. Now and in front of your neighbors. If you won't, then I *will* tell the law, and I'll go as high as I have to. It's not just you who'll go to prison, you know. Vincent and Carey will, too. You've got a choice, and you have to make it now. The house goes, or the truth about Peaslee comes out."

The boilers are clanking now, men are advancing with the hoses, and others have hatchets to break open the walls and ease the mounting pressure inside. But Pick turns in rage and calls out a few names. He stops them all with a flat hand, like a traffic policeman. They pause, tense with vexation. Teddy the foreman jogs over to Pick. "What's the species of delay, here, son? You better make a move."

"No," Pick says. "I'm making a deal. I've made one. Let it burn."

Let it burn? All around her people repeat his words. "He says let it all burn." "I'll be goddamned." "He's letting the house burn."

It is dusk now. When did the sun go down? Esther has been transfixed by that other sun, the brutal radiance gathering itself inside the thin siding of the house. Its whiteness is grayed now with night and smoke; the windows, packed with fire, are all one can see.

The Two Forks buckaroos are trying to come forward, but they are held back by a man with a gun. It is another of Ben's brothers, she guesses. Do any of the others know what she and Ben have been to each other? Does Michael, seeing her at Pick's side, think she has betrayed his brother, chosen his enemy? She wants to go to him. *Don't think it. I'm still*— But is she? What is she? She sees that some of the Two Forks buckaroos are barefoot and a couple have dabs of shaving soap unwiped from their faces. They stand with folded arms or hands in pockets, heavy and simple, like Greek letters signifying rage. This is their home. Some of the spectators from town are weeping. Let it burn.

"That glass is like to blow," someone near Esther says. "Better all get back."

The fire creates its own wind, and the wind rises and roars, bullying. Esther's skirts are sucked toward the flame, and she steps backward. Something strikes her temple lightly, but burns—she can smell her acrid hair. She brushes the thing away in panic, and her hand comes away streaked with soot. She turns her back and trots some distance away, to where Lobo is being held now by a boy from town. She rests her face for a moment on the horse's shoulder, but he is not hers. She longs for Duniway. I want my horse, she thinks, and then, I am a girl who wants her horse. I am different from what I was.

Now the house is respiring. The whole façade heaves. The fire has found some inside weakness, some tender joinery, and has worked at it. There is a moment when the panels of the siding seem to stand away from the frame of the house and pause in the air, like great sheets of suspended paper, and then they begin to turn, to topple and descend, this way, that way, and everyone draws back even farther and the standing horses jostle in their traces. For a moment, as the fire roars and the siding falls, one can see a hard sketch of the structure, floors and walls and staircases in cross section. Pleasant place, luxurious place, where one could move from room to comfortable room and be sheltered.

Then the onrush of air intoxicates the fire, and it bounds up and strikes without strategy, careless, drunk and pillaging, a legion without an officer. Around them, the desert is flat, quiet, and dim, paused in time. But Two Forks is chaos and cannot be saved.

At the fire wagons, one of the hoses, long unused and now pumped full of pressured water, bursts a hole, and water sprays up and falls downward, yards short of the fire itself. With all that light burning at their faces, the spectators are themselves at once speckled, splattered by water. Esther's arm and back are wet. She hears Marguerite again: *Where is the fountain?*

Vincent has come up. He has a bag of things he has saved. Esther can see the frame of one of the tintypes of Pick's parents. He puts his hand on Pick's shoulder and agitates him a little, back and forth. They stand all together, Pick and Esther and Vincent and Michael Cruff. All the faces are darkened with char, and it's possible that the water on some faces mixes with tears as well as sweat, for Pick's mouth pulls down hard, and when Michael speaks again, there is a crackle in his voice. He says, "Maybe if you commence ranching again, you'll think some about how you go about it. You broke up your own town, Pickett. The Cruffs are just the rock you broke it on."

When it has all fallen, a mess of crossed black beams and horrible coals, Esther makes a wide circle around to the back of the house, away from the spectators. Nearby, the remaining fire wagon is drenching the roofs of the bunkhouse and barns. The floor of the kitchen where she worked with Vincent is buckled, a glowing, irregular pavement. The heat is still fierce, but it pulses, and she can get fairly close. She takes the bullet from her shoe and the ring from her pocket. It's funny that the bullet just fits inside the ring, making a strange little machine, a neat contraption of metal with no apparent use. She fingers them for a moment with her sooty hands. She takes a last look at the ring, its bright little pearl, its pond and willow tree. Then, covering her face with one hand, she takes a few steps toward the house and casts ring and bullet into the wavering, blinding coals.

Pick has seen her gesture. He comes out of the dark as a silhouette against the golden ruin. His face is sooty and stippled with welts where he has been burned by cinders. "I wish you wanted that ring," he says.

"I know." She feels teary for the first time this whole awful day. "I wish I *could* want it."

"Well, Esther. I guess it's Idaho for me. I'll have to start with something little."

"You won't build this one again?"

"Naw. That house was for some other fellow than the one I

turned out to be." He kicks a tuft of grass, blackened with ash. "You gave up the bullet, too."

"I couldn't—denounce you. Even for Joe."

"You could have kept it, in case I ever go wrong again. In-surance."

"Then you'd be a hostage. People have to do right on their own. Nobody can make them."

"I hope I can do it," he says. "I used to look across the desert at your light. I thought, There is someone who can understand. But I should have known even you couldn't forgive what hap-pened. I wouldn't want you to."

She tries to show him that she is sorry, that she knows his losses are monstrous. "Thank you for asking me to be with you." She extends her charcoaled hand.

He takes it, squeezes it, and drops it again. He gives a short, clouded laugh. "Aw, well, Blackbird. You're welcome."

45

FINALLY IT RAINS, a deep, dense rain cutting sluices in the mud. While Half-a-Mind's three murky ponds swell and leak and form one lake again, Esther keeps to her cabin, writing. No longer to her mother, though. These letters are to the living. She asks Mr. Fleming if he will hold off the renewal of the warehouse contract for a month, as she is at present unsure of her plans. She writes to school friends at home, long neglected. When she takes her letters to town, finally, she sits on the edge of the raised boardwalk and waits for the mail carriers. With some self-consciousness they put her letters into their canvas bags, but they don't have any for her. She sent Ben the telegram ten days ago, and nothing has come. When she seemed not to write, to have gone silent, he must have washed his hands of her. It's hard to believe that his flushed, seeking face could have become closed and cold. But she has seen what people can be like. Where shall she go then? Chicago?

The sky lifts and clears. Half-a-Mind's mud precipitates, and the lake is a glamorous polar blue. When Esther goes to town for the auction, she finds that the schoolhouse will not hold the crowd that has bent itself on Joe Peaslee's goods, and the event has been moved to the church. Horses are tied thick at the rails, and the yard is choked with buggies and wagons, right up to the stone border of the graveyard. Vincent says, "I never saw a turnout like this, not even for Fourth of July." On the steps of the church and in its shade families sit on tablecloths and picnic. Homesteaders, mostly done with harvest, recount the taking to their neighbors in bushels and pounds. It is a bit thin this year, but they are happy to have anything. They mourn again what was lost to that mean frost. Cattlemen are freshly shaved. Their steers are in the hands of the drive bosses now, and they can do nothing but hope for safe trails and high prices at the terminus. Relief and accomplishment make men's voices boisterous and women more relaxed than usual— they kneel and even recline on the picnic blankets, somnolent and smiling. After the rain, autumn skies have appeared—haze high in the blue is gathering into feathery horsetails.

"Going to bid?" Vincent asks her as he uncinches Lester's saddle. It seems too heavy for him. He has trimmed his beard, but he is still stooped.

"I don't think so. I only have two dollars with me."

"Two dollars! Let me show you something." He lifts out the old buckskin bag from his pocket, in which he kept his gold. "Look in there."

She opens the bag. Instead of the irregular chunks and grains of ore, the bag holds a mess of coins. "My goodness."

"I took it up to Peterson and had it assayed. Twenty-six ounces, and I got close to five hundred dollars for it."

"What will you do with it?"

"Don't know. Maybe I'll build a library and they can name it after me. Did you hear, by the by, that Cecil's shutting down the newspaper? He's leaving Century. Got himself some position in entertainment down Reno way."

"Yes."

"Maybe a certain prank wounded him. His reputation as a newspaperman. So he's getting out of the business."

"I don't think it was only me. He wanted to leave." She pauses to work it out. "I was sorry that I should deceive him so, when he taught me so much."

"Well, I suppose you did right enough. And blame me if that wasn't some verbiage you put down. I liked it on that account alone."

"Vincent, I wonder if I could hire you to build something?"

"What do you need?"

"A traveling box to keep a cat in."

Vincent takes off Lester's bridle and halters him before he answers. "I guess I could do that. But that means you're leaving us, too."

"You don't have to build it if you don't want to."

"I'll do it. But keep your money, or see if there's something in that auction you want to remember Joe by."

"I've already taken the yellow cat."

"Still." He spreads his saddle blanket on the ground, and they sit down. "So Pick told you what happened."

"Yes."

"I'd like to make you my apology."

"You don't need to make it to me."

"Try and stop me. I shouldn't have been there in the first place, and I knew it. I guess I been looking out for Pick and doing for him since his dad died, and I didn't know when to fall back and let him go it alone. I should have told the sheriff, but I didn't do it. And now it's too late to do the right thing. They all worked it out without me."

"It must have been awful."

"Koerner should hang."

"I daresay he never will."

"Good luck anybody finding him. Maybe Pinkerton's could. I used to think it was a good thing, out here, that people could just up and go. Oh, it was different out here than in the East. All different kinds mixing. Some whole family off a farm in Nebraska, some kid who saw an advertisement in a magazine in Boston. Some people had money and bought land or started hotels, and some took claims. People came out to get married and people came out to avoid it. Everybody could just shift. If a gambler's luck was bad, he became a schoolteacher for a while. A fellow you knew as a cheat in San Francisco could rise up to Congress by way of the copper business in Montana . . ."

"Did that happen?"

"I'm just saying it might have. I won't say there weren't lots of fights and schemes, but we all wore the same shoes. Now it's . . . well. Not the same shoes anymore. And there's no place to disappear to, really. You've got to be the same person your whole life, and that means you have to be a big person to start with. Well, ain't it the dickens. We gone and settled up the whole country. A little while ago we were just two handfuls of farmers, five Indians, and a sprinkle of soldiery. Ain't it the dickens."

In the church, Gordon Cecil is talking to the auctioneer, and in a few moments the auctioneer clears his throat and makes an announcement. "I have something new to offer you, ladies and gentlemen. It's not from the Peaslee estate. Mr. Cecil, here, informs me that he is closing up shop in Century and wants to sell his press. He's got an offer on it already, for a hundred and twenty-five dollars. But before he takes it, he wants to give his neighbors a crack. Take it into consideration. Anybody can give upward of one hundred fifty can walk away with the press and its accoutrements and a wagon to carry it. I'll give you a few minutes to think about that."

Esther surveys the crowd. Phelia and Elijah Jacob, Carey Stoop, his mother, his sister and nieces and nephews, Lenore and Patsy Duncan and their parents, Alfred and Ida Schmidt and Gerald and Johann and Louisa, Violet Fowler and May, and behind them Maudie, who seems to be escorted by Odell Underwood's younger brother. Sheep and cattle people and homesteaders from other towns, and a few buckaroos, too old or injured to join the drives. And there on a bench are Delores Green and Fred and the baby. The baby is walking! Esther's amazed smile appeals to him, it seems, for he tick-tocks over to her on stiff legs, his dimpled hands held high and wide for balance. She gives him her finger, and he toddles back to his parents, pulling her with him. Delores looks up. Her dark eyes are shadowed with fatigue, and under them her cheeks are burnished from work outside. "Miss—Esther. I'm pleased to see you. I haven't seen you for some weeks."

"It's been a . . . busy . . . summer, hasn't it?"

"Summer. Year."

They laugh together in rueful understanding. Esther says, "I was happy to have the map Marguerite made. Thank you for sending it."

"Yes. She was proud of that."

"She is the cleverest of children."

"Isn't she?" says Delores. "That has been my only wish, that she should go to school and stay there. I don't know if it was the right one, now. Perhaps I should have kept her with me after all." She brightens with courage. "But soon we will have her back. The auctioneer has agreed to put up our alfalfa among Joe Peaslee's lots. If it sells today, we will be on our way to Klamath tomorrow. Our debt will be paid, and we will have our girl."

Esther begins to offer her best wishes, but Delores has more to say. She begins to speak, stops, and tries again. "I have wanted to know you more. At first I thought you were just—oh, young. Perhaps spoiled. That was my fault. I thought someone of Pick's family could do anything she wanted, could just go wherever she wanted to, on a whim. Then later, when you were so kind to my little girl and I wanted to truly know you, I still couldn't, because I had heard for sure that you were wearing his ring. I couldn't be a friend to someone and conceal from her . . . well, a man's failings. And I thought of course that you wouldn't much want to know someone who had been at Two Forks the way I was. It would have been strange if you did."

Fred screws up his face a little but shows no other discomfort. Delores's past is no mystery to the man who loves her.

Esther finds herself quickened to honesty. She crouches in front of Delores to speak to her. "It didn't matter to me, as it turned out. It doesn't now, I mean."

"No?"

"And it's gone. Two Forks, I mean."

"Yes. That's a shame. Ferris built it in hope of something."

The auctioneer pops his gavel down onto the pulpit and says, "Lot one, my friends! Tea and teacups and linen towels!"

In a few seconds he has two dollars for lot one. Does he hear five? Five it is, how about seven, seven, seven? He's got seven, does he hear nine, he has nine, who has nine for lot one, Mrs. Jacob has nine, who has ten—Odell Underwood goes ten, does Mrs. Jacob have eleven? No? Eleven once, eleven twice, and Odell Underwood gets lot one. See Mrs. Fowler at the table there to pay.

So the hoard is distributed. The Jacobs take most of the tack, including horse blankets, but they have to pay for it, since plenty of others are bidding. Pick might have made a bid on such a lot, but where is he? Is he somewhere in this crowd? There is much milling near the door. Someone buys all the flour except for an opened half a bag, and someone else buys that. Odell Underwood buys the lot of Joe's unlabeled bottles, and Jane Fremont buys a bundled hoe, rake, and saw. The handsome gleaming plow that occupied a front corner of the store near the stove is sold to a boy from Jack-High, and lots of people find this interesting, for what claim does he mean to farm? Isn't he terribly optimistic? Perhaps he has something down on the new train line.

Esther has wished for this sweeping of Joe's things, but now it hurts. People who never knew him take possession of stacks of shirts and overalls, boxes of ribbon, crackers, spices, sacks of onions, pens, razors, pads of paper. Books go in small lots, the books she read sitting by the front window, to be taken out to some ranch house or claim and lost forever. Things she never really noticed in Joe's—a wheelbarrow that had been hung high on the wall of the front room—are purchased and trundled away. She looks down at Delores and is somehow reassured. People may be dispossessed, rejected, buried, but they rise back up, as grass through the earth, as growing children, as accreted wisdom. Joe is not all gone.

"Now, you know it's got a few years on it, but what'll it cost you new, I ask you? Who's getting this bargain?"

It is the Liberty. Esther has two dollars in her skirt pocket. What if no one wanted it, and she could buy it for two dollars? But she doesn't move. Dr. Bloucher from Peterson buys the Liberty for fourteen dollars.

"Do you think he is composing his memoirs?" says Jane, who has appeared at Esther's other side.

"Yes. Chapter One: How I Became a Liar."

The day after the fire—a week ago now—Esther hadn't wanted to be alone, and she walked over to Jane's claim. Jane was hauling water for her turnips and beets. "Let's go in," she said. "It's hot." She gave Esther a towel dipped in water to wipe her dusty face, then listened as Esther recounted all that had taken place. When she told of Pick's confession, to her surprise, Jane was nodding. "Carey was here," Jane said. "He told me the same story. After he read the letter in the *Intelligence* and after the fire, he couldn't stand not to tell me. He is broken about it. As he should be. I could see he was troubled before now, but I didn't understand why."

"Can you ever—do you think he is a bad man? Have your feelings for him changed?"

Jane had unpinned her hair, and it lay in russet hanks on her shoulder. She picked up a comb and pulled it through several times before answering. "He is too passionate—in that weakness he has gone nearly to the devil. But he has left that path. He has begun a new way, one of self-governing, and he has told Pick what he is doing. Maybe I shouldn't be, but I'm soft toward his errors. He is certainly soft toward mine."

"Is it the same? A mistake in your past, surely, but—"

"Well, listen. He knew I was cold, and he wondered why. Then he grew a little older and understood that I was ashamed, and then, older still, that I was ashamed because I was terribly proud. And *that* he thinks is funny." Her smile is shy, self-mocking, and abruptly radiant. "We are two broken creatures that together can make one that works. I don't know why I'm sure of it, but I am." She repins her hair swiftly and looks like the old, austere Jane again.

"I *am* glad."

"I see you, too, have at last made a choice." She pointed to Esther's neck, where the necklace no longer hung.

"Yes. Whether there is anything further between Ben and me, I couldn't keep it anymore."

Now the bulky items and large lots have all been purchased, and the auctioneer stops a moment to confer with Fred Green. He raps his gavel and calls out that the Greens' sixty bales of sun-cured alfalfa are on the block, and the starting price is—

Whether people feel snug with their own harvests or came unprepared to buy or transport hay, Esther cannot tell. But despite the beseeching of the auctioneer, there are no bids at the starting price. The alfalfa is taken off the block. Delores leans her cheek on the baby's head. Marguerite will have to wait.

It is a bitter disappointment. Esther's throat trembles. When Delores looks up at her, she is shy, feeling she has no standing to mourn, but Delores takes her hand, and for a moment they knit their fingers together. Marguerite is Pick's child, whether or not he claims her, which makes her Esther's cousin, her distant but true little cousin. And the baby is Marguerite's brother, and is Esther's cousin, too, and so Fred is Esther's cousin, and Delores's mother is, and the Paiute grandmother and the uncle with one foot, and all of the other Paiute. And who knew who their cousins were—who are also Esther's as well? Are they cousins, back in time, with the Filipinos now holed up in their mountains? Who've made children with the Spaniards who fled them? And the Moors who had children with the Spaniards and were driven away? The world is a net of cousins. The wolf is cousin to the lamb.

"Now's the time for who wants the press. It's a Rutger and

Lane stop-cylinder rotary, nine years old and as good as new. Mr. Cecil's throwing into the bargain the big old spring wagon that'll haul the press. It's heavy, but it's more portable than your room-size presses and more efficient than your handpresses. It can throw off—what is it, Cecil?—seven hundred sheets an hour, depending on the durability of your shoulder turning the wheel. Then we have type stick and type, paper and inks and plates, all included."

A peculiar freshening comes over Esther, a lurch, a casting open of doors. I could do that, she thinks. Make a newspaper. She knows she could. And this thought, though new to her, is apparently not new to someone else, for Vincent is standing beside her. He holds back his beard and shows her the sack of coins and says, "Listen. I got an idea. You and I are going to do something for Joe." Then he lifts his hand to the auctioneer.

46

ESTHER LOOKS AT THE BILL OF SALE, turns it over, and even smells it. She owns the press. She can write what she thinks is true. She can print it and sell it. People will learn what they need to know.

It is late afternoon now. The auctioneer is hoarsening, but his demeanor has become more and more playful and bright as the items to be sold have become smaller, more individual, strange and rare. Some people are packing their things to leave, the Greens among them. The baby is asleep on Fred's shoulder.

The auctioneer is holding something in his fingers and twirling it, as a music-hall performer might twirl a cane. "A dollar. A dollar only. Come on now," he says. "Doesn't anyone want to view the heavens? Must I go down into nickels and dimes on this remarkable device?"

It is Joe's spyglass. Esther thinks of the two dollars in her pocket. Oh, Joe, who looked out and felt his back twinge and loved and feared everything!

"Wait a minute, there."

Esther turns at the sound of this voice. Pick—for it is he—has come through the door backward and is awkwardly calling over his shoulder, which makes it hard to hear him. But most of the people present give an exclamation and begin talking. In a moment the reason becomes clear to Esther. He is lifting Marguerite Green through the doorway, over all the men who are seated on the floor, and instead of putting her down, he keeps all seven chunky years of her in his arms. Their faces, close together, are father and child.

Delores stands up, and Fred, shifting the baby, does, too.

"He paid them," says Fred. "He's brought her home. Don't say a word, Delores. We can pay him back in hay."

Delores puts her hands to her face, then drops them and reveals she is weeping. "I'm glad, I'm glad."

Someone says, "I'll give six bits for that telescope."

Pick lifts his chin at Delores and Fred. Marguerite rides high on his arm, enjoying her view of the assembly and surveying the people like a princess. She waves to her mother.

"Well, Mr. Pickett? It's a dollar to you," calls the auctioneer. "Doesn't our Century girl want to examine the planets?"

"Yes," Pick says. "Our girl does."

47

CAREY STOOP is taking Jane Fremont home, and he quells his sunny joy long enough to ask Esther if they might carry her at least as far as the turnoff to Half-a-Mind. They don't talk much. The buggy wheels click on the rocks. The sun is still warm on the black metal, but evening is coming. Jane and Carey sit close to each other.

Esther is fatigued. She wants to go back to her claim, to her cabin, to her bed, to drop her dress and petticoats in a circle on the floor and sleep, sleep, sleep. If only her mother were there to hold her, to bring her a drink and sit on her bed. But her mother has died. She didn't want to, but she couldn't help it, and there is nowhere Esther can go where her mother or her father or Joe Peaslee will be.

She leans her head back on the folded buggy top. If only a machine could be invented that would capture something of what a person was. With automated fingers it might etch a life in grooves and patterns on a blank waxen ball. Then we could run our hands over it and feel there both what we'd lost and what we'd not yet learned. The beloved would be part restored—the skills, the faults, the tastes, the raptures and disgraces. The days, too. Afternoons of sunny indolence, a few desperate mornings. And what if we could run our hands over the wax and feel the body there, the boundaried softness that turned out to be so transient, the poignant original we failed to love enough? Wandering over such a recording, our hands might even recollect the face, that impossible, mobile mask, the wall that is also window, the flesh inseparable from spirit. And the voice, the voice as well—

Such machines do exist, of course. Of all longing's requests, this one may be fulfilled. The recording may be played, and the voice indeed restored. But, she thinks, though the pitch and accent and even the breath between the words might be saved, still, the sound alone is not enough. We don't want to hear that Mary had a little lamb or that a boy once stood on a burning deck. Four score and seven years? What do we care for history? We want to have recorded one thing only: our name, spoken in love. *Esther, is that you?*

From the junction she walks the last half mile. When her cabin and yard come into sight, there is the yellow cat lounging on its back in the shade of the shed. But she can't make out what a certain gray patch is—it looks like a shingle has fallen down from the shed roof and is swinging on its nail. And when she is closer still, she can see something white down in Half-a-Mind, as if a large bird has alighted there. Puzzled, she hurries.

It's only a moment, really, before it all becomes clear. The gray patch is the face of the mare Duniway, who has put her head out over the door of the shed. She is holding two stalks of hay limp in her lips, as if she is much too overworked and can't be bothered to chew. In the lake is someone who has ridden all day, many days, riding late, falling asleep over his reins. Who has come in faithfulness and in hope to see her face and take it in his hands. He floats on the lake in the year's last heat. Oh, me, too, she thinks. She pulls at the neck of her shirtwaist and flies down the path. I will swim with you.

PART SIX

FURTHER ON

48

IT HAS BEEN MANY YEARS since Esther wrote to her mother, as she did that year. Sometimes she looks at those letters, to remember just when this or that happened, to combat the distortions of memory, for she tries to tell the truth in her mind as well as in her business. Every couple of years she unties the white string, which has proved to be of remarkably good quality.

Concerns other than her past, of course, have pressed their claims. There have been disasters and world's fairs, styles, inventions, movements, frauds, and obfuscations. The war abroad sputtered on. Aguinaldo was captured, the Philippines subdued. McKinley, extending his hand to greet a supposed well-wisher, encountered the bullet of a distressed immigrant workingman. This assassin, dead by electrocution, was drenched in acid and buried, and his letters were burned.

To many of these stories Esther applied mind and hands. She lived for some time in Salem; later she put the press to work in Spokane. There was a newspaper near Eugene that ran for several years, and another in Santa Rosa, where she had four employees. In many of these places she earned a reputation for niceness about her appearance, which rested largely on the fact that she always wore gloves. Her children knew, if others didn't, that she wore them to cover fingers always marked with ink.

As time wore on, she wrote fewer letters to Century and received fewer in return. And then she was no longer writing to Century at all, for no one lived there anymore. The railroad went twelve miles to the west, with depots at Failing and Jack-High, and within a year or two the town disassembled itself. The Schmidts closed their livery and went to Eugene. Gordon Cecil became the mayor of a small town in Nevada and was apparently very popular. Odell Underwood, always resourceful, opened a new saloon in Failing. Ferris Pickett and Vincent went to Idaho, though Pick came back now and then to visit Marguerite. Vincent wrote Esther that he liked the beautiful lakes and was contented, and when he died in his sleep, Pick was good enough to write and tell her. After Maudie's wedding, Violet took May and went to Idaho, too. Perhaps there she got her wish. Esther didn't know.

Now Jane Fremont—though that was never her name and is her name no longer—has written again, and among other news she says that Marguerite Green, having finished medical work at the university in Salem, is treating the ill at a sanatorium in Portland. To think of that child grown up—and more than grown up, for she is twenty-four—floods Esther with memory, makes her catch her breath. She has sat all morning staring out the window, which is swung wide over the sunny street. The tall, befrilled house across the steep street has been painted this week in fresh blue and gold, and behind it the sky outblues it effortlessly. She hears the periodic clang of the streetcar and the tolling from the mission, and if she cranes her neck a bit from the desk, she can see the bay, bearing ships like huge, somber tea trays on its taffeta green. San Francisco is a lovely city despite what it now suffers: whole men traveling to Europe, maimed ones being returned.

Yes, poor Century, now only silvered boards breaking apart in the heat, settling into the sand. Not even the bones of Joe Peaslee anchor it there, for they lie in Pennsylvania, gathered home by a cousin and interred near those of his family after such a long time away. A secondary school was built on the Two Forks site, serving the children of Failing and Jack-High, which by arrangement with the state draws part of its revenue from selling hay and water off Half-a-Mind. Jane writes that she and Carey have been there for meetings and shows with their sons Charles and Gregory, and that Charles will begin there next year. Delores and Fred prospered with their chicken business and added turkeys and pheasants. Their horses are the most beautiful in the county. The baby, Weston Green, has grown almost into a man, too. He is quieter than his sister, Jane reports, and a serious farmer. He devised an irrigation system out of a series of wells and a kerosene pump, and he and his father grow abundant hay, which Carey buys for his stock. Carey has thoughts of running for the state legislature.

Jane and Carey are still on the Stoop ranch, but they are oriented now toward Peterson, and the Century road is almost unused. The buildings of Century have been stripped, the hitching rails carried off. The school bell was sold to a church in Prineville. No one even visits the town anymore, except for young people bent on an eerie picnic. One can still go into the hotel, duck between cobwebs, and tap at the telegraph key.

How can it be that a place of energy and promise and industry could vanish? Is it natural? No. But it is possible for towns to consume themselves. To become something no one wishes any longer to defend.

One of her clearest memories, now, of that time, is the evening Ben came back for her. They went up on the bluff, leading Duniway, to retrieve Ben's abandoned wagon, and at some moment they stood at the edge of the precipice and saw it all: Half-a-Mind shimmering, clacking with birds, the smoking black patch of Two Forks, the tiny yellow trapezoid of field where Joe Peaslee was found, and the town, mere lumps on a disappearing horizon. She was braced in the pungent wind off that sea of sage, Ben beside her. He held her arm as she leaned out and looked down on her claim and, like others before her, relinquished it. It was one of the things she never wrote down, but never forgot.

Yes, after a time a girl no longer records everything that happens to her. She can see that in her own daughters. It is because such an account implies an ending, and who, orphan or not, would seek that? Let one not be delivered into an ending, even a happy one. Let one not tell everything—whether she and Ben remained together, or separated and met again, or never met again, whether her daughters are his daughters, their young brows hilariously dire, whether when he went to France last year and was killed while putting up a pontoon bridge, it was Esther who mourned hardest, and still mourns. There is no ending, happy or not, and no one is completely lost. She consults them every day of her life, those who loved or wronged her, those who lived and strove beside her, for they are herself. She is their document. What did her mother, Joe Peaslee, Pick, Half-a-Mind, and the yellow cat mean to her? She cannot say it. She can only be it. She walks about, and she is their book.

For how large the mind is! The whole desert is nothing to it. Whoever grasps territory on a plain of dust, a green island, or a rich field in France grasps sand. That old settlement is finished, and liberty must move inside, to be found in the mind. O that inexhaustible Oregon we each enclose. And Century is tiny, after all. Look how the mind can hold it, rock it, like a child.

ACKNOWLEDGMENTS

My gratitude to these people and organizations (as well as to those unnamed who've also provided support, insight, and solace to me as a writer): Merle Kelley; Jim and Emily Keesey; Dan and Deborah Keesey; Linda and Charlie Schrader-Patton; Christopher, Nicholas, and Austin Keesey; Fiona and Sophia Schrader-Patton; Alex Gaiser; Ilsa Gaiser; Ellen Benton Wahler; Lynne Raughley and Peter Ho Davies; Marshall Klimasewiski; Zachary Lazar; Allyson Goldin Loomis and Jon Loomis; Sheila Donohue; Averill Curdy Murr and Naeem Murr; Danielle Chapman and Christian Wiman; Geoff Rogers; Tom Byrnes; Jackie Hiltz and Todd Gherke; Kaylee Muckey and Jayksen Muckey; Shannon Jones; Ellen Fagg Weist; Judy Berck; Tom Osdoba; Paul Winner; John Brandon; Michael Sledge; Katharine Andres; Jonathan Veit; Miriam Erickson; Deborah Eisenberg; the Iowa Writers' Workshop; the Fine Arts Work Center in Provincetown; the National Endowment for the Arts; the Yaddo Foundation; the MacDowell Colony; the English Major in Writing at Northwestern University; Mark Krotov, Steve Weil, and the entire publishing team at Farrar, Straus and Giroux; my colleagues at Linfield College and in the Linfield English Department, especially Lex Runciman; and my many lovely students, past and present.

Special thanks to Julie Barer for the care she has shown me, the superb advice she offered on the manuscript, and the faith and vigor with which she pursued opportunities for it, to Jonathan Galassi, whose willingness to take on a late-blooming first-time novelist is truly gracious, and to Courtney Hodell, whose sustained affection for and insightful scrutiny of the book have been no less than valiant.

Most of all I thank Christopher Gaiser, my champion, closest comfort, and favorite wit, and Lee Begole Montgomery, superior writer, editor, and advocate, and beloved boon companion.

A Note About the Author

Anna Keesey is a graduate of Stanford University and of the University of Iowa Writers' Workshop, and her work has appeared in a number of journals and anthologies, including *Best American Short Stories*. She's the recipient of a National Endowment for the Arts Creative Writing fellowship and has held residencies at MacDowell, Bread Loaf, Yaddo, and the Fine Arts Work Center in Provincetown. Anna has taught English and creative writing, most recently at Northwestern University and Linfield College in McMinnville, Oregon.